"Thanks again, Ro..." Goldie said.

He stared at her for a moment, ... and left.

Goldie closed her eyes and remembered the homeyness of Rory's rambling farmhouse, the cute grins of his two boys—wait, the cute grin of the youngest boy, since the older one had seemed a bit sad—and the way Rory's eyes crinkled when he smiled. And she imagined the kind of woman who could be part of that lovely picture. The kind of woman who baked cookies and kept the house neat and played kickball with the boys in the backyard. That kind of loving, caring, motherly type of woman.

And then she reminded herself that she'd come to Viola, Louisiana, to help her grandmother, not get involved with yet another man who probably didn't know the meaning of the words *trust* and *commitment*.

No matter how kind Rory Branagan had been, and no matter how much her heart was telling her that this man might just be different from all the rest.

With over seventy books published and millions in print, **Lenora Worth** writes award-winning romance and romantic suspense. Three of her books were finalists for the ACFW Carol Awards, and her Love Inspired Suspense novel *Body of Evidence* became a *New York Times* bestseller. Her novella in *Mistletoe Kisses* made her a *USA TODAY* bestselling author. Lenora goes on adventures with her retired husband, Don, and enjoys reading, baking and shopping…especially shoe shopping.

Pamela Tracy is a *USA TODAY* bestselling author who lives with her husband (the inspiration for most of her heroes) and son (the interference for most of her writing time). Since 1999, she has published more than twenty-five books and sold more than a million copies. She's a RITA® Award finalist and a winner of the American Christian Fiction Writers' Book of the Year Award.

Together Under the Tree

New York Times Bestselling Author

Lenora Worth

&

USA TODAY Bestselling Author

Pamela Tracy

2 Uplifting Stories

The Perfect Gift and *Once Upon a Christmas*

LOVE INSPIRED
INSPIRATIONAL ROMANCE

Recycling programs
for this product may
not exist in your area.

ISBN-13: 978-1-335-42991-9

Together Under the Tree

Copyright © 2022 by Harlequin Enterprises ULC

The Perfect Gift
First published in 2009. This edition published in 2022.
Copyright © 2009 by Lenora H. Nazworth

Once Upon a Christmas
First published in 2012. This edition published in 2022.
Copyright © 2012 by Pamela Tracy Osback

For questions and comments about the quality of this book, please contact us
at CustomerService@Harlequin.com.

Love Inspired
22 Adelaide St. West, 41st Floor
Toronto, Ontario M5H 4E3, Canada
www.LoveInspired.com

Printed in U.S.A.

CONTENTS

THE PERFECT GIFT

Lenora Worth

To the Unity Sunday School class—
for all their good and perfect gifts.

Every good and perfect gift is from above,
coming down from the Father of the heavenly lights,
who does not change like shifting shadows.
—*James* 1:17

Prologue

The man and the two little boys stared down at the disheveled woman asleep on the big Ultrasuede couch in their living room.

"Is she a princess, Daddy?" six-year-old Tyler asked, his dark eyes going wide. "My friend Emily is always talking about princesses. She's a girl, though." He shrugged. "I don't know much about that kind of stuff."

"She's not a princess, silly," his older brother, Sam, answered with ten-year-old authority. "And she shouldn't be here. Isn't it illegal to enter someone's house when they're not at home, Dad? Besides, she's ruining our couch with her wet clothes."

Rory, still in shock from finding the woman there in the first place, stopped staring and went into action. "It's okay, Sam. She looks hurt." He gently nudged at the woman's arm. "Ma'am, excuse me? Wake up, okay?" When the woman didn't move, he panicked. "Lady, can you hear me?"

"She's asleep," Tyler pointed out. "Maybe she needs a blanket."

Rory pushed away the blanket his son offered. "Let's make sure she's all right first." He bent and carefully rolled the woman over from her stomach to her back, then felt for a pulse along her neck. She had a pulse. That much he knew. He could feel it through the softness of her skin. And she was wearing an intricate gold-chained square locket that fell across her V-necked sweater with each movement of her breath.

"Is she dead?" Sam asked, his curiosity with all things crime-related making Rory wince. The kid had been that way since his mother had been killed three years earlier in a convenience-store robbery.

"No, son. She's breathing. But something is definitely wrong."

Rory carefully examined the woman for broken bones or any other signs of injury, then turned her face around so he could inspect it. And that's when he saw the blood matted in her dark blond hair just above her left temple.

"She don't look so great," Tyler remarked.

"No, she doesn't," Rory replied, grabbing his cell out of his pocket. He immediately called 911 and explained the situation. "We found a woman in our house, unconscious and bleeding from a head wound. She needs medical attention."

After giving his address to the dispatcher, Rory hung up and turned to his two quiet, curious sons.

"Now you can hand me the blanket, Tyler."

His son shoved the plaid comforter toward him, the boy's big eyes wide with wonder—and a keen interest. "Daddy, if she lives, can we keep her?"

Chapter One

Two hours earlier

Icy rain pounded the windshield then fell away like tiny diamonds from a broken necklace.

"It never sleets in South Louisiana!"

Goldie Rios hit her hand on the steering wheel of her compact vehicle, wondering how a perfectly good Saturday in early December had gone from a day of Christmas shopping and a late dinner to driving down this dark, deserted road all by herself.

Nervous and tired, she grabbed the locket she always wore, clutching it briefly with one hand before taking the wheel of the car back with a tight grip. Oh, yes. She remembered with belated bitterness how her day had gone from bad to worse. She'd just dumped another loser of a boyfriend, and right in the middle of a swanky uptown restaurant at the mall near Baton Rouge. The whole place had gone silent, the only sound Goldie's seething response to Loser Number Five's whining excuses for being seen with another woman one hour before he'd met Goldie for dinner.

The woman was not his sister, his mother, his aunt or his niece. And Goldie was pretty sure she wasn't his grandmother, either, since the cute blonde clung to him in a way that bespoke intimacy rather than family bonds.

She should have listened to her friend Carla—*before* Carla called her from the other end of the mall and told her to casually walk by the pet store. She'd warned Goldie that this one was too smooth, too confident and too good-looking, but Goldie wasn't good at listening to other people's advice. Carla was right. He was in the pet store, buying a cuddly Chihuahua while he cuddled the cute blonde.

Busted.

Goldie watched, horrified and hurt, from behind the Gingerbread House at Santa Claus Lane, while the man she'd been dating for six months kissed another woman. And bought her a dog. He'd never once offered to buy Goldie a dog. In fact, he'd told her he was highly allergic to animals. So after waiting for him to meet her for dinner, Goldie smiled, chatted with him, ordered spaghetti and meatballs and then "accidentally" dumped half her meal onto his lap before telling him that they were finished. It was a standard metaphoric mode of dumping a boyfriend, but now she understood why a lot of women took this route. It made a statement to the world and it made her feel good.

Or at least it had until she'd left the mall in tears.

After driving for an hour in rain that turned to sleet, she'd realized she'd somehow missed the main exit to

Viola, Louisiana. Now she was trying to get home through the back way. Bad idea on a night like this and considering she wasn't all that familiar with the roads around here. If she hadn't been so depressed and distracted, she might have thought long and hard about the sanity of taking this remote shortcut. Too late now.

Easing the little car along, Goldie sent up a prayer for safe travels while the radio personality announced yet another road closing due to icy conditions.

"If you're inside, stay there," the perky broadcaster advised. "If you're traveling, stay on the main roads."

Goldie sputtered a reply. "You don't say."

She was not on a main road. And the sleet was getting heavier while the temperature was dipping below freezing. Soon these roads would be slick with ice. Her cell phone rang but since she had both hands glued to the steering wheel and the service out here was questionable at best, Goldie ignored it. Probably Carla calling for details about the breakup. Or maybe Grammy wondering why she wasn't home yet. But she didn't dare talk on the phone and drive in this mess at the same time.

Goldie listened as the "Jingle Bells" ring tone died down, her eyes misting as a wave of loneliness hit her square in her soul. "I guess I'll be alone again this Christmas," she said out loud just to hear herself talking.

No puppy dog for her. And no more snuggling or cuddling with Number Five, either. Five losers in five years. Could her life get any worse? She'd been making the same old mistakes with men since she'd graduated from college and worked in Baton Rouge. Now she'd just have to focus on doing her weekly column on being organized long-distance from Viola while she stayed with her recuperating grandmother through the holidays. In spite of coming here to help Grammy and in hopes of finding some true meaning in her life, Goldie was as confused as ever. Some advice columnist she was. How could she tell other people how to stay focused and organized when she couldn't even keep a man? When would she find what she was looking for— that perfect fit in a relationship?

And why did that matter so much, anyway? She'd never been one to chase after the dream of marriage and family the way some of her single friends did. By Goldie's way of thinking, relationships were highly overrated. So why did she keep dating the wrong men? Maybe so she *could* break up with them and prove her theory? And keep her heart safe in the process?

She held to the steering wheel as she came to a curve, the trees crouching across the road causing her to lose sight of the asphalt. And that's when she hit the patch of slick black ice. The car lurched then shimmied before suddenly changing direction. Screaming, Goldie tried to remember how to steer into the skid, but it was too late. Her car kept slipping and sliding until it went into a careening, screeching turnaround. She looked up, her scream now locked inside her throat, as the car headed right toward the wide trunk of an ancient cypress tree.

The alligator was cooperating. The humans all around the eight-foot reptile, however, were not.

"I want him gone, Rory."

"Me, too. I can't sleep at night, knowing that creature is hibernating right here at my dock. Rory, can you just take him outta here?"

Rory Branagan shivered in his waterproof work boots and his insulated raincoat. His gaze moved from the sedate alligator buried in a self-made bunker of water and mud near the bank to the couple standing in the icy wind. In the yellow glow from the security light, he could see the fear in the couple's eyes. "I understand, Mr. Johnson. But this gator is just doing what alligators do in winter. He's hunkering down for a good long rest."

Alfred Johnson kicked his cowboy boots into the sleet-covered grass near the shallow pond behind his house. "His snout is sticking up out of the water. 'Bout scared my poor wife to death. He coulda grabbed little DeeDee and ate her whole."

"He's not that hungry right now, sir," Rory observed, shaking his head. "And your poodle shouldn't be out here near the water anyway." At least not on a night like this one. And surely these nice people knew that if they lived on a bayou, they were bound to see alligators.

"Good thing I was holding tight to DeeDee," Mrs. Johnson stated, completely ignoring Rory's advice. "Now, it's too cold and wet out here to be arguing. Are you gonna rustle this thing outta here and get him away from my family?"

Rory looked down at the big leathery snout sticking out of the water, thinking Marge Johnson might be petite but she was fiercely protective of the things she loved. That included her family and that barking pile of white fur she called DeeDee. Well, he couldn't blame the woman.

"I think this one here was 'icing' his snout because of

the sleet and this frigid water, Mrs. Johnson. He probably wouldn't hurt you as cold as it is out here, since he's not interested in food right now. But if this weather clears and we get some warmer days after Christmas, he could pose a problem."

"So get him," Mr. Johnson instructed, his tone as sharp as the crystals of sleet hitting Rory's broad-brimmed rain hat. "I don't want that gator showing up for Christmas dinner later this month."

"And I don't want him around my grandbabies," Marge insisted, shaking her head, her hair so stiff with hair spray Rory could see tiny ice particles shimmering like a crown on her head. "We've got kids coming home for the holidays and I've got too much to do. I can't be worried about my grandchildren out here by the water."

Rory nodded, steeled himself against a messy job and thought it was nights such as this that made him wish he was in another line of work. But his job as a nuisance hunter for the Louisiana Department of Wildlife and Fisheries paid the bills. And he loved his work on most days. This wasn't a typical day in Louisiana, though. It rarely got this nasty around these parts during the winter. But the sleet was getting heavier by the minute. The forecast for the next couple of days didn't look promising. A rare but sure ice storm was coming, whether Rory liked it or not.

And that old gator was getting real cozy in his nice little cave here on the shore of Mr. Johnson's shallow, marshy pond. If Rory didn't help the poor creature, Mr. Johnson might take matters into his own hands and just shoot the reptile. Rory's conscience couldn't allow that to happen. Nor could his job with the state.

"I'll see what I can do," Rory told Mr. Johnson. "Let me just go to my truck and get my equipment."

"Fair enough," Mr. Johnson replied, satisfied for now at least. "Go on inside, Marge. You're shivering in your wader boots out here, honey."

Rory stomped up the slope toward the driveway, listening to Marge's concerned questions as her husband guided her back to the house. His vibrating cell phone made him stop at the back of the truck.

"What's wrong?" Rory asked into the phone. The call was from his house and that meant trouble. Having two boys ages six and ten with no mother always meant trouble.

"It's all right."

As always, his mother's voice was calm and firm. "Mom, are you sure?"

"Yes, I'm sure. I just wanted you to know that we're headed over to my house. The boys were getting bored waiting on you and I need to get home anyway to bake cookies for the youth Christmas party at church this Tuesday. Now I have two eager helpers. We're going to make some with cinnamon and sprinkles and lots of icing. That's where we'll be. I offered to let them spend the night but they wanted to be home with you in case this sleet turns to snow. Something about making a gigantic snowman first thing in the morning. You can pick them up when you're done."

Rory smiled at his sons' high hopes. "Are you sure you can make it back in this weather?"

"Rory, I've lived on Branagan Road for over thirty-five years. I think I can drive the mile from your house to mine, son."

"Of course you can." His mother didn't take any bunk and she sure didn't listen to anyone's advice. And that was one of the main reasons Rory loved her.

"Don't worry so much," Frances Branagan declared. "Now let me get on home before it does get worse."

"Thanks," Rory said, appreciation coursing through his chilled bones. "You're my favorite mom, you know that?"

"I love you, too. Be safe."

He hung up, spoke a prayer of gratitude for his dear patient mother and then set about figuring how to wrestle the unfortunate alligator snoozing down in the pond.

Goldie's feet were cold. She sputtered awake, then groaned as she glanced around. She was in her car, in the dark, on an unfamiliar road. And her head hurt with all the viciousness of two fencers slicing each other to the death, the clanging and banging of her pulse tearing through her temple with each beat of her heart.

She'd wrecked her car. In the ice storm!

Moaning, she pushed at the air bag surrounding her, glad that it had at least saved her from going through the windshield. Then she touched a hand to her head. It was wet and sticky with blood. Weak and disoriented, she groped for the seat belt then after slipping it loose, moaned again when the restraint lifted from her bruised midsection. Automatically reaching for her locket, she clutched it tight. She had to find her phone and call for help.

Her phone, which earlier had been in the seat with her purse, was nowhere to be found now. And she was too dizzy to go digging under the seat.

What should she do? She had to call someone. With great effort, she tried to open the door. After what seemed like hours, the door cringed ajar and a blast of arctic air flowed over Goldie's hot skin. Taking in the crunched front end of her car, she held on to the door as light-headedness washed over her again. She managed to stand, to find her purse. But the phone was lost in the recesses of her shopping bags, notebooks and laptop case. And even if she could find it, she probably wouldn't have very good service.

Goldie gave up on the search and, still woozy and confused, stood and glanced around the woods. She saw a light flickering through the trees.

"A house," she whispered, her prayers raw in her throat. "Maybe someone can help me."

Without giving it much thought other than to find warmth and aid, she slowly made her way along the icy road, her purse clutched to her chest, her head screaming a protest of swirling pain. It was the longest trek of her life and none of the walk made any sense to Goldie. Her brain was fuzzy and her pulse was on fire with a radiating pain. All she could think about was getting out of this freezing sleet.

"Must have a concussion," she voiced to the wind.

When she finally made it to the front door of the house, she was cold, wet and numb with shock. But she knocked and fell against the cool wood, her prayers too hard to voice.

No one came to the door.

So, desperate and beyond caring, she pushed away from the door and continued along the wraparound porch, holding the fat wooden railing until she reached the back of the big farmhouse. Then she fell against the glass-paneled door of the inviting home. Her eyes tried to focus on the Christmas tree sitting in front of the large bay windows and the embers of what looked like a recent fire sparking in the big fireplace.

Goldie wanted that warmth. So she knocked and tried to call out. But no one answered. With one last hope, she jiggled the handle, thinking to herself that she was about to do some serious breaking and entering if she couldn't get any assistance.

And then, the door flew open and Goldie fell through, landing on the cold wide-planked wood of the floor. With a grunt of pain, she crawled to a sitting position then kicked the door shut. Her gaze scanned the big, cozy room and landed for a quick, painful moment on the massive couch across from the still-warm fireplace.

That big brown sofa looked like paradise right now. She's just rest for a minute, then figure out what to do.

Seeing stars that weren't on the tree, Goldie crawled over, pulled herself onto the cushioned pillows and grabbing her beloved locket to hold it close in her hand, and promptly passed out, facedown.

Chapter Two

She had to be dreaming. Goldie sighed in her sleep, glowing warmth moving through her tired bones. She squinted toward the face hovering over her.

The man had dark brown hair and pretty golden eyes but the frown on his face made him look fierce and almost savage. What was he doing in her dream?

Goldie's eyes flew open, pain shooting through her temple like an electrical charge when she tried to sit up. "Where am I?"

"It's okay," the fierce-looking man assured her, pushing her down on the soft pillows. "The ambulance is on its way. You're going to the hospital."

"Hospital?" Goldie tried to sit again but the room started spinning and she felt sick to her stomach. Falling back on the pillows, she asked, "What's wrong with me?"

"You gotta boo-boo."

She closed one eye then slanted the other one toward that tiny voice. A miniature version of Fierce Man stared at her with big, solemn eyes.

"What kind of boo-boo?" Goldie asked, not so sure she wanted an ambulance or an audience. "What happened?"

"You've been in an accident," the man recapped, shooing the little tyke out of the way. "You hit your head."

For a minute, Goldie just lay there staring at her surroundings. This was a nice enough place, but she had no idea how she'd wound up here. "Where am I?"

"This is my house," the man explained. "But don't worry about that right now. Do you remember anything?"

"No." Goldie closed her eyes, hoping that would help the dizziness spiraling through her brain. "I don't know."

"Did you walk here or drive maybe?"

And then she remembered she'd been in a car. Images of that car swirling out of control rushed through her mind. "Yes. Yes. I was in a wreck on the road." She took a deep breath to stop the nausea rising in her stomach. "I lost control and then my head hurt so much. I couldn't find my phone so I got out of the car and I saw the light."

"You broke into our house," came yet another male voice. A different one. This one was more pronounced and angry.

"No, the door was open," Goldie replied, deciding to look at Fierce Man instead of that accusing little person, whoever he was.

The man glanced from Goldie to the boys huddled around her feet. "Did MeeMaw forget to lock the back door?"

The bigger of the two boys shook his head then looked down at the floor. "No, sir. She told me to do it. I was the last one out. I thought I heard it click."

Goldie watched, triumphant because she'd told the truth and now so had the real culprit, as the man's brooding frown changed to a look of complete understanding and forgiveness. "It's okay, son. That old door sticks all the time. I need to see about making it more secure. That happens to me a lot, too."

Goldie thought that was the sweetest thing, the way this man was shouldering the blame for the malfunctioning back door. "I'm glad it wasn't closed," she remarked on a raw spasm of pain, hoping to ease the boy's embarrassment. "I was so cold. And my head hurt a lot."

"So she didn't break in," the tiny one mouthed to the older one, obviously his brother since they looked almost identical. "You need to tell her you're sorry."

"I thought she did," the older one revealed, his hands fisting at his sides. "It looked that way." He didn't say he was sorry.

"Okay, you two. Enough," the man interceded in an authoritative voice. "Step aside and give the nice lady some space."

The boys backed away, their eyes curious and cute.

"I'm so sorry," Goldie apologized to the man. "I didn't mean to pass out on your couch."

"You're hurt," he replied, cutting her the same slack he'd just allowed the boy who'd accidentally left the house unlocked. "Just lie still until we can get you some help."

"How long have I been out?"

"I'm not sure," the man answered. "We got home

about fifteen minutes ago. Do you remember anything else?"

She moved her head in an attempt to nod, but the pain stopped her. "My car hit a patch of ice and went sliding right into a tree. A big tree."

"Could have been worse," the man theorized, surveying her. "I think you're okay except for the bang on your head. Must have hit the steering wheel pretty hard."

"It's all fuzzy," she admitted. Then, in spite of her pain and her odd circumstances landing on his couch, she remembered her manners and said, "I'm Goldie Rios."

He smiled at that, sending out a radiant warmth that brought Goldie a sense of comfort and security. "I'm Rory Branagan and these are my sons, Tyler and Sam."

"I'm Tyler," the little one added, grinning.

Sam didn't say anything. He seemed downright sad as he stared at her. Sad and a bit distrustful. How could she blame him? He'd come home to find a strange woman bleeding on his furniture.

"It's good to meet all of you," Goldie responded. "And thanks for being so kind to me."

Rory's soft smile shined again, making Goldie wonder if she might yet be dreaming. This man was a sensitive father. And probably a considerate husband. And for some reason that her hurting brain couldn't quite figure out, that bothered Goldie. Trying to think, she realized she couldn't remember much but the accident. Where had she been? And where was she headed?

The sound of a siren broke Rory's smile and brought Goldie out of her pounding thoughts. He jumped up and went into action while she blinked and closed her eyes.

"I think your ride is here." Then he glanced at his sons. "And so is a patrol car. You'll need to give the police a report, nothing to worry about."

Goldie could tell he'd added that last bit for the benefit of his sons, since their eyes grew even wider. The little one showed excitement, but the older boy's eyes held a dark, brooding anger.

If her head hadn't hurt so much, Goldie might have been able to figure that one out. And get to know Not-so-fierce Man a little better. She was certainly content to stay right here in the light of that great smile. But she was in pain, no doubt. And although she wasn't sure if she needed to go to the hospital, she didn't have much choice. Her car was probably totaled and she was too dizzy to stand up. Then, in a clear and concise image in her mind, she remembered her grandmother.

"I need to let Grammy know," she noted. "My grandmother."

"Sure. What's her number?" Rory replied. "I'll call her right now."

Goldie rattled off the numbers, glad her brain was beginning to cooperate. "Her name is Ruth Rios."

Rory let out a chuckle. "You don't say? I should have made the connection when you told me your name. I know Miss Ruth. She goes to my church. So you're her granddaughter?"

Goldie nodded. "I just came here a few weeks ago to help her out. She's been recovering from hip surgery."

"Yeah, we heard that and since she hasn't been to church in a while… I'm sure sorry." He gave her an apologetic look. "I should have gone by to see her."

"She's doing better," Goldie informed him. "But I

know she's worried since I'm not home yet. I was supposed to be there hours ago."

"I'll call her, I promise," Rory reiterated as the paramedics knocked on the door, followed by one of the three police officers serving Viola.

Goldie nodded, her mind whirling with pain and confusion. "Don't let her get out in this weather. She doesn't need to come to the hospital." After that, she didn't get much of a chance to say anything else to Rory. She was too busy being examined and questioned, both of which left her tired and even more confused.

The paramedics checked her vitals, asked her all the pertinent questions and concluded yes, she might have a mild concussion. And the officer seemed satisfied that she'd been in a one-car accident and that she hadn't been drinking. He and Rory both assured her they'd have the car towed. So she was off to the hospital.

"I appreciate your help," Goldie mumbled to Rory as she was lifted up and hustled onto the waiting gurney.

"Don't worry about that," Rory commented, following her stretcher out into the chilly night. "Take care, Goldie."

"Thanks," she mumbled again as the ambulance doors shut. She could just make out his image as he talked to the police officer.

But as she lay there with two efficient paramedics fussing over her, Goldie wondered if she'd ever see Rory Branagan again.

Doubtful, since she wouldn't be staying here in Viola much longer now that Grammy was better. And double doubtful since she didn't attend church with Grammy.

Or at least, she hadn't yet.

* * *

The next morning, Goldie hung up the phone by her hospital bed to find Rory standing in the door of her room, holding a huge poinsettia in a green pot.

"Uh, hi," he said, the big red and green plant blocking his face. "The nurse said I could come in."

Goldie grinned then motioned to him. "Hi, yourself. I just talked to Grammy. She said you were so nice last night, calling her and keeping her informed. And that you wouldn't let her get out in the weather even to come visit me."

He lifted his chin in a quick nod. "She was pretty stubborn about doing just that, but I called her neighbor and asked her to sit with your grandmother. Then I contacted the hospital to check on you. Only, they didn't want to give me any information. So I phoned your grandmother again and explained it to her, since she was your next of kin." He laughed, took a breath then asked, "So how are you?"

"I'm fine," Goldie reported, her heart doing an odd little dance as he set down the plant and came closer. "You didn't have to go to all that trouble."

"No trouble. Me and Miss Ruth go back a long way. I once rescued an armadillo out of her backyard."

"Excuse me?" Goldie reclined against her pillows, taking in his crisp plaid flannel shirt and sturdy jeans. She didn't think it was possible that he still looked so handsome, even in the glaring morning light, but he did.

"I work for the Department of Wildlife and Fisheries as a nuisance hunter. I get calls to trap wild animals, anything from armadillos and snakes to alligators and even the occasional black bear."

"You're kidding?"

He looked downright sheepish. "No, that's my job."

"Isn't that sorta dangerous?"

He grinned again. "Not as dangerous as forcing myself to come to the hospital in an ice storm to check on you. And mind you, it wasn't the storm that scared me."

He did seem a bit uncomfortable. He fidgeted with the water jar and rearranged her drinking cup. And Goldie's impish nature clicked on. "What, you don't like hospitals?"

"That and... I'm a bit rusty on talking to women."

She filed that comment away to study more closely later. He had two little boys so he was obviously a happily married man. Disappointing but comforting in a strange way. He looked like the kind of man who belonged in a family.

Nobody liked hospitals but the expression in his eyes told her maybe he'd had some firsthand experience with this kind of thing. Maybe she'd ask him about that, too, but right now, she only wanted to put him at ease. "I'm easy to talk to on most days and I really like the flower."

"It was the only thing I could find at the superstore on the highway."

"It's pretty, but again, you didn't have to come see me."

"I promised Miss Ruth." He shrugged. "And I wanted to make sure you were all right."

Goldie stared at the plant. "I have a slight concussion, but they're releasing me this afternoon. I just have to rest for the weekend and take over-the-counter pain reliever. No ibuprofen though, since it can cause some sort of bleeding—doctor's orders." She motioned to a paper on the bedside table. "I have a whole list of instructions on all the things to watch for after a concussion." And she wondered if one of those things was a rapid pulse, and if Rory or her head injury was the cause of that symptom.

"So, what about your confusion and memory loss?"

She slanted her throbbing head. "I still can't quite remember much more about the accident or what I was doing most of yesterday, but I'm okay. The doctor said I might not ever remember all of it. He just warned me of dizziness and confusion at times. But hey, I'm that way on a good day."

He fingered one of the vivid red poinsettia leaves. "Your car was full of shopping bags."

"You've seen my car?"

"I had it towed, remember?" He seemed embarrassed. "I guess you don't. It's at a nearby garage. But I got all the stuff out of it. It's in my car right now. I can take it by your grandmother's if you want me to."

Goldie shook her head. "You're amazing. What's the catch?"

"Excuse me?" he asked, echoing her earlier words to him. "What catch?"

She shrugged, wincing at her sore muscles. "You just seem too good to be true."

He lowered his head. When he looked back up, his eyes were dark with some unspoken emotion. "Oh, I'm not, trust me. I just walked across the woods last night with the policeman to check on your car and then I notified a friend who owns a body shop to tow it. After you file your insurance report and get the go-ahead, he'll give you a good estimate—that is if you want him to fix the car."

Goldie decided not to question why he deflected the compliment. "Can it be fixed?"

"Maybe." He stood quietly and then said, "I hope I didn't overstep—having him pick up the car."

Goldie shook her head. "No, not at all. I just didn't need this to happen right now. I'm here to help Grammy and I depend on my car to get me around. Just one more thing to deal with."

He inclined his head in understanding. "Maybe you can rent a car or drive your grandmother's."

Goldie laughed. "Her car is ancient but it does move, barely. Grammy says it has one speed—slow."

His smile was back. "I see you have her sense of humor."

"Keeps me sane."

He seemed amused then said, "Well, I guess I'd better get back to the house. I left my sons with my mother—again. That poor woman never gets a break." His smile was indulgent. "We made two snowmen— one in our yard and one in hers."

She looked out the window. "Did it snow last night?"

"Yeah, a pretty good dusting. The ground is covered white and we were able to get two passable snowmen."

"Are the roads okay, then?"

"The roads are fine now. I had to be careful driving into town, but the sun melted most of the ice. However, we could have another round tomorrow." He turned toward the door then whirled. "Hey, do you need a ride home?"

Goldie didn't know how to respond. This man seemed to know what she needed even before she voiced it. That was very disconcerting to a woman who was used to being independent and confident and…alone. "I hadn't thought about that. I sure don't want Grammy trying to find someone to drive me, even if the roads are clear."

"I can take you right now."

He really was a sweet man. "I haven't been released yet. The doctor said later today."

"I'll come back and take you home, then," he confirmed, holding up a hand when she tried to protest. "I just have to help the boys do some things around our place. We have a small herd of cows and they need checking on and we all have chores to do, but they can stay with my mom while I take you to your grandmother's house."

"I don't want to impose."

"I insist. Your grandmother's worried about you and I don't mind. I'll call her."

"I can call Grammy," Goldie asserted. "I'll tell her you're bringing me home. They said midafternoon, after I see the doctor one more time and he signs my release."

"So, I'll be back around three."

Goldie had to ask. "You said your mother watches the boys a lot? Does your wife work?" And where had his wife been last night?

"I don't have a wife," he corrected, the light going out of his eyes. "She…died a few years ago."

Wishing she'd learn to keep her curiosity to herself, Goldie looked down at her hands. That probably explained his aversion to hospitals. "I'm so sorry."

He didn't comment. He just nodded his head again in a silent acknowledgment. "I'll see you at three."

"Okay. Thanks again, Rory. For everything."

He waved goodbye then shut the door.

"Nice going, Goldie," she whispered to herself. If her head hadn't been so sore, she would have hit her forehead in disgust. Why was she accident-prone with herself and her mouth?

Instead, Goldie closed her eyes and remembered the homeyness of Rory's rambling farmhouse, the cute grins of his two little boys—wait, the cute grin of the youngest of his two boys, at least—and the way Rory's eyes crinkled when he smiled. And she imagined the kind of woman who'd once been a part of that lovely picture. The kind of woman who baked cookies, kept the house neat and played kick ball with the boys in the backyard. A loving, caring, motherly type woman.

And she reminded herself she was not that kind of woman even if she did have a compulsion toward being organized. Besides, she'd come here to help her grandmother, not get involved with yet another male even if this one seemed to actually understand the meaning of the words *trust* and *commitment*. In spite of her accident and her fuzzy memories, she somehow knew she had a very good reason for not wanting a man in her life—no matter how kind Rory Branagan had been to her and how much her heart was telling her that this man just might be different from all the rest.

Chapter Three

Her locket was missing.

Frantic, Goldie searched all around her bed and the bedside table, then buzzed for a nurse. She glanced at the clock. It was almost time for Rory to come and take her home, but she couldn't leave without her locket. When the bubbly RN rushed into her room, Goldie was just about out of the bed.

"Don't try to get up by yourself," the nurse objected, holding Goldie's arm. "Do you need a bathroom break?"

"No, I... I can't find my locket," Goldie replied, willing herself not to cry. "It's on a gold chain—it's a filigree-etched square with a porcelain picture of a Louisiana iris and a tiny yellow butterfly. Somebody must have taken it off me when they brought me in."

The nurse opened drawers and went through the nearby closet. "Here's the bag that came with your personal belongings. Want me to check inside? It might be in your purse."

Goldie nodded. "If you don't mind."

She watched closely as the nurse searched her leather

purse then rummaged through Goldie's clothes from last night. "I don't see anything like that, honey. Maybe you gave the locket to someone for safekeeping before you came here?"

"No," Goldie replied, trying to think. Had Rory removed the locket last night? Or had she lost it? She couldn't remember. What if someone had taken it? She'd never forgive herself if something had happened to it.

"Just relax and I'll ask at the desk," the nurse advised, trying to reassure her as she handed Goldie her belongings.

Goldie bobbed her head. "Ask everyone. I have to find it. It's very old and has a lot of sentimental value."

"Okay." The nurse walked toward the door. "I'll see what I can do, but you know the hospital isn't—"

"I know—not responsible for the loss of valuables," Goldie repeated. "I understand."

But she wanted her necklace back. She had to find it. So she waited for the nurse to leave, then she carefully got up to search on her own. She made it to the end of the bed but she stood up too quickly. Her pulse quickened as blood rushed from her head and made her dizzy.

And that's when Rory walked in and grabbed her just as she reached for the bed for support.

"Hey, hey," Rory urged, guiding Goldie back to the bed. "Where you going, sunshine?"

"My locket," Goldie explained, squeezing her eyes shut to stop the stars flashing through her brain. "I... I think I lost it."

He gazed down at her. She looked so young and innocent, lying there devoid of makeup. Her hair wasn't exactly blond, more burnished and gold than a true blond. It shimmered like silky threads against her cheeks while the square patch of gauze just over her hairline shined starkly white. The frown on her face only made her look more like a lost little girl than a determined woman.

"I remember your locket. You were wearing it last night. At least, I saw it when I turned you over on the couch."

"I was?" She sat up again. "Maybe I lost it at your house."

"I'll look when I get home," he said. Because this woman had disrupted his life to the point that he was worried about her *and* what she meant to him as a man, he asked, "So what's the deal with that pretty locket, anyway?"

She looked away, toward the window. "My daddy gave it to me before he went to war during Desert Storm. It has a picture of me and him inside it. He never made it home."

"Oh, wow." Rory felt bad for being so nosy. "I'm sure sorry to hear that. No wonder it means so much to you."

"It does and it's very old. It belonged to his great-great-grandmother. And my grandmother gave it to him to give to me on my twelfth birthday. It's kind of a tradition in our family. Grammy says good things happen to the women who wear that locket. So far, that hasn't exactly been the case with me."

Rory hadn't pegged her for being traditional nor for feeling sorry for herself, but under the circumstances, he could certainly understand why she looked so down. And he could sympathize with her need to find the piece of jewelry. "I'll look over the house and in the yard, too. I'll get the boys to help."

"I'd appreciate that." She stared at the ceiling. "I've made such a mess of things. Wrecking my car, losing my necklace. I need to get my life together somehow."

Rory could tell she was fighting back tears. "Listen, your car might be fixable and…well, we'll probably find your locket. Just be glad you're okay. That wreck could have been much worse."

She looked over at him, her smile bittersweet. "I guess I am acting a little over-the-top. And you're right. I'm still here and Grammy needs me. It's just that was one of the few things my daddy ever gave me. My parents were divorced so I didn't get to see him much."

"That's a shame," Rory replied. "I'm blessed that my parents had a great marriage. My mom's a widow now, but I had a pretty good childhood. Nothing major—just lots of good memories."

She smiled again. "Yes, you are blessed. I've never had that. We transferred all over while my dad was alive and in the army, then my mother moved us around a lot after the divorce. Grammy was the one who kept me grounded and safe, even if she and my mother don't always see eye to eye."

"And where's your mother now? Should I call her?"

She shook her head. "No. That's okay. I'll give her an update when she checks on us. She's traveling overseas, one of those long tours with a bunch of her friends—a big Christmas extravaganza. Angela likes to travel and she rarely calls home."

Rory thought her daughter did not like that arrangement. In spite of her pretty curls and her soft smile, he sensed loneliness in Goldie. And he wondered how long she'd been searching for a safe place to lay her head. "Hey, let's get you home to your grandmother. She's told me she's got a big pot of homemade chicken soup simmering on the stove just for you. And fresh-baked corn bread to go with it."

"Grammy's answer to anything is chicken soup," Goldie said. "And she makes the best. She puts home-made dumplings in there."

"I take it you like her cooking," Rory replied, grinning.

"I like food, period." She laughed then grimaced. "And if I stay with her much longer, I won't be able to fit into any of my clothes."

Rory thought Goldie looked just perfect, but he refrained from making such a flirtatious comment since they didn't really know each other. Yet.

Then he told himself not to even think along those lines. He had enough to keep him busy, what with the boys, his mother and his work and, well, a man got lonely just like a woman did, he reasoned.

But he didn't need to think about that right now.

"Has the doctor been by?" he asked, suddenly ready to get out of here.

Goldie waved toward the hallway. "Yes. I'm sorry, I guess you're ready. I was waiting on the nurse. She's checking around for my locket."

"Oh, okay." He tapped his knuckles on the food tray. "Got everything else together?"

"Yes. One of Grammy's friends brought me this change of clothes. I sent your poinsettia home with her."

He noticed she was wearing a sweater and some

wide-legged sweatpants. "I could have brought that. I didn't even think about clothes."

"You've done more than enough," Goldie said. "Besides, I think Grammy sent Phyllis to check on me and bring back a thorough report. And if I know my grandmother and Phyllis, they probably tag-teamed my doctor to get the whole story on my injuries."

"Are you sure you're up to going home?"

"Oh, yes, I'm ready to get into my own bed." She lifted up. "Let's go to the desk and see where that nurse is."

Rory helped her. "Are you still dizzy?"

"No. I think I just got up too quickly before. And we're not telling the nurse about that little episode. It wasn't the awful dizziness I had after the wreck. I have work to do and I need to get back to it."

"Oh, I don't think you need to worry about work. It's the weekend."

"I have a deadline," she explained. "I write a syndicated advice column. It's mostly about organizing your house and keeping your life straight—something I haven't been doing lately. And I'm already pushing things with my boss by working long distance."

Rory gained a new insight. "A column? That's interesting."

"Not as interesting as being a nuisance hunter," she retorted, standing on wobbly legs.

Rory laughed at that. "We'll have to compare notes on that some time. I could use tips on organization and keeping things straight and orderly in my life, that's for sure."

"And I've always wanted to track down an alligator and wrestle it until I can tie its mouth shut," she teased.

Rory got a picture of this petite woman holding down a ten-foot reptile. It made him smile.

"Don't think I can do it?" she asked as they made it out of her room.

"I have no doubt," he replied, not willing to argue the point with an injured woman.

"And I think you'd be pretty good at doling out advice," she replied. "At least, I think women would listen to you no matter what you say. They'd follow your advice based on your smile alone."

That made him take notice. Giving her the best smile he could muster, he prompted, "So, you like my smile, huh?"

She laughed, a soft pink flush coloring her cheeks. "I do when I'm not seeing two of you."

"Are you okay?"

"I'm fine. I just wish I hadn't lost my locket. Let's get out of here, though, so you don't have to wait."

"Not so fast, young lady."

They turned to find her doctor and the nurse who'd been in her room trailing them down the hallway. "You need to be in this. Standard hospital policy."

Goldie glared at the wheelchair. "Oh, all right." Settling herself into the chair, she turned to the nurse. "Did you find my locket?"

"I'm afraid not, honey," the nurse replied. "I'm sorry. Everything that came in with you should be in that bag the paramedics put your personal things in."

Goldie clutched her purse and the plastic bag labeled with her name. "Maybe somebody dropped it in here and we just didn't see it. It could be in the pocket of the jeans I was wearing yesterday."

"We'll look when we get you home," Rory suggested, hoping to distract her from tossing out the contents of her purse and the bag right here. Or refusing to get home to some rest. She looked so upset, he wondered if she shouldn't stay in the hospital another night.

She didn't answer. She was too busy digging around in the deep recesses of her big leather purse, pulling out various labeled little sacks of all sorts. She had a bag for everything inside that larger bag. "I sure hope I can find it."

"We'll keep looking," the nurse said, waving to them.

When they got outside, Goldie had that lost expression on her face again.

"They won't find it," she said. "Somebody probably stole it. It's pretty valuable, considering how old it is. But I don't care about how much money it can bring. I just want it back."

Rory could understand her frustrations. And her disappointment. He hoped he could find that locket for Goldie, but he had his doubts, too. Even though it hadn't snowed more than a couple of inches last night, a piece of jewelry could easily become lost in all the mush. He'd have to go over the yard and house with an eagle eye.

After getting Goldie into his car, Rory started out of the parking lot and onto the main highway. "So where did you live when you're not in Viola?"

"Baton Rouge," she answered, her gaze on the road. "Wow, I see patches of snow in the trees. And the ground is still covered. It's so beautiful even if it does hurt my eyes."

"It was pretty cold last night. Some of that could freeze up again later." Trying to get to know her better, he continued, "And what did you do in Baton Rouge? I mean, how long have you been writing the column?"

"Since college," she replied. Then she turned to look at him. "I went to school at LSU and got a degree in communication. I wasn't sure what I wanted to do. I had written a column for a school newspaper and that experience gave me a chance to write a column for a paper in Baton Rouge. Because my most popular columns were on organization and how to get your life on track, I got promoted to the lifestyles section and after three years, the column became regionally syndicated. But I do feature articles, advertorials and fillers, too. I don't make a lot of money, but I enjoy my work. I've always been highly organized so it's nice to use those skills in my job."

"Kind of like that woman on television my mother likes so much. I can't remember her name but she does a cooking show."

Goldie knew of the woman in question. "No, more like a Southern version of the modern woman—you know, busy, stressed, working all the time both in the home and out of the home and needing to fold the laundry and cook a decent meal then finish studying a business report. I interview a lot of women to get the best tips."

"My wife was like that," he said, then wished he hadn't mentioned Rachel. He didn't like to talk about her.

Goldie gave him a nod. "Your home reflects that. I'm impressed that it was so neat."

He shrugged. "My mom was over last night, cleaning for me. You should have seen it when I left yesterday morning."

"Oh, your mother. Well, I'm sure she loves helping out."

"She's been a blessing…since…since Rachel died. She's a big help with the house and the boys. I guess that works two ways since we lost my dad a year ago. She likes the company."

"I'm sorry about your wife and your dad." Goldie didn't say anything else. She just stared out at the road ahead.

Thinking his past tragedies were sure a downer and not the best approach to impressing a woman, Rory was glad when they pulled up to her grandmother's tiny brick house. He didn't need to worry about impressing a woman, anyway. "I'll help you get in and say hi to your grandmother."

Goldie waited for him to come around the car then slowly lifted herself out to face him. "I might as well warn you, Rory. She's gonna want you to stay and eat. But you don't have to. That is, unless you want to, I mean."

Rory smiled down at her, thinking soup and corn bread was mighty tempting right now. Especially if he'd get to sit across the table from Goldie.

Then he remembered his boys waiting at his mother's house and he thought about Rachel, how much he still missed her, and he wondered why he was even thinking about another woman.

"I'd better get on home," he told Goldie as he helped her up the two stone steps to the porch.

"Nonsense, Rory Branagan," came the sweet but firm voice from inside the open door. Ruth stood there holding on to a walker. "After all you've done for Goldie, the least we can do is give you a good meal. Now come on in here and have some dinner. I insist."

Rory looked from Goldie's "I told you so" grin to Ruth Rios's twinkling eyes and realized he was trapped between longing and duty. And that was not a good place for a man.

Or at least he didn't think it was.

But he went into the house and shut the door anyway.

Chapter Four

"More coconut pie, Rory?"

"No, ma'am." Rory glanced over at Goldie, shot her a smile then looked back at her grandmother. "I don't think I can eat another bite. And I really need to head on home."

The man was fidgety. Goldie had noticed that earlier today in the hospital, only then she'd chalked it up to his memories of his wife's death. But now, he just seemed like a caged animal wanting out. Did she make him that nervous? Or was he just used to being outside, cornering some varmint instead of sitting with two women as if he were a member of the garden club?

"Grammy, you know Rory has two boys. And they're probably wondering where their daddy is."

"'Course I know all about his boys," Ruth replied, pursing her lips in that Grammy way. "I've taught both of them in Sunday school. Adorable."

Rory laughed at that. He had a deep laugh. A steady laugh. Goldie liked the sound of it.

"I wouldn't exactly call them adorable now. They can

be a handful, that's for sure. Which is why I'd better relieve my mom. She's had them for two days in a row."

"Do you go out a lot?" Grammy asked, her tone as innocent as the fresh snow still outside.

Rory looked shocked then shook his head. "No, not on dates or stuff like that. I had a call last night from the Johnsons. They spotted an old gator snoozing under the icy water near their dock. Mrs. Johnson wasn't happy."

"I reckon not," Grammy agreed, clearly fascinated. "How'd you catch him?"

Rory tapped his fingers on the table, no doubt ready to be on the road and away from two curious females. "Well, I didn't want to have to kill him, so I just put on my waders and went in and roped him."

"You hear that, Goldie? Roped an alligator, all by himself. You ever heard of such?"

Goldie gave Rory an apologetic smile. "Can't say that I have, Grammy. I'd be afraid I'd lose an arm or leg, going into water with an alligator."

Rory shook his head. "He was hibernating. An easy catch. I loaded him up and tagged him—we like to keep records on how many we catch and release."

"So you did release him?" Goldie repeated, suddenly as fascinated as her grandmother.

"We try to release as many as we can. But sometimes, we have to shoot 'em."

"That's too bad," Goldie said, imagining this soft-spoken man shooting to kill. He might be soft-spoken right now but she could picture him as an expert hunter. Why did that make a little shiver slink down her backbone?

"She never did like to see any of God's creatures hurt or dying," Ruth murmured, her hand over her mouth in a mock whisper. "She'd bring home every stray out there if I let her."

Goldie couldn't argue with that. "She's right. I love animals. But I've never been in one spot long enough to even have a gerbil, let alone a dog or cat."

"She's kind of a nomad," Grammy offered up. "A wandering soul."

"What she means," Goldie interpreted, wishing her grandmother wouldn't talk about her personal inadequacies so much, "is that I can't seem to settle down."

"Well, you've been all over," Grammy argued, pouring Rory a second cup of coffee with automatic sweetness. "Traveled all over Europe and the whole United States, this one."

Goldie nodded. "That's why I like working at the paper. I can go anywhere I want and still get my column submitted on time. Plus, I pick up ideas and suggestions for my readers when I travel and with technology, it's fairly easy to do feature stories on the road, too."

Rory was now the one who seemed fascinated. "I've rarely left Louisiana. Is it fun, traveling around all the time?"

Goldie felt the scrutiny of his gaze. The man's job sure suited him. He looked like he could track down the wildest of animals.

"It…uh…can be fun, yes. But Grammy's exaggerating. My parents moved me around a lot when I was growing up, so that's what I'm used to. Then I did some traveling on my own after high school and college. Just summer tours." Sending her grandmother a warning glance, she added, "But I'm here in good ol' Viola for a while."

"And I'm grateful to have her," Grammy acknowledged. "She's taken good care of her old grandma, let me tell you. And even though I'm up and around, using my walker, she insists on staying through Christmas. So we have a few more weeks with her."

"That should be a blessing for you, Miss Ruth." Rory got up. "I hate to leave such good company, ladies, but I have to get home." He looked down at Goldie. "I'm glad you're okay and I'll search for your locket the minute I get home."

Grammy's gaze centered on Goldie's neck. "You lost your locket, honey?"

"I've misplaced it, yes," Goldie echoed, her smile waning. "I hope I dropped it at Rory's house last night. I've explained to him how much it means to me."

Grammy didn't seem too concerned. She patted Goldie's hand. "Well, lockets can be replaced. You can't."

Goldie pushed the cobwebs of regret out of her mind, deciding to think positively. With a wry grin, she said, "I am one of a kind."

Grammy laughed at that. "You sure are."

Rory just stood there, smiling his soft smile, his eyes so tigerlike, Goldie could almost feel sorry for alligators and armadillos.

"I'll walk you out," she said, getting up. Glad the dizziness wasn't back, she slowly made her way around the antique mahogany dining table.

"Don't overdo it now," Grammy warned, but Goldie caught the gleam in her grandmother's eyes.

Rory took her arm. "You don't have to see me to the door. It's cold out there."

"I just wanted to thank you again, for all you've done," Goldie said, a rare shyness taking over her tongue.

"Not a problem. Just be careful next time an ice storm hits, okay?"

"That might not happen again in a long time," she replied, being reasonable. "But that's the way things go for me—the first ice storm in Louisiana in years and I wind up on the worst road in the state."

"Well, if it does happen again and you find yourself out near Branagan Road, you know where I live."

A rush of something warm and satisfying moved down Goldie's spine. "Yes, I sure do."

"I'll call you if I find the necklace," he said, throwing up a hand in goodbye.

"Okay."

She shut the door against the cold wind, bright red felt Christmas bows lifting out from the wreath she'd made to hang there, and she wondered if she'd ever see her necklace again.

And if she'd ever see this man again.

He planned on seeing her again.

Rory wasn't sure if it was the chicken soup or the coconut pie or the blondish curls, but somewhere during the hour or so he'd spent with Goldie and her grandmother, he'd decided he'd like to get to know Goldie Rios a little better. Only he wasn't so sure how to go about that.

I'm rusty on this stuff, Lord, he thought, his prayers as scattered as the frigid wind. He hadn't considered dating anyone since Rachel's death. In fact, he'd believed that to be an insult to his wife's memory. And to her love for him and their boys.

But maybe he'd been wrong about that. Maybe the boys needed a mother's touch. His own mother was a pretty terrific substitute and the boys loved her dearly, but well, a man needed a wife. Especially a man trying to raise two active sons. Telling himself to slow down, Rory pushed contemplations of finding a wife out of his mind. That would be wrong—to automatically think of Goldie in those terms when he'd only just met the woman.

Right now, he wouldn't think beyond getting to know her. One day at a time, he reminded himself. After all, she was the first woman who'd even made him stop to consider dating again. And maybe he was just caught up in the whole thing—finding her on his couch, hurt and frightened, seeing that lost expression in her eyes when she told him about her locket and watching her wince as her grandmother bragged on her, going into detail about her life.

Goldie was obviously a smart, capable woman.

But from the look of things, she wasn't anywhere near settling down to one man. One man with two rambunctious children.

"I'd better find that locket and get it back to her before I do something really dumb," Rory said to himself.

Like ask her out on a date or something.

But that urge might be tougher to control than wrestling a gator had ever been.

"Grammy, I know that look," Goldie said after Rory had left. "You're up to matchmaking, aren't you?"

"The thought never crossed my mind," Ruth teased, her smile causing her dimples to deepen. "But you have to admit, Rory is a fine-looking man. And a good, solid Christian, too."

"I don't doubt that," Goldie replied. "He does seem like a good person."

"And nice-looking, right?"

"Can't fault him there, either."

"And he is single and lonely, bless his heart."

"Yes, bless his heart," Goldie echoed. "But, Grams, you know I won't be here that long now that you're better. I have to go back to Baton Rouge after Christmas."

Grammy shook her head, her silver curls glistening even if they were too clipped to move. "You know, you don't have to go back to that big city. You could stay here awhile longer. You said so yourself—you can do your work from anywhere."

Goldie put the rest of the pie in the refrigerator. "Yes, I did say that. But I have an apartment in Baton Rouge and I have friends there. And I do have to show up at the paper for editorial meetings and planning sessions and such. My boss has been very kind in allowing me to work from here but he won't let that go on forever."

Ruth slapped the lid on the plastic container of leftover soup. "Of course you have to get back one day, darlin'. But it's been so nice having you here with me. Not that I need you to hover over me, but you do make for pleasant company."

Goldie counted to ten, telling herself not to let that grandmotherly guilt get her all confused. "I love your company, too. And that's why I agreed to stay through the rest of December. But come January one, I'm going home."

"You're too tough," Ruth said. "Too stubborn and

too tough. Men don't always appreciate those qualities in a woman."

"I'm not looking for a man," Goldie retorted, stung by her grandmother's words. "Now, are we going to watch that classic movie I rented the other day, or are you tired?"

"You're the one who just came home from the hospital," Ruth proclaimed in a gentle tone. "How're you feeling?"

"I feel okay," Goldie admitted. "No dizziness and just a few fuzzy memories."

"Oh, don't forget to call your friend back," Grammy said, heading for the small den at the front of the house. "She was really worried about you, especially since you and what's-his-name had a bad fight."

Goldie's eyes widened as memories came floating down on her like snowflakes. She'd been at the mall, eating dinner with what's-his-name. The same one who'd just bought a puppy for another woman—in the same mall. Some things weren't worth remembering. "I'll call Carla, then start the movie," she said.

But she didn't reach for the phone right away. Instead, she stood there looking out the kitchen window, listening to her grandmother's wind chimes hanging on the small back porch playing a tune in the night breeze. The yard was illuminated by a bright yellow security light and the trees danced and swayed, soft white flakes of leftover snow shivering to the ground with each blast of wind. It had snowed in southern Louisiana.

Nothing normal had happened to her over this last weekend. Ice. Snow. Another breakup—okay, that was normal. Then the car wreck. And she'd wound up in a stranger's house, hurt and confused. A stranger who'd turned out to be a nice man with two cute kids. What were the odds of that happening? And to her, of all people?

And to top it off, she's lost the one possession she treasured above anything else, her golden locket. Good things were supposed to happen with that locket, but so far Goldie could only count her "good things" on one hand. While she could count her not-so-good relationships breaking up on the other hand.

I've had too many disappointing tries at finding a soul mate, Lord. So I won't get my hopes up again.

She might have lost her precious locket to Rory Branagan. But she would not lose her heart.

Rory walked up the path to his mother's rambling ranch-style house, missing his dad. It was times such as these he'd go into his dad's big workshop out back and have a man-to-man discussion on doing the right thing. However, he wasn't here anymore. But Rory could talk to God, asking for strength and guidance, and he could talk to his mom on most subjects. At least he had his faith to get him through the rough spots.

And he was in a rough spot tonight, for sure.

Of all the houses, how'd she wind up in mine?

He'd been limping along, getting things done and taking care of his boys. He'd managed to restart his life after Rachel had died. For his boys' sake he'd prayed for God to ease the anger and the bitterness of his wife's senseless death, had even tried to forgive the person who'd taken her life. But not once in the last long months had he ever asked God to send him a replacement. Because no one could replace Rachel.

And it hurt him to even think in those terms.

But he still couldn't get Goldie Rios out of his mind.

"You gonna turn into an icicle, standing out there on the steps, son."

Rory looked around to find his mother at the door, her shawl clasped around her shoulders. "Hey, Mom. Sorry I'm so late—again."

"Get in here," Frances ordered, her smile indulgent and full of a mother's love.

Rory knocked the mud and dirty snow off his boots. "Where are the boys?"

"In the back den, watching one of those children's movies you keep me supplied with. We played some games, had some chili for dinner and now they're quiet and absorbed in watching talking animals going on all kinds of adventures."

He shut the door then took off his down jacket. "Mom, am I taking advantage of your good graces?"

Frances pulled her shawl more tightly around her shoulders. "Rory, haven't we had this conversation before? You know how I feel about those two. I don't mind helping out."

"But you have a life," he countered, guilt weighing at him. "I could find a sitter occasionally."

"Don't you dare," Frances replied, motioning to the kitchen. "C'mon. I just made hot chocolate."

Rory followed her into the neat, whitewashed room. He'd helped his father redo the cabinets and tile in this kitchen. "Maybe I should spend more time with them."

"That can't hurt," Frances reflected, handing him a mug of the steaming chocolate milk. "Sam acts out now and then."

"Has he been giving you trouble?"

"Nothing I can't handle," Frances replied. "He gets a little smart-alecky at times but I think he just misses his mother. And...he's growing up so fast."

"Then I do need to spend more time with them."

"You have to work, son. And I don't mind being the disciplinarian, as long as I have your permission on that."

"You know you do. But I'm gonna make sure I get home on time—as many days as I can. And I'll do more with them on the weekends. We've got soccer and baseball again in the spring at least."

"That's good, but your job is unpredictable. Just keep doing the best you can and God will take care of the rest."

Rory looked around the corner toward the den where Sam and Tyler lay curled in the sleeping bags Frances kept here just for them. He loved his boys with all his heart and each time he looked at them, he missed their mother.

"What's wrong, anyway?" Frances asked. Then she put a hand to her throat. "Is it this woman? The girl you found in your house last night?"

Rory could never hide anything from his mother. He shrugged. "She sure did shake up my normal routine."

"I'll say. It was mighty nice of you to give her a ride home from the hospital."

"I did it for Miss Ruth. You know she's been down with hip replacement surgery. Goldie's staying with her until she's well again."

Frances looked doubtful. "That sounds like a nice

gesture but surely this girl won't be around much longer, right?"

Rory knew what his mother was saying. Goldie would go back to Baton Rouge soon and therefore, he had no business getting involved with her. "I think she's staying through the holidays."

Frances put down her empty cup. "Hmm. Holidays have a way of making everything look so lovely, don't they?"

Then she turned and headed into the den, leaving her son to wonder what in the world she was talking about. Did his mother think he was going to have some holiday fling then just go back to life as usual once the new year came?

Didn't she know he wasn't that kind of man?

Yes, she did. But she didn't know what kind of woman Goldie Rios was and that was why she'd made such a pointed statement to him.

And she might be right. Because Rory knew that just like the fresh snow that had fallen last night, things could turn ugly come the light of day. And he had his boys to protect.

No time to even consider getting to know Goldie Rios even though he'd been thinking of doing that exact thing.

He'd just search for her locket and leave it at that. It was the best thing to do, all the way around.

Chapter Five

Dear Goldie:
How do I get rid of the clutter in my life? My
house is a wreck and so is my love life. I can't
help but wonder if the two are connected—Shipwrecked in Serepta

A few days later, Goldie stared at the email question, thinking she could use some advice on that subject herself. While her topics mostly concentrated on
rearranging furniture and adding plants and flowers to
make a room "pop," her readers sometimes threw her
a curve ball by combining messiness in their homes
with messiness in their personal lives. And this was
one such question.

"Talk about timing."

Well, she owed this reader an answer and she also
owed her publisher a column for this week. And her
blog needed updating. So she'd better come up with a
concrete, logical answer. Did she dare tell her readers
about her accident and her blow to the head? And that

she'd been rescued by a wonderful man but she was too afraid to flirt with him and get to know him?

"Maybe later," she said out loud. She didn't want to overload her loyal followers with the shaky details of her own troubles. She'd just answer this question to the best of her abilities, based on her own instincts and tons of research from experts.

She'd keyed in "Dear Shipwrecked" when a knock came at her bedroom door.

"Yes?" Knowing it was her grandmother, Goldie tried to sound upbeat. Grams didn't like downers or whiners.

"Are you going to church with me? It's Wednesday-night dinner and devotions."

"No, Grams. I have a deadline." And since she'd only had one quick phone call from Rory, telling her he hadn't found her locket anywhere on his property, Goldie couldn't even use that excuse for trying to see him at church. Besides, that would be just plain wrong. Even if she wasn't exactly a regular church attendee, she wouldn't use a church supper as an excuse to see a man. Would she?

It didn't matter. He probably was way too busy during the week to come to Wednesday-night dinner and devotionals anyway. That was mostly for the senior adult crowd that Grams hung with. Which made Goldie even more determined not to go as the poor still-single granddaughter of Ruth Rios. She'd get too many questions and innuendos from well-meaning but clueless senior citizens.

Ruth opened the door, the smell of vanilla lotion wafting into the room. She was dressed and ready, wearing a bright red Christmas sweater with gold metallic threads shooting through it. Leaning on her walker, she said, "It's my first time back at church since my surgery, honey. I'd really like it if you came with me."

Goldie pushed away from her laptop. "You can't go to church, Grams. You can't drive yourself yet. Doctor's orders."

"I'm not," Ruth corrected, her handbag already on her arm. "You're driving me. So you might as well stay and eat and hear Reverend Howe's devotional, too."

"But I'm not ready," Goldie replied, her gaze lingering on the big cup of coffee she'd just poured. "I'm in my sweats."

"All the more reason to hurry up and get dressed," Ruth proposed. "It's casual, so you don't have to fuss."

"But I thought Phyllis usually picked you up for church events anyway. Didn't she do that a lot before your surgery?"

Ruth's expression bordered on agitation. Placing her hands together over the bars on her walker, she explained, "Phyllis is way across town running errands and I'm not going to make her go out of her way when I have a perfectly good driver staying here in my home."

Goldie knew defeat when she saw it. And it shined brightly triumphant all over her grandmother's face. She also knew that Phyllis being across town didn't mean a whole lot, considering how small this town actually was. But when Grams got a notion in her mind, it didn't go away.

Goldie let out a sigh. "I'll be ready in ten minutes."

"Good." Grams shut the door with a soft victory swish.

Goldie stared down at her computer, wondering why she couldn't just tell her grandmother no sometimes. But she knew the answer to that. Grams had depended on Goldie for a long time now, since Angela wasn't in the picture as far as being a caring daughter-in-law. And Goldie depended on Grams to be her grandmother and mother, since Angela wasn't a caring mother, either. It was a mutual, unspoken rule around here. And even though Goldie had traveled a lot herself, she'd settled down to a pretty normal routine after she'd taken the job in Baton Rouge. Her work was just flexible enough to allow her travel time if she needed it and sometimes she did travel on assignment. It worked for her. And that was why she was here in Viola.

So she could be near Grammy, to help her.

And so Grammy could return the favor.

That was why Goldie was now rushing to throw on a green sweater and a black skirt and matching boots. Eyeing herself in the mirror, she decided there wasn't much she could do about the big bandage covering one half of her head, so she grabbed a wool hat with an embroidered blue and green flower woven into its seams, hoping that it would add some dash to her church-going ensemble.

"I'll get back to you later," she promised Shipwrecked.

After she figured out how to fix the clutter that seemed to be blocking her own nonexistent love life.

Rory watched as Goldie entered the church fellowship hall with her grandmother. Goldie held Ruth's arm, taking time to let her grandmother push her walker slowly up the aisle. They stopped to greet people, Ruth hugging and laughing while Goldie hung back as if she'd just walked into a dark forest. She actually looked afraid. But the cute hat made her look jaunty in spite of that lost expression on her face.

Goldie Rios obviously didn't like venturing into unknown territory. But the woman was supposed to be a world traveler and Rory knew that took courage and smarts. So why did she seem so out of place in Viola?

Or was she just out of place inside a church?

He kept watching her while his mother watched him. The boys were safely behind closed doors enjoying a tailor-made children's program and their own dinner, so for the next hour, he didn't have that responsibility. It was kind of nice to just watch a woman, to study her habits, to get to know her through her expressions and her body language.

Whoa! Rory reminded himself Goldie wasn't one of his wild animals, even if she did have that deer-in-the-headlights expression on her pretty face.

"Rory, it's rude to stare," his mother whispered in his ear.

He glanced at Frances, saw the disapproval in her eyes and wondered if he didn't have a new kind of war on his hands. His mother, usually so serene and even-tempered, seemed determined to thwart his attempts at flirting with a woman. Or at least with this particular woman. "Mom, I found her hurt and unconscious in my house last weekend. And she lost her necklace, probably at my house somewhere. It's natural that I'd want to make sure she is all right."

"She looks fit as a fiddle to me," Frances noted, her

tone full of sarcasm. "And I'm sure she has a lot of jewelry, so quit worrying about that locket."

If they hadn't been in church, Rory might have retorted something back, but he wouldn't get into this
with his mother in the Lord's house. He could understand her need to protect him, but he was a grown man.

"I'm a grown man," he said before he could grab
his tongue.

"I happen to know that." Frances aimed her chin toward Goldie. "And I'm pretty sure she's noticed, too."

He grinned at his mother. "I hope so."

Frances gave him a sharp-edged glare but didn't
voice any hostile words. Thankfully, the preacher entered the building and quieted everyone so he could
bless the meal of beef stew and biscuits provided by the
Women's Prayer Group. That ended any further conversation regarding Goldie Rios.

But Rory did take his time looking at her when he
buttered a biscuit or passed the dessert brownies. And
when she glanced around after she'd settled her grandmother in a chair at the end of the long table across from
Rory, her eyes locked with his and he smiled a greeting.

Goldie nodded then turned to face front and…never
once looked back during the entire meal or Reverend
Howe's interesting devotional.

Rory *was* here. Goldie kept thinking that as she ate
her stew and chatted with Grammy's friends. He was
here and even two brownies hadn't helped stifle her curiosity. He'd told her that he attended her grandmother's
church and even though the thought of seeing him here
had crossed her mind several times as she'd hurried to

get ready, Goldie hadn't figured he'd actually show up on a Wednesday night. She folded her devotional sheet and put it in her purse, wondering if she should say hi to Rory. She'd kept her mind on the reverend's talk but the whole time she could almost feel Rory's eyes centered on the back of her head.

Or rather, on the back of her hat.

"Goldie, are you ready?"

She turned to find Grammy staring at her with a fixed expression. Everyone else was getting up to leave now that the closing prayer was over. "Oh, sorry. Yes, I'm ready."

"Did you have an extra prayer on your mind?" Grams asked sweetly. "Reverend Howe could pray with you."

"You could say that," Goldie replied, standing to help her grandmother into the aisle. Pushing the walker toward Ruth, she added, "But I'm good, Grams. I don't need to talk to the preacher."

"I'm so glad you came with me tonight, honey. You could use the Lord's centering in your life, you know."

Her grandmother might just have a point. The devotional had helped Goldie in a weird kind of way. Reverend Howe had talked about worrying, or rather, how to stop worrying—based on a passage in the book of Matthew. Goldie could use that advice, for sure. She did worry; she worried about keeping things in order. She worried about her job and never missing a deadline. She worried about being on time and trying to look and do her best. She worried that her best wasn't good enough. And she worried that this was it—this was as good as her life was going to get.

But why? What did worrying accomplish, except

more worrying? Turning some of that over to the Lord might just do the trick if she gave it a serious shot, at least. But right now, she was really worried about whether she should avoid Rory or say hello to him.

Then she remembered she had a legitimate question to ask him. She could ask about her locket—again—just in case. Which was good, because he was coming up behind her on the aisle. She caught sight of him when she turned to greet one of her grandmother's friends.

"Hi." Rory pulled Goldie to the side, smiling at her and hoping to wipe that look of unease off her face. "How are you?"

"I'm good," she said, brushing at her hat. "Grams kind of sprung this on me, so I didn't have much time to style my hair."

"And you're hiding the bandage, right?"

"You got me there. It's not a pretty sight."

"I like the hat."

She touched it again. "Thanks. It did keep my head warm."

She must be too warm; she had a nice flush going on. "No more dizziness?"

She looked uncertain then shook her head. "No, not from the concussion, at least."

Her blush indicated maybe he could be the reason she was getting a little light-headed. And for some reason, that made him feel the same way. "Well, I just wanted to say hello. We're going home to finish homework."

"Oh, homework," she repeated, clutching her purse to her side. "I guess with two kids, you'd have a lot of that. Hey, did you happen to look for my locket again?"

He glanced down at the patterned carpet in the church hall. "Every time I've had a chance. I didn't find anything outside the house but we have a lot of leaves that need raking. And I did search again in the den and kitchen. Even took out the vacuum cleaner and hoped I'd hit on the necklace that way. Found a lot of lost toys and coins, but no necklaces. I'm sorry."

"Okay. I guess I've lost it for sure this time."

Surprised, Rory asked, "Have you misplaced it before?"

"No, not really. I have a spot for it back at home—right on top of my dresser. But here, in Grammy's spare bedroom, I just have a small travel case and I usually put it in there. I like things to be in their proper place."

She sure got all flustered when things weren't right where she expected them to be, or so it seemed from the few times he'd been around her. "Uh-huh."

Crestfallen, she lifted her chin in a brave front. "I've been known to toss it in there amid all the other jewelry I have with me, though. But it always turns up."

"Well, don't give up on it yet. It might be underneath the couch cushions and I just haven't touched on it yet."

She gave a shaky nod. "I owe you a new cushion, too."

"You do?"

"Yes. I'm pretty sure I left a bloodstain on your other one."

"I did put it in the laundry room. But it was already pretty messy from pizza and ice cream stains."

She smiled at that. "Well, Grammy's giving me the eye. This dinner was one of her first big outings, so I'm sure she's tired. I'd better get her home and all tucked in."

Rory could imagine Goldie tucking her grandmother into bed and making sure Ruth was comfortable and safe. That image made his heart soften into a pile of mush. He was about to tell her goodbye when he felt a hand on his arm. Rory's mother smiled at him. "The boys are getting restless."

"Oh, sorry, Mom. I'm coming." Rory looked back at Goldie. "Goldie Rios, this is my mother, Frances Branagan."

"Hello, Mrs. Branagan," Goldie greeted, reaching out a hand to his mother, her eyes bright with sincerity and curiosity.

Frances took her hand and smiled at her. "So this is the famous Goldie. How are you doing? No more head pain, I hope."

"I'm fine," Goldie reassured, grinning. "Just a few stitches and an ugly bandage."

To her credit, Frances was the very essence of politeness. "I'm glad you're all better. You gave Rory and the boys quite a scare."

A rush of little feet stopped the conversation. "Hey, it's her. The pretty lady who almost died on our couch!"

Rory winced as everyone around them turned to look after Tyler's loud announcement. "Tyler, use your inside voice," he cautioned.

"Too late for that," Frances pointed out, her tone firm but indulgent. "Tyler, it's time to go."

But Tyler was now clinging to Goldie's sweater. "You didn't die, did you?"

"No, I'm alive and well," Goldie said, her eyes wide with wonder and embarrassment. Then she leaned down. "And I do appreciate all your help."

Tyler grinned up at her. "All I did was stand there and get in the way."

That made her laugh. And caused something like a delicate snowflake to shimmy down inside Rory's soul.

Goldie looked up at Rory and Frances. "He is adorable, just like Grams said."

Frances let out an unladylike snort. "Yeah, right."

Sam walked up, his expression bordering on hostile. "Dad, I've got math to do."

Rory shot his oldest son a warning look. "Sam, don't be so rude. Can't you say hello to our friend Goldie?"

Sam stared at Goldie, but refused to acknowledge her. "Can we go now?"

Frances pulled at Sam's shirt collar. "Not until you show some manners, young man. Your father wants you to say hello."

"Hello!" Sam yelled an exaggerated holler, causing even more people to stop and stare.

Goldie's smile looked pasted on this time. She shifted her gaze from Sam to Rory then back to Sam. "Hi, Sam. It's good to see you again. And at least I'm not seeing two of you tonight."

Sam did a fake laugh. "Ha-ha. That's funny."

Rory felt the red all the way down to his toes. This was going from bad to worse. And he'd only stopped to greet Goldie at church. Imagine what his family might do if he did actually ask the woman out on a date.

He knew the answer to that. They'd all make him pay one way or another. Was he so wrong to want to get to know Goldie better?

Giving Goldie one last apologetic glance, he said,

"I guess we'll see you later. I'll keep looking for your locket, I promise."

"Oh, okay then." She waved to him as Tyler and Sam dragged him down the steps. "Thanks."

Sam pulled away to turn and stare at Goldie. "We don't have her stupid necklace, Dad."

Rory pushed the boys into the car then closed the door on his mother's questioning expression.

Then he got in, took a deep breath and announced, "I guess I won't have to worry about ever dating a woman with you three around. Y'all embarrassed Goldie in there."

"I tried to be nice," Frances replied, her tone low and pensive.

"I just wanted to keep her," Tyler reminded them. "But y'all wouldn't let me."

"I hate her," Sam retorted, glaring at Rory in the rearview mirror. "And I'm sick of hearing about that dumb necklace she lost."

Frances gasped. "Sam, that is no way to talk."

Rory turned in his seat. "You and I are going to have a long discussion on manners when we get home, son. You know better than to talk like that to an adult. In fact, we don't talk to anyone in such a bad tone, ever."

Sam hung his head, his lips jutted out in a firm pout.

Frances gave him a hard stare then shrugged. "I'm sorry, Rory."

"Yeah, me, too."

Rory cranked the car and left the church parking lot. But he did notice Goldie in the glow of the outside church lights, watching as he drove away. And he could only imagine what she must be thinking.

Chapter Six

Two days later, Goldie was thinking of Rory Branagan. Again.

"I have to stop this," she whispered to herself as she fingered her hair. The gauze bandage was gone, but she did have a sore spot underneath the new part in her hair. And it was itching.

Just like her curious mind was itching with questions. Such as, why did she feel so drawn to this man? And why did one of his sons want to adopt her while the other one seemed to hate her? And what about his mother? Bad vibes there, no doubt. Was Frances Branagan being overly protective or did she see something in Goldie that didn't impress her enough to want Goldie to get to know her son?

Can't blame her, Goldie thought as she wrapped up the ending paragraph of her blog. She'd already sent her weekly column, and yes, she'd answered Shipwrecked's question with authority and aplomb, the point being if your home is cluttered then you probably have underlying emotional clutter to clear out, too.

But what if you ran screaming from clutter and messy situations? Goldie wondered. She'd been doing that for most of her life. And she knew, deep in her soul, that all the moving around and traveling had only worsened her compulsive nature. And now, she'd made a career out of keeping clutter at bay.

When are you going to delve into your own over-packed mess of emotions? The voice in her head played that loop over and over again while Goldie just kept pushing it away.

She looked at the tidy little room that had become her haven over the last few weeks, taking in the blue-and-brown-striped curtains and deep brown bedspread with the blue flower sprigs she'd bought at the super-store on the highway. Her gaze moved over the matching canvas baskets and containers she'd placed on an old bookshelf next to the many research books she had brought with her. The dainty old desk she'd found in the shed out back had been restored to a sky blue. Her laptop and a white pencil holder sat pristinely on the desk, her papers stacked and sorted and arranged just so by her open spiral-bound day calendar. A brown vase of freshly cut mums left over from Grammy's fall garden brightened the room. And the one picture on the wall reflected a rocking chair set against a white porch, the blues of the flowers along the brown steps in the picture perfectly matching the color scheme of this room. She'd done that, made this room her home for now. Until it was time to move on.

She'd come here after Grammy's surgery and re-organized almost the whole house in between trips to the hospital and then later chauffeuring Grams to the rehab unit, working at her laptop in the lobby while Grams went through therapy. Grams had come home to a better-organized house, her shock evident even when she'd thanked Goldie for making everything so convenient for her.

And Goldie had gotten two columns and three blog posts out of the whole makeover, passing on tips and suggestions to her readers with delight. Not bad. Not bad at all.

But there was still that tangled mess inside her mind that needed to be sorted. And thinking about Rory only made the tangle even crazier—and harder to unravel.

Her laptop dinged with a new email. Goldie glanced at it then opened the message.

Dear Goldie:
Thanks for the advice you gave to "Shipwrecked in Serepta." I feel the same way sometimes. I'm not a very neat person but I'd like to have more control in my life. I've tried sorting through magazines and catalogs with plans to just toss them, but they always seem to pile up around me again. Sometimes I order things I don't even need or want. How can I stay on top of all the trash that seems to accumulate in my house and stop buying things I don't really need?
—Buried in Bossier City

Goldie stared down at the words on her screen. She'd have to carefully consider this, do some research with the experts and get back to Buried. Because this was about more than just catalogs and magazines and all the pretty enticements such things offered. This was about having an orderly life and making sure all the stacks and stacks of junk didn't bury the real issues. Whatever the real issues might be.

She saved the message then grabbed her cell phone and stood to go outside. Maybe a short walk would get rid of this restlessness. Passing where Grams sat knitting as she watched the evening news, Goldie tossed a wrap over her shoulders and called out, "I'll be in the backyard getting some fresh air if you need me, Grammy. I have my phone so you can page me."

Grammy shifted then held up her own phone. "Got mine right here handy." Giving Goldie a glance, she added, "It's a Friday night. Shouldn't you be out with people your own age?"

Goldie laughed out loud. "In case you haven't noticed, there aren't a whole lot of people my age living in Viola."

Grams chuckled. "What about your friend Carla from Baton Rouge? She could drive up and spend the weekend here with us."

"Yeah, I'm sure Carla will jump right on that idea." Then because Grams looked confused, she said, "It's okay. I'm fine. We'll watch a movie after supper, okay?"

"If I can stay awake that long," Ruth replied.

Goldie went out the back door, her boots hitting against dry leaves and crunchy winter grass. It was just hitting that cold time of evening when the sun officially became a golden glow behind the horizon and dusk blanketed the air with a crisp intensity. That time between work and coming home, she thought. She tugged the long wool wrap around her neck. Maybe she should have grabbed a jacket, but she'd only be out here a few minutes.

Then she heard a sound coming from the concrete canal just beyond her grandmother's property line. Such canals and aqueducts were common in flood-prone, flat Louisiana. But that sound wasn't so common. It came again, a yelp of pain. Deciding there must be a wounded animal down there, Goldie pushed through the trees and shrubs and glanced across the chain-link fence. Then she saw a movement in the bramble where a puddle of old mud, tree limbs and leaves had pooled near one of the drains.

Another yelp caused her to gasp. A black and white puppy was down there and from the looks of things, the poor baby had become trapped in some washed-up rope and old vines. "Hold on, little fellow."

Goldie didn't hesitate. She immediately ran to the crooked chain-link gate and opened it, determined to make her way down the side of the slippery canal so she could untangle the shivering animal below. But the concrete ditch was steep and still moist from the storm. She held on to an old vine, hoping to use it for leverage so she could shimmy down the side of the concrete embankment.

"Hold on, little puppy. I'm coming."

The vine broke, sending Goldie right into the pile of tangled vines and wet, muddy leaves. With a whoosh, she hit bottom hard, landing right next to the trapped puppy. The dog started yelping, excitement and fear causing the scared animal to step back. But his little paw was all caught up in the mess.

"Hold on, baby," Goldie cooed after she'd caught her breath. "Let me see if I broke anything."

She sat there, the wetness seeping into her jeans causing her to shiver and groan. "This doesn't feel so good." She would be bruised but she was probably all right. At least she hadn't hit her head again. Reaching across to the shaking little dog, Goldie lowered her voice. "It's okay, fellow. I promise. I'll get us out of here somehow."

But when she looked back up at the solid wall of aged concrete, she wondered at her own good sense. Why hadn't she thought to bring a rope or a ladder at least?

"I guess we're in trouble," she confessed to the hyper dog. Trying anew to gain the animal's trust, she held her hand out, palm down, so he could sniff her knuckles.

The trembling little dog lifted his nostrils from his spot but didn't try to come any closer to Goldie. "I assure you I'm on your side," she said, looking around to see what she could do.

Dusk was setting in right on time. Cold air penetrated her wet clothes. Her lightweight sweater and wrap didn't help much. Her clothes were now sagging with mud. She could probably grab a vine or a low branch from one of the cypress trees but she was afraid that wouldn't hold her weight.

"Any suggestions?" she asked the anxious puppy.

He growled and yelped.

"I see. You're no help."

Goldie grabbed her cell phone out of her pocket. She'd have to call Grams to send help. And she had a feeling she knew exactly who Grams could call.

The nuisance hunter.

* * *

Rory had just finished washing the dinner plates when the phone rang. Glancing at the clock, he let out a sigh. And hoped he wouldn't be called out tonight. He'd been looking forward to a quiet night with the boys.

"Hello," he answered, bracing himself.

"Rory, it's Ruth Rios. I need your help."

Rory smiled in spite of his dread. "Not another armadillo, Miss Ruth?"

"No, not this time. It's Goldie. She's somehow gotten herself stuck in the drainage canal behind my house. She was trying to get to a little puppy and now they're both stuck. She's okay but she can't get back up the wall. Something about carrying the dog and too much mud and everything being slippery. I can't do anything to help her and she can't stay out there all night."

"I'll be right there," Rory said. He hung up the phone then turned to the boys. "C'mon, you two. We've got a mission."

"You're taking us with you?" Tyler asked, his big eyes going wide.

"Yep. Your grandmother is out with her church group tonight. And this should be an easy job. Y'all might get to help."

Sam didn't look so sure. "I have homework."

"Bring it with you. You can stay inside with Miss Ruth and finish up while I help Goldie."

Hostility oozed from Sam's pores. "We're going to that woman's house?"

"Yes, Sam, we are. Now don't argue with me. Just get your coat, your books and lesson plans and let's go.

It's cold out there and Goldie is stuck in a ditch with a puppy."

"A puppy?" Tyler grabbed his down jacket. "You said *we* might get a puppy, remember?"

"I remember," Rory replied. He'd held off getting a pet for the boys because they were rarely home during the weekdays. And he wasn't so sure his sons were ready for that kind of responsibility. Maybe taking them on this rescue mission wasn't such a hot idea. "Let's just go help Goldie and Miss Ruth and we'll talk about that later."

"Maybe we can have *this* puppy," Tyler suggested, his tone relentless in its enthusiasm. "I'd like that."

Rory pinched his nose with his fingers. "Get in the truck, son."

The boys hopped into his big truck, one scowling and one smiling. It was gonna be another long night.

Goldie heard the roar of a truck's engine. Looking over at the dog she'd dubbed Spike because he reminded her of the Peanuts cartoon character that was Snoopy's cousin, she grinned. "Cavalry's here, Spike. We'll be inside by the fire in about five minutes, tops."

Spike had inched closer but he still shivered with resistance. But his yelps had turned into whimpers now.

"I know you're cold and scared," Goldie whispered, her hand reaching out to the dog, "but I'm here with you and Rory is a highly trained expert. He'll get us out of this, I promise." She stared up at the evening star over her head. "And so will God. God loves all creatures, you know. Even scruffy little dogs."

Spike whimpered then yelped with a more positive enthusiasm this time.

"Good. You understand. I like that in a dog."

"Well, aren't you two cozy down there."

Goldie turned to find Rory grinning at her.

And what a grin. His expression held amusement and concern all in one good-looking package. Or maybe what was left of the muted early-evening light was playing tricks on her. "Hey there. 'Bout time you got here."

Rory shook his head. "Why is it that I always find you in a dire situation?"

"Just call it the *Perils of Pauline*," Goldie said, shrugging. "I could have found a way back up but I didn't want to leave Spike down here by himself."

"Of course not." Rory motioned behind him. "Tyler, stay right there. We might need you to help with…uh… Spike when we bring these two up."

Tyler peeked over the fence. "Hey, Miss Goldie. You found a puppy?"

Goldie nodded. "Sure did. And we've gotten pretty close over the last half hour. I think he's hungry and cold. And so am I."

Rory opened the gate then brought Grammy's ladder through. "Goldie, can you walk? I mean, you didn't damage anything, did you?"

"Nothing but my pride. That wet concrete doesn't have a lot of traction."

He looked around. "I can see that. I'm gonna unfold the ladder and hold it for you to come up, okay?"

"Okay, but what about Spike?"

"Will he come to you?"

"He might. He's still a little skittish, though. And I have to get him untangled, if he'll let me."

Rory turned to Tyler. "Son, run in the house and ask Miss Ruth for a piece of cheese. Tell Sam to get it for her."

"Okay." Tyler took off.

Rory faced Goldie. "I could come down there myself and try to free him."

"No, don't do that," Goldie argued. "He's just now gotten used to me. You'd probably scare him all over again. Maybe the food will help. If not, then you can give it a try."

"Okay, 'cause as much as I'm enjoying this lovely scene, I promised your grandmother I wouldn't leave you in this ditch."

Goldie smiled, happy for the company even if she was frozen solid. "So, are most of your Friday nights this exciting, Rory?"

"Not before you came along," he replied, that grin still intact. "You know, you're becoming more of a nuisance than any animals I've ever had to hunt."

"Sorry," she mumbled, his teasing words stinging her with a bite that beat the cold. "I didn't want Grams to call you, but she insisted you were the best man for the job."

He laughed at that. "I can't say I've ever had to rescue a human being before, that is—"

"I know, before I hit town. I'll try to be more careful after this."

He slanted his head. "If you didn't scare me so much with your mishaps, I'd tell you to keep it up. At least it's an excuse to see a pretty lady now and then, bleeding head and wet mud and yelping dogs aside."

"Very funny."

But those words hadn't stung at all. No, his *flirting* words poured over Goldie, warming her to the core in spite of his intentional references to her accident-prone existence. But the man did have a point. She always seemed to be in some sort of predicament in spite of touting herself as organized and completely together.

Then Tyler came running with the hunk of cheese. "I had to get it myself. Sam wouldn't help. But Miss Ruth told me right where to find it in the refrigerator."

The warmth left Goldie's soul. Sam didn't like her. And that could be a big problem since she didn't have a clue about handling a little boy. She didn't even have such a great track record with the big boys, either. So why was she even bothering with the idea of getting to know Rory better?

She stood and held out a hand to catch the cheese Rory tossed down. Then she turned to Spike, enticing him with the food. "Okay, fellow, you have to help me out here." She leaned close and whispered, "'Cause I think I could really fall for this one and I shouldn't do that for oh, so many reasons."

Spike barked at her then tugged to be free from his constraints. Seeing that as a good sign, Goldie carefully scooted toward the little dog, broke the cheese into tiny pieces and held out her hand again.

Spike strained toward her and licked her knuckles then after sniffing, ate the cheese from her hand. When he was finished, Goldie carefully lifted the squirming animal up and worked to free his paw from the twisted vines and coarse old rope that had snared him. Spike fidgeted and yelped a bit, but he looked up at Goldie with trusting eyes until she had him free.

"He's fallen for you," Rory said, his tone muted and low as it echoed out on the night air.

When Goldie turned around to stare up at him, she thought she saw something there in his glistening eyes.

Something that excited her even while it confused her.

"I know how you feel," she said to Spike. Then she scooped up the little dog in her arms and dragged her aching, wet self toward the ladder.

And took the hand of the man waiting there for her at the top.

"Good to see you again, Goldilocks," Rory teased as he lifted her onto the grass.

Goldie swallowed the lump in her throat. "Thanks for coming, Rory. Thanks again for helping me."

Rory tugged her wet wrap away then took off his own down jacket and wrapped it around Goldie and Spike.

"Let's get y'all inside to the fire."

Goldie looked down at Spike again, the warmth of Rory's jacket cocooning them like a security blanket.

"We're safe now, little fellow."

And she knew that she was safe, even if this man could be a big danger to her tattered emotions.

Chapter Seven

"Rory, that's a nice fire."

Rory put another log on then turned to smile at Ruth. The tiny lights on the Christmas tree by the window twinkled almost as much as her eyes. "I've had lots of practice." He sat down on the couch beside Tyler. "How's that hot chocolate, son?"

"Good," Tyler said. "Almost as good as MeeMaw's."

Ruth laughed at that. "Grandmas always make the best." She glanced over to the tiny dining table where Sam sat reading a book, his brow wrinkled with a scowl. "Sam, would you like some more hot chocolate?"

Sam eyed Rory, saw the warning look Rory shot him then said, "No, ma'am. Thank you."

Goldie came into the living room, wearing clean clothes and carrying Spike in her arms. "I have a new shadow," she proclaimed, smiling down at the now-clean puppy. "I managed to wipe him down with a wet rag at least. Think I got most of the mud and leaves out of his fur."

Tyler rushed over. "Can I pet him, Miss Goldie?"

"Sure," Goldie responded. She sank down on a floral ottoman by the fire. "Just be careful. He's still kind of scared."

"I wonder if he got lost," Tyler said, carefully rubbing Spike's thick hair. "Or maybe somebody left him."

"I hope not," Ruth said. "It's not nice to leave a helpless little animal out in the cold on a night such as this."

"What kind of dog is he, Dad?" Tyler asked, still petting Spike. The dog settled into Goldie's lap and held his nose up to Tyler, obviously deciding he had yet another new friend.

Rory grinned. "I'd say he's a Sooner, son."

"What kind of dog is that?" Tyler asked.

"He'd sooner be one breed as another," Rory replied, winking at Goldie.

She laughed then held Spike up in the air. "You hear that, boy? I think you've been insulted."

"He doesn't care," Ruth stated. "He's safe and warm now and that's all that matters."

"Are you gonna keep him?" Tyler inquired of Goldie.

She looked over at Rory. "I'd like to, but I won't be able to take him back to Baton Rouge with me. My apartment doesn't allow pets."

"Then you oughta just stay here with Miss Ruth," Tyler claimed in a reasonable tone.

Rory saw Goldie's reaction to that. She got all flustered and fidgety. Which meant she wasn't planning on sticking around any longer than necessary.

"Tyler, Miss Goldie lives in the city and she's a very busy woman. She doesn't have time to keep a dog."

Goldie lifted her eyebrows in protest. "I didn't say

that. I just said my lease agreement clearly states no pets."

"You could move," Tyler said, intent on helping out with this situation. "Or you could just give Spike to me. I'd take good care of him. Sam could help, right, Sam?"

"Yeah, whatever," Sam said, his tone full of disdain.

Rory watched Goldie's reaction to his eldest son's rudeness, wishing he could figure out what Sam's problem was. But he knew the boy had struggled since he'd lost his mother and no amount of talking to the church counselor or asking God for mercies had seemed to help.

Maybe adopting a dog would. "Sam, would you be willing to help take care of Spike if we took him?"

Sam slapped his book closed, but his eyes did grow wide with interest. "I don't care. Maybe."

"I care," Tyler said, jumping up to clap his hands. "Can we take him home, Daddy?"

Rory looked from Sam's frowning face to Tyler's hopeful one. "Not tonight, boys. We're not prepared and it's too late to get supplies tonight."

Of course, he could rustle up a doggie bed and some food easily enough but he wasn't ready to make a commitment until he figured out what to do about Sam's surly response. He wanted to teach his sons responsibility but first he'd have to see if Sam was willing to go the distance and help Tyler with the dog.

Goldie stood up, holding Spike close. "I have an idea. How about I keep him here with me and Grams until it's time for me to go back home after Christmas? That way, we can enjoy him and make him feel secure. And in the meantime, you can buy whatever you need to set up a home for him and maybe your daddy can go over some rules with you on how to care for an animal. How does that sound?"

Tyler looked confused at first then turned to Rory. "Dad, would that be okay?"

Rory shot Goldie an appreciative nod. "That just might work. But first, we have to convince your brother that he'd help you take care of Spike. Sam, you hear that?"

Sam glared at the little dog. "I don't care, I told you already. It's just a dumb animal." He went back to pretending to read but Rory noticed he glanced at the puppy a couple of times.

Ruth raised up in her chair. "Sounds as if Sam doesn't like dogs. I've never known a boy not to want a puppy." She shrugged, acting indifferent to Sam's attitude. "Oh, well. I guess if this plan isn't approved by all the Branagan men, then I might wind up with Spike as my only companion once Goldie goes back to Baton Rouge. And me old and hardly able to walk. I'd have to get a sitter for the little fellow every time I go to therapy. And I can't even lift the poor animal. I'd worry constantly that he'd get loose and run away again. On the other hand, I could certainly babysit Spike for whoever else he winds up with. That would be easier on me—and Spike, too, I imagine." She let out a long, dramatic sigh. "I guess after Goldie leaves, I'll have to put an ad in the paper to find him a suitable home. If only—"

"I didn't say no," Sam countered, his tone quieter now. He rubbed a hand across his nose. "I'd have to think about it some more and find out what needs to be done, is all."

Ruth clapped her hands together in glee. "That

sounds like a logical process. Rory, you never told me
how smart Sam is. He's taking his time so as not to rush
into this lightly and I think that's very wise. Taking care
of someone else is hard work, as we adults well know."

Rory wanted to kiss Miss Ruth. Instead, he glanced
over at Goldie. "So you're gonna keep Spike for now?"

"Yes, I am," she agreed, nuzzling the dog. "He's really a sweet puppy." Then she looked at Sam. "But when
it's time for me to leave, I hope y'all can take him. And
I hope you'll bring him back to visit Grams now and
then. That would make me feel better."

Sam eyed Rory, his scowl gone for now. But the frustration and disappointment showing on his face was
almost worse than any scowl. "What if he belongs to
someone else, Dad? Then we'd have to give him back."

Rory's heart hurt for his son. Maybe Sam was afraid
to love again. Rory sure knew that feeling.

Ruth let out a gasp before Rory could respond. "See
how smart he is. Sam's right. Maybe we should ask
around before we go making plans for our new friend."

"I'll do that," Goldie said. "I'll put out flyers around
the neighborhood and ask some of the neighbors if
they're missing a pet. Good thinking, Sam."

Sam lowered his head again. "Can we go now, Dad?"

"Yes," Rory said, getting up. "It is a school night.
Did you get all your lessons done?"

Sam nodded. "Miss Ruth helped me with some of
the spelling."

"Did you thank her?"

Ruth bobbed her head. "He certainly did. We had
a nice visit, too. Although I couldn't figure why he'd

want to sit here with an old lady while y'all were out there, rescuing Spike."

Sam lifted his gaze toward Goldie then lowered his head. "I just wanted to get my homework done."

Rory motioned for the boys. "C'mon, you two. Let's get going." He waited until they'd both located their jackets. "Tell Miss Ruth thanks for the hot chocolate then head to the truck."

"Thanks," they spoke in unison.

After the boys gathered their things, Ruth pulled herself up and grabbed on to her walker, giving both of them a one-armed hug. "I think I'm going to bed. Good night all."

Rory glanced from her slowly departing form to Goldie and the dog. "Boys, go ahead now. I'll be there in just a minute."

Sam gave him a skeptical look. "Dad—"

"Go, Sam. Now."

Sam and Tyler went up the hall and out the front door.

"I'm sorry about Sam's attitude," Rory told Goldie.

She nodded. "I understand. He's a little boy and he misses his mother. He thinks I'm a threat to that—to all of you. I don't have to be a psychologist to see that."

"I miss her, too," Rory replied. "Tyler's still too young to grasp what happened, but Sam—he was older and he saw what it did to me. I guess some of that rubbed off on him."

Goldie handed him Spike. Taking the dog, Rory rubbed the soft fur on the animal's back and was rewarded with a lick on the face. "Maybe a dog would help."

She stared over at Spike. "He is adorable." Then she addressed Rory. "Grams told me what happened with your wife. A robbery, Rory, such a senseless crime. I can't imagine what you must have gone through."

Rory didn't like to talk about this, but he felt Goldie needed to understand. "She just went for some milk and eggs. She was baking and I had promised I'd get the stuff on the way home. But I had an emergency and so she went herself. The boys were at a Scout meeting. I was gonna pick them up then swing by the grocery store. Instead, she went to a convenience store near our house to save time. And she got shot, right there in the store. Her and the store clerk. The clerk survived."

He couldn't look at Goldie, so he held tightly to the little dog and stared down into Spike's dark, expectant eyes. "Maybe a dog *would* help."

He heard Goldie's sharp intake of breath then looked up at her, seeing the anguish on her face. "Goldie, I—"

"You don't owe me any explanations, Rory." She took the dog back. "Thanks for saving Spike and me."

Rory didn't know what else to say. They didn't have much of a chance, him and Goldie. He knew it and she knew it. There was just so much between them. So much left unsaid. Grief and distance and circumstances and life. But he did know that since he'd met Goldie Rios, something inside him had changed. He stared at the fidgety little dog then glanced at Goldie. "Some things are worth saving, no matter the cost."

Spike pressed his nose against Goldie's sweater. Rory looked at her, his gaze holding hers. She didn't speak. She just stood there. Rory had the sudden urge to kiss her. He held his fists to his sides, telling himself that kissing her would only make things worse. "I guess I'd better go before the boys hijack my truck and run it into the bayou."

She smiled at that. Then she turned serious again. "Rory, it's okay. Really. I understand."

Rory clinched his fists again. "No, it's not okay. I should be able to ask you out on a proper date. But—"

"But you have two little boys and you have responsibilities and…you're still grieving." She held Spike close. "And I'll be going back to Baton Rouge soon anyway."

"It's only an hour's drive."

"But we're still a long way from that."

He stepped close then. "But while you're here…"

"While I'm here, let's just leave things the way they are, for everyone's sake, okay?"

"Could you just tell me this, then? What if…say things were okay and I did ask you out on a date? Would you go, I mean, if we didn't have all these complications holding us back?"

She glanced down at Spike then back up and into his eyes. "If things were different, yes, I'd go out with you. But I remembered what happened the day of my wreck. I'd just broken up with a man who bought a puppy for another woman the same day he was supposed to have a romantic dinner with me. That kind of scars a girl, if you know what I mean."

He nodded. "Yeah, I get that." Then he pointed to Spike. "But look at you now. You have your own puppy."

"Only I had to get him the hard way."

"Or maybe God sent him just in time. You saved this little dog, Goldie. You think I'm the one doing all the rescuing around here, but I think you've got that all backward. You're pretty good at rescues yourself."

"No, I'm pretty good at bluffing my way through life."

"So you're telling me you're just a big joke? A sham?"

"Something like that."

He finally gave in and leaned close. "You are so wrong on that account, Goldilocks. I've felt more alive since you've come in my life than I have for months now. And that's a sure sign that I need to focus on my boys a little more, that I need to feel alive for them. So I thank you for making me see that."

"Whatever I can do to help."

He saw the disappointment in her eyes but he heard the message in her words. He did need to focus on his boys. And that was that.

"Take care of Spike."

"I will," she said, her tone full of resignation. "And I'll bring him to the boys whenever it's time for me to leave, I promise."

Rory nodded then turned toward the door. He'd hold her to that promise, if only because it would give him one more chance to see her again before she walked out of his life forever.

Goldie lay curled in bed, Spike snuggled on an old blanket right beside her. Amazing how a lost little animal could bring out all her maternal instincts. But it was the scowl of a lost little boy that was keeping her awake tonight. That and the hurt expression in his daddy's eyes whenever Rory looked at her.

He's drawn to me, she thought, her hand stroking

Spike's fur. *And I feel something.* She'd never felt so much so quickly with the men she'd thought she cared about.

Lord, what's happening to me?

She'd come here to help her grandmother, to do the right thing in her wayward mother's absence. She'd come here for a temporary time, determined to keep up with her obligations and to do her job, determined to keep the fragile order in her life, the order that kept her sane, content and committed. But what kind of order did she really have? She had traveled when she only wanted to settle down. She had organized and arranged when in her mind, her life was in disarray and disrepair. She missed her father, longed for her mother, loved her grandmother. Believed in God even when she didn't dare darken the doors of church unless forced to do so. She felt alone, so alone at times that the intensity of it pierced her very soul.

"What's happening?" she asked in her prayers. Was she so busy trying to make things perfect that she'd missed making things right?

Spike made a cute little snoring noise. The dog knew he was safe now, and he felt secure in his slumbers. Someone had heard his pleas, had listened to his distress. Goldie longed for that kind of security.

Some things are worth saving.

Rory's words came back to her, there in the silence of a winter night. And she wondered if he was sending out his own plea for help.

Do I try to save him, Lord? Or do I just walk away before I get hurt again?

Goldie didn't have any answers for that. But she'd

sure been willing to fight for this lost little animal. Wasn't Rory worth fighting for, too? Weren't Rory and his sons worth saving, same as little Spike?

"Uh-oh." Goldie sat up, causing Spike to do the same. Her whole system was now on high alert. Spike sensed her confusion. He nuzzled his way onto her lap then tried to lick her face.

Her instincts told her that she needed to fix this situation, to make it right. But her heart told her that she couldn't make something perfect out of something that was broken, maybe beyond repair. How did she find the perfect solution for a grieving man and his two confused little boys? Grams always said to pray, just pray.

And so Goldie did. For a long time. She poured out her thoughts to God and asked His guidance. She waited for the peace of an unburdened heart, the peace that Grams seemed to possess even in the worst of circumstances. Finally, drained and tired, she grabbed at the covers then burrowed deep underneath the blankets, Spike yelping at her to let him in. Goldie brought the little dog close beside her again and watched as he settled down, but it was a long time before *she* finally went to sleep.

Chapter Eight

"I was beginning to think I'd never see you again."

Carla McCoy walked around Goldie's bedroom in her grandmother's house, picking up knickknacks as she admired the new decorating scheme. Spike followed Goldie's best friend, sniffing at her loafers each time she stopped, his little paws skidding on the hardwood floor.

"I've been right here," Goldie replied from her spot on the bed. She patted the comforter and laughed as Spike took a running jump toward her. "Except for that fateful night I went to the mall to do some shopping and, oh yeah, caught my boyfriend with another woman."

"You need to get out more," Carla said, her short red shag falling around her ears. "You sound kind of bitter."

"I'm not bitter about having to be here with Grams," Goldie replied. "But yes, I'm a tad frustrated about my ex-boyfriends."

Carla plopped down beside her. "So that's why you've been as quiet as a church mouse for the last week or so. You lying low, hoping to hide out here in little Viola forever just because of some man who didn't know a good thing when he saw it?"

"Just through the holidays," Goldie retorted. "I'm not hiding out but I am lying low. That's been the plan since Grammy had her surgery, anyway. I'm staying here until Angela gets back from her grand tour of Europe. And then I'm sure my mother will be ever so eager to check up on Grams now and then."

"You're bitter about your mother, too, aren't you?"

Goldie thought about that for a minute. "I'm not mad that she traipsed off to Europe even after Grams fell and broke her hip, no, because that's how Angela deals with things—she runs away. And I don't mind one bit hanging out with Grams. I've been doing that most of my life and I love it."

Carla tilted her head, her golden bell earrings making a tinkling sound. "But?"

"My daddy loved Grams. I mean, she was his mother and all that. But my mother and Grams? Not so good. Friction every time they get together—like sandpaper hitting rough rocks or something. So technically, it wouldn't have been a good mix—my mother here with her mother-in-law for weeks on end. Mama thinks Grams is too straitlaced and churchy, and Grams thinks Mama is too loose and flighty, if you know what I mean?"

Carla let out a hoot of laughter. "I don't know about your mother, but your Grammy is one of the coolest people I've ever met, Goldie. How could anyone not love Miss Ruth?"

"My mama loves Grams," Goldie countered. "She just can't be in the same room with her for more than five minutes. I mean, Grams is settled and sure of things while my mother is scatterbrained and not very capable of making a coherent decision. So that's why I have to run interference."

"But you can't run interference forever."

Goldie shrugged. "I can and I will. It's what family is all about. I've always been the peacemaker, the one who kept my mother organized and on track and the one who stuck by Grammy because she was so organized and on track. I took over where my dad left off, I reckon."

"You've done a good job, considering Miss Ruth doesn't have anyone else to help her out." Carla twirled her hair with a finger. "I know she has lots of church friends and that's good, but family is important. Family is just better."

"And that's why I'm here," Goldie said, her thoughts drifting to Rory and his duty to his family. "I'm blessed that my job allows me to work from home a lot and that my boss at the paper was willing to permit this extended long-distance work relationship, so I was the logical choice."

"Not a lot of granddaughters would do that, you know," Carla replied, getting up to roam around again. Spike took that as a sign he needed to do the same.

Carla scooped the little dog into her arms. "You are so cute," she told Spike. "And much more understanding and interesting than most men, I must admit." She leaned close to whisper to Spike, "I'm so glad my friend here has you to talk to while she's…uh…lying low."

Goldie grinned. "I didn't have much choice since no one responded to my flyers or queries. I couldn't abandon the poor little fellow. And Grams loves him, too."

Carla stroked Spike's back. "You seem to like it here."

Goldie looked at her friend, making a face. "I think I needed this time away from Baton Rouge. It's been good for me, taking things easy over the last few weeks." She shrugged. "And that's probably part of the reason Loser Number Five was buying a puppy for another woman in the mall in the first place. I neglected him and his fragile ego."

"Did he bother to come here and see you, before you spotted him with her?" Carla asked.

"He came a few times and we'd go out to dinner, but I knew something was up," Goldie admitted. "We never were a sure thing from the beginning, but I held out hope."

"Don't we all," Carla said, putting Spike on the bed then turning to unpack her weekend bag. Spike stood on his hind legs and nosed into the bag, but she pushed him away.

"Is that why you decided to come and visit?" Goldie questioned, glad to see her friend but still wondering what Carla was doing here when she preferred the night-life in Baton Rouge over a quiet weekend in the country.

"I'll tell you all the latest tonight, after we do our nails, eat popcorn and watch sappy movies," Carla promised. "But I do have some good news. I think I've actually found a man I can settle down with."

Goldie got up and touched a hand to her friend's sweater sleeve. "Oh, then I have to hear the details on that."

"All in good time," Carla said. "I just need some solid advice. I'm kind of scared I might make a mess of things."

"That would be my department," Goldie quipped.

"We'll talk later," Carla repeated. "I promise."

"Okay, whenever you're ready to talk. In the meantime, I'm glad you called and I'm glad you came. Want to go get Mexican for dinner?"

"Can you leave Grams?"

"I can now, yes. She has her cell and I have mine, just in case. And she has one of those emergency necklaces. She wears that all the time."

"Mexican it is, then," Carla agreed. "Besides, the restaurant isn't that far away, is it?"

"Nothing in this town is that far away," Goldie said through a grin. But her grin faded when she thought about Rory's house just a few miles down the road. Best not to remember the big Christmas tree and the pretty kitchen. Or the fact that Rory was usually in that kitchen every night, trying to be a good father to his boys.

Carla grabbed her purse. "I'll just freshen up and then I'll be ready. And, Goldie, when we get to the restaurant, I want *you* to tell me all about this nuisance hunter you keep mentioning in your calls and emails. That can't wait until later and lights out. I have to know all of it ASAP."

Goldie shook her head. "I was hoping you wouldn't ask about that."

Carla laughed as she headed toward the bathroom. "No such luck, girl. There's something in your voice whenever you mention this new man in your life."

Goldie heard the bathroom door shut then turned to stare at her reflection in the dresser mirror. "Something's there, all right." She just wasn't sure what that something was.

She thought about all the reasons she shouldn't get involved with Rory Branagan—his grief, his sullen older son, his disapproving but well-meaning mother, Goldie's own aversion to yet another failed relationship, her job in the city, her need to stay organized and in control.

Not a whole lot going for them.

If you didn't count the way just seeing the man made her go all soft and gooey inside. Or the fact that he'd rescued her twice now and always made her feel safe and secure by smiling at her.

She looked down at Spike. "Or you, little bit. I can't forget that you are the tie that is binding Rory and me together right now."

Because she would soon be handing off Spike to Rory, for safekeeping. Her heart might also go with the little dog when that handoff took place.

And then she'd go back to the real world and her loneliness again.

The loneliness had never bothered him this much.

Rory stared out at the looming night, wondering what to do with himself. His sister had brought her kids from Dallas to visit with his mother and his boys. Becky had offered to give both Rory and Frances a night off by taking her two girls and his boys out for pizza and a movie. Frances was doing her last-minute Christmas shopping.

Which left Rory alone on a Friday night.

He could wrap presents or watch a game on the sports channel. Or he could just stand here staring out the window, wondering what Goldie was doing tonight.

But that wouldn't do and thinking about Goldie made him much lonelier.

He went to the Christmas tree, smiling at the collection of ornaments they'd gathered over the years. Two "Baby's First Christmas" balls with the dates of his sons' births printed on them in gold make him remember when his children had come into the world. He looked over the tree, searching for the "First Christmas Together" ornament his mother had given to him and Rachel after they'd gotten married. It was white porcelain and had two little bears dressed in snow clothes kissing. Rachel had loved that ornament. Then he noticed the picture ornaments showing his boys at various ages. Rory touched a hand to each one, his memories as warm and vibrant as the fire that roared in the fireplace. Why were the holidays so hard?

He closed his eyes to lift up a prayer for peace and control. He had to be strong for his children, had to be understanding whenever Sam acted out or Tyler cried in the night for his mother. The horror of Rachel's death still haunted Rory, filling him with guilt. Life was so precious. It could all change in one minute. He thought about the night he'd found Goldie right here in this room.

What if she'd died that night?

He would never have known her pretty smile or her dry wit. He wouldn't have been able to watch her golden curls rustling like twirling silk around her face. He would have never seen her cuddling Spike, the sight of that simple sign of affection causing his worn, tired heart to swell and pump a little faster. He would never have known Goldie.

"What do I do now, Lord?" he asked out loud. "Should I listen to my heart, or keep cool and just let her go?"

Rory didn't have the answers to those questions and tonight, he didn't want to think about next year and Goldie going back to Baton Rouge. Besides, Baton Rouge wasn't that far away and he was sure Goldie would come and visit Ruth more often now. Wouldn't she?

He'd just have to take things slowly and leave it all in God's hands. What else could he do?

You could be a little more aggressive, a little more proactive, he told himself. *You could go after Goldie.*

He could, but he wouldn't.

Rory stared up at the tree again, the faces of his boys smiling, gap-toothed and innocent, back at him.

No, he wouldn't pursue Goldie. He had to think of his children. But what if having Goldie in their lives could make a positive difference for his boys?

Rory had never thought of that, considering how surly Sam had been around Goldie. But Tyler wanted to keep Goldie in their lives. Which one was right?

Only time and God's grace could answer that question.

The phone rang, jarring Rory out of his thoughts.

He answered it on the second ring.

"Hey, buddy, you and the boys want to go for Mexican?"

It was his friend Kip Lawrence. "Hey, Kip. The boys are off with my sister. I'm on my own, but now that I think about it, I am hungry."

"Good. Penny abandoned me to go shopping—

again," Kip replied, laughing. "I told her I might catch up with you since it's been a while. We need to plan a hunting trip."

"That sounds good," Rory said. "What time?"

"As soon as you can get to The Taco Mesa. I'm starving."

"I'll meet you there in fifteen minutes," Rory said, glad to have a friend tonight. "Thanks for calling."

He hung up, smiling. *Thanks to You, too, Lord, for getting me out of the house.*

He freshened up, then hurried to his truck, praying the whole time. Maybe if he prayed enough, he'd rid himself of his grief and guilt and all his erratic thoughts about Goldie Rios.

The Taco Mesa was booming tonight. All around them, people were laughing and eating. The bright, colorful Christmas lights lining the ceiling and walls illuminated the merriment in tiny spotlights of blue, yellow, red and green. Goldie had just bitten into her chips and hot sauce when she looked up and saw Rory walking in with another man.

"Oh, boy," she said, dropping her hand. There was no way to hide since they were seated in a booth right by the door.

"What is it?" Carla asked, glancing around to where Rory stood waiting for a table. Then she shifted so fast she almost knocked over her water glass. "Is that him? Is that the famous nuisance hunter?"

"Shh," Goldie instructed on a low whisper. "He'll hear you."

Too late. Rory looked across the room and right at

her. Caught, she could only wave and smile. "Oh, great. He's coming this way."

Goldie didn't know whether to be excited or sick to her stomach. She wanted to see Rory; she didn't want to see Rory. What was wrong with her? Since when had she become so indecisive and self-conscious?

Since she'd first woken up on his couch and seen that unforgettable face hovering over her like some knight in armor come to her rescue. Well, she didn't need rescuing now, did she?

No, but maybe the knight in question did. Because at this moment he looked about as anxious and confused as she felt. Even if he was smiling.

Chapter Nine

"Uh, hi."

Rory didn't know what else to say. He wondered if the good Lord was trying to hurry him into a relationship with Goldie or make him more patient. Either way, he was here and so was Goldie. And she looked great, except for the flush of surprise brightening her face. That flush actually made her look pretty, but the awkward frown accompanying it made Rory realize she probably felt as uncomfortable as he did right now. He hated making her feel that way but what was he supposed to do? Ignore her? That would be even worse.

"Hello." Her laughter was as brittle as the tortilla chips on the table. Then she waved a hand toward the redhead staring pointedly up at him. "Uh, Rory, this is my friend Carla McCoy. You've heard me mention her."

Rory nodded, extending his hand to Carla. "Yeah. I think we talked on the phone once after Goldie's accident."

Carla shook his hand then smiled. "So you're the one who found her? The famous nuisance hunter?"

Rory put his hands in the pockets of his leather jacket. "Yeah. Good thing she found our house. It was a miserable night."

"Thank you for helping her," Carla said. "It's nice to meet you."

"You, too." Rory glanced back at Kip. "Well, I'm here with a buddy. Guess I'd better get back to him." He looked down at Goldie. "It's nice to see you again."

"Good to see you," she replied, her eyes going a deep green.

Before he could spin around and get away, Kip came over to the table. "Hey, Rory, Penny just called and she's finished shopping. Do you mind if she joins us for dinner?"

"No, I don't mind," Rory said. Then he looked back at Goldie. "This is my friend Kip Lawrence. We thought we'd grab a bite since my boys are with my sister and her kids. She's visiting my mom this weekend."

Kip nodded hello. "And my wife was out shopping," he interjected, laughing. "I guess she ran out of money."

Carla glanced from Rory to Goldie. "Well, since you're here and your wife is on the way, and we've all now been properly introduced, y'all want to sit with us?"

Goldie and Rory both spoke at the same time.

"I don't think—"

"Better not—"

Rory looked over at Kip. The gleam in Kip's eyes told him this wasn't going to be easy. Goldie's friend Carla had that same gleam. The let's-see-where-this-matchmaking-is-going gleam.

"Oh, c'mon," Carla pleaded. "I never get to meet

any of Goldie's Viola friends. We don't mind, do we, Goldie?"

Rory watched as Goldie shifted and squirmed. She didn't want him to sit down with her, or maybe she did but she was afraid to say so. And he should just decline the invitation but he didn't want to do that, in spite of all his prayers to the contrary. "We don't want to interrupt," he offered, giving Goldie an out.

She shot her friend a stony glare then smiled up at him. "Y'all are welcome to eat with us, if Kip's wife won't mind."

"Are you kidding?" Kip replied. "She'll be glad for the female company. Besides, everyone in town's talking about how Rory here became a hero the night you had your wreck. She'd be mad as a wet hen if I passed up an opportunity to meet the woman Rory found on his couch."

Rory cringed then shrugged. "Sorry. I guess the word's gotten around, even if the story has taken on a life of its own."

Goldie lifted her eyebrows then looked at Kip. "Small-town grapevines have a tendency to embellish things, but yes, Rory did call 911 that night. And he's been a good friend since."

Kip slapped Rory on the back. "You're just that kind of guy, aren't you?"

"Yeah, I guess I am," Rory replied, wishing he'd stayed home and made a sandwich.

"All right then," Goldie replied. "It's settled. Just pull up some chairs and we'll get the waitress back over here."

Rory grabbed a chair from an empty table and swung

it around so he'd be near Goldie. Might as well take advantage of this chance encounter. "You don't mind, really?" he said on a low tone for her ears only.

She gave him one of her famous Goldie looks. "No, I don't mind but…"

"But we're friends, Goldie. Just friends. So don't go all radar on me and look as if you'd like to bolt out the door."

She shook her head, her curls bouncing. "From the expression on your face, I thought maybe you were the one wanting to turn around and walk back out the door."

He smiled at that. "I did think about it."

They looked up to find Kip and Carla staring at them. Carla grabbed the bowl of chips and shoved them toward Kip. "Hey, I bet you've got pictures of your kids in your wallet. Let me see them."

Kip obliged but he grinned over at Rory while he fished out the pictures.

"I'm sorry." Goldie lowered her head as she gave her friend a frown. "You have to understand, Rory's more used to saving me from bad situations than eating chips and hot sauce with me."

Kip lifted his head. "You mean there's more to this story?"

Goldie nodded. "I got trapped in a drainage ditch with a puppy a few days ago. Grams insisted Rory come over to help us out. Now I have a puppy named Spike and after I go back to Baton Rouge, Spike gets a new home with Rory and his boys."

"I love happy endings," Kip quipped with a hand to his heart. His grin made Goldie laugh but Rory thought about cuffing his friend on the ear.

Carla leaned forward. "You know, Goldie's always been accident-prone. We met in grammar school and when we both got new bikes for our birthdays, she took off on hers and had a wreck and broke her left arm." She shrugged. "Of course, a broken arm didn't stop her from riding her bike that summer. And from getting a skinned knee from yet another mishap." She grinned over at Goldie. "Then she moved away and came back later when we were in high school and we took up right where we'd left off. We got our driver's licenses together and—"

"And I promptly backed my mom's minivan into another car at the apartment complex where we lived," Goldie finished. "I think I was grounded for about a year after that."

"I had to do all the driving for a while," Carla added. "Then they moved again and, well, no telling what kind of things she got into while they were away."

Rory laughed at that. "I'm glad Carla's here. She can update me on *all* your previous accidents. Or at least the ones she actually witnessed."

"Uh, not a good idea," Goldie said. "I wasn't that bad. And can we please change the subject?"

Carla ignored that plea then gleefully launched into childhood tales of daring deeds that had apparently gotten both of them in trouble.

In a few minutes, Kip did the same with Rory's past, telling the group grand tales of their adventures hunting, fishing and swimming all around the area. "Rory though, he always wanted to capture animals and release them back into the wild or take them to some animal preserve instead of just hunting them down for sport. He sure is in the right profession."

Kip looked up to find a leggy brunette grinning down at him. "Are you bragging about the adventures of Kip and Rory again?"

His eyes crinkled in a smile then he looked sheepish. "This is my lovely wife, Penny. Have a seat, honey."

Penny nudged Rory. "Good to see you. It's been a while."

"Yep." Rory introduced everyone and soon after the waitress rushed their orders through and brought the food out so they could finally eat.

Rory looked at Goldie, glad that the conversation soon shifted from their personal lives to more current events and the upcoming holidays.

She looked just about as relieved as he did.

"That was nice," Goldie told Rory as they all stood outside the restaurant, the chill of the December night a sharp contrast to the warmth of the lively restaurant.

"It was," Rory replied, his eyes holding hers. "You know, we might be able to do this again, just the two of us, on a real date or something."

Goldie's pulse did a jagged little dance. "Are you sure about that? I mean, we did decide…"

"We didn't really decide anything except that we could be friends while you're here. And friendship never changes, right?"

She glanced over at Carla. Her friend was chatting with Kip and Penny as if they'd been friends forever.

"No, it doesn't." She wanted to be Rory's friend, but she wasn't sure how to do that. It seemed a letdown when she thought about all the other possibilities, but she did care about him and she liked being around him.

Then she said something that surprised her. "I just don't have many male friends."

"Well, now's your chance to give it a try. You know, men are perfectly acceptable as friends. We've even been known to shed a tear or two during sappy movies."

"I do know that. It's just that in my case, I usually want more and it backfires and then I'm left alone again."

He leaned close. "I didn't leave you alone when I found you that night in my house, did I?"

She shook her head. "No."

"And I didn't leave you alone when I found you and Spike in that ditch, did I?"

"No, but you were just being you. Doing your job. You're that kind of man, Rory. The kind who rescues God's creatures."

"Sometimes, it's not that simple," he said. "Sometimes I have to take an animal down."

"Oh, well, then—"

"Relax. I've never taken down a woman before."

"You might be tempted if you stay around me long enough."

"I'll take my chances." He glanced over at their friends. "I'll call you next week, okay? We can spend time together and enjoy each other's company, nothing more unless we both feel ready to take that next step. No pressure."

"Okay." She shifted, stomping her boots against the pavement. It would be hard to honor that "no pressure" clause but she sure did want to try. "We'd better go. Grammy's by herself."

"I'll be in touch." He tipped his hand in farewell then turned to Kip and Penny. "I'm ready."

After goodbyes and some more ribbing, they parted ways. Goldie got into Carla's little economy car, huddling in her wool coat.

"He's adorable," Carla noted, cranking the car and shivering while she waited for the heat to kick in.

"Adorable?" Goldie had to giggle at that.

"Well, yeah, in that rugged, outdoorsman-type way," Carla replied. "I mean, let's face it, girl, you usually go for the corporate image type."

"Yes, and how's that been working for me?" Goldie quipped.

"I see your point." Carla whipped out into the scant traffic on the main street running through Viola, the flash of red and green illuminated wreaths on each streetlamp brightening their way. Across the square a huge palm tree sparkled with twinkling white lights, two giant synthetic snowmen grinning and looking just a bit out of place underneath the tropical tree. "Do you like him?"

"Of course I like him," Goldie admitted. "It's just that I don't see a future with him."

"Why not?"

"I have to get back to Baton Rouge, for starters. And I don't think he's the kind of man who would go for a long-distance relationship."

"It's not that far from Viola to Baton Rouge. Just hit I-10 and go east for about an hour, depending on traffic."

"I know the way," Goldie replied. "But I don't know the way into Rory's world. The man lost his wife to a violent crime and he has two little boys. He's a real family man."

"Wow."

She heard Carla's shivering intake of breath. "Yeah,

wow. And the older son—Sam—he doesn't exactly want me in their life. But it's not about me. That little boy has a right to be mad at the world. He lost his mother." She leaned against the door. "And I lost my locket after the accident."

Carla held the steering wheel then glanced over at her. "You didn't tell me about that."

"I don't want to talk about it. I don't know where I lost it. I've looked in the spot where I had the wreck, searched my messed-up car at the garage and Rory's checked all over his house and yard. Someone could have taken it at the hospital, I just don't know."

"I'm sorry you lost your locket but what does that have to do with you and Rory?"

Goldie didn't know how to explain it. "It's just that Grams always told me the locket was special. She said it would bring good to me because it was so filled with love and family ties. And my daddy put the picture of me and him in there for that very reason. So I guess I set my high hopes on always having that locket as a security blanket or a reminder of all the good in the world. And now, it's gone. Grams said the locket isn't important— it's the love behind it that counts. It's the strength of the Lord's love that will bring the most good in my life."

She shrugged, knowing she could tell Carla any-thing. "It's silly, but I was sort of drifting before I came here to help Grams. I guess I'm getting restless in Baton Rouge. So I thought maybe a change of scenery would get me back on the right track. I still like my work and I've met my deadlines, even out of the office. But I just had this funny notion that if I left for a while maybe Loser Number Five would miss me enough to actually make a commitment. And instead, I find him buying a dog for another woman on the very night we're supposed to see each other for the first time in weeks. And then, I have this wreck and I lose my necklace."

"On the same night you find the perfect man—or rather, the perfect man finds you. I do see your dilemma, yeah."

Goldie heard the sarcasm in her friend's words. "I'm overanalyzing this, aren't I?"

Carla tapped the wheel. "Just a bit. And so because of all of the above and especially because you lost your locket, you think you can't be happy with Rory?"

Goldie bobbed her head. "I know it doesn't make sense but that necklace was my lifeline. I wanted to pass it on to my own daughter one day. And now it's out there somewhere, lost or sold or sitting in a pawn shop."

"Have you looked in any pawn shops?"

"We don't have one here, no."

"Oh, I guess that would be kind of fruitless, then."

"Yes and that's how I feel about Rory and a relationship—fruitless, pointless, end of discussion."

Carla pulled the car into the driveway behind Ruth's old sedan. "I never knew you were such a pessimist."

"I'm being realistic," Goldie replied, her pulse sounding an oncoming headache. "I just don't see how Rory and I can have any type of relationship other than friendship. It's not the right fit—he's not my type, I'm certainly not the stay-at-home-and-make-cookies type and we have different goals as far as our futures. I don't see how it can ever work."

Carla sat with her hands on the wheel, the car quiet now. "You don't think you're cut out to take on a man with two kids? Goldie, you're the queen of the organized life. You tell other woman how to handle everything from kids to animals to mothers-in-law and still maintain a perfect house. But you're not willing to take on all that yourself?"

"I guess not. I'm a big fraud, aren't I?"

"I didn't say that. I read your column and I've seen you in action. You know how to whip any room into shape and your advice is solid. In theory, at least."

"Well, in theory, I don't think I'm the woman for Rory, so there."

Carla bit her lower lip, deep in thought. "But would you like it to work?"

"I don't know," Goldie admitted. "I care about Rory and I'd like to get to know Sam and Tyler a little more. But his mother and he are close and I don't think she approves of me, either. It's just not the best situation to test my happily-ever-after skills. And besides, I'm still a little wounded by the incident at the mall and the spaghetti-in-his-lap breakup that followed."

"Sounds like you've found lots of excuses for not moving forward on this."

"Not excuses, realistic problems, Carla." Goldie didn't want to talk about it anymore. "Hey, what about you? You said you'd tell me everything about your new man."

"Yes, I said later when we did the girlie things."

"Well, let's go inside, don our PJs and get started," Goldie said, opening her door. "I need to concentrate on someone besides myself."

"Good," Carla replied. "Because I've been dying to tell you more but I wanted to wait until the right time." She got out of the car and came around to meet Goldie at the front door. "Goldie, I really think I've found the one. You know, when I said I think I've found the right man?"

"Yes, and I'd like to hear the whole story." Goldie eyed her friend then saw the glow surrounding Carla there in the porch light. "*The one?* Really?"

"Yes," Carla reiterated, clapping her hands together. "I think I'm in love, finally. But just like you, I'm afraid to admit that. I could mess up things, too."

Goldie took in that declaration and the doubt in her friend's words then stared at Carla. "First of all, you won't mess up. And second, why didn't you say something earlier? Besides, hey, I have to meet this man."

Carla put her hands on Goldie's arms. "I… I didn't want to rub it in since you've been so down."

Goldie saw the regret in her friend's eyes. "Don't be silly. You know I'm not that way. I'm happy for you, really."

But when she hugged Carla close, she had to work hard to put on a happy face so she could celebrate with her friend.

Because Goldie couldn't help but wonder why this kind of happiness couldn't happen for her, too. *Maybe because you keep pushing it away,* that voice in her head retorted.

Maybe so. But Rory did say he was going to call her.

That notion gave her the courage to stand back and smile at her friend. "Let's get inside so you can tell me everything. And I'll give you the best advice possible— on the house. And in theory, of course."

Chapter Ten

The next morning, Goldie awoke to her cell phone ringing. Turning, she grabbed the humming device while trying to fully wake up. She and Carla had stayed up half the night talking about men, just like they used to do in high school talking about boys.

"Hello," she said in a dry-throated whisper.

"Goldie, thank goodness you're there. I need help."

"Rory?" Hearing the panicked sound of his voice brought Goldie fully alert. "What's wrong?"

"It's my mom," he said. "My sister just called. They're rushing her to the hospital. Becky thinks she had a heart attack."

"Oh, no."

Goldie glanced over at Carla. Her friend lay in the bed with one eye open then mouthed, "What?"

"It's Rory," Goldie explained with a hand to her phone as she sat up on the bed. "What can I do to help?"

"Becky and I need to be at the hospital but we don't have anyone to leave the kids with. Could you...?"

"I'll be there as soon as I can," Goldie replied.

"Thanks. I couldn't think of anyone else. Most of my mom's friends aren't good with this many young children. And I couldn't get anyone else on the phone—everyone's out Christmas shopping. I… I thought at least the boys kinda know you."

"I'll be there," she promised. "I'll bring Carla with me. She comes from a big family, so she's used to lots of kids."

"Good. I'll send Becky on behind the ambulance then I'll wait for y'all."

Goldie hung up then whirled around to Carla. "You have to come with me." She quickly described the situation. "I don't know a thing about entertaining little boys."

Carla got up, pushing at her hair. "Well, we'll figure it out together. They mostly like to eat and fight and throw balls—stuff like that. Don't worry."

But Goldie was worried. About Rory and his mom. If something happened to Mrs. Branagan—she didn't want to think about that right now. Spike came bouncing into the room then hopped up on the bed. "Maybe we should take you, too," Goldie added as she went about combing her hair and getting on her jeans and a sweater. "Dogs and boys just naturally go together, don't they?" And the boys needed to adjust to Spike if they were going to adopt him after Christmas.

Carla nodded then yawned, her sleepy eyes like two slits. "We shouldn't have stayed up half the night gabbing."

Goldie was wide-awake. "Too late to worry about that. I'll make coffee once we get to Rory's."

Grams came to the door. "What's wrong?"

Goldie told her the news on her way to the bathroom. "Grams, you might want to alert the prayer warriors at church."

"I sure will," Grams said. "Do you want me to come along?"

Goldie almost said no then turned. "Would you like to? I mean, just so I don't worry about you if I have to stay all day? We'll take both cars and that way, if you get tired, Carla can bring you home."

"Of course," Grams declared. "I'm already dressed and I've had all my medication. Just let me gather a few things. I can sit at Rory's house same as here, I reckon. Or better yet, we'll make some soup for later. They'll all need their nourishment."

Goldie nodded then hurried away. When she came back into the bedroom, Carla looked up at her. "He trusts you with his children," she noted. "I think that must mean something."

Goldie shook her head. "He panicked. I haven't been around them that much. I was the first person he thought about."

"Exactly," Carla said, her smug expression belying the seriousness of that one word.

"After he'd tried calling other people," Goldie replied, throwing on a heavy sweater and warm booties.

"Still, you were high up on the list, apparently."

Goldie wasn't sure how to take that. What did Rory normally do in such an emergency? Who would he have called if she hadn't been available? Maybe he'd never had such an emergency before. He did depend on his mother a lot whenever he was called away, but she'd never heard him mention any other babysitters.

Well, now he's beginning to depend on you, too, she thought. Maybe Carla had a point.

Grams materialized with her walker and a big tote bag in the attached basket. "I think Carla's right, honey. Rory respects you and he knows you'll take care of things for him."

Goldie heard the hopeful tone in Grammy's voice. "Your hearing sure is intact," she said, searching for her purse.

"And so is my eyesight," Grams replied with a serene smile. "It's all gonna be all right. God is always in control."

Carla grabbed Spike, holding him close. "That's right. Grams knows these things."

"I just hope Mrs. Branagan is all right," Goldie murmured. "Now let's go."

Goldie helped Grams into her car and waited as Carla backed out first so she could follow. Spike barked at Carla's car as they passed.

Goldie said the same prayer over and over. *Let her be okay, dear Lord.* She couldn't think beyond that. She'd help Rory, no doubt, no questions asked. As for the meaning behind his request, it was simple, really. He'd been worried about his mother, nothing else.

And yet, her heart burned with a strange warm, sappy emotion in spite of her cynical nature. Rory had called on her to rescue him this time.

That was sure a first.

"I'm sorry," Rory apologized, ushering Goldie and her little troupe into the house. "I just didn't know where else to turn." He waved a hand in the air. "The house is a mess. The boys are getting dressed and Becky's girls are watching cartoons. I've explained things to them, but it's just not good."

"It's okay," Goldie said, seeing the glaze of worry in his eyes. "Just go and be with your mom. Grams and Carla will be here to make sure I don't blow up the oven or flood the house."

That almost brought a smile to his face. "All right. I'd better hurry. I've left numbers on a pad on the counter, just in case. And you have my cell number."

"Go," she ordered, pushing him toward the back door.

"Rory, we'll be praying," Grams said, giving him a hug.

"Thanks, to all of you." He gave Goldie one last look then headed out the door.

Carla glanced toward the den. "I'll go see how the girls are doing."

Spike squirmed out of Grammy's arms then headed down the hallway, barking.

Two bedroom doors opened wide as both boys came rushing out.

"Spike!" Tyler's eyes, so like his father's, gleamed with delight. "Hey, Sam, Spike's here."

Sam looked up at the three women and reached down to pet Spike then turned back toward his room. Goldie decided she'd have to be the one to handle this. It was now or never for her and Sam. And she so wanted to make it work.

"Hey, Tyler, my friend Carla says she wants to make some cookies. Can you help her find stuff in the kitchen?"

Tyler bobbed his head. "Can Spike come?"

"Sure." Goldie watched as the puppy skidded up the hallway behind the little boy.

Grams nodded. "Go ahead. I'll go get to know Becky's girls."

Goldie glanced around the house, seeing it with new eyes since Rory's mom hadn't been here to clean. The hall tree by the back door was cluttered with sports equipment and muddy sneakers. Book bags lay open and grinning right by the shoes. Jackets and coats of all sizes and shapes lay piled like hay bales on the walnut bench seat and on top of every available bit of space. Dirty dishes lined the counter. A cereal box sat bent and open right by the forgotten milk. She hurriedly put away the milk and closed and put away the cereal. She'd tackle the rest later.

This place does need a woman's touch, she thought. Rory's mother did her best but now that effort might have caught up with her. Goldie closed her eyes and asked God to take care of all of them.

Then she went to Sam's bedroom door and knocked. "Sam, it's Goldie. May I come in?"

No answer.

She tried again, tapping gently against the wood. "Sam, I just want to talk to you."

Finally, the door crept open and Sam stood there, the expression on his face somewhere between pouting and defiant. "I'm okay."

Goldie inched the door open then surveyed the room. It held the standard bunk beds and sports posters, a bookcase and a basket full of various balls. Clothes, shoes and books cluttered the floor. Goldie picked up a black and white soccer ball. "Do you play soccer?"

He nodded then plopped down on his unmade bed. Goldie itched to straighten the room but knew that would be a mistake. "And I guess you play baseball, too, huh?"

Another nod. And then words so quiet, she almost didn't hear them. "My mom used to come to all my games."

That simple statement almost broke Goldie's heart. How could she fault this kid for his attitude? He'd lost his mother when he was still so young. How horrible that must have been for them. Goldie thought of her own mother and suddenly felt the urge to hug Angela close, flaws and all. She wished Angela would come home for Christmas so she could just talk to her, at least.

"I bet your mother was sure proud of you."

Sam didn't respond. He just sat there staring at the bookshelf. Goldie sat silent, wishing she knew what to say.

"Is my Grandma gonna die?" he finally asked, his head down.

How should she answer that? Deciding to be honest, Goldie cleared her throat. "I don't know. Your dad will call us and let us know what the doctors say. But I'm going to hope and pray that your grandmother will be all right. You can do that, too, you know. It's okay to say a prayer."

He looked at her then, his big eyes devoid of any kind of hope. "My mom died. It was too late to pray for her."

Goldie had to restrain herself from gathering him close. "I know, honey. That was a hard blow. A terrible thing." She sat still, not daring to reach out. "There's just no easy way to deal with that, is there?"

He shook his head. "I miss her."

"I'm sure you do."

"I don't want Grandma to die," he said. He turned to stare up at Goldie. "I'm sorry."

Goldie wanted to take him into her arms and reassure him that it would be all right. For the first time in her life, her maternal instincts kicked in and went into full-power mode. And she knew at that moment, if she ever had a child of her own, she would protect that child with a fierce heart. But right now, she wanted to protect *this* child.

"Don't be sorry for being honest, Sam. None of us likes seeing people we love die. I was so worried about my Grams when she fell and broke her hip. Grams is this amazing woman who knows that we have everlasting life after death—eternal life with God."

Sam shifted away. "No, you don't understand," he pleaded, his voice rising.

Goldie tried again. "But I do—"

He got up, fisted his hands. "I'm not talking about that. I don't want Grandma to die but you don't know— Dad doesn't know what happened. I did something really bad."

Goldie's heart started beating triple time. "What do you mean?"

"It's my fault," Sam confessed. "I caused Grandma to have the heart attack. I know it was my fault."

Rory stood by the doors to the ICU, watching as doctors and nurses rushed by. No one had come to talk to him and Becky yet and his sister was beside herself.

"We should hear something soon," he said, reassuring her for about the tenth time.

Becky nodded. "I still can't believe it. One minute we were standing there wrapping gifts. I left the room to check on the kids—the girls were fighting as usual—and when I walked back in, she started clutching her chest and then she fell to the floor. I was only gone about five minutes. I was so scared. I tried to talk to her but she wasn't making any sense. She couldn't speak. It was horrible."

"I'm just glad you were there with her," Rory said, closing his eyes, his hand on his sister's arm. "I don't get it, either. She's always been so healthy. Dad was the one we had to watch and worry about."

"*She* watched and worried," Becky replied. "Maybe it's catching up with her. First Rachel's death and then Dad. It's hard for any of us to bear."

Rory nodded. "She took both hard. We all did. And then, I started depending on her way too much."

Becky put her hand over his. "You've done a good job with the boys, Rory. Anyone can see that."

"Mom helped a lot, though," he said. "I leaned on her too much. I didn't want to take advantage of her and I should have just hired a sitter right away, so we could adjust, but you know Mom. She insisted everything was fine. I should have insisted—"

Becky shook her head. "No, Mom wanted to help. She loves the boys. If I'd let her, she'd have the girls here half the time, too."

He smiled at that. "Yeah, I guess we can't beat ourselves up for this, but I just don't know what provoked her into having a heart attack—if it was a heart attack."

Becky shook her head. "I've always heard heart attacks are like a silent killer among women."

Rory glanced down the hall. "I wish the doctor would come out here and tell us what's happening."

Becky glanced at the buzzing cell phone in her hand. "That's William. I'd better give him an update."

Rory watched as his sister poured out her heart to her husband then assured him that he didn't need to drive all the way from Dallas to be there. "Just wait until I have more information," Becky said. "I might need to stay here awhile longer and you'll need to come and get the girls if I do."

Rory thought back over the night he'd gotten the call about Rachel. He couldn't even remember getting to the hospital, couldn't remember his mother taking the boys out of the room so he could tell his dying wife goodbye. He just remembered seeing Rachel lying there, so pale and so still…and then she was gone. Just like that.

Things could certainly change in a heartbeat. He knew that firsthand. He'd seen that firsthand. He thought about Goldie and how she'd come into his life and again, he thanked God that she had found warmth and comfort in his house that night.

Goldie.

She'd made it through. And for some strange reason she'd made it into his life. Today, he'd thought of her when he needed help. But had he been wrong to call on her, to depend on Goldie to help him?

Or had he been right? Exactly right?

Rory didn't have the answers to his own questions and right now, he could only take a breath and thank God that Goldie had come through for him. He wouldn't forget it. He'd make it up to her when this was all over. And he wouldn't waste precious time wondering what was wrong or right or how to handle the complications.

He'd just enjoy the gift God had shown him. The gift of finding hope again.

Then he looked up to find Becky waiting for him, her phone silent now.

"Rory, the doctor wants to talk to us. It wasn't a heart attack. It was a stroke."

Chapter Eleven

Goldie sat staring out at the gray winter day, glad she'd done most of her Christmas shopping. Today was the last Saturday before Christmas. If she had to spend it inside, at least Rory's house was nice and warm.

And clean now, thanks to Carla and Goldie.

They'd cleaned, baked, made soup—Grams insisted on soup, of course. And now they were waiting for the biscuits Carla had whipped up to rise and brown. Rory could come home to a good, hearty supper and a warm, sparkling-clean house.

If they could just keep the four kids from messing it up again.

Carla was at the kitchen counter talking quietly on her cell phone with her new man. Tyler was asleep on his bed after helping with the cookies and the biscuits, Spike curled up by his side. The girls were sprawled on the den floor by the fire, reading books and listening to their separate headphones and Sam…well, Sam was still in his room. He had come out a few times—to eat, help clean up, play with Spike and stare up at Goldie, his heart in his eyes. And his future in her hands.

Goldie now knew why he was so sure he'd caused his grandmother's attack. But she couldn't tell anyone. She'd promised Sam. She'd also urged him to tell his dad the truth. Why the boy had decided to trust her, of all the other people in this house, was beyond Goldie's comprehension, but he had. And she thanked God he had, while she tried to understand his reasoning.

Now, the question remained. Would the child do the right thing and tell his father the truth?

"What's wrong, honey?"

Goldie glanced up to find Grams hovering nearby on her souped-up walker. The tennis balls on the base of the walker's legs added traction and the garland of berries and red flowers looping around the basket added holiday festivity. Becky's daughters had insisted on decorating the walker to give it some Christmas cheer.

But right now, Gram's didn't seem to be in a festive mood, in spite of the sweet smile on her face. And because she knew that smile meant business, Goldie answered, "Nothing. Just worried."

"Are you hungry?"

Goldie looked up at her Grammy, love filling her heart to the breaking point. "No, Grams. After a sandwich, three oatmeal cookies and two cups of coffee, I'm good until dinnertime."

"Okay. Do you want to talk?"

"About what?"

"About Rory and your feelings for him."

"I don't have feelings for him."

"Oh, yes, you do."

Goldie glanced around to make sure they were alone and that the girls still had their music piped into their ears. "Grams, what are you talking about?"

"I told you, I'm not blind. I saw it the minute Rory brought you home from the hospital. And I'm not completely deaf even if I do have to wear a hearing aid now and then. I hear it in your voice and in his. You two have something stewing, that's for sure."

Goldie couldn't deny it. "I care about Rory. He's a nice man—"

"It's more than that," Grams said. "I've never known you to go out on a limb for anyone other than family, child. But you didn't hesitate this morning. You came to Rory's aid and you've done a good job of corralling all of us here today. It must be love, or at least the beginning of love."

Goldie closed her eyes to find patience. "Grams, you can't go around saying things like that. It's complicated. Rory is a friend and he needed us."

Grams backed up to sit in the chair across from Goldie. "I'm not announcing it on the evening news, so don't worry. Complicated? How so?"

Goldie waved a hand in the air. "Look around. The man has two children and a mother who's sick. And he's a widower."

Grams slanted her eyebrows. "Your point?"

Goldie leaned close to whisper. "My point is—I'm not cut out to be an instant mother and the man's still grieving his wife. Besides, with his mother being sick now, he's going to have a whole lot to deal with and right here before Christmas. I don't think he'll be in the mood to woo me."

"But it's the perfect time for you to be a good friend to him."

Goldie tried to be patient. "I'm doing that right now."

Grams sat silent for a minute, gazing at the fire, the picture of innocence. Then she patted the arm of her chair as if following the beat of some silent song. "Do you want to be wooed?"

Goldie knew her grandmother could be stubborn since she'd inherited that same trait, but she sure didn't know the woman could be so intuitive. Grams had read her very heart. But Goldie wasn't ready to concede that fact.

"I don't know," she admitted. "I make a mess of relationships. I've been through a lot of bad ones lately."

"Maybe because you've been looking for love in all the wrong places," Grams quipped.

"That's my life," Goldie shot back. "Like the lyrics of a country song."

"Country songs are deeply rooted in real-life feelings. You should listen to the local station more often. That and our wonderful gospel station."

"I'll make a note," Goldie teased, giving her grandmother an impish grin. Then she leaned back in her chair. "Sam has some issues and I don't know how to handle that."

"You talked to the boy earlier," Grams reminded her. "What came of that?"

"I promised him I'd keep that between him and me," Goldie replied. "I have to honor that promise, but I did urge him to talk to his dad."

"Trying to win his trust—that's a good start."

"No, just trying to stay out of things," Goldie said,

even though what Sam had told her put her square in the middle of a bad situation. What should she do?

Again, Grams seemed to read her thoughts. "Prayer, darlin'. Prayer will bring answers."

"Is it truly that easy?" Goldie asked, wanting with all her soul to be as sure as her grandmother. "I do pray but it seems so halfhearted and I seem to pray only in emergencies."

Grams shook her head. "Being a Christian isn't supposed to be easy, honey. But prayer brings comfort and answers—answers that the Lord knows are already in our hearts. We just have to get clarity and prayer helps with that, but you have to rely on God's strength during both good and bad times, not just as a last resort."

"So, you think God listens to each and every prayer?"

"Of course I do. God's arms are wide open enough for everyone, even you." She winked. "And so are mine."

Goldie leaned over to kiss her grandmother. "I'll keep that in mind, too, Grams." Then she whispered, "Do you ever pray for Mama? Do you ever pray that she'll come home just to see if we're both okay?"

Ruth's lips twisted in a frown. "Every day, honey. I'm stubborn that way. Even though your mother and I are worlds apart, I still love her. I love her because she loved my son and their love brought me you and that's reason enough to easily forgive her ways."

"Grams, you amaze me," Goldie said, grinning. "I'm gonna pray for her, too. It can't hurt."

"That's for sure."

The phone rang and Goldie rushed to get it. Carla came into the den, her own phone in her hand. She closed it, watching Goldie.

"Hey, it's me," Rory said.

He sounded so drained. "Hey. Any word?"

"Yes, but it's not good. She's suffered a mild stroke but the doctors say she should have a full recovery. It was a TIA—transient ischemic attack—I think is the official term. They think she's had several over the last few months and this was probably the worst. No permanent damage since we got her to the hospital so quickly, and thankfully, she takes an aspirin every morning anyway, so that probably helped. But the chance of a second stroke is high, so they want to keep her in the hospital and on medication for now. She might need some therapy—something about comprehension and memory. They're going to do a few more tests and get her on the right medicine and a new diet."

Goldie wished she could say something to make him feel better. "Rory, I'm so sorry. But I'm so glad you acted quickly this morning. Listen, just stay there as long as you need. Everything is fine here."

"Are you sure? Becky and I were talking and one of us can come home to relieve y'all."

"Maybe later," Goldie said. "Just stay there with your mom for now. Grams sent Carla to the store and we've been baking and cooking all afternoon. We have vegetable-beef soup for supper and also cookies and biscuits." She didn't tell him that she'd scrubbed down the kitchen, washed three loads of clothes and pretty much reorganized the whole pantry.

"And the kids?"

Goldie thought about Sam. Rory didn't need to worry about that right now. "They're all okay. Settled down and cozy. We're going to wrap some gifts later."

"I need to finish my shopping," he replied on a sigh. "Christmas is just a few days away. But Mom's gonna need both Becky and me for a while."

"I can help with that, too."

"Goldie, I can't expect you to do everything. I've been doing it all for a long time now. I mean, Mom helped a lot…"

He stopped. The silence spoke of his pain.

While Goldie hid her own. But this wasn't about her hurt feelings at hearing him snap at her. His frustration wasn't toward her, after all. "She's going to be okay, Rory."

"You know you can't promise that." He went silent then said, "I'm sorry. I'm just tired and worried."

"I understand."

"I think you truly do, Goldilocks. You've been through this kind of stuff yourself with your grandmother."

"Grams said we need to pray and I'm gonna listen to her. She's very wise, you know."

"She's the best," he replied. "Thank her for me. And, Goldie, when things are better, I intend to take you out—just the two of us. To thank *you*."

"That sounds nice, but not necessary," she said, wondering why she'd said that. But it was true—a date with Rory sounded wonderful—and the first step was admitting she was drawn to this man.

"Good. I'll hold you to that. I just hope everything goes okay with Mom."

"It will, Rory. I don't know your mother that well, but she strikes me as a strong, determined woman. And she's still young enough to recover."

"You're right there. She's tough."

"So you have to be tough, too. And don't worry about us. We're fine. Stay there as long as you need to."

"Thanks. I feel better knowing everything's okay back home. I'll keep you posted."

She hung up, her thoughts on Frances and her recovery. Then she thought of Sam. After giving Grams and Carla a report about Rory's mom, she said, "Grams, I'm going to check on Tyler and Spike and see how Sam's doing. He might be persuaded with another one of Carla's cookies to come out of his room again. And he'll want to know about his grandmother."

"Good idea, honey. I think I'll just recline here on this nice, soft couch and get a few winks."

Carla nodded then whisked the girls up. "Hey, how about a nature walk?"

"It's cold out there," the oldest one remarked.

"Good for you to get some fresh air," Carla replied. "Let's look at natural stuff to make a holiday centerpiece. And while we walk, I'll explain about what happened to your grandmother. She's going to be fine, but you need to know what to expect."

That seemed to do the trick. The girls ran toward the door, throwing on jackets and hats as they went.

Goldie guided her grandmother over to the couch. "Lie down. I'll wrap this blanket around you."

Grams leaned against the pillows, causing Goldie to remember she'd ruined one of them the night of her accident. Making a note to get a new one for Rory for Christmas, at least, she found the plaid comforter and put it over Grams's legs. "Rest."

Grams smiled, already drowsy. "I'll pray myself to sleep."

Goldie did a little more tidying, fluffing pillows and picking up magazines. She could hear Carla laughing with the girls in the backyard as she talked about her boyfriend. Goldie wanted to feel jealous, but she didn't have it in her heart to be that way. Carla deserved a good man, someone to love.

And maybe she did, too. But first, she needed to see how Sam was doing. She headed down the short hallway then tapped on the door. When she didn't get a response, she carefully opened the door, thinking maybe he was already in bed. But the room was empty and Sam was nowhere to be found.

Goldie turned and went across the hall to Tyler's room. He was fast asleep but Spike saw her and bounced off the bed.

"C'mon, boy," she said. "We need to find Sam."

Where had the boy gone? Was he hiding out because of what he'd done? Or had he run away from home, hoping to spare himself from having to confess to his father?

I can't call Rory, she thought. She'd just look around the house and yard. Maybe Sam had gone outside. But she would have seen him coming through the house since both the front and back doors were in plain sight of the open den and kitchen.

Tyler was safe and Grams was dozing. Goldie grabbed her jacket and stepped into the backyard, motioning to Carla. Spike headed toward the girls, barking playfully. "I can't find Sam," she said softly so the girls couldn't hear. They were busy breaking magnolia leaves from a nearby tree.

"What?" Carla brushed at her hair.

"Sam isn't in his room. Have you seen him out here?"

"No, but we only made it as far at this tree. We're going to spray these leaves gold."

"That's great, but I have to find Sam."

"Oh, of course. What should I do with the girls?"

Goldie glanced over at Lauren and Regina. "Hey, you two, have you seen Sam anywhere out here?"

"No, ma'am," they both answered. Spike barked his own reply. "He's pouting."

"He's not in his room," Goldie replied, walking toward them. "Did he tell you why he was mad?"

Lauren shook out the shiny green leaves she'd gathered. "Sam's a little rude. He never smiles. I don't know what's wrong with him."

Goldie shot a glance toward Lauren. "He's just confused and…he misses his mother. And now his grandmother is sick. Cut him some slack, okay?"

Regina twirled around. "Is Grandma gonna be all right?"

Carla nodded. "Yes, we think. Remember I explained she'd had a tiny stroke. She's in good hands and the doctors know exactly what kind of treatment to give her. She just might need to take it easy for a while."

"Will she be home for Christmas?"

"We hope so," Goldie offered, unsure what to say next.

Carla pushed at Goldie. "Go look for Sam and I'll take care of these two. I'll watch for him." Then she whistled at Spike. "C'mon, boy. Let's play in the leaves."

Goldie hurried down the long driveway, searching through the cypress trees and old oaks, calling Sam's name as she went. She checked in the storage shed behind the house and down by the bayou. She walked out onto the short pier and stared into the woods and out into the dark water. Was Sam doing this deliberately since he'd confessed all to her earlier? Was he afraid of being punished?

I told him he'd have to be the one to tell his dad the truth, Goldie reminded herself. Why would he bolt now?

Then Goldie reached into the pocket of her jeans and pulled out her returned locket, her fingers rubbing against the tiny porcelain frame.

"Where are you, Sam?"

How in the world could she explain his son's disappearance to Rory if Sam didn't show up? How could she tell him that Sam had found her locket the night she'd had her wreck and that the boy had been hiding it since then?

And that his grandmother had discovered the missing locket this morning right before she'd had her stroke.

Chapter Twelve

After calling Sam's name over and over, Goldie went back into the house. The sun was going down, the chill of early evening causing her to shiver as she knocked dirt off her boots. She'd have some major work to catch up on when she got home tonight. But right now, she wasn't too worried about that. And in spite of all the new and exciting things happening all around her— things she couldn't explain—she now had a better perspective on how to answer a lot of the questions she got. That would make her editor at the paper happy. Firsthand experience always provided the best resource.

But Goldie would keep most of what she'd learned dealing with Rory and his sons to herself for now. It was too personal to share in an advice column.

Getting back to finding Sam, she hurried through the house.

Grams was up and watching an old movie. "There you are. Everything all right?"

"Have you seen Sam?" Goldie asked, praying the boy was somewhere in the house.

"No, but then I just woke up a few minutes ago. You can't find him?"

"No, and I've looked all over the yard and even in the woods. I'm getting concerned but I don't want to call Rory."

"Are you sure you've looked everywhere? Young boys can hide out in the oddest of places. Your father used to do that a lot."

Goldie backtracked in her mind. "Everywhere but the master bedroom." She walked over to the sofa. "Do you think I should look in there?"

"I would," Grams replied. "I can't imagine why he'd be in there, but maybe he figured that would be the one place no one would look."

"Good point," Goldie said, heading down the hallway toward the back of the long house. Since the door to Rory's room had been closed before, she hadn't gone in there and she hadn't allowed anyone else to do so, either. But now, she didn't have a choice.

She didn't bother knocking. Instead, she carefully opened the door and stared into the dark room, her eyes adjusting to the late-afternoon shadows. And there on the floor sat Sam. The boy had pictures strewn all around him.

"Sam, didn't you hear me calling you?" Goldie asked, wondering if she was able to help this troubled child.

Sam glanced up and shrugged, his eyes big and solemn. "I'm sorry. I didn't want anyone to know where I was."

Goldie let out a sigh of relief. "Well, you had me worried sick. I was just about to call your father."

Sam looked down at his hands. "I'm not supposed to be in here."

"I see. So I guess this is one more thing we're not going to tell him." She sank down on the floor beside him, her gaze skimming the haphazard bed linens and the masculine clothes scattered around the big room. She caught sight of a dainty jewelry box sitting open on the dresser, its baubles frozen in time. Averting her eyes, she told Sam, "You know something, you can't keep doing this. Your daddy loves you and he's got a lot to deal with right now. You could be a big help to him if you'd just try to talk to him. And if you can't do that, then maybe you need to talk to someone else to make you feel better."

Sam finally looked right at her. "You didn't tell him about the locket?"

"I told you I wouldn't," she repeated, wishing she could figure this child out. "You have to, though. He needs to know what you did and why you did it." She'd like to know that herself.

Sam's gaze held a mixture of trepidation and defiance. "He'll be mad at me. He's always mad at me."

Shocked to hear that, Goldie picked up one of the pictures and saw the image of Sam's mother staring back at her. Rachel had been a pretty woman. She could see Rachel's eyes whenever she looked at Sam. "Why does he seem mad at you?"

"I don't know. He just doesn't talk to me very much. I wish he'd talk about Mom more, but I don't want to make him sad."

Goldie couldn't imagine this little boy's pent-up pain.

"Maybe you just need to ask him about her. He might not realize you need to hear things about her."

"I can't."

Goldie decided to try another tactic. "Can you tell me why you took my necklace?"

He shifted through some pictures then tossed them back in a box. "I don't know. I found it by the couch and I just didn't know what to do with it."

"Did you know your daddy was looking for it?"

He nodded his head. "I was afraid I'd get in trouble for not showing it to him right away, so I didn't say anything. Is that a sin?"

Goldie needed someone much wiser to answer that question, but right now, Sam only had her. "It's a sin to lie, yes. But technically, you didn't lie. You just withheld information. So maybe it is a sin. Any way you look at it, it's not good. You need to come clean."

"Then I'll feel better?"

"You should. Your dad loves you and he's not going to hurt you. He might punish you but in the end, he'll be proud that you did the right thing."

He looked back at the pictures. "I thought maybe I could take the locket and put it on her grave—for a Christmas gift. Christmas isn't as fun as it used to be."

Goldie's heart shattered. This little boy had a whole lot going on underneath those thick bangs. "That's a nice thought but your mom wouldn't want a stolen locket on her grave. And, Sam, she wants you to have fun at Christmas. She wants you to laugh and play. You're a little boy—you've got a lot to laugh about."

He looked back at his mom's picture. "I want Daddy to laugh, too."

"But he does, doesn't he?"

"Some. But it's kind of fake, I think."

Goldie felt her legs going numb from sitting there crossed-legged but she couldn't move. "Well, let's think about this. Putting a necklace that doesn't belong to you on your mother's grave sure won't make him any happier, now will it?"

"I didn't do it, anyway. I was afraid he'd see it and be really mad. I hid it and then Grandma found it in that bag where I'd put it and then she got all upset and dizzy."

Goldie watched his face, saw how hard he was fighting his emotions. "Sam, you didn't cause your grandmother to get sick. It was something inside her, something already not right. She had a very light stroke but she has good doctors and she's going to need medicine and some therapy. But you can't pull any more tricks like this, okay? She doesn't need that kind of stress."

"So it *is* my fault?"

Goldie wanted to sink into the floor. "No, no. I just mean she has to take things easy so it would be nice if you didn't…if you could… I think you need to let your dad explain what needs to be done."

He sat silent, staring at the pile of pictures. "Do you hate me?"

Goldie shook her head. "Of course not. I want to be your friend and I'm so proud of you for confiding in me about the necklace. You know, in a weird way, you've given me such a wonderful gift." She took the necklace out of her pocket and put it around her neck, her fingers brushing over it. "This necklace is very special to me because it has a picture of me and my dad inside. I lost my dad when I was young, so I know how you feel."

He gave her a doubtful look. "I saw the picture. Did you cry when he died?"

"Yes, a lot. My mom and I both did."

"My dad cried at the funeral. I remember. I cried, too. Tyler was too little. Grandma held him all day."

Goldie shut her eyes to the image of what that poignant memory must have been like. "I remember my mom crying at my daddy's funeral, too. That's tough to watch." Then she reached out a hand to Sam, hoping the boy would respond. "You know it's okay to cry, don't you?"

He pushed away. "I'm not a baby."

"Crying has nothing to do with being a baby," she explained. "It hurts when someone we love dies. Tears are God's way of allowing us to be sad. But tears also allow us to heal our hearts, too."

He went into withdrawal again. Goldie had to wonder if Rory even knew how bad things were with his oldest son. She'd have to talk to him about this, somehow. But right now she had to think of something to bring Sam out of his self-imposed shell. Picking up one of the pictures, she said, "Hey, I have a great idea. Have you ever done any scrapbooking?"

Sam balked at that. "That sounds stupid."

"You don't even know what I'm talking about," she retorted, her tone playful. "But if you want to do something special for both your parents, we could make a weatherproof picture to put on your mom's grave and we could make something very special for your dad and your grandmother for Christmas. A scrapbook is like a picture book, but we'd add little things and maybe write something special by some of the pictures. And it can be just from you. A present from Sam. How about that?"

He acted unimpressed for a few seconds. Then he said, "Will you help me?"

"I'd love to," Goldie replied, her hand still near his. She wasn't sure when she'd get this done but she'd find the time. "It'll be a big surprise." Then she nodded her head. "I'll explain to your dad that I need to borrow you for a couple of hours one night next week, okay? That way he won't think I've kidnapped you or something."

Sam didn't say anything but he finally took her hand, shaking it as if they'd just made a business deal. "Will Spike be there?"

"Of course. He'll probably want to chew on a few of my scrapbook pages."

"Okay."

"Okay, then." Goldie closed her eyes for a minute, thanking God for allowing her to help this lost little boy.

And when she opened her eyes, Sam was actually smiling.

Rory went in to see his mother before going home.

"Hi," he said, taking her hand.

Frances gave him a drowsy smile. "Hi."

She could talk; that was a good sign. The doctors had explained she might have to deal with some memory loss and relearn her thought processes.

"Mom, I'm going home to check on the boys and Becky's girls. Becky's staying here tonight."

Frances shook her head. "Both go home. Now."

Seeing her struggle with her thoughts broke Rory's heart. "But—"

"No but. Go." Then she raised her eyebrows. "Who's with children?"

"Goldie and Miss Ruth."

At first, Frances looked confused, her expression twisting as if she were in pain. Then she settled back with a sigh. "That girl—"

"Yes, Mom. That girl. She's been great about this. And she's been with the kids all day long."

Frances smiled lopsidedly at that. "Make or break."

Rory understood what she was saying. "If she can survive a day with the boys, will you cut her some slack?"

Frances moved her head in a tiny nod. "Might."

Rory laughed at that, feeling better. "Thanks, Mom. I'll go talk to Becky and see if I can convince her to go home with me."

"Do it."

Rory had to laugh again. Even from a hospital bed, with wires attached to her, his mother was still barking orders and being firm. That attitude would help her to recover, he hoped. He prayed.

"Wait."

He turned at his mother's soft call. "Do you need something? Are you in pain?"

She shook her head. "Don't want…to be…pushed aside."

Rory saw the single tear moving down his mother's face. "You won't be pushed aside, Mom. You know how much we all depend on you. But you do need to get well."

She squinted. "Goldie."

"What about Goldie?"

"I didn't like her…taking over."

Rory suddenly understood. "Mom, she's not taking over. We're just friends and right now, neither of us is sure where that might lead. You need to rest and get better. Don't worry about Goldie."

"Not worried anymore."

Rory watched, amazed, as his mother managed a weak smile. "Go home."

"Yes, ma'am." His mother had given him her blessings. And in spite of worrying about her health, he felt as if a great weight had been lifted off his shoulders.

After telling Becky about their talk and convincing her to leave with him, Rory waited until his sister had told Frances good-night. Becky followed him home in her car, planning on picking up the girls to take them back to Frances's house.

When he pulled up to the house, Rory felt a gush of warmth seeping into his cold bones. The Christmas tree was sparkling just inside the window. Soft lighting flowed throughout the house, making it seem homey and welcoming. He stopped, his hands on the steering wheel.

It had been such a long time since he'd just sat looking at his house. This had been Rachel's dream house and he'd been heavily involved in building it. His dad had helped and so had several of his friends. After they'd moved in, she'd fussed and fixed and made it a home.

But the day she died, all the warmth had left this house. Rory had tried so hard to keep things the way she'd want them, for the boys. And his mother had done her best to help him. But his heart had become cold and hard and unyielding. He lived for his sons and he worked to keep the memories and the grief at bay.

The holidays were so hard without her here.

Then he looked through a window and saw another woman standing in his kitchen. A burnished-blond-haired, green-eyed woman prone to getting herself into sticky situations. That woman had come to his aid without question today.

He watched as she laughed and smiled down at one of the boys. When Sam turned around, Rory heaved a great breath, tears forming in his eyes.

Sam was smiling up at Goldie.

She'd won over his son, just as she'd won over him.

He fell for her right then and there.

Goldie glanced around. She'd heard a car and now she saw Rory's truck out in the driveway. "I think your dad's home," she said to Sam.

The boy's eyes widened. "Are you gonna tell him?"

"Not my place," she said. "I'm leaving that up to you. But I strongly suggest you tell your Dad what you did and why. He'll understand."

Sam didn't look so sure. "Okay," he said, his eyes downcast. But then he glanced up at her and smiled in such a sweet way, Goldie fell for him right then and there.

Was this how it felt to be a mother?

She squelched the tears misting in her eyes.

She'd sent Grams and Carla home so Grams could rest in her own house and take her medicine. The girls were drawing at the dining table and Tyler had awoken from his nap and was playing with his toy trucks by the fire. The house was sparkling clean in spite of four kids messing it up every hour on the hour, and the soup and biscuits were still warming on the stove.

She and Sam had been choosing which pictures to include in the scrapbook. She'd found a folder in his room and put the photos in it to keep them safe. And she'd promised Sam she'd get back with him so he could help her make the keepsake in time for Christmas.

"Now remember, I'll figure out a way to get you out of the house and over to Grams to work on our special project."

"Okay," he said. "Do I have to tell Dad tonight? About the locket?"

Goldie smiled down at him but held firm. "You tell him when you think the time is right. Your dad loves you, Sam. He'll forgive you."

The back door opened then and Rory walked in. "Well, look what a pretty picture—you two busy in the kitchen and everyone else quiet and settled."

Goldie's heart did a little jig of delight. She could get used to seeing him walk through the door every night.

Then she remembered this wasn't her house or her door. And Rory wasn't hers to claim.

But the way he looked at her with a hint of promise in his eyes made her wish for things she couldn't have. She put that wish out of her mind for now.

"How's your mother?"

"Feeling good enough to shoo me and Becky home. Becky's right behind me."

"I sure am," his dark-haired sister said as she rushed

through the door. "Oh, Goldie, I can't tell you how much we appreciate this." Becky stopped, glancing around. "What did you do to the house? It looks different."

Tyler ran up to Rory. "We cleaned up. Miss Goldie showed us how to stay organ-nized."

"Organized?" Becky asked, correcting him with a grin. "Well, well." Her girls rushed up to hug her close. "Did you two help?" They bobbed their heads and both started talking at once.

"We had such a good time. Carla helped us make a wreath from nature and we—"

"We helped with the soup and we learned how to label containers and roll socks into neat piles…"

Goldie blocked out all the banter, her eyes focused on Rory. He seemed pleased but he also seemed sad. Was he remembering other homecomings, with Rachel standing here?

Sam had been holding back but now he came around the counter. "Is Grandma gonna get well, Daddy?"

"Yes, she is," Rory said, dropping his jacket on the hall tree bench. "She just has to rest and do some special exercises to get back on track. Her mind's a little fuzzy right now."

Tyler made a face. "Does that hurt?"

"No," Rory said, "not like a stomachache. But it's scary for her. She might have to learn some things all over again."

"Will she miss Christmas?" Tyler asked, tugging at Rory's jeans.

Rory scooped his son up in his arms. "We hope not. But if she's not home, I'll take y'all to see her and give her a present, okay?"

"Okay."

Sam shot Goldie a covert glance. He'd want to have their surprise ready for his grandmother. Goldie smiled at him, conveying her promise with a wink.

After more explanations and reassurances about their grandmother's health, Becky thanked Goldie again and took the girls back to Frances's house.

"Stay here," Rory told Goldie. "I'll get the boys in bed and then we can talk."

She nodded, unable to sit still. Her whole being was humming with awareness. Rory was home and she had to admit it felt so nice imagining being a part of this family.

But do I have the right, Lord?

Goldie didn't know how to handle this sudden rush of feelings. She had too many things to consider. Her job, his children, his mother and about a million other reasons why she should just leave now.

But when Rory came back into the den, his eyes glinting gold in the firelight, Goldie became quiet and still. She couldn't leave him now.

So for once in her tidy, carefully organized life, she didn't try to rearrange things or fix things.

She just stood and stared across the room at the man she was falling in love with.

Chapter Thirteen

"Come and sit," Rory ordered, pointing toward the couch.

Goldie did as he asked, waiting for him to find a spot next to her. "Do you want some dinner?"

He glanced toward the stove. "Maybe later. Right now I just want to sit here in the quiet with you."

"You look tired," she said, acutely aware of the way his gaze flickered over her. "I'm so sorry, Rory. I hope your mother will be better soon."

He let out a long sigh. "Yeah, me, too. I had a lot of time today to think about what might have caused this."

Goldie looked away, toward the fire. She wanted to tell him about Sam thinking it was his fault, but Rory had enough to deal with right now. And she'd promised Sam she wouldn't rat him out to his dad. Her locket was safely hidden underneath her turtleneck sweater for now and that was all that mattered. She'd found it again.

So instead she tried to reassure Rory. "I read about strokes—looked up some information on the internet. It sounds as if this is very treatable."

"Yes, that's what the doctors say." He leaned forward, his hands clinched together. "I just hope I didn't drive her to this. The boys can be a handful, as you've probably figured out already. But Mom's always a trouper. She helped out right from the beginning." He rubbed a hand across his forehead. "I was pretty messed up the week or so after the funeral. Mom was a rock."

"I can't even begin to understand," Goldie said, the quiet in the room insulating them like a blanket. "It must have been horrible."

"It was." He gazed at the fire, his features shadowed and closed. Then he turned to face her. "I wanted to thank you, Goldie. For what you did today. I don't know why I called you—I shouldn't have. You don't even know my kids that well. But now, I'm glad I did." He took in his surroundings. "Becky was right. The house looks different. Even my two boys seem different. You're the one who made that possible. I'll never forget that."

Goldie didn't know how to respond. Was he hiding his anger that she took over his home, or did he truly appreciate what she'd tried to do for him? He didn't seem angry right now. He appeared sincere and humble, as if he'd actually seen this home for the first time without the veil of grief covering his eyes.

To ease the darkness of her own thoughts, she said, "I was born a neat-freak so it's second nature for me to rearrange and file away and sort things. But I didn't mind. And Grams and Carla enjoyed it, too. We laughed and cleaned, cooked and played games, broke up fights and kissed boo-boos, and even though a mixing bowl got broken and the dog and kids tracked in dirt and leaves, we managed to survive."

"Which one of them broke the bowl?"

"Oh, that would be me, of course. I might be neat but I'm also accident-prone, as you've noticed."

He grinned at that. "Glad it was just a bowl. And I'm glad you're not hurt or stuck in a ditch."

"Me, too." She put a hand to her mouth, stifling a yawn. "Excuse me."

Rory shook his head, smiling. "And you're probably just as tired as I am."

She chuckled. "I think I'll sleep soundly tonight."

He sat back, relaxing against the couch. "Funny how people come into our lives, huh? Of all the couches in the world, I'm glad you passed out on mine."

She looked down at her hands. "Are you sure? I mean, I've been nothing but trouble, don't you think?"

He turned so she could see his face. "I'm beginning to like trouble." Then he glanced around. "Where is that little pile of fur that follows you around?"

"Spike? He went home with Grams and Carla, even though Tyler really wanted him to stay. He loved running around with the kids but I think he's probably snoozing away right now, dreaming of chasing the kids around the yard and hiding in a pile of leaves."

"Are you really going to give him to the boys when you go back to Baton Rouge?"

She nodded, hating to think about leaving Rory and his children and Spike. "I promised." When she looked over at him, she could see the reflection of her own thoughts in his eyes. Did he want her to stay?

Goldie's pulse lifted and skipped at that hope. "I

guess I should get home," she said, overwhelmed with a whole passel of new feelings. If she sat here much longer, she might do something really dangerous and tell Rory she didn't want to leave.

"Don't go yet," he pleaded, his gaze saying, "Don't go, ever." Or maybe she was just wishing he'd say that to her.

"Aren't you tired?"

"I was. I am. But I don't want you to go. That soup smells good but I hate eating alone."

She smiled, hoping to ease the pain behind his words. "Then I won't leave just yet."

He took her hand in his. "Are we having a date here?"

She glanced around. "Well, we are alone and I'm not in a crashed car or a drainage canal and I'm conscious and alert."

"Are you seeing two of me?"

"No." One of him was way more than she could handle at this point. "I just see you, Rory. Only you."

"And what do you see, when you look at me?"

The deep intensity of that question threw her and she worked to form her thoughts. "I see a good man who's been through a terrible ordeal. I see a man who loves his children and cares about his family. I see a strong man, determined to take care of everybody." She felt his hand tighten on hers. "And I see a man who also needs to remember to take care of himself."

She watched as he closed his eyes and laid his head back on the puffy couch. Goldie had to fight the urge to reach up and push at the little curls settling across his forehead. Her fingers lifted toward him.

Then he opened his eyes and looked at her. Goldie

put her hand down by her side. "I pray every night to do the right thing, for my boys, for my job, for the people I love. But what if that's not enough?"

Goldie wanted to tell him so many things, but she couldn't form the right words. "I think you just have to put one foot in front of the other," she said. "You have to keep moving, Rory. And you need to keep praying." Then she glanced toward the hallway where the boys slept. "But you might want to reach out to the boys a little more. I think Sam needs to talk to you, really talk to you. Or maybe you need to talk to him."

At first, he seemed shocked and angry, a nerve twitching near his mouth as he gritted his teeth. "You picked up on that?"

She nodded, afraid she'd only made him feel worse. "Well, yes. I mean, we both noticed he wasn't exactly thrilled when I entered the picture. But today, I think Sam and I reached a truce of sorts. He's just afraid and confused. And he wants to please you so much. I remember being the same way with my dad."

"Did Sam say something to you today? Something about me?"

Oh boy, did he ever. "We just had a long talk and he kind of warmed up to me. But he blames himself for what happened to your mother."

"Why would he feel that way?"

Realizing she'd let that slip without thinking, Goldie scrambled for words. "I guess because he's the oldest and he thinks he's supposed to be more responsible. I told him it wasn't his fault." To convince him further, she said, "Don't worry. We talked it through and he seems much better now. We're working on a special

Christmas gift for you, by the way." Then she put a finger to her lips. "It's a big secret so you have to really act surprised."

Rory turned toward her, his hand still on hers. "I saw him smiling, when I pulled up. I saw you two there through the window and my son was smiling. I don't know what happened between y'all today but I want to thank you again. And you're right. I do need to spend more time with him." Then he touched a finger to her head. "Even after having a concussion, you've still got a pretty good brain inside there, you know."

"And here I thought my head was full of air."

He leaned close, the richness of his golden-brown eyes capturing her in a heady warmth. "Goldie…"

She didn't hear anything else. She just heard him calling her name as he leaned toward her. And then, his lips met hers and she was lost, lost in a longing that caught her breath and made her feel whole again. Rory was kissing her. And she didn't want him to ever stop.

Rory pulled away to stare over at her. "Wow."

Goldie couldn't read the tone of that "Wow." Was it a good kind of wow or an "I've-made-a-huge-mistake-here" wow?

"Is that good or bad?" she finally asked, her words low and shaky.

"Good," he said, his hand on her arm. "And bad."

"Clarify things for me, please."

"It was good, too good." He shifted away. "I don't know how to handle this. Is it too soon? Is there a rule book for a widower kissing another woman?"

Goldie shook her head. "I give advice on getting

things in order but I've never had to answer that question, Rory. I guess it all depends on what you feel inside."

He got up to stand with his back to the fire. "Right now, I'm feeling all kinds of things. Guilt and joy, both at the same time. Pain and happiness, all mixed together. I feel like I'm betraying Rachel but I feel like I've just come alive again myself. Is that wrong?"

Goldie stood and headed to the kitchen. "You need to eat."

He followed her, turning her to face him. "Don't go getting all busy on me. We need to talk about this."

"What's there to talk about?" she asked, wishing she could tell him about her feelings. "You're still in love with your wife and that's part of what I like about you. You're the kind of man who stays faithful, Rory. Faithful to God and family and friends. And here I come, messing with all of that. Do you want me to tell you this is wrong? How can I when it feels right to me?"

He let go of her arm. "You've been out there, though. You know more about this kind of thing than I do. I only knew and loved one woman and that woman is gone now. This is all new for me."

"I've had a few relationships, yes, but honestly, I've never dealt with this before, either. None of my ex-boyfriends compare to you—and technically, I haven't even had a date with you yet. How do you explain that?" She turned to the soup on the stove.

"Is *that* a good thing?"

She pulled the foil off the biscuits. "You tell me. Is this good between us? Or are we just asking for trouble? I like you, Rory. But we know what we're up against. I have a fairly good job in Baton Rouge and I'm pushing things with the paper as it is, doing my job long distance and through email. And even though Baton Rouge is not that far away on the map, we're worlds away from each other in our lifestyles. I've been moved from pillar to post most of my life and you're as settled as a cypress tree, roots and all."

"So I'm like an old tree?"

She glanced back to find him smiling at her. "You know what I mean. Besides that, I might have made headway with Sam but your mother wasn't that thrilled about me from what I could tell. And now, you've got a lot more to deal with."

"You mean my mother's stroke?"

"Yes. She's going to need assistance and since you live right here, most of that responsibility will fall on your shoulders."

"I know that and I'm more than willing to take care of her, but that doesn't mean we can't at least continue to get to know each other, does it?"

"But we only have a few days left."

He nodded, his expression solemn as he thought about what she'd said. "We can call and email each other and you'll come now and then to see Ruth, right?"

"Yes, but—"

"Yeah, so, I think we're looking for excuses to fail. Or maybe you're just looking for excuses. Maybe you don't want this because you'd have to deal with my mother and my boys and my life."

"That's not what I'm saying," she protested. But she had to stop and consider that if she decided to let him into her life, she'd have to become a part of his—the way it was and the way it would be. She couldn't ask him to change his life very much. She'd have to be the one doing most of the changing. "I don't know, Rory. I just don't know."

He stared across at her, silent and still. "Then I think that's your answer. Maybe you're *not* ready for this. Maybe you're not ready for me."

Goldie dipped his soup into a bowl and put two biscuits on a plate then poured him a glass of iced tea. "Eat your dinner."

Rory sat down on one of the high stools near the kitchen counter. He pushed the soupspoon around in the chunky beef and vegetables then lifted it to his mouth. After eating a couple of bites, he gazed across at her. "I can't say that I blame you."

Goldie wanted to shout out her fears and her doubts. "What if I'm wrong for you?" she asked. "What if I can't be the woman you think I might be?"

"I can't answer that," he said, taking a biscuit and buttering it. "But I do know this—you've made me smile again. You made Sam smile again. I know this might sound way out there, but I believe God puts certain people in our lives for a reason. And somehow, by the grace of God, you showed up here, Goldie. Here in this house that was sad and gloomy in spite of my best efforts. You've brought something new and bright into our lives. And I can't see anything wrong in that." He chewed his biscuit then said, "And you don't have to be a certain way for me. I kind of like you just the way you are."

"But I'm not Rachel," she explained, getting to the crux of the matter. "I'm not her, Rory."

He dropped the biscuit, his eyes glazing hot. "You don't have to be. I'd never expect you to be her. No one can replace Rachel. But God has a plan for my life. And maybe you're part of that plan."

"And what about *my* life? Is He up there planning things for me, too? Did He drop me down in this little town for a reason?"

"You came to help your grandmother. Isn't that reason enough?"

She sank back against the counter. "It should be. I love Grams that much. I might get fired, but she needed me."

"Not many people would take that stance."

"We've always helped each other."

"And what about your mother?"

"She's out of the picture."

"Have you talked to her since she left for Europe?"

"Just through email. Phone calls across the Atlantic are expensive."

"You miss her."

"Yes, but why are we talking about my mother?"

"Maybe that's part of God's plan, too."

A fire of frustration burned inside her. "Well, I have a plan, too, Rory. I plan to go back to my safe little world and do my job. I'm good at that one thing, at least."

"You might be good at more than that, Goldie."

"And how am I supposed to figure that out?"

"That's between you and God, I reckon."

She looked down, unsure what to say next. Then she felt the weight of her locket against her skin. When she'd lost it, she thought only bad would come of it. But now, she had it back and all because a little boy wanted to remember his deceased mother at Christmas. It was a twisted logic but in a strange way, Sam's need to do something special for his mother had brought Goldie and him closer together today. It was as if God had somehow forced both of them together. Or was she just grasping at hope? Rory's mother had a stroke; that certainly couldn't have been part of God's plan.

But it made them stop and think about how things hadn't been going along as well as they'd thought.

Maybe Rory was onto something. Maybe God had been working on both of them and she was just too blind to see that. But how could she be sure?

"You're right. This is between God and me. And I'll have to be the one to figure it out."

Rory pushed his finished soup away then got up. "Well, let me know when you do get things all figured out."

Goldie could tell she'd hurt him. "I'm sorry," she said. "Look, it's late and you've had an awful day. Just get some rest."

He lifted his chin a notch as she walked to the door and gathered her coat and scarf. "Thanks again."

She could tell from his tone that she'd messed up. Was he mad at her because she had cold feet or because she wasn't so sure about the God part of all of this?

"I'll see you later."

"All right." He walked her to the door then pulled her around. "We can make this right, Goldie. It might take some time but we've got time."

She stared up at him, wishing she could get this all straight and tidy in her mind and in her heart. "Or I could make a mess of things for you, Rory. I don't know if I'm willing to take that risk."

His eyes flashed with fire. "Or maybe you're just not willing to take on the three of us—my boys and me. Maybe we just don't fit in with your perfectly controlled life."

His words hurt her to the core, cutting off her breath and her hope. "You know something, Rory, you really need to get over this notion that you're a burden on everyone around you. Have you ever stopped to think we're all here to help you because we care about you and those children? Or have you just been so wrapped up in misery, you can't even see the suffering of your own son?"

He backed away, shock making him go pale. "You have no reason to say that. You don't know anything about my son."

Goldie swallowed back the painful lump in her throat. "I know enough, Rory."

Then she turned, left his house and hurried to her car. And she didn't dare look back, because if she did, she would return to him and hold him and tell him she was sorry. And she'd tell him that she'd gotten to know Sam really well today.

And that she'd found her locket, too.

Chapter Fourteen

Christmas Eve

Rory stared out the window, taking in the dry leaves and the bare gray trees surrounding his property. He had a beautiful piece of land here, full of cypress and pines, oak and sycamore trees. Just a few weeks ago, these woods had been full of bright oranges and brilliant yellows, the leaves turning with a perfect symmetry almost overnight.

And now, most of the leaves were scattered to the wind. And so was his spiraling and chaotic life.

Because of Goldie.

Fitting, even her name made him think of the changing seasons. He'd lost Rachel in the spring on a perfectly beautiful night where the dogwoods glowed white and ethereal in the surrounding woods. He'd mourned her through Easter and the worst parts of summer. He'd lost her through someone else's brutality and now that person was serving a life sentence in prison. But in some ways, Rory was serving that same sentence, too.

If I'd only been able to go to the store for her that night, he thought over and over again. If only. He'd asked God to give him answers but he knew he'd find the answers in heaven. But right now, he was still here on earth. And he was falling in love with a woman who was completely different from his wife. A woman who was afraid to lose control and let him love her.

Lord, is it possible to love two women at the same time?

Rory had never felt so torn in his life. Since work had been kind of slow due to the winter season, he was at odds all the way around. He'd raked leaves with the boys, trying to bring Sam out of his own mourning. He'd even taken them with him on a quick run to get a doe out of a mud pit, just to have them near. Christmas was hard on all of them but this year with his mom sick, it would be especially hard. Frances always fussed and cooked and spoiled them. Rory knew he'd failed his boys in the most important way. He'd neglected to actually talk to them about their mother.

Goldie had been right on that account, but he'd been too angry and hurt to tell her so.

I'm trying, Lord, he said on a fervent prayer. *I'm trying. I'll give up Goldie if it will bring me closer to my boys. It's the only thing I can do. It's the right thing to do.*

"And I'm that kind of man," he said to himself, his tone sarcastic and bitter.

Maybe if he concentrated on keeping busy, he could find a way to work through all these strange feelings. He wanted Goldie in his life but he wasn't sure he was ready to accept that he was in love with her. And she sure wasn't ready to accept that, either. So instead of standing here brooding on it, he made a list and set out to cook Christmas dinner tomorrow for his sons and his mother.

Becky would bring her family over after Christmas to spend some time with their mother but right now, it was up to Rory to make things special. Frances had improved enough to come home, on the condition that she'd rest and let everyone else spoil her for a change. Rory thought that was a good idea.

When he heard a car in the drive, he opened the back door and waved at the friend who'd taken the boys along with her children to see the live nativity village set up behind the church. The boys rushed in, throwing hats and jackets here and there, excited about petting a real donkey and two baby lambs.

"Mrs. Evans said you helped find the animals for the nativity scene, Dad," Tyler exclaimed, clearly impressed.

Sam chimed in. "I told my friends you know a lot about animals." His eyes shone bright with pride.

Rory let out a held breath. Maybe his older son was slowly healing in his own way. The minister and the church counselors had told Rory that children were more resilient than adults when it came to grief. He hoped that was true. But he couldn't forget that Goldie had helped Sam, too.

Even if she wasn't speaking to Rory, she'd kept her pledge to Sam to help him with his big surprise. She'd picked up Sam the other night, waiting in the car for him to come out. Rory had waved to her and she'd just smiled and waved back, her eyes devoid of any joy.

Putting that image away for now, he said, "Hey, I have an idea and I need y'all to help me. I want to cook Christmas dinner for Grandma and bring it to her tomorrow. What do you think?"

"Can she get out of bed?" Sam asked, swiping a hand across his red nose.

Rory nodded. "She's okay physically. She just has some memory and coordination problems. But she's doing fine and she's already started her therapy sessions. Her friend took her to the first one yesterday. But we'll go there and cook so she won't have to lift a finger."

"What's a cordon-nation problem, Daddy?" Tyler inquired.

"It means she might have trouble remembering how to spell and read. Her thoughts get all mixed up so she has to learn some things over again."

"I can help her read," Tyler offered. "I can read pretty good."

"I know you can," Rory replied, smiling. The boys had become very protective of their grandmother since Frances had come home yesterday. And Becky was staying through the New Year so Rory could get a break.

"Who's with Grandma now?" Sam posed the question as he nabbed a cookie from the jar on the counter.

"She has a day nurse," Rory explained. "We thought that would be a good idea since I had to finish up some work today. And she has friends coming over tonight to visit, since she can't go to the Christmas Eve service at church. We'll visit her later, too. But tomorrow we can give the nurse a rest. Right now we need to make this list and buy groceries." He grabbed a pen and a notepad.

Tyler shrugged. "I wish she hadn't got sick."

"Me, either, buddy, but sometimes things like this happen."

"Like when Mom died?" Sam guessed, his eyes going dark again.

Rory almost went back to his old standard way of brushing off hard questions. But instead of repeating that things just happened and changing the subject, he clarified, "Yes, son. Like that. It hurts a lot but we have to keep on keeping on." He ruffled Sam's hair. "Your mom would want us to do that. She'd want us to have a good Christmas and she'd tell us that we're blessed because we have each other."

Tyler looked up at Rory. "Is Miss Goldie coming over for Christmas?"

"Maybe," Rory replied. He wanted to see her on Christmas day. He had her gift. "I hope we get to see her again before she goes back to Baton Rouge."

"She's supposed to bring Spike, remember?" Tyler said, his expression hopeful.

"I remember, son."

Sam glanced around then back to Rory. "Daddy, I… I need to tell you something."

"What?" Rory asked, dread building up inside him. Did Sam want to talk some more about his mother's death?

Sam gave his little brother another glance. "Not right now, though."

Rory took that as a hint. "Hey, Tyler, why don't you go and wash your hands for lunch. I'll call you when it's ready."

Tyler shrugged again. "I can't see any dirt on my

hands, but whatever." He took off running toward the bathroom.

Rory had to smile at that. Tyler sounded like an echo of his older brother. When he turned back to Sam, the boy looked so dejected Rory touched him on the shoulder. "You know you can talk to me about anything don't you, son?"

Sam nodded, his head down.

Rory took him over to the couch. "Let's talk, then."

Sam let out a long sigh, his hands in his lap. "I did something bad."

Surprised at that solemn admission, Rory playfully pushed at Sam's shirtsleeve. "Like what? Did you get in another fight with your brother over the game remote?"

Sam shook his head. "Worse than that."

"Okay, so you forgot to pick up your dirty clothes again."

Sam didn't respond. He sat staring at his hands.

"Just tell me now, Sam. Let's get it out in the open."

Sam finally looked up at him, the expression on his face mirroring the doubt and fear in his eyes. "I... I found Miss Goldie's locket."

Rory let out a chuckle and a big sigh. "You did? Well, that's nothing to be so sad about. Where'd you find it? Where is it now? We need to let her know right away."

Sam shook his head. "She knows already."

That cut the chuckle right out of Rory's throat. "What?" He realized Sam had seen her this week. He must have given her the locket then.

But Sam's frown was full of despair not pride. "I told her about it the other day when she was here with her friend and her grandma."

"You did?" Wondering why Goldie hadn't mentioned it, he stared at his son. They must have found it when they were out playing in the leaves and maybe Goldie just forgot to tell him. "Why didn't y'all tell me?"

Sam fell back against the couch, his chin jutting out. "Miss Goldie said I had to be the one. She said it wasn't her place."

Rory put two fingers to his nose, pinching the throbbing pain developing there. "Okay, let's start from the beginning, Sam. Tell me what happened with the locket."

Sam looked at the Christmas tree. "I found it the night Miss Goldie had her wreck."

A great weight settled like an anchor in Rory's stomach. "That was about three weeks ago. And you knew we were searching for it. Are you telling me you had it the whole time and didn't say anything?"

"Yes, sir."

Now he could at least see why Goldie hadn't brought up the locket the last time he'd seen her. And he suddenly understood very well that she indeed knew more about his son than he did. She'd been protecting Sam.

Rory looked at his son, wondering what else he didn't know. "Sam, you heard how much that necklace meant to Goldie and you saw me looking for it everywhere around here. Why did you feel the need to hide the locket, son?"

Sam finally glanced up, his eyes brimming with fear and doubt. "I thought I'd put it on Mama's grave. It was so pretty and… I wanted to just put it on her grave but I was afraid you'd get mad at me. So I…hid it."

Rory bit his lip, his own emotions swelling until he

thought he'd burst. He had to repeat the whole thing just to make sense of it. "So even though you knew it was wrong to hide the locket, you kept it because you wanted to put it on Mommy's grave?"

"Yes, sir."

"But, Sam, even though that was a thoughtful thing to do for your mother, you know that was wrong, don't you?"

"Yes, sir. Miss Goldie told me that was sweet but since the locket didn't belong to me, it was better to give it back to her. She said Mom wouldn't want stolen jewelry on her grave."

Rory listened to his son's words, trying to piece this puzzle together. "And Miss Goldie promised not to tell me, right?"

Sam bobbed his head. "She said I had to tell you and that you loved me so you'd forgive me. Is that true?"

Rory's heart hammered an erratic cadence deep inside his chest. "Yes, of course that's true," he assured him, reaching over to Sam. "I love you." He held his son close, feeling the tension radiating from the little boy's body. "But you understand that what you did was wrong?"

"Yes, sir."

Rory closed his eyes, remembering his harsh words to Goldie. "What made you decide to give it back to Goldie?"

Sam pulled away, his eyes full of moisture. "'Cause MeeMaw found it in one of the Christmas bags and when she asked me about it, I told her I'd put it there and she got really upset and then—"

"And then she got sick, right?"

Sam nodded again, tears falling down his face. "I didn't mean to make her mad or get her all sick. I just hid it there until I could take it to Mama. I wasn't trying to be mean, honest, Dad. I just wanted Mama to have it. I didn't want Miss Goldie around. I wanted Mama."

Rory gritted his teeth against the tears pricking at his own eyes as he pulled his son back into his arms. "I know, son. I know." He kissed Sam's dark curls. "I miss her, too. And while putting the locket on her grave would have been a nice gesture, you were wrong to hide it. You understand that now. And you did the right thing, telling me the truth, okay?"

Sam's muffled reply sent ripples of love and shame throughout Rory's system. He'd failed his son. He should have talked to Sam more about Rachel, about her death and everything that had held them apart since then. But he'd been so busy trying to be normal, trying to put one foot in front of the other like everyone had told him to do, that he hadn't noticed his son's suffering.

Well, Goldie had noticed and instead of getting angry and berating Sam for literally stealing something that was very precious to her, she'd turned things around and forced the issue by befriending Sam and convincing him to tell his father the truth.

How did he thank her for that? For giving his son back to him, for showing him that his heart wasn't completely broken after all? How could he ever convince her that she belonged in his life? Goldie would make a wonderful mother to his children. He could see that so clearly now. Somehow he had to convince her of that.

Wiping at his own eyes, he held Sam by the shoulders. "So Miss Goldie has her locket?"

Sam nodded. "She put it on after I gave it to her. She was really glad to have it back." He looked up at Rory, a new light shining in his eyes. "And you know what, Dad? I felt better, telling her the truth."

"I'm sure you did. I'm so proud of you. Your mom would be proud, too."

"That's what Miss Goldie said."

"And you two, are things better between you now?"

Another bob of the head. "She's helping me…" Sam stopped, his mouth dropping open. "Never mind. It's a surprise."

"A good surprise?"

"Uh-huh."

"Then I can live with that." Rory reached out a hand to Sam. Sam offered his own and Rory shook it, man to man. "I *am* proud of you, son. You confessed to something you did and you told me why you did it. You and I both are blessed because your mother was a wonderful woman and she'd be so touched that you wanted to put something nice on her grave. She knows you did the right thing and you need to remember that."

Sam blinked then sniffed. "Will God forgive me, too?"

"Of course He will," Rory confirmed. "God always gives us a second chance to make things right."

Sam's expression lifted and changed right in front of Rory's eyes, his frown relaxing into a soft smile. "I like Miss Goldie. I didn't at first, but I do now. I'm sorry I hid the locket."

"Well, it's all over now," Rory said. "And, Sam, you didn't cause MeeMaw to get sick. She was already ill, so unhealthy that something went wrong inside her brain.

But she's going to be better soon. I promise you, this is not your fault."

Sam lowered his gaze again. "Miss Goldie told me that it's not anybody's fault. Does that mean what happened to Mom isn't your fault, then?"

That one hit Rory right in the heart. "I guess it does. But why... How do you know that I blame myself?"

"You said it," Sam replied. "I heard you telling MeeMaw that one day when you were sad. I heard you and so I thought... I thought that if we do bad things, then something bad happens to people because of us. You told MeeMaw that if you hadn't been late, you could have gone to the store for Mama and she'd still be alive."

Rory listened to the heartfelt words coming out of his son's mouth and silently prayed to God to take this burden from his son. And him. "I shouldn't have said that, Sam. I was just confused and I missed your mama."

"Miss Goldie said you still love Mom. Do you?"

"Of course I do. I'll always love your mom. And I do wish I could have been the one who went to the store that night but I have to stop blaming myself, don't I?"

Sam nodded. "I don't blame you. I don't blame anybody."

Rory ruffled his son's curls. "I'm glad to hear that. I think it's time you and I both stop punishing ourselves for things we can't control, okay?"

"Okay." Sam settled back again. "I hope Miss Goldie comes on Christmas. Then we can give you the present I made. And we get to see Spike again."

"I hope so, too, son," Rory said, nodding. "In fact, I'm going by there on my way to get groceries and invite her and Miss Ruth for dinner. What do you think about that?"

"That's okay with me," Sam replied, the relief on his face evident.

But it was a heartbreaking relief for Rory. How long had his son carried this burden, wondering if his own father was to blame for his mother's death, wondering how to love a man who couldn't forgive himself?

Rory thought about Christ dying on the cross and remembered the burden had already been lifted, from his shoulders and from his son's, too. Because of another son long ago who'd been willing to keep the burden of sins on His back. So men such as Rory could sit here by the fire and hug their own children close, knowing they were forgiven.

It was sobering and humbling and Rory thanked God he'd finally seen the truth there in Sam's eyes.

And he wanted to thank Goldie, for rescuing him from his own doubts and despair. He sent out a prayer that she'd forgive him for being so pigheaded and for pushing her so hard. Loneliness and confusion had clouded his vision.

His head was clear now. And he wanted her in his life.

"Are you gonna go see her?" Sam asked, tugging at Rory's sleeve.

"I am. But I can't leave you and Tyler here by yourselves. I guess y'all will have to go to the store with me. And to see Miss Goldie, too."

Sam got up, a new energy radiating around him. "I'll go tell Tyler." Then he turned around. "We never had lunch, Dad."

"No, we didn't," Rory said. "How about we see if Goldie wants to go for pizza with us *before* we buy groceries?"

"Okay."

And with that, his son ran down the hallway to get his brother. While Rory sat staring at the twinkling star on the Christmas tree.

Chapter Fifteen

Goldie pulled her grandmother's car up to the curb at the Baton Rouge Metropolitan Airport, her hands clammy on the wheel. Was she crazy to be here? It was Christmas Eve, after all. Glancing around, she wondered for the hundredth time if she'd made the right decision.

"Well, I'm here now." Goldie got out of the car and looked around. A crowd of holiday travelers rushed by, suitcase wheels grinding on the hard, cold concrete.

She pulled her leather jacket close then checked her watch. She was on time. She only hoped the flight would be.

And suddenly, she saw her mother coming through the terminal at a fast pace, tugging her bright purple suitcase behind her. Angela was wearing all black and carrying a shiny patent black-and-white-patterned tote to match.

Goldie braced herself. She still couldn't get over the shock of her mother's phone call from the Atlanta airport early this morning.

"I'm coming home, honey. Pick me up in Baton Rouge at two o'clock. Don't be late."

And just like that, Goldie's world had gone into a tailspin. Her wayward mother had decided to surprise them with a Christmas Eve visit. On the one hand, Goldie thanked God for this gift of a second chance. On the other hand, Goldie wished she could run, get on one of those planes and fly away from her troubles.

But no, that's what her mother did. Goldie always stayed behind and kept things organized. Goldie always put everything in its rightful place, even her love life.

Grinding her teeth against the cold, she took a deep breath. She'd organized her grandmother's house and Rory's house, and managed to keep her work organized and never missed a deadline. She'd answered Buried in Bossier with a new insight and she'd dashed off a holiday organization tip sheet that her editor at the paper was raving about. In fact, she was so efficient she always got through the worst of circumstances, like losing the man she loved, with noble aplomb.

This week, she'd helped Sam make two small scrapbooks, rearranged her grandmother's pantry yet again and bought colorful storage bins for all the Christmas decorations that she would take down before she left for the city and her own tidy little apartment.

But what was she supposed to do with her mother?

"Hi, Mom," Goldie called, pasting a smile on her face when her mother emerged onto the sidewalk. "I'm here."

"Why, you sure are. I knew you'd be right on time. You just don't have it in you to be late, do you, suga'?"

"And it's great to see you, too, Mom."

Angela tossed her own wavy burnished-brown hair and laughed. "Hello, darlin'." She hugged Goldie close. "You're so thin."

"And you're so blunt."

Goldie put her mother's suitcase in the trunk then got in the car. Angela tossed her tote in the back. "What on earth are you doing driving this old gas-guzzler?"

"My car's in the shop."

Angela pulled down the sun visor, saw there wasn't a mirror and frowned. Snapping it back up, she turned to Goldie. "Why? What's wrong with it?"

"Oh, major damage to the front bumper, the hood and some missing parts that fell out when I hit a tree."

"You hit a tree? How on earth did that happen?"

"The roads were icy."

Angela gave her daughter a long, glaring look. "Ice? In Louisiana? Honey, are you sure you're feeling okay?"

"We had a big ice storm about three weeks ago and yes, I'm sure. I hit a bad spot and, well, I wrecked my car. But I'm okay. Just got a knot on my already-hard head."

And fell in love with a not-so-perfect family.

Her mother's blue-green eyes slanted like a cat's as she studied Goldie's head to make sure she was all right. "I guess I've missed a lot."

"Why'd you come home so soon, anyway?" Goldie asked, trying to be patient, trying to be thankful.

Angela waved a hand in the air. "Well, honey, there I was standing looking up at the Eiffel Tower. It was beautiful. You know, Paris is the City of Lights."

"Yes, I've heard that."

"Well, I got this awful feeling. I got homesick. I

wanted to see the Christmas lights in Natchitoches and the cute little lights in Viola and I wanted to drive up to Shreveport and do the whole Trail of Lights from Shreveport and Bossier City all the way over into Jefferson and Marshall in Texas."

Goldie nodded, pretending to understand. "And so…"

"And so, I booked a flight home. And just in time for Christmas. And wait until you see what I brought you."

"Mom, I've never known you to be homesick."

"I know. It floored me, too. But, honey, I'm getting old and ornery, and I just want my own bed, my frayed pajamas and I don't want to see another tour bus for a long time."

Goldie smiled over at her mother. "I'm glad you're home, Mom."

Angela patted her hand. "And besides, your grandmother sent me an urgent text message. Something about a man named Rory putting you all in a tizzy."

Goldie almost lost control of the car. "Grams knows how to text?"

"Yep. Pretty good at it, too. I had to ask a teenager on the tour what she was saying. Who knew 'RUP' means 'read up please' and 'WAY' means 'where are you?' When I didn't answer at first, I got another one saying '4COL,GTHM AEAP.'"

"What does that mean?" Goldie asked, sick at her stomach. She texted a lot herself but even she didn't know all the shorthand.

"For crying out loud, get home as early as possible," Angela explained with a shrug.

Since she was stopped at a red light, Goldie gently

banged her head against the ancient steering wheel. "I can't believe this."

"Well, aren't you glad to see me?"

"Yes," Goldie replied, too stunned to say anything else.

"Now before we get back to your grandmother's house, let's stop in Lafayette, have a nice cup of Louisiana coffee and talk about this Rory. And I want to hear everything." She winked. "After all, isn't that what a mother is for?"

Rory pulled up to Ruth's house with high expectations and sweaty palms. He'd gone to the grocery store first so he wouldn't have to rush this. So he and the boys had spent two hours in the crowded place, making sure they had all the ingredients for a passable meal. He'd finally fed the boys in the snack bar, promising them a nice meal later, hopefully with Goldie.

"I don't see Miss Ruth's car, Dad," Sam said.

"Neither do I," Rory replied. "Let's just go check since we're here."

They all piled out of the truck. Rory could hear Spike barking inside the house. That was a good sign at least.

But the woman who opened the door wasn't Goldie. Or Miss Ruth.

"Uh, hi," Rory said. "Is Goldie here?"

The woman gave him a once-over look that might have served for sizing up a rodent. "No and your knock probably woke up her grandmother."

"I'm sorry," Rory apologized, lowering his voice. "I just wanted to talk to Goldie."

"Well, you can't," the woman declared. "I'm Phyllis,

Ruth's friend. Goldie called me to come and stay with her. Goldie went to Baton Rouge."

With that, the woman slammed the door in his face.

"She wasn't very nice," Tyler said, looking down at his sneakers.

But Rory didn't care about the woman's rudeness. He only cared that Goldie had left. On Christmas Eve. Without saying goodbye.

"She didn't bring Spike to us," Sam said, his chin jutting out. "And she promised." He stared at the door. "And what about— Never mind."

Rory knew what his son was thinking. She hadn't even bothered to make sure Sam got the presents he'd made for Rory and Frances.

"How could she just leave like that, Dad?" Sam asked.

Rory hated the disappointment in his son's question. But he felt that same disappointment inside his heart.

"I don't know, son. Maybe she had an emergency."

"Yeah, right." Sam was back to his old cynical self.

And Rory couldn't blame the boy. A crushing weight settled on his chest as he guided his boys back to the truck. Goldie had bolted; she'd run away without even giving them a chance. Or maybe she'd left because he hadn't really given her a chance.

Goldie pulled into the driveway, a great exhaustion weighing her down. She'd poured out her heart to her mother, something she wasn't used to doing.

But even after tears and ranting and hoping and discussing, and even though she was drained, she'd appreciated having her mother to talk to. And to sagely tell her, "Go find the man and tell him you love him, honey. The rest will all just have to work itself out."

What a Christmas this was turning out to be.

They walked in to find Phyllis fussing as she wiped at the tile floor in the kitchen. "That dog of yours had an accident."

"I'm so sorry," Goldie said, mortified. Phyllis was a dear friend to her grandmother but she wasn't the most pleasant person in the world. "Let me finish cleaning that."

Phyllis lifted up with a groan, her bright red sweat suit reminding Goldie of Mrs. Claus. "Where's Grams?"

"She's just getting up from her nap," Phyllis said, already gathering her things. "But for the life of me, I don't know how she got any rest. Dogs barking, people knocking at the door—"

"Who stopped by?"

"Oh, a man and two boys. I think I've seen him at church. Young, nice-looking but kind of dense. I told him you'd gone to Baton Rouge and he just stood there with his mouth open."

Goldie looked at her stunned mother. "Rory."

"Rory," Phyllis echoed with a triumphant smile. "I knew him. Just couldn't remember his name."

"Rory was here?"

Phyllis stared across the room at Goldie. "Yes, that's what I said. Now you're looking daft, just like he did."

"That's because she's in love with him," Angela asserted, impatience fueling her declaration. "Phyllis, why don't you stay awhile. I'll go get Mama Ruth up and give her a big old hug, and we'll make a pot of coffee and I'll get out the goodies I brought for y'all."

"You brought me something?" Phyllis asked, looking dumbfounded.

"I sure did," Angela replied. Then she grinned. "Now who's looking daft?"

Phyllis waved a hand in the air. "Good to have you back in town, Angela."

"Good to be back." Angela looked at Goldie. "Go while you can, honey. And don't look back."

Goldie grabbed Spike and did as her mother told her. For once.

She pulled up to the house and sat in the car, an anxious Spike right beside her, watching as the man and the two little boys laughed and talked inside the kitchen. Across the big, open room, the Christmas tree sparkled with hundreds of tiny blinking lights. The wreath on the French door glistened from the tall security light out in the backyard and up over the trees, a bright star shined as a beacon to the world.

A beacon to all of those who had lost hope.

"You know something, Spike? I've come full circle."

The little dog hopped from his spot on the old blanket into her lap, waiting for her to finish. "This all started when I saw my boyfriend holding a little puppy—and another woman. That scene, as awful as it was, brought me to this scene, and you." She stroked the little dog then hugged him close. "I like this scene better."

Goldie got out, determined to get this relationship organized. Spike barked his excitement and three dark-haired heads came up. Then she heard footsteps and watched as the boys rushed to open the door.

"Spike!" Tyler ran out, reaching up to the little dog. "You came back."

Goldie giggled and handed Spike over to Tyler. "Of course he came back. I promised, didn't I?"

Sam stood to the side. "That woman told us you'd left."

Goldie glanced from Sam's hopeful face to Rory's surprised one. "Well, that woman didn't have the Christmas spirit and so she didn't take the time to explain things. I didn't go back to Baton Rouge for good. I just went to pick up my mother at the airport. She came home for Christmas."

Rory's eyes met hers, a faint smile replacing his frown. "That's good, isn't it?"

"It is good," Goldie said. "And I'm sorry y'all thought I'd left you. I'd never leave without saying goodbye and giving you Spike."

Sam nudged her. "What about…?"

"Right here." Goldie patted her big bag. "May we come in?"

"Sure," Rory agreed, grinning now. "You're just in time. We visited my mom and then we ordered pizza."

"How is she?"

"She's doing pretty good. Glad to be home. My aunt came up from New Orleans to spend the night with her and we'll all be there tomorrow. I'm going to cook."

"Wow. That sounds like fun."

He shut the door then glanced to where the boys were playing with Spike. "Goldie, I—"

Sam came running up. "I told him, Miss Goldie. About the locket."

"Yes, he did," Rory said. "And we're both sorry for what we put you through."

Goldie smiled down at Sam then pulled out her necklace from under her blouse. "It's over now and I have my locket back. And I think Grams was right. It did bring me good, but it's not so much about the jewelry. It's about finding the good in my own life—God's blessings and His plan for me."

Rory's gaze washed over her, understanding coloring his eyes in a rich gold that rivaled the lights on the tree. "Can you stay awhile?"

"I sure can." She leaned down to Sam. "After supper, we'll give your dad his gift, okay?"

Sam nodded. "I'll get out the paper plates."

They ate and laughed and chatted. Goldie told them all about her mother and how Grams had texted her.

"She called in reinforcements?" Rory asked.

"I guess so. I can't believe Grams knew how to text anyone and that my mother came all that way for me."

"I can," he replied. "We need to talk."

"Not before presents," Tyler declared. "You promised we could open one tonight, remember?"

"I do."

"It's okay," Goldie said. "I can stay awhile."

They went over by the tree and Tyler opened a remote-control car. He went off to try it out in the hallway. Sam opened his—an LSU jacket. Then he looked at Goldie. "Now?"

"Now," she repeated, reaching into her bag. She handed the two boxes to Sam. "The green one's your grandmother's. And the red one is your dad's."

Sam put the green one under the tree then sheepishly handed the other one to Rory. "For you, from me."

"Thanks, Sam." Rory quickly opened the box then lifted out the scrapbook inside. Goldie watched, holding her breath. Sam came to sit by her, reaching out for her hand.

The look on Rory's face as he studied the pages made her fall in love with him all over again. His eyes went dark and then turned bright and moist. He moved his fingers over the photographs of his family, his eyes scanning the words written there in Sam's broad handwriting.

"I remembered some of it and Miss Goldie helped me with the other stuff."

Rory looked up, his fingers moving over a wedding picture, a baby picture of each boy, a T-ball game, Sam at bat, a beach vacation and a family Christmas picture taken at church. After seeing several more pictures, he swallowed and tried to speak, then swallowed again. "This is the best gift I've ever been given, Sam. This means the world to me and so do you and your brother. Thank you."

Sam beamed with pride. "We made MeeMaw one, too. With pictures of Grandpa and Mom and you and Aunt Becky and the girls and us. And we have a picture to put on Mom's grave."

"I know MeeMaw will love hers, and so will your mom." Rory reached out, his arms opening for Sam. "I love you, son."

Sam rushed into his daddy's arms while Goldie discreetly wiped at her eyes. While she watched them, she held her locket and thanked God for leading her to this family.

* * *

An hour later, Rory came up the hallway from tucking in the boys and Spike and found his kitchen clean and his living room tidy.

"You've been busy."

"Sorry. Habit."

"It's a nice habit." He stared at her, sitting there on the couch where he'd found her. She was so still. Goldie rarely sat still. "So…"

"So," she said. "Here we are."

"You came back."

"I did."

"But you're leaving again, right?"

"That depends." She leaned forward, her gaze holding Rory's. "We could take things slow, see where it goes, okay? That is, if you're still interested in that kind of arrangement."

He grinned at her nervousness and her formality. "I think I can live with that. I'm not in a big rush."

"Me, either."

Rory fell down on the couch. "Who am I kidding? I'm in a really big rush." Then he kissed her, showing her the urgency of that rush.

"Wow," she said when he let her go.

"Is that a good wow?"

"Yes, very good. Taking things slow is highly overrated anyway. And you kissed me again."

He reached for her hand. "Yes and I know what kissing you did to me the first time. It threw me. But in a good way."

"Glad we clarified that." She pulled away, her hand touching her necklace. "It sure threw me, too."

Rory took one of her hands back in his. "I'm sorry about how I treated you the other night."

"I'm sorry I couldn't tell you the truth about my locket."

He kissed her again. "You promised Sam. And you were right. He and I had a good long talk and things are better, so much better. So there. All is forgiven."

Her smile became radiant. "Yes, all is forgiven."

"I still owe you a real date."

"I'll hold you to that."

He gave her a quick peck on the cheek. "So, will you bring your mother and grandmother to Christmas dinner?"

"Are you sure? Won't that be a lot on your mother?"

"She wants you both there and I won't let her get too tired. Besides, she said you're practically family now."

"She did? When did she say that?"

"Today, when I told her I loved you and somehow, I was going to make you mine."

"You told her that?"

"I did. I do—love you." Then he jumped up. "I forgot. I have your present."

Her green eyes sparkled right along with the tree lights. She carefully opened the tiny box then lifted the lid. "Oh, Rory."

"It's a locket," he said, grinning. "To replace the one I'd thought you'd lost."

Goldie rubbed her fingers over the round gold medallion then opened it. "It's beautiful. I'll have to get a picture to put in here."

"But you found *your* locket."

She pulled him down beside her and hugged him tight.

"Yes, I certainly did." She kissed him then put her hand on her heart. "And I think it's right here. I guess I just had to find a way to open it."

Rory pulled her hand up to his lips, kissing her fingers. "So, I know the way to Baton Rouge."

"That's good. And I know the way home."

Rory's heart opened and filled with hope. He stared down at the little picture book on the table, knowing he'd make new memories with Goldie. "I love you, but I think I already told you that."

"I love you, too."

"You owe me a new couch pillow."

"It's in the car. Grams helped me make it." She got up. "I'll go and get it."

But Rory pulled her back. "Oh, no. You might fall into a hole and I'd have to come dig you out."

"Good point. But you'll like the pillow. It says 'Home, sweet home' on one side and 'Go, LSU' on the other."

He tugged her to the fire so they could hug each other close while they looked at the Christmas tree.

"Don't leave me, Goldilocks."

"I won't," she promised. "I went about it all the wrong way, but at last I've found the right man."

He laughed then kissed the top of her head. "Think you can handle me and the boys?"

"I think so." She leaned up, her gaze holding his. "In fact, I think this family is just right for me. A perfect fit."

"Merry Christmas," Rory said.

"Merry Christmas yourself."

They stood there for a long time, holding each other as they looked beyond the tree, out the window and up into the night sky, their hopes pinned on the star guiding them toward the perfect gift of God's grace and love.

Finally, Rory whispered, "Hey, you know anything about putting a bike together?"

Goldie grinned. "No, but I'm willing to learn. And I can organize all the parts for you."

"Let's get started, then," Rory replied, his hand in hers.

And from the smile on her face, he knew Goldie was finally ready to do just that.

* * * * *

ONCE UPON A CHRISTMAS

Pamela Tracy

To my vintage shopping buddies
and fellow English teachers:
Marianne Botos, Lyn McClelland and Stacey Rannik.
You guys keep me stylish and sane. Thanks so much!

For the Lord searches every heart
and understands every motive behind the thoughts.
—*1 Chronicles* 28:9

Chapter One

"I didn't hit her." Small arms folded across his chest, bottom lip at a salute, five-year-old Caleb McCreedy looked ready for battle.

Only three months into his kindergarten year and he'd managed what his two older brothers hadn't.

A trip to the principal's office.

"My lunch box hit her," Caleb finished. He made a face and paused as if in deep thought.

John Deere baseball cap in hand, Jared McCreedy shifted uncomfortably on one of the hard brown chairs in the too small office and frowned. His youngest son was no stranger to battle. He had the example of two older brothers. They, however, knew better than to bring it to school.

Mrs. Ann Tyson, principal of Roanoke Elementary for all of three months, turned to Jared as if expecting him to do something besides sit and listen as the story unfolded. Although his memories of being in trouble a time or two should have helped him speak up, they hadn't.

All he could do was frown.

"On purpose!" This outburst came from Cassidy Tate, a loud, little girl with wild brown curls.

The principal cleared her throat, not because she needed to, Jared could tell, but to let Cassidy know she'd been out of line. Then Mrs. Tyson glanced at the referral in her hand.

Jared took the time to study Cassidy. He'd heard about her many, many times from his middle son who sat behind her in a second-grade classroom.

Cassidy tore my paper.

Cassidy pulled the head off my LEGO and now I can't find it. Never mind that Matt wasn't allowed to take LEGOs to school.

Cassidy keeps following me.

"I like her," Caleb informed the family every time Matt shared a "Cassidy" story. With Caleb, it was a love/hate relationship. Caleb loved her when he wasn't throwing lunch boxes at her, and Matt, although he wasn't allowed to hate, avoided her at all costs.

Cassidy's mother, Maggie Tate, sat on the brown chair right next to Jared, but she didn't look uncomfortable. At one time or another she must have spent time in a principal's office, too, because she seemed to know exactly what to do, how to sit and what questions to ask. She looked in control, something he wanted very much to feel at the moment.

Since his wife's death, Jared had tried for control but realized that his idea of being in control didn't mesh with the chaos of his three sons, each with varying needs and each missing their mother.

He wished Mandy were here.

When the principal finally set down the referral, Maggie was ready. "Are you sure it was on purpose?" She didn't raise her voice, change her expression, or so much as clench a fist.

"I'm sure." Cassidy glared at Caleb who was trying hard not to wriggle in a couch designed for much bigger people.

That couch hadn't been here the first time Jared had visited this office. He'd been five years old and had taken something that hadn't belonged to him. He no longer remembered what.

The next time he'd stood before the same principal's door, it was because the principal, Billy Staples, wanted permission to take something from Jared.

Jared remembered what. As oldest son, albeit in junior high, he'd willingly given his permission for his mother and Billy to marry.

Mrs. Tyson leaned forward, and Jared could see her fighting back a smile even as she said, "He did throw the lunch box up in the air on purpose. Three times. Along with five other little boys. The lunch aide asked them to stop. Two did. The aide was on her way over to intervene, yet again, when Caleb's lunch box hit Cassidy in the face."

"I wasn't aiming for her face," Caleb insisted, his voice breaking. "We were trying to see if—since our lunch boxes had peanut butter on them—they would stick to the roof if we threw them hard enough."

"Ceiling," Cassidy corrected.

Beside him, Maggie made a low-pitched, strangled

sound. If Jared hadn't been sitting so close to her, he wouldn't have noticed. She was a master at keeping calm.

"But the fact that you might hit someone is exactly why the aide asked you to stop," the principal said patiently.

"And you didn't listen," Jared added, finally getting his voice.

"But—"

"No buts."

"If you'd packed me leftover turkey from Thanksgiving, like I wanted," Caleb accused, "this wouldn't have happened. Turkey doesn't stick."

"Caleb!"

Caleb had the good sense to stop talking.

Cassidy looked from Caleb to Jared before saying, "See, Mama, I told you it wasn't me."

Now that Jared looked again, the woman in question didn't look old enough to be so in control of the situation, let alone a mama, or a business owner. Yet, she was all three. This past summer, Joel, Jared's younger brother, had done some work on her vintage clothing shop. Because Joel's fiancée wanted a vintage wedding, Joel had spent a lot of time talking about vintage clothes and about the shopkeeper. His description hadn't done Maggie Tate justice.

Her deep brown hair fell in a blunt cut that was shorter than he liked and barely reached her shoulders. When she'd walked into the principal's office, five minutes late and looking non-repentant, he'd noted the short gray-and-red dress that gave him a chance to admire a nice pair of legs encased in some sort of black tights. Black clunky shoes with ridiculous heels finished the outfit.

City girl.

She'd probably been chatting up a customer in her store when she'd gotten the call from the school. He'd been in the field wrapping up corn harvest.

She smelled of some sort of jasmine perfume; he smelled of sweat.

"...not the first time for either of them," Mrs. Tyson was saying.

"What?" Jared straightened up. He'd missed the first half of the sentence.

Again came the half smile and Jared knew the principal was enjoying this. Maybe because Jared's stepfather had been principal of Roanoke Elementary for thirty years and some parents still went to him first, only to be redirected back to Mrs. Tyson. Maybe because Mrs. Tyson had heard about the McCreedy boys, and their escapades, even though more than a decade had passed since they'd been students here. Maybe because Mrs. Tyson knew the color in Jared's cheeks wasn't because Caleb was in trouble but because it had been far too long since he had admired a pair of legs.

"I was talking about throwing lunch boxes. This is not the first time for either of them."

Maggie looked at Cassidy. "Were you throwing lunch boxes, too?"

"Not today."

"But some other day?" Maggie insisted. "Did you hit Caleb with a lunch box some other day?"

Cassidy's lips went together. The answer was in her expression. Yes.

The principal's brows went together. Clearly, this was the first she'd heard of it.

"Why did you tattle," Maggie asked, "if you've done the same thing to him?"

Caleb and Cassidy exchanged a look, no longer adversaries, now conspirators.

"She didn't tattle," Mrs. Tyson said. "The aide did and the aide had plenty to say. Seems that while Caleb was removed from the lunchroom and escorted to his teacher, Cassidy hid his lunch box and doesn't seem to remember where."

Jared closed his eyes. Caleb's teacher was soon to be Jared's sister-in-law.

"We'll take care of this at home," he said firmly as he stood, giving Caleb a look that said *we're going.* "I promise you that."

"We'll find the lunch box," Maggie quickly offered. "Or—" she shot Cassidy a glance that could only mean trouble "—we'll buy him a new one from *your* allowance."

Cassidy's mouth opened to an exaggerated *O.* That quickly, Caleb was back to adversary.

"If he threw the lunch box at her, she's not buying him a new one," Jared argued.

"People." One word, that's all it took when it was an elementary school principal.

Ten minutes later, Jared stood outside the principal's office door tightly holding Caleb's hand. Maggie and her daughter were still inside.

"This is my baddest day." Caleb didn't even try to fight the tears. Of Jared's three boys, he was the one who cried freely, whined often and ran full tilt from the time he got out of bed until he fell back into it. He argued the most, too. But, Caleb was also the one who still climbed on Jared's lap, laughed until tears came to his eyes and who knew the name of each and every animal on the farm.

If they didn't have a name, Caleb gave them one.

"I doubt that," Jared said calmly. "We'll talk later. Now, don't start whining."

"I can't help it. I really want my lunch box. It's my favorite."

Jared pictured the lunch boxes sitting on the kitchen counter. Grandpa Billy packed them every morning. Ryan's was a plain blue. Nine-year-olds no longer needed action figures or at least his didn't. Matt's was Star Wars. Caleb's was Spider-Man.

"We should go buy a new one," Caleb suggested. "There's a really cool one—"

"No, we should go to the cafeteria and see if the lunch ladies found it."

Caleb followed, feet dragging. "I don't want to go there."

Of course he didn't. The principal had just assigned him a full week of wiping down tables instead of going to recess. Jared intended to do the same at home along with no television for a week.

The cafeteria hadn't changed all that much since Jared's years. There were still rows of tables with benches that could be levered up to make mopping easier. Large gray trash baskets were in the four corners. Right now, decorations of snowflakes and wrapped presents were taped to the walls. Snowmen and Santas shared messages of "Don't Forget our Winter Program."

No way could Jared forget. He'd recently been put in charge of props. In just a few weeks, Caleb would be dressed like an elf and singing with his class. Ryan actually had the part of Santa. Matt would pretend to have a stomachache the night of the program. According to the note sent by Matt's teacher, he had the role of delivering presents to people in the audience.

Smart teacher.

"You start in here," Jared ordered. "I'll go in the kitchen."

A few minutes later, Maggie Tate joined them in the search. She poked her head in the kitchen door. "I'm so sorry. She'll be wiping down lunch tables with him."

Jared almost bumped his head as he looked up from the cabinet he'd been going through. "That's okay."

She nodded and then went into the cafeteria, presumably to search.

Jared was on his fifth cabinet when he heard the giggles.

He followed the noise to the cafeteria and stopped. In the middle of the lunchroom tables stood Maggie and the two children, all of them looking at the ceiling. In her hand, she held Caleb's lunch box. Jared could see the peanut butter smeared all over it.

Finally, Maggie hunched down and shook her head. "Caleb, it would take a lot more peanut butter to make it stick."

"I wondered about that," Caleb admitted.

"I can go find some peanut butter," Cassidy offered.

Maggie simply shook her head again, smiled at Jared and sashayed past him into the kitchen where she washed the offending lunch box before handing it to Jared.

For a brief moment he'd been worried she'd gone looking for peanut butter.

Maggie helped Cassidy into her coat and out the front door of Roanoke Elementary. Together they walked the mere block to Maggie's shop Hand Me Ups.

Well, Maggie walked; Cassidy did more of a sideways hop with a scoot and jiggle follow-up.

"I don't think it's fair that I got in so much trouble," Cassidy said after a moment. "I didn't throw my lunch box at him, and we found the lunch box right where I hid it. And I only hid it so he wouldn't throw it at me again."

"But you didn't tell people where you hid the lunch box when they asked. That was wrong."

Cassidy contemplated, for all of thirty seconds. "But, if I gave it back, he might have thrown it at me again."

"Once adults were involved, that wasn't likely. You were wasting our time. I might have missed a customer at the shop. And I'm sure Caleb's dad had work to do. Plus, even you admitted he didn't exactly 'throw' it at you."

"Oh, yeah."

"And, what if the lunch box was gone when we went back to get it?" Maggie asked.

"He could have one of mine."

Cassidy had two, both pink and both secondhand, one with Dora on it and the other with Cinderella. Cassidy's greatest wish was to get rid of both of them in order to buy a new one with a pony on it. Maggie doubted Caleb would be inclined to accept either.

"No, if the lunch box disappeared, we'd be getting him a new one, with your piggy bank money."

"But I have to use that money to buy presents!" Cassidy's scoot and jiggle stopped for all of a moment. Then, she was on to a new subject: one where her piggy bank wasn't in danger and there were other problems to solve. "Am I pretty?"

"Getting prettier every day."

"Today, Lisa Totwell said that she was the prettiest girl in class and that I was second."

"Well," Maggie said carefully, "do you want to be the prettiest, or is it okay if Lisa is?"

"It's okay if she is. She's my best friend, you know. Cuz we're both the new students in second grade this year. Everyone else has been here forever."

Yesterday, Brittney Callahan had been Cassidy's best friend. Before that, it was Sarah, a girl Maggie had yet to put a last name or a face to.

Didn't matter. Maggie was thrilled at how quickly Cassidy was fitting in—maybe fitting in a little too well. Coming to Roanoke, Iowa, was the right choice. For both of them.

"Cassidy, you know that Caleb is only in kindergarten, right?"

"Yep."

"Maybe you need to play with the kids in your own class."

Cassidy stopped so quickly, she nearly stumbled to the ground. "No way, Mom. Caleb is my friend, and he's fun. Plus, he's Matt's brother."

Matt McCreedy was the subject of many a conversation. He was the only one in Cassidy's second grade who hadn't been given best-friend status, and Maggie suspected Cassidy might be going through her first crush.

Now that Maggie had met Matt's dad, she figured he and Matt were cut from the same cloth—rugged, sturdy denim. Caleb seemed to be cut from a different sort of cloth.

Which meant that Mr. Jared McCreedy didn't understand his youngest son's creative personality.

"We'll talk about it later." Maggie didn't want to dwell on the plight of the misunderstood child.

She'd been one—an army brat with an errant mother and a father who was used to giving orders and having them followed with a "Yes, sir. Right away, sir." Her dad was a man who tried hard, but one who definitely didn't understand girls.

"Mom, you've got that look on your face again," Cassidy complained. "Did I do something?"

"Yes, you did something. You got sent to the principal's office for the second time, and I had to leave work to come deal with it. After taking most of last week off, I really needed to spend time in the shop."

Cassidy suddenly was very involved in staring at a crack in the sidewalk.

Maggie wasn't deterred. "School's only been in session three months. Next week is December and if you don't…" Her words tapered off as a black truck drove by. Actually, she was glad for the interruption. She'd been about to bring up consequences, such as not attending Christmas activity at the church this Friday night or even the school's winter play and the possibility of Cassidy not appearing in it.

Don't threaten unless you mean it.

"Look, Mom!"

Jared McCreedy sat tall and oh-so-serious-looking behind the wheel of the Ford diesel truck. His three sons, the oldest in the front, two more in the back, all looked at Maggie and Cassidy. Caleb waved. Except for Matt, none of the boys appeared as serious as their father.

Cassidy frowned. "They have a dog. His name is Captain Rex."

Something Cassidy asked for quite often, usually after figuring out that there was no way her mother would even listen when asked for a horse or a baby brother.

"Yes, they have a dog."

Cassidy's letter to Santa—not mailed because it wasn't finished—had a dog in it, second on the list, right after a pair of red boots. Cassidy wouldn't be getting a dog. The McCreedys had something Maggie and Cassidy did not: *a house and yard.* Maggie thought of two more things the McCreedys had: *horses and baby brothers.*

And family. They had plenty of family. They hadn't had to fly to New York to celebrate Thanksgiving with her disapproving mother-in-law—the only relative who cared even to invite them.

The McCreedys, Maggie knew, had roots that ran deep in Roanoke, Iowa. She hadn't seen Solitaire Farm, their place, but she'd heard about it and could picture what it looked like.

Big white house with a huge porch, complete with a swing and a rocker or two. Long driveway, winding its way to the front door, cars parked, meaning a large family. A barn. Lots of green, green grass to run across and trees to climb. Room to breathe. Plenty of animals, especially horses and, of course, acres of corn and soybeans.

Except for the corn, soybeans and animals bigger than a dog, what Maggie imagined was pretty much a portrait of one of her goals: a real home for Cassidy.

Too bad this farm was owned by a man who reminded her of her late husband, Dan, thinking of his duty above all else. Because, if Jared McCreedy had been a different kind of man—softer, more jubilant and easygoing—maybe Maggie would have engaged in a little flirting.

What would it have hurt?

It had been a year.

Not a chance. Jared even looked like Maggie's late husband: tall, thick dark brown hair, and almost black piercing eyes. Both men were capable of walking into a room and suddenly making the room seem small. There were a few differences. Dan wore fatigues while Jared wore jeans and a flannel shirt. Dan had to wear his hair at a precision cut while Jared's was long enough to cover his ears. Dan was always clean-shaven. Jared had a five-o'clock shadow that made Maggie think about how good whiskers felt during a kiss.

Whoa.

Been there, done that, not a chance Maggie wanted to deal with a man so intent on being in control that he didn't know how to have fun.

Or appreciate the concept of getting a lunch box to stick to the ceiling with the help of a little peanut butter. Maggie smiled when she pictured the abject horror on Jared's face when he spotted the sticky lunch box. No, Jared McCreedy was not her ideal man. No sense of thinking about him at all.

Chapter Two

It had been a tough week thanks to Monday's phone call from the principal. And now once again, thanks to a Friday phone call from Caleb's teacher, Jared was standing in the hallway of Roanoke Elementary.

He checked his watch. He had at least a dozen things to do today, starting with figuring out—since he was here—what props were needed for the school's Christmas program. The father who had been in charge was now working extra hours and Beth, the woman he was about to see, had asked Joel, her fiancé and Jared's brother, to help.

Joel had a rodeo, so right now, Jared was it.

But that had nothing to do with his visit today. No, Beth had something to say about Caleb, his youngest, who was responsible for Jared standing in the school's hallway at four in the afternoon on a working day.

Through a window in the door, he could see Beth sitting at a small table. Someone else's mom had her back to the door. So, maybe Caleb wasn't the only one in trouble. Both women seemed overly fascinated by some paperwork spread out on the small table.

He didn't intend to let any more time pass doing nothing. He needed to gather his boys, find the teacher in charge of the program, talk shop and head home. There was still an hour or two of Iowa daylight, and he had things to do and was already behind. He opened the classroom door and stepped in.

"Jared." Beth Armstrong—Miss Armstrong to his son, Beth to him—twisted in her seat, looking surprised.

Funny, she'd called his cell phone and left a message requesting this meeting.

Then she glanced at the large clock just over her desk. "Is it that time already?"

"That time and then some," Jared said, finally figuring out who was sitting with Beth. Hmm, she didn't have a child in Beth's class. Had something else happened between Caleb and Cassidy?

His future sister-in-law didn't even blink, just nonchalantly walked over to where Jared stood. "Sorry, I was looking at pictures of wedding dresses and time got away from me. You know Maggie, right?"

"Away from us," Maggie Tate agreed as she closed magazines and reached for some loose pictures, "and, yes, we've met."

When Jared didn't respond, didn't say that keeping him waiting was okay, Beth grinned. She was getting entirely too good at teasing him. He could blame the fact that she was about to become his sister-in-law, but truth was, he'd known her most of his life. This time, she simply told him something he already knew. "Patience is a virtue."

"Whoever coined that phrase wasn't a single father of three with a farm to run," Jared retorted.

"And I didn't realize that you were standing outside waiting for Beth." Maggie finished loading the papers into a canvas bag and made her way to the door. Jared couldn't help but think her small frame looked right at home in the five-year-old wonderland of kindergarten.

His mouth went dry, and the annoyance he felt at being kept waiting almost vanished.

Almost.

Then, the young woman, her eyes twinkling, spoke again. "Patience is a virtue, have it if you can. Seldom found in a woman. Never in a man."

Beth clapped her hands, clearly pleased that someone else shared the same opinion.

All Jared could think was, *great, another female with a proverb.* The only sayings he knew by heart were the ones his father said, and they were more advice than quips. Jared's personal favorite: always plow around a stump.

He doubted the women would appreciate his contribution.

"Maggie's helping me find my wedding dress," Beth said.

"You're a wedding planner, too?" Jared asked, forcing his gaze from Maggie's deep green eyes. He had no time for a pretty face. And he was more than annoyed.

"Wedding planner?" Beth looked confused.

"I'm willing to add that to my list of occupations,"

Maggie said. "But, at the moment, no. I'm just a shop owner and seamstress trying to keep a customer happy."

Her shop, Jared knew, was all about vintage clothing, which explained the red velvet skirt. Who wore red velvet? Maybe Santa. Jared suppressed the smile that threatened to emerge. This woman was as alien to his world as, well, as an alien. Her skirt, tight at the knees, reminded him of one Marilyn Monroe had worn in an old movie he'd watched. She'd topped it with a simple white shirt and wide black belt. It was colder today than it had been on Monday. Maybe that's why she had on a tiny, red sweater.

She'd freeze going out to the car.

Square-toed boots completed the outfit and kept Jared from admiring her legs the way he'd just admired her figure.

Good.

Frilly city girls made no sense to him.

Plus, she looked like she was ready to assist Santa or something.

"When I finished talking with my daughter's teacher," Maggie explained, "I checked to see if Beth happened to be alone. I'd brought some samples for her to look at." Her voice was louder than Beth's, stronger, and with an accent he couldn't quite place, but definitely not Midwestern.

"I need to fetch Cassidy before she thinks I've forgotten her." Maggie carefully slid by Jared, grabbed a coat from on top of a student's desk and hurried toward the exit. "I'll get going and let you have your time."

"See if you can find me something like the first one we looked at," Beth called.

Jared didn't say anything, just held open the door so Maggie could exit gracefully.

"I really am sorry," Beth said. "Time got away from me. And I do need to talk with you."

Jared folded himself into the small orange chair Maggie'd just vacated. A fragrance that didn't belong to five-year-olds or their teacher lingered—that jasmine smell again. He waited while Beth went to her desk and rummaged through a stack of papers.

Jared did his best not to hurry her. Unfortunately, the seconds ticked on and Jared started imagining all the suggestions she had for him. She probably wanted him to work with Caleb more. Jared got that, and would love suggestions, especially when it came to time management and incentives.

He stared at a bulletin board with a group of Christmas trees, stickers acting as ornaments, all bearing the names of Caleb's classmates.

Caleb's ornament read *C-A-B*. The *B* looked ready to fall down. Jared's youngest son hadn't bothered with the *L* or the *E*.

"Caleb behaving? I've asked him every day since Monday. He claims his light's been green."

Jared understood the traffic light system. Green meant Go, everything good. Yellow meant Pause, we need to think about this day and perhaps discuss how it could have been a bit better. Red meant no television, or no video games, or no LEGO bricks, depending on which kid decided not to obey the rules.

Beth didn't answer, but finally found whatever she was looking for and came to sit down with Jared. She laid a few papers in front of him. "Caleb is trying very hard to behave but he complains a lot about his stomach hurting. He asks to go to the bathroom often."

"He does that at home, too," Jared admitted.

"Behavior is not why I called."

She took a breath, and suddenly Jared got worried.

"It's still very early," Beth said softly, "and maybe if I hadn't been around since Caleb was born, I'd wait. But, the music and PE teacher have both come to me with concerns, also. Jared, it's not that he's misbehaving, but he's having trouble focusing, not just your typical trouble, either. Caleb can't wait his turn, he bursts out with answers and he's unable to sit long enough to complete a single paper."

For a moment, Jared had trouble wrapping his mind around what Beth was saying. Yes, of his three boys, Caleb was the most energetic. Okay, downright wild at times. Jared saw that and somewhat blamed himself. After his wife, Mandy, had died four years ago, Jared had buried himself in the farm. For the first year, he'd walked around in a black fog. The three years that followed were a transitional period. He should have been paying more attention to Caleb.

But Caleb was still very young, only five.

"I think you need to schedule an appointment with your family doctor, see what he thinks. Honestly, Jared," Beth continued, "I'm hoping it's just immaturity, but if it's not, I want to get help now so that first grade and beyond are easier. We might need to think about having some testing done and maybe seeing a developmental specialist."

"Developmental specialist?" Jared's tongue felt twice its normal size. Judging by his inability to say more than one or two words, he felt more like an observer to this conference than a participant. He shook his head and wished—like he wished almost every day—that Mandy were here instead of him, making these decisions when it came to this part of parenthood. Mandy always seemed to know what to do.

"Jared?" Beth said.

He looked at her, desperately trying to think of a response. "I think Caleb is fine," he finally said. "He can count to a hundred. He's been able to add and subtract single digits since he was three. You've trained my brother well. He's been helping all the boys with math while they work at Solitaire's Market."

"I know, Jared," she said softly. "Caleb likes numbers."

He scooted back the chair and stood. "Do you have anything else you need to tell me?"

She looked at him, and he saw in her eyes so many shared memories. She'd been his late wife's best friend and truly loved his sons.

"Caleb's a charmer, but you already knew that."

Jared nodded, wanting more than anything to get out of this room where everything was in miniature and the dominant smell was no longer jasmine but crayons, glue and children. He needed to get home, back in the field, where he could wrestle his oversize tractor and surround himself with the land, McCreedy land, and the rich smell of dirt that would not forsake.

Beth stood and held out yet another piece of paper, this time not one with Caleb's scribbles. "It's the developmental specialist the school recommends, just in case."

"I didn't even know the town was big enough to have a developmental specialist."

"It's not big enough," Beth said. "You'll have to go to Des Moines."

"That's over an hour."

And still Beth held out the paper. He took it because he'd neither the time nor the inclination to argue. He went into Des Moines maybe once every two or three months. "I'll think about it," he finally said.

"You know," Beth said thoughtfully, "you might want to talk to Maggie. She's a friend and she's told me to give her name to any parent needing help. Her daughter Cassidy's just two years older than Caleb and has problems with focus, too. She's already walking the path you're about to travel."

"I work best alone," Jared said.

As he closed the door behind him, he heard her utter one word.

"Liar."

Maggie pushed her chair away from the kitchen table and rested her elbows on the windowsill. She could feel the cold coming through the pane but she didn't care, at least not enough to move. Tiny slivers of aged gold paint flecked onto the sleeves of her pink sweater. She did care a bit about the moisture gathering in the center of the pane. It meant she needed to replace the window.

One more thing on her list.

Just a month ago, Roanoke, Iowa, boasted a distant sea of green, orange, red and yellow leaves that Maggie could see from her second-story window. The sight of so many trees, some stretching over residential streets, never failed to take her breath away.

Because the view belonged to her.

Today, the trees stretched their empty, dark limbs like waiting fingers saying, *Where's the snow? We're waiting.*

It was *her* town. Just like the trees, she intended to put down roots, grow, thrive, make a home, never leave.

Please let this be a forever kind of place.

Even now, in the predawn light, her town was waking up and starting its day. Just like she was doing.

Across the wide street was a drugstore. It had the old-timey chairs but the only thing the owner served up was Thrifty ice cream. Maggie dreamed of a soda fountain. Next to it was a hardware store that Maggie avoided because the only things she liked to fix simply needed a needle and thread. Then there was an antiques store she couldn't resist. The owner, one Henry Throxmorton, was unlocking the front door. He had a newspaper under his arm. She'd never seen him smile, but she knew his wife was sick a lot. Maybe that was why.

Just two days ago, Maggie had found in Roanoke's Rummage—an awful name for an antiques store if you asked Maggie—the pair of red cowboy boots she'd been looking for. Looking unloved and extremely dusty, they'd been on the bottom shelf of a bookcase. There was no rhyme or reason to how Henry arranged his store. But, had they been on display, maybe some other enterprising mother would have found them.

All it took to make them look almost new was a thorough cleaning with saddle soap and then applying a cream-based polish of the same color. They were already wrapped and under the Christmas tree.

On the same side was also a small real estate office. Maggie sometimes dawdled by the front where there were pictures of homes for sale. The ones with big lawns attracted her the most, but she didn't really do yard work. The ones with no backyards didn't appeal at all.

Looking at the photos also exposed a curiosity Maggie had finally acted on. Her mother had been born in Roanoke in 1967. Could one of the houses have been her childhood home? Maggie didn't have a clue. All she remembered of her mother was a woman who smoked cigarettes and cooked a lot of noodle soup.

Maggie hated noodle soup.

Life had handed Maggie's mother an itinerary that she didn't intend to follow. It included the destinations marriage and motherhood. The only reason Maggie knew about Roanoke was her mother's birth certificate. Natalie had been seven pounds, six ounces, and twenty-one-inches long: a live birth, Caucasian. She'd been born to Mary Johnson. Either Mary had chosen not to put down a name for the father or she hadn't known who the father was.

So, some help that was. In Roanoke, Johnson was the second-most popular name, nestled between Smith and Miller.

Moving to Roanoke to find a connection to an errant mother was akin to looking for a needle in a haystack and made about as much sense. But Maggie had two choices. Stay in New York with Dan's mother or strike out on her own.

She didn't regret her choice and there was nothing

wrong with living above one's place of business. It was very convenient in fact. But Cassidy needed a backyard, a place to run, a swing set, the dog she kept asking for. No, not the horse. And Maggie wanted her own bedroom.

Maybe in a few years.

Maggie shook off the daydream. This morning was a school day and tonight was a holiday party at Beth's church. Cassidy had begged to go, had already planned what to wear. Maggie had too much to do to dawdle in front of the window any longer.

After brushing off the paint—she really needed to do something about sanding and repainting—she scooted back to her computer and started to push away some of Cassidy's school papers. Why they were on Maggie's desk, she didn't know. Cassidy's stuff seemed to have a mind of its own and liked to spread to every nook and cranny of their tiny apartment.

Cassidy's letter to Santa was under a page of math homework, and it looked like her list had grown to three. Underneath the word *puppy* was added *baby brother*.

Great, another item that couldn't be purchased at a discount store. Cassidy needed to start thinking of affordable alternatives or the red boots would be it.

If only the red boots could bark and be named Fido.

While Cassidy slumbered, Maggie—sitting next to the old wall heater and thinking about turning on the oven—updated the store's records on her computer. Under her breath, she reminded herself that any small business needed four years to establish. Right now, thanks to her alteration business, she made enough to pay the bills and a few, very few, extras. Oh, it caused some late and restless nights, but with the economy the way it was, Maggie was just glad she had a way to make a living. So what if she went to the library instead of the bookstore. So what if they ate hamburgers instead of steaks.

Maggie had enough money for the essentials.

The used red cowboy boots under the tree were proof of that. She'd priced new red boots. Not this Christmas. Good thing hugs were free.

Finally, at seven, Maggie turned off the computer and headed for the kitchen to make breakfast. Cassidy still slept and Maggie wouldn't wake her until the blueberry pancakes were ready, one large circle for a face, two small ovals for ears, then banana slices for eyes, a strawberry nose and raisin teeth.

It was a tradition that Maggie knew would end all too soon as her little girl grew up. Just when Maggie picked up a spoon, the doorbell rang.

Maggie quickly glanced at the calendar on the refrigerator. Two reminders were penciled in.

The only pickup Maggie had today was Rosalind Maynard. She'd wanted Maggie to find a 1930s denim chore jacket for her husband. They were getting their photo made for their seventieth wedding anniversary. Apparently, Rosalind's husband came from a long line of farmers. His parents had also had a seventieth photo taken way back when, and George Jr. wanted to look like his dad, even down to the jacket.

It was the second notation that made Maggie frown. Yesterday, Jared McCreedy had called. He wanted to talk. She'd agreed, and she'd said any morning was good, but she hadn't planned on this *soon*.

No, not possible. This morning was too soon for it to be Jared.

She hoped.

Quickly, Maggie hurried down the stairs and skidded, barefoot, across the cold, wooden floor. Maybe she could open the door, usher in Mrs. Maynard, grab the jacket, ring up the sale, usher out the customer, and still get her kid fed and to school on time.

Only it wasn't Mrs. Maynard.

Jared McCreedy stood on the threshold, three boys by his side and cap in hand. He didn't say a word when she threw open the door. He pretty much just stared.

His son Caleb wasn't so shy. "Wow, I think you like pink."

"Hush," Jared said.

Hiding a smile, Maggie stepped back and let the entire clan in.

"Pink is a good color," Maggie said to Caleb, "which is why I'm wearing it. I call this my Jane Fonda look." Granted, leg warmers were very seventies, but she did own a vintage store, so she could get away with it.

"I like red," Caleb admitted.

An older boy shook her hand, the only McCreedy she hadn't met personally, and then sat on a chair right by the entry and whipped out some sort of handheld gaming device.

"That's Ryan," Caleb announced. "He's in fourth grade."

Matt looked around suspiciously. "Where's Cassidy?"

"Upstairs asleep."

"It's time to go to school." Matt was completely aghast.

"I was just making her breakfast when you rang the doorbell. We're fast eaters and dressers."

Matt, way too mature for a second grader, clearly had more to say on the subject, but Jared jumped in. "We don't need to be keeping you. I saw your lights on, we were running early, and I don't know what I was thinking stopping by unannounced. I'm so sorry. I can stop back by once I've dropped the boys off at school if that's okay. I got up at five and thanks to the party tonight at church, I have a whole list of things to do. That's no excuse, though. I simply forget the rest of the world can sleep in."

It had been a week since she'd last seen Jared. He still managed to have that my-time-is-too-valuable-for-this look on his handsome face, but right now there was a hint of something else, maybe humbleness.

"I get up at five, too, Monday through Friday," Maggie responded. "It's when I do the books. That way my evening belongs to Cassidy."

Jared shook his head. His dark hair, combed to the side, didn't move. He opened his mouth, but instead of addressing Maggie, he looked past her and said sternly, "Caleb, those stairs do not belong to you."

Halfway up the stairs Caleb paused indecisively, but before the little boy could make a decision, a loud thump, the sound of something breaking and then a howl came from above.

"Cassidy," Maggie breathed.

The only McCreedy who beat her to the apartment's kitchen was Caleb.

Cassidy stood in the middle of the room crying. Pancake batter splattered her pajama bottoms, the floor, the counters, the refrigerator door and even the ceiling. The bowl was in pieces.

"Now that's a mess," Matt said from behind her.

Jared's snort could have been dismay, agreement, or it could have been him holding back laughter. Maggie couldn't see his face.

"Don't move," Maggie ordered. Quickly she stepped amid the batter and shards, lifted her howling child under her arms and carried Cassidy into the bathroom. Flipping shut the toilet lid with her foot, Maggie stood her daughter on top and asked, "Are you bleeding?"

Cassidy continued howling.

Maggie knew neither cajoling nor scolding would have any effect. So, in a matter-of-fact voice, she reasoned, "Matt, from your class, is here. Do you want him to tell your friends that you're a crybaby?"

Cassidy stopped.

"Now," Maggie went on, gently wiping the tears from Cassidy's face, "are you bleeding?"

"Yes."

"Where?"

Cassidy searched desperately for some blood.

After a moment, Maggie nudged in a patient but firm voice, "Where do you hurt?"

The fact that Cassidy had to stop and think proved what Maggie already knew. Cassidy wasn't bleeding and she wasn't hurt. She was scared and embarrassed. The best cure for that was not a bandage but a hug.

Hugs were free.

A minute later, Cassidy was in her room changing

into her school clothes and Maggie was in her kitchen trying not to stare as a tall cowboy, too tall for this tiny kitchen, cleaned up pancake batter.

Chapter Three

After eating a second breakfast, because Maggie offered and it seemed polite and, okay, Jared needed something to do with his hands, he ushered everyone down the stairs and out to his truck.

"Really," Maggie insisted. "Cassidy and I can walk to the school. We always do."

"We're already late," Matt protested.

"I want to walk," Caleb volunteered.

"Matt's right," Jared said. "We're already late. Plus, there's something I'd like to ask you. I don't know if I'll have another chance to get away."

Jared's sons quickly piled in the backseat. Matt and Ryan sat by the coveted windows, while Caleb was more than annoyed to be in the middle. Cassidy, looking way too pleased, climbed in the front, quite content to be in the middle. She snapped on her seat belt and looked at Jared as if he were Santa, the Tooth Fairy and the Easter Bunny all rolled into one. Jared knew the look well. It usually meant the kid using it was about to ask for something.

"Why don't you have a girl?" Cassidy asked, once he'd put on his own seat belt and started the truck.

The snort from the backseat might have been Ryan or might have been Matt. For the first time, Jared got what Grandpa Billy meant when he said *the apple didn't fall far from the tree.* It was all Jared could do not to snort, too. The only obvious non-snorter was Caleb because the five-year-old said, "Yeah, Dad, I want a sister. We can name her Molly."

"We don't need a—" Jared stopped, suddenly realizing that not just one but both females in the front seat were staring at him.

"We have a girl," Jared revised. "Her name is Beth, and she'll have to be in charge of giving you girl relatives."

"But—" Caleb started to say.

Jared held up one hand. "End of conversation."

"Dad has to be married in order for there to be a sister," Ryan told Caleb.

"And Dad doesn't like girls," Matt added.

Jared almost drove off the road. Where did Matt get that idea? As for Maggie, she was looking away from him and out the window. He could tell by the way her cheeks were sucked in and her lips were puckered, that she was doing all she could not to laugh.

"Why don't you like girls?" Cassidy asked.

"I do like girls," Jared assured her, "especially ones who eat blueberry pancakes and ones who show me exactly where to park."

Cassidy giggled and pointed to a visitor's spot right by the front walkway of Roanoke Elementary. "Am I a visitor?" Jared asked.

"Yes," Cassidy decided. "Because you're not a kid and you don't work here."

"Good enough," Jared agreed.

A moment later, both he and Maggie had signed their children in as tardy and watched as all of them, clutching late slips, scurried to their classrooms.

Well, Matt didn't scurry. He looked at Jared accusingly. The only thing worse than being late, to Matt's way of thinking, was being late alongside Cassidy Tate.

Jared had never stopped at Roanoke's only coffeehouse just to have coffee. What he was paying for two cups could buy a whole pound, not that he would have. He didn't like coffee. Plus, the concept of just sitting around, doing nothing, felt strange. He resisted the urge to fidget.

"You always come here after dropping Cassidy off at school?" He shifted in the brown hardback chair and stretched out his legs. They didn't fit under the tiny table.

Maggie took a sip of something that was more chocolate than coffee and nodded. "As often as I can. It's my one treat before I open the store for the day. Usually, though, I'm alone so I sit here and write in my journal. Or I read. Do you like to read?"

He hadn't been asked that question in almost fifteen years, not since high school. "I read the Bible."

"Oh."

She visibly recoiled, her withdrawal so tangible it made him stop thinking about where to put his feet and how much he'd paid for the stupid cups of coffee.

"When I have time," he added, hoping to get her to relax, "I read the newspaper."

"Online or paper?"

"A little bit of both."

Instead of looking at Maggie and trying to figure out why his reading the Bible could put such a look of vulnerability—or fear?—on her face, Jared took a drink of his coffee. Bitter stuff, downright nasty. Good thing the cup wasn't that big.

He decided to get right to the point. "Beth has pretty much insisted that I come talk to you."

"And here I thought you just stopped by because you knew I needed help with breakfast."

When she smiled, it about made him want to forget the real reason he had stopped by. But, only for a moment. "She thinks you can give me some ideas on how to help my son Caleb. He's having trouble at school."

Maggie was already nodding. "I told Beth she could send anyone my way. When Cassidy started having trouble in school, I felt so alone. My husband wasn't around and when he was, he didn't really understand. For months my only friends were the specialists and the books and articles I was reading practically every night on how to deal with Attention Deficit."

He looked at her empty ring finger and desperately tried to remember what Joel had said about why a Mr. Tate wasn't around.

"I'm not sure that anything is wrong with Caleb," Jared said finally. "I think I just need to be stricter and—"

He knew the moment he lost her. Her smile flattened. Her stare was suddenly focused on something other than his face. His late wife, Mandy, used to get the same look on her face, usually when he was saying something about why the living room wasn't picked up or why they were having hamburger for the third night in the row. It was only when Mandy got sick and couldn't do anything that he realized just how much she'd been doing.

And how clueless he'd been.

"Look," he backtracked, "Caleb is just five. He lost his mother when he was not yet two, and he pretty much lost me for almost a year. That he can focus at all is a miracle. I want to be a good dad. Beth says you have more parenting tips than Dr. Spock."

He was trying to be nonchalant, but he was out of his comfort zone. He was used to women who wore comfortable shirts tucked into jeans. She wore enough pink to be a flamingo. She didn't look old enough to be a parent, let alone one who gave advice when the going got tough.

"The most important thing I can tell you is don't be afraid to ask for help, take all the advice that is offered and also be willing to sacrifice to get it."

"Sacrifice?"

She nodded. "Time mostly."

Something Jared didn't have in abundance.

"You asked me for advice," Maggie reminded him. "Funny, but it all goes back to something we talked about the first time in Beth's classroom. Here's the truth. When dealing with Caleb, patience isn't a virtue, it's your only barrier between sanity and chaos."

Great, Jared thought, because if he remembered correctly, she had told him, upon that first meeting, that patience was *seldom* found in a woman and *never* in a man.

"I was really hoping," he said, "that you'd give me some concrete advice. You know, an earlier bedtime, maybe he needs to eat more fruit." Jared was grasping at straws and trying to remember everything he'd looked for on the internet.

She shook her head. He had an idea that whatever concrete advice she gave would be hard, harder than he could do.

"An earlier bedtime is always good. What kind of advice do you really want? I mean, is Caleb having trouble finishing homework? Sleeping? Does he worry a lot?"

Unfortunately, the only thing that didn't ring true was worry. Caleb didn't have a care in the world, especially when it came to homework.

"He gets stomachaches more than my other two and spends more time in the bathroom. Other than that, he's a normal kid." Thankfully the cell phone he'd never wanted and now couldn't live without saved him from having to say anything else. He wasn't prepared for her questions, and he knew her advice would be near impossible to follow.

"This is Jared," he answered. It only took a moment to hear about the latest catastrophe facing those in charge of the church party.

"Absolutely," Jared promised. "I'll head home now and get some more." Never before had he been glad to hear that he hadn't brought enough hay for a maze. By now, he should be an expert on mazes.

He couldn't help it. After he disconnected the call, he checked his watch again.

This meeting was over.

And Maggie Tate was looking at him as if he'd disappointed her.

For some reason, it bothered him.

"Mom, Mom, Mom." Cassidy rarely said *Mom* only once. She usually said it three or more times just because she could.

"I'm getting dressed."

"But I'm ready. Did you know that this outfit would look much better with red boots?" Cassidy didn't expect an answer. She just looked at the two presents under the tree: one really small, the other really big. Neither looked the size of cowboy boots.

Maggie was no dummy. She'd wrapped the cowboy boots in a box five times their size.

"For now, your regular shoes will have to do. And, Cassidy, if you keep interrupting me, we'll be late."

Cassidy had put on her good clothes the moment she had gotten home and had been chanting "I'm ready" for almost three hours.

Maggie applied a layer of red lipstick that matched the red of her Norma Jean wool-blend winter dress. The weatherman predicted snow, and although it hadn't arrived yet, cold temperatures had. Maggie wanted to be prepared for the worst and a fully lined frock would do the trick.

At least on the outside.

The inside, *her insides,* had a completely different need—one that pretty clothes couldn't mask. She'd not stepped foot in a church for a year, not since Dan died.

It's not a church service, Beth had insisted. *It's just*

a party. No Bible study and we'll be singing Christ-mas songs.

It wasn't Beth's invitation that was getting Maggie to church. It was Cassidy's, "But, Mom, all my friends will be there."

It's not a church service, Maggie told herself. *And even if it turns into one, I can just take a bathroom break.*

Maggie's biggest fear was letting God get close.

Because that would stir up a memory Maggie was trying desperately to bury, one that involved Dan and injustice.

"Cool," Cassidy approved when Maggie finally made it to the living room. "I'm ready."

"I feel cool," Maggie agreed. Only, really, she didn't. Ever since Jared had taken her out for coffee this morning, broached the subject of Caleb needing help—*of Jared needing help*—and then chauffeured her home, she'd felt a bit off.

As if she'd left something undone.

It was usually mothers who'd come to Maggie to ask quietly if meeting with a developmental specialist had made a difference. They'd often thrown out tidbits of how their own children were behaving as if hoping Maggie would say something like, "Oh, that's just typical kid behavior. I doubt you need to do all I'm doing."

But Maggie wasn't a specialist and wouldn't offer any advice as to what someone else's child needed. Early on, she had discovered that sometimes the mothers hoped she'd give them ideas on ways to "fix" their children.

Their children weren't broken. Cassidy wasn't broken. There was no fix. All Maggie could do is share what had worked and what hadn't worked for them.

Patience worked, but it took time. Losing her patience didn't work and took even more time.

"Mom, Mom, Mom."

"What?"

"Can I have some hot chocolate?"

"No, they're serving a meal at the party. I've already paid the five dollars, and I want you to eat real food."

"Hot chocolate is real."

"Real sugary," Maggie agreed.

"But—"

"Get your heavy coat, plus mittens. Then grab your backpack. I think there will be prizes and candy. Let's go."

She'd diverted Cassidy. Taken the child's mind off the hot chocolate and on to something else, something Cassidy wanted. End of problem.

It worked, this time.

Something else that worked for Cassidy was walking—well, Maggie walked, Cassidy skipped—to the church, waving at people who passed by.

As they turned onto Calver Street, Maggie could see the Main Street Church ahead. The parking lot was already fairly full. A few stragglers were exiting their cars. In the back, she could see the hay bale maze Jared and his crew had been working on. A campfire was already burning. Plus, she could also see a horse pulling a wagon full of kids.

Good thing the storm was holding off and the weather was cold but not freezing.

Near the wagon ride was Jared's big black truck,

tailgate down, and even though the festival was starting, a group of men were still unloading bales of hay.

All day long she'd been thinking about the man, how his presence had filled her kitchen, how wonderful all the noise had been, and—

"Caleb told me about this maze. His uncle, Joel, designed it. They started it yesterday, but something happened and they had to fix it. I think Matt's daddy didn't bring enough hay the first time. He had to go back for more."

Aah, that's why coffee and conversation was cut short.

They reached the parking lot and hurried toward the entrance.

The horse neighed, a distant sound that echoed in the early-evening chill and beckoned Cassidy. "Mom, Mom, Mom. That's what I want to do first!" She sped up, her hand automatically reaching back for her mother and dragging Maggie along.

That's when Jared McCreedy exited the front door of the church, Caleb's small hand in his. Caleb was dragging his feet, practically falling in an effort to halt his father's progress. A constant stream of "No, No, No" came from his mouth. Heading to the side of the building, away from the crowd of people, Jared bent down and starting talking.

Maggie couldn't hear the words, but she knew by Caleb's bowed head that somehow the little boy had gotten in trouble. And Jared McCreedy was doing what good fathers across the world do. He was shepherding. He was offering wisdom. He was trying to teach right from wrong.

As Maggie entered the church, she could imagine Caleb arguing with his dad. It didn't take any imagination at all to picture Jared. He wouldn't be open to an argument, especially coming from his youngest son.

"Welcome, we're glad you could join us!"

Maggie shelved her musings about Jared for a moment and smiled at the woman greeting them. Upswept hair, perfect makeup and wearing an outfit that could have come right out of Maggie's store.

"Is that Lilli Ann?" Maggie asked.

The woman turned. "Where?"

"I mean the designer of your vintage suit."

The woman checked her outfit. "Oh, this is just something I threw on. My sister sent it from Des Moines a few years ago. She said it just looked like something I'd wear."

Too bad. So far in Roanoke there'd not been a true fashionista who could talk Crepe Fox Fur or gold-tone pearl buttons.

Safe topics for in a church foyer when you really didn't want to be there.

"Let me take your coats," the woman offered.

It's not a church service, Beth had insisted. *It's just a party. No Bible study and we'll be singing Christmas songs.*

"No," Maggie insisted. "We're fine. I'll hang them up." If she hung up her cocoa leather and shearling coat, she'd know right where to get it if she needed a quick getaway.

Not that her coat could get lost amid the heavy leather jackets and box-store offerings hanging on the rack. None of tonight's attendees seemed to be into double-breasted fronts and huge collars.

"Have you been here before?"

Maggie knew what was coming next: an invitation to services.

"Excuse me." Maggie pulled Cassidy in front of her. "We need the restroom."

"Right over there."

After a thorough washing of her hands—not because they were dirty but because Maggie needed to get her bearings—and several deep breaths, all while Cassidy urged "Come on, Mom, Mom, Mom, pleeeeee-ase," Maggie headed for the foyer again. The woman who'd greeted her was already at the door with some other victim.

"There's a horse," Cassidy reminded.

"Perfect." The horse was outside. To Maggie's way of thinking, being outside a church was much better than inside a church.

As they made their way to the line for the horse and wagon rides, first picking up plastic cups of hot chocolate, Maggie noticed that Jared and Caleb were still standing at the side of the church.

Cassidy, though, was all about Cassidy. In a nanosecond, Maggie was holding both their drinks while Cassidy charged full speed ahead. She would have made it, too, if a toddler hadn't suddenly veered in her way.

Cassidy recalculated, turned left, stumbled, went down, seemed momentarily stunned, but then hopped up and without so much as a backward glance at the toddler who had deterred her, got in line.

It was that magical seven-year-old energy.

Nope, Maggie thought for the second time, she wouldn't change a thing about Cassidy. Every nuance was part of the precious package that Maggie loved, unconditionally.

Looking behind her, she watched Jared with his son. At one time, Maggie had been a prayer warrior. If that were still true, she'd be praying that Jared McCreedy was the kind of father who would soon figure out the same thing about his youngest son.

But Maggie no longer prayed. She'd seen firsthand the power of answered prayers and it terrified her.

Chapter Four

The Main Street Church certainly drew a crowd. Maggie recognized customers, parents of Cassidy's classmates and even Henry Throxmorton, the owner of the antiques store from across the street who never seemed to smile. He wasn't smiling now, but he was sitting at a table across from two other men—both knew how to smile—and looking as comfortable as she'd ever seen him. His wife, looking frail but content, sat next to him.

Only six months in Roanoke and already she knew a few faces. For the first time since entering the church doors, Maggie relaxed. She could do this.

Maggie quickly purchased a few tickets and followed the path Cassidy had already taken—sans the toddler. How Cassidy knew her way around, Maggie didn't know. In a matter of minutes, they were both in line for the horse and wagon. Never mind the cold! There were a handful of adults and a crush of kids under ten, most of whom Maggie did not know, but Cassidy did.

With mittens on and hats down over their ears, Cassidy and Maggie rode in the wagon bed, singing Christmas songs at the top of their lungs along with anyone else foolhardy enough to be outside in the freezing weather.

Joel McCreedy, Jared's brother, added a deep bass from his position at the reins. He listened to the kids' suggestions for songs, told jokes and even paid attention as little ones shouted their lists for Santa Claus.

Joel was easygoing, not like his older brother. With a devil-may-care glint in his eyes and I-can-do-anything attitude, the younger McCreedy brother had quickly won over both Maggie and Cassidy this past summer while he worked on remodeling the store that became Hand Me Ups.

Still, it was the older brother that Maggie couldn't seem to forget.

After three go-rounds, the cold soon drove the Tate women inside to the crowded fellowship hall where the food smelled as inviting as the people were. It only took a moment before Cassidy claimed she was warm again and stood at one of the large windows staring longingly at the horse toting around yet another group of revelers.

Not a chance. Maggie was so cold her teeth hurt.

"Joel said that when the crowd dies down, I can sit up front with him. Then it would be fair." Cassidy stood so close to the window that her breath frosted the glass.

Maggie was no dummy. "Which means we'll be here until cleanup."

"Yes," Cassidy said brightly.

Just as Maggie was ready to open her mouth, squash that idea—

"We can always use help with cleanup."

Trust Beth Armstrong to walk by at just the right

moment. Her arms were full of paper plates, cups and napkins. Matt McCreedy followed her with a stack of plastic forks. He tripped over his untied shoelaces and the forks hit the ground. Maggie and Cassidy gathered them up and followed Beth and Matt to the kitchen.

"I'm not quite sure where Jared's gotten off to." Beth joined the workers in the kitchen. "He's supposed to be helping with serving. He never shirks his duty."

"Dad's busy," Matt volunteered.

"Doing what?"

Matt gave the typical kid reply. "I don't know."

Maggie bit her lower lip. She knew how busy Jared was. She also believed Beth's words about Jared and responsibility. Her husband had been like that, putting duty first. Could be Jared had lost all track of time and didn't realize how cold it was. If Jared and Caleb were outside, then maybe now was the perfect time to start interfering.

Helping.

She wasn't interfering.

"Watch Cassidy for just a moment, will you?"

In response, Beth set Cassidy to putting plastic dining ware into separate containers.

Stepping outside the kitchen and once again into the fellowship hall, Maggie quickly looked around. No Jared. She headed for the foyer, still full of people in varying stages of taking off coats, putting them back on. Most laughing. No Jared.

She really hadn't been expecting to find him in either place.

Then, exiting the church, she rounded the corner and

found both Jared and Caleb leaning against the building, both of them looking half-frozen.

"We'll go in when you calm down," Jared was saying.

"Noooooooo."

Maggie had to give Jared credit, he didn't lose his temper at Caleb's belligerent whine nor did he give in. His voice, however, was sharp when he said, "I'm sure getting cold."

"Nooooooo." If anything, the whine got louder. Jared winced and stood his ground.

"I'll bet you're getting hungry, too," Maggie announced as she rounded the corner, hoping she was doing the right thing, slightly nervous at intervening.

Helping, she was helping.

She wished someone had been around when she was first going through this.

"Cassidy's been looking for you, Caleb." Maggie looked at Jared, trying to gauge whether he wanted her help or wanted her to back off. His expression was unfathomable. But, judging by the way he gritted his teeth, he did need help—whether he wanted it or not.

"Seems your Uncle Joel has promised a hayride with a couple of kids sitting up front," Maggie continued. "She thought you'd like to go with her."

Happiness for a moment, back to anger and then doubt all flickered across Caleb's face.

"That would be fine with me," Jared encouraged. His hands were shoved deep in the pockets of his tan coat. A black knit cap was pulled over his head, low enough so Maggie couldn't see his eyes, but not so low that it did a good job of protecting his face.

Caleb pushed himself away from the church, a little clumsily since he had on a heavy coat—just like his father's but definitely a size too big—and boots that were also a little too big for his feet. It looked like hand-me-downs were alive and well at the McCreedy house. Without a backward glance, Caleb trotted toward the horse and wagon.

Maggie turned. She needed to get Cassidy pronto.

"Wait!" Jared said.

"Just let me get Cassidy out there to meet him. It's important that I keep my word." She hurried inside, fetched Cassidy, and rushed toward the horse and wagon.

A moment later, she promised Joel that she'd have the children's tickets after he made the round. Caleb, used to both the wagon and Joel, hopped right up on the front seat. Cassidy scrambled alongside him. Both children shouted *Giddy up!*

Maggie headed to the side of the church, albeit hesitantly. Thanks to his winter hat, she'd not been able to read his expression and wasn't one hundred percent sure he'd appreciated her interference.

Her help.

But Jared—sensible man—had already gone inside and was taking his place carrying hot dog buns to the serving area. No way did Maggie want to talk to him amid all these people.

There was a short line at the table where two women sold tickets. A jar with money inside had a photo of a family and in black marker were the words: all proceeds to go to needy families.

Nostalgia, unwelcomed and unwanted, hit Maggie

like a surprise kick to the back of the knees. Three years ago, she'd been the church woman sitting at the table collecting the money. Sixteen years ago, she'd been a member of the "needy family" club.

Maggie took a deep breath. Tonight she was close to being the needy family again and as far away from the church woman as she could possibly be.

It's not a church service. It's just a party. We'll be singing Christmas songs.

But Maggie could never forget, no matter how she tried to place her memories of Christmas on a back burner for Cassidy's sake.

Christmas was not the best time to venture inside a church, and not because they collected for needy families and not because Maggie no longer prayed.

It was because it had been a December day that she'd received word that her husband had been killed in the line of duty. It had also been a December day that Maggie's mother had walked out on her daughter and husband.

I'm strong. I can do this. I will do this.

Maggie managed to buy the tickets with minimal words and—her legs still feeling weak—backed away from the table and just stood in the middle of the crowd looking at the walls.

I'm strong. I can do this. I will do this.

The walls behind the ticket sellers were awash with Christmas drawings made by the kids. Santas of varying sizes, some even skinny, tumbled across the walls. Snowmen chased them. Snowflakes, some resembling pumpkins, came in amazing colors.

Cassidy didn't have an offering on the wall as Maggie didn't let her attend church.

Maggie left the fellowship hall. She needed something to chase away the memories of the past. She needed away from all the "Merry Christmases." It was somewhat calmer in the hallway. The Bible classroom doors were shut, but the area teemed with people and, yes, their minds were on Christmas.

Tables were set up, and a craft business seemed to be thriving. Joel could wait a little longer for the tickets. And, she knew if she wasn't there when he finished the round, he'd just take the kids again.

Low on funds, Maggie bypassed the spiral-bound cookbooks that were for sale next to a display of beaded jewelry and went straight to some knitters and crocheters who might consider selling their goods on consignment in her shop. What she really wanted was crocheted soda can hats, but she'd make the request after seeing which of the crafters wanted to work with her.

While the ticket takers on the inside were collecting money for needy families, the crafters were all about collecting money for the church camp. They were thrilled at having another avenue to make money.

There was also a husband and wife team selling photo identification badges for kids. He was flanked by an artist and a clockmaker. If she'd had some spare cash, she'd buy a few presents.

Maybe next year they'd let her set up an area and sell vintage clothes. She could do a great business in the kids department.

That did it. Just a few thoughts about work and next year. Some of Maggie's anxiety ebbed. Enough so that when Cassidy came barreling around the corner shouting, "I couldn't find you!" Maggie was able to pick up her daughter and swing her saying, "I'll never wander far. You'll always be able to find me."

Cassidy didn't know how true those words were. She also wasn't willing to slow down to look at such grown-up temptations as jewelry and identification tags.

"How did you get away from Joel?" Maggie asked.

"We went around three times and then Joel said for Caleb's big brother to bring me to you," Cassidy explained. "There were lots of kids in line. We weren't being fair."

The sound of laughter and the smell of food wafting from the fellowship hall were a magnet. Cassidy pulled Maggie through the door and into the room crowded with people both eating and playing games.

Maggie wasn't a bit hungry.

Neither apparently was Cassidy, except for wanting a bag of popcorn which she didn't get.

In the back of the fellowship hall there was a coloring table, a face-painting table manned by Beth, and a fishing game. Cassidy looked, paused, and passed by saying, "Maybe I'll get my face painted, later."

Outside, the cold slapped at Maggie's face. Cassidy zoomed to the maze and latched on to the McCreedy boys, to both Ryan and Caleb's joy and Matt's consternation. After one turn making their way through the labyrinth, Maggie knew why. Ryan was overjoyed because he surrendered Matt and Caleb into Maggie's supervision. He disappeared with his friends toward an impromptu football game played with bigger boys and a few fathers.

Caleb was overjoyed because he just plain liked girls, Cassidy especially.

"Nothing makes Matt happy," Cassidy confided after their third time going through the maze.

"I want to go help Beth," Matt said.

Maggie looked in through one of the windows. Beth had a line ten kids deep. "Beth's busy at the face-painting booth," Maggie said. "We'll see if the line dies down soon, and then you can go help her."

An hour later, Cassidy and the boys were out of tickets and Maggie was guiding them back to the fellowship hall and the food line. Matt and Caleb ran ahead, Cassidy on their heels. Maggie wasn't quite as fast. But, the closer she got, the slower her feet became.

Once again, Jared had a towel in his hand and was cleaning up a mess. Only this time it wasn't pancake batter. It was ketchup.

She didn't have time to look away before he glanced up and caught her staring.

She could only hope he realized that she was fixated on the ketchup spill and not him.

Too bad hot dogs were a staple at Solitaire Farm because after tonight, Jared wasn't sure he could stomach the smell ever again. This wasn't his first time helping with the church's Christmas party, but it was his first time without Mandy. The last few Christmases had been hard.

Jared's helpers were ambitious and laughed a lot, but they really weren't much help. They got sidetracked on conversations, mostly football scores or whose house had been broken into recently—seemed there'd been quite a few thefts. They took too long taking orders, because every customer was a friend. They forgot where stuff was stored, even though most had attended the Main Street Church for decades and this wasn't their first time in the kitchen. And, most of all, they were clumsy.

Even worse, when they spilled things, they were more likely than not to leave the spill where it was than to clean it up.

Jared had just sent home Sophia Totwell. She had claimed a hurt ankle; he figured she was as tired of the hot dog smell as he was. Plus, she'd seen her husband and two kids wandering around, looking lost.

"I wish you'd talk to him," Sophie said to Jared as she untied her apron. "You've been farming a long time. Give him some advice on how to make money as well as spend it."

Kyle Totwell didn't want to hear what Jared had to say. He'd moved onto a broken-down farm, purchased way too many cows for his ability and finances, and was now suffering.

"Dad, can I have a hot dog?" Caleb skidded under the table, managing to rearrange the tablecloth and knock a handful of napkins to the ground. Matt picked them up and stayed on the correct side of the food counter.

"One hot dog, no bun, coming up," Jared said. He nudged Caleb around the table to stand next to Matt. He just knew his voice dripped with patience. Surely Maggie would notice how in control he was. "You want one, too?" he asked Matt.

"Yes."

"And you?" he asked Cassidy.

"I don't like buns, either."

Maggie came to the edge of the table, guiding Cassidy away from the tablecloth and smiling at Jared as if this morning hadn't happened.

"Thanks for what you did earlier, and thanks for taking my boys around," he said.

"They were no problem. We had fun."

He'd noticed. Maybe that's why he'd been so attuned to the ambitious, laughing lot in his food court. He'd been wishing he was with Maggie and the kids.

"I'm sorry I left the coffee shop so abruptly this morn—" he started.

"Nothing to apologize for," she finished. "Some topics are harder than others."

"What are you guys talking about?" Matt wanted to know.

"Grown-up talk." Jared quickly made four plates, two with just hot dogs and two with buns, potato chips and a homemade chocolate chip cookie.

"I want a choc—" Cassidy and Caleb chimed in unison.

"Only after you eat the hot dog," Maggie said. "And then only half."

"Dad, you always give me a chocolate chip cookie," Caleb complained.

"Now might be a good time to change."

Little adult that he was, Matt had already made his way to a table and was eating his hot dog, sans ketchup—before touching anything on his plate. He did not look overjoyed when Cassidy and Caleb joined him. He did, however, astutely move his plate so his cookie was out of his little brother's reach.

"How many times did they go through the maze?" Jared asked.

"I stopped counting at seven."

Jared's next words came out before he had time to think. "You have more patience than I do." Immediately, he wanted them back. Her smile slipped a little, just enough so he knew she was thinking about this morning.

She, indeed, did have patience because instead of pointing out the obvious, she simply said, "I'd better go see what the kids are doing and make sure they eat."

He watched her walk away, her hips sashaying in such a way that Jared wondered how such an old-fashioned red dress could look so appealing.

Maybe because it wasn't the dress.

Chapter Five

It was nine and the game lines still boasted one or two kids. Cassidy leaned back in the chair, and let Beth Armstrong's paintbrush create an image on her cheek that would soon become red cowboy boots.

Beth had more paint on her than most of the kids, and she looked ready to drop.

"I take it the Christmas party's a success?" Maggie stood slightly to the side, gently swaying with Caleb on her hip, and watched as Beth created her masterpiece.

"It always is. This year seemed really good. I heard one of the women say we raised almost five hundred dollars. There was never a moment the face-painting booth didn't have a kid."

"Me, either," Maggie agreed. "There was never a time I didn't have a kid." She switched Caleb from her left arm to her right. Good thing he was a small fellow or her arms would be more on fire than they already were.

"He's sure taken to you," Beth observed.

"This morning we had a whole conversation in the

car about his dad not having a girl. Caleb seemed to think they needed one."

Cassidy giggled.

"Now, you're going to have one boot bigger than the other. Don't move," Beth scolded Cassidy before turning to Maggie. "I heard all about you taking a ride in Jared's truck. Caleb is a natural reporter. You'd think the ride went on for days. Then, too, there was something about pancake batter."

"Yes," Maggie admitted, "this morning was not my finest hour by any means. A good-looking guy stops by my place and winds up doing kitchen duty because Cassidy spilled a bowl full of pancake batter."

"On accident," Cassidy asserted.

"Then, Jared takes me out for coffee, so we can talk, and I find out he doesn't drink coffee—serious flaw, by the way—and then he gets the call about some hay emergency at church so he doesn't even get to finish the coffee that he didn't like."

"I'm glad he took my advice. Jared really needed to talk to you. He probably figures suffering through a cup of coffee a small price to pay."

"We didn't really get to talk."

"Well, you must have connected somehow. Everyone in town's going to be talking about how you chauffeured Matt and Caleb around."

"My having them is more Ryan's doing." Maggie shifted, trying to get Caleb into a better grip. It had been a long time since she'd held a sleeping five-year-old. "We ran into them at the maze and he transferred the care and feeding of these small animals to me."

"We're not animals," Cassidy protested. "I'm a cow-boy—I mean cowgirl."

"They're animals," Jared agreed, coming up from behind. "We're closing down, and I get to take a break before cleanup. Anybody want a last-minute hot dog? We're giving away the leftovers." He didn't look surprised when no one took him up on his offer.

Gently, he tried to take Caleb from Maggie's arms.

But Caleb, even in sleep, was already comfortable and he wasn't letting go. His hands curled into Maggie's shirt and his head nestled tightly into her neck.

"I think he likes me," Maggie said.

"He just likes girls," Cassidy reminded her.

"Now you're going to have part of a boot all the way to your nose," Beth said. "Stop moving. I'm going to need to do some boot repairs here." She nodded toward Caleb. "Why don't you guys take him to the nursery? He'll be more comfortable. I'll finish with Cassidy while you're gone."

Jared nodded, already turning to head from the gym. Maggie followed, letting him open the doors for her. The hallway was almost empty. The crafters had packed up what was left. The stragglers were either helping with cleanup or children of the cleanup crew. Almost everyone said something personal to Jared. More than a few introduced themselves to Maggie even while raising an eyebrow.

Small towns were the same everywhere.

After a moment, they were at the nursery's door. Jared hit a dimmer switch that allowed him to adjust the light. Just able to see, he headed past a few rocking chairs, a changing table and to a crib. "He won't be happy waking up in one of these, especially if one of his brothers finds out."

"Then we won't tell them."

Maggie gently rubbed Caleb's back. He was heavy against her chest and smelled of sweat and hot dogs and little boy.

Maggie figured his father smelled of sweat and hot dogs and big boy.

"You know your way around this church," Maggie remarked as she lay Caleb down. "This nursery reminds me of a church in Lubbock. I spent many a sermon sitting in it while taking care of Cassidy."

"So you do go to church? I've never seen you here."

It was too late to erase the words. Blame them on an overload of nostalgia. Maggie tucked the blanket over Caleb. "At one time I went to church. I don't see the need now. Although, your church is lovely. I like how everyone interacts. I was never at a congregation long enough for the members to get to know me."

"I'd hate that. Why did you move so often?"

"My husband was military."

"Was?"

Maggie busied herself by brushing a strand of Caleb's hair out of his eyes and tucking him in yet again. After a moment, Jared sat in one of the rocking chairs and said, "You don't seem to have trouble fitting in. Beth thinks highly of you and so does my brother."

"They have to think highly of me." Maggie turned to face Jared. "I stock the kind of clothes Beth likes, and I paid your brother in cash for the work he did on my shop and plan for him to do more."

Jared laughed. The sound was deep and showed

Maggie a side of the man she doubted many saw. Most of the time, like when he was trying to meet with his son's teacher, or clean up messy pancake batter, or drink coffee, or even push hot dogs at a church function, he came across as way too serious.

"I think I need to think highly of you, too," he confessed.

"Why?"

"I watched you with Caleb tonight. He and Cassidy were like twins, running here, running there, running everywhere. You kept them in sight, you kept them in control and never once lost your patience."

"I've had years of practice—first with my dad, who expected me to practically salute when he issued an order, and then with my late husband."

"Your husband expected you to salute?"

"It's a military thing. And, no, Dan didn't really expect me to salute. It was more like Dan expected Cassidy to follow orders like the men he led. It wasn't happening and watching him lose his patience only inspired me to keep control at all times."

"That couldn't have been easy."

Maybe it was the late hour, maybe it was the man who so needed to understand how to be patient, maybe it was just that Maggie needed to talk.

"When Dan was still alive and home on leave, Cassidy would purposely break her pencil while doing homework. She'd let the pencil roll to the ground and claim she couldn't find it."

Jared nodded.

"I'd put away all Cassidy's toys while we tried to do homework, but Cassidy was, is, just as happy playing with—and even licking—a salt shaker or just folding a work sheet into a paper airplane. She makes killer paper airplanes."

"Caleb won't sit still long enough to notice the salt shaker let alone make a paper airplane," Jared contributed. "Plus, he asks to go to the bathroom every few minutes. Once, I thought I heard him throw up."

"By the time we figured out that Cassidy had Attention Deficit behavior—not disorder, not yet—Cassidy refused to work with her father."

Jared was silent, and Maggie could only hope he was thinking: *I can't let this happen to me.*

"Dan always turned the activity into a battle, forgetting that doing battle with a five-year-old girl didn't necessarily mean there'd be a clear winner."

The single window in the nursery let in a long, gray shadow that emphasized the empty rockers, the mural of Noah's Ark on the wall and the cribs. A forgotten diaper bag was by the changing table. The room was so quiet that Maggie could hear Jared breathing.

"Tell me what to do," he finally said.

"What do you mean?"

"I mean besides learning how to find time and balance it with patience, tell me what to do. I'm committed. I want to help my son. I appreciated you interfering earlier—"

"I wasn't interfering. I was helping." In a moment, she'd opened her purse, and took out a piece of paper and wrote down the name of two books. "Here are the titles of the two books that helped me the most. Call me if you have any questions. I don't have the right answers, and believe me, I made plenty of mistakes. But I can tell you what works best for Cassidy and me."

Jared nodded and took the paper from her hand. His fingers were warm against hers. His eyes sincere. But, in the back of her mind, she could see Dan looking just as sincere, hear Dan saying the same thing, *Tell me what to do. I'm committed. I want to help.*

Problem was, Maggie'd had a lifetime of watching people fail who claimed to be committed: first her mother and then her husband.

At least this time the person destined to fail wasn't someone Maggie loved.

Early Saturday morning, after chores and while the rest of his family still slumbered, Jared got on the computer—for once his high-speed internet actually worked—and ordered the books Maggie had suggested. He followed that with about twenty minutes of finding the perfect directions for building a hay feeder.

Time and patience, Maggie had said.

December on Solitaire Farm meant a bit more time: time to do all the things, like building a hay feeder that Jared had put off during the busy season. The best thing about this feeder was the cost, possibly under five dollars. It could be built out of scrap plywood. What he didn't use, he'd take to the school for props. He hadn't planned to start the feeder today, but after last week with Caleb getting sent to the office and then the conference with his teacher, and then last night with Maggie, well, Jared had plenty to think about. Since there was nothing to plow, and he had lots of thinking to do, he needed to do something with his hands.

Already fully dressed, Jared merely put on his heavy parka and hat before heading for the barn. There was a slight misting of ice on the porch. The soles of his work boots barely noticed. The cold air momentarily stung his hands and he buried them in his pockets. According to the almanac, winter wouldn't arrive for another three weeks, but God's timeline didn't care what was predicted.

Jared's father had been a master at predicting snow. He'd laughed when Jared asked how. The same man who'd taught Jared "Always plow around stumps," had also advised, "If a cat washes her face o'er the ear, 'tis a sign the weather will be fine and clear." He'd followed that with, "When clouds look like black smoke, a wise man will put on his cloak."

Stepping off the bottom porch step, Jared turned and looked at the home he'd grown up in. It was all his now, since Joel had sold his share right out of high school. Owning a farm was a lot of work. Some of Jared's neighbors hadn't quite figured that out. There were a lot of wannabes moving in, like the Totwells who'd purchased an old farm just five miles east of Solitaire Farm. They'd named it Roanoke Creek even though they didn't have a creek. The father, Kyle Totwell, was always showing up on Jared's door with questions. Fool kid—same age as Joel—purchased cows, lots of cows, before he knew how to care for them.

Jared was primarily an Iowa row crop farmer. He raised a few animals because his father had, but scaled way back—just what his family needed. Joel was set on changing that. Joel liked the live-animal part of farming, like Kyle Totwell did.

There was something amusing about a family who thought farming a romantic profession, a way to get back to nature. The smell of manure was as back to nature as one could get. As for romantic...there was nothing romantic about getting up at four in the morning, dressing in the dark so as to not wake anyone and then heading out into the cold.

Jared couldn't imagine doing anything else, living anywhere else, but since Mandy died, the fear of failure—not having enough time and not having enough heart—had settled like a seed in his stomach that sprouted, grew, retracted, only to hibernate just waiting for the opportunity to rear its head again.

"Dad, I sure wish you were here now."

It had been a while since Jared had paid lip service to his dad's memory. The last time had probably been the day after Mandy's death when he'd found himself on his knees next to their bed, now his alone, and Jared had beat the sheets with his fists, silently screaming, "Why? Why? Why?"

He, like a child, had wanted his dad that day. His dad would have been the only one who would have chanced entering the bedroom, would have known the words to say when, really, there were no words.

Jared tore away his eyes from the two-story farmhouse that housed his sleeping family, a family that depended on him.

Depended on him not to fall victim to the winter doldrums.

Hands in his pockets, Jared walked across the yard. His dog, Captain Rex, named by one of the boys, came from wherever he'd been and settled companionably alongside. Except for an occasional sound from where the cows stood, the Iowa morning was silent.

Silent and cold.

Almost every farmer Jared knew experienced winter frustration. Most worked jobs off the farm to keep things going. Jared hadn't wanted to, so he'd done the next best thing. He'd opened a small market at the edge of the property right where the rural road met the intersection into town. It had been Mandy's idea, and she'd kept it up when she was alive. Billy had helped after Mandy's death. It provided some income, not much. Then, last year, Joel finally realized he was needed at home.

Joel was a natural shopkeeper as well as a gifted carpenter and took Solitaire's Market to a new level. He pretty much changed the shed Solitaire's Market was occupying into a log cabin that sold more than produce. His girlfriend, Beth, Caleb's teacher, had a say. So, along with some very nonfarm items, like oil paintings and homemade soap, Jared now met the needs of his customers' children. For a mere dollar, they could travel through a real corn maze. The maze at last night's church Christmas party was nothing compared to the permanent one next to Jared's—make that Joel's—store.

To Jared's amazement, people came from as far as Knoxville. Just a few weeks ago, Joel and Beth had decorated the maze for Thanksgiving. Fake turkeys, cardboard pilgrims and Indians, and a giant cornucopia were all part of the experience. When kids and their parents exited, they were given an ear of Indian corn with a tag advertising Jared's farm tied to the end. He made almost as much money on the maze as he did selling pumpkins and other produce. And, he wouldn't have sold as many pumpkins without the maze.

He turned on the light in the barn. This was one of the few places where Mandy's ghost behaved. She'd helped out here, sure, but not very often. Her place had been inside and with the boys.

Which is now my place, Jared reminded himself. Being both mom and dad wasn't easy, but it was rewarding, and yes, it was getting easier—thanks to Beth.

Beth, Mandy's best friend.

Beth had been around forever, first helping with Jared's wedding, then baby showers and finally when Mandy got sick.

Jared had been busy working the farm. He'd accepted whatever Mandy wanted.

Now, he wished he'd chosen time with Mandy over time on the farm. The farm was silent and cold, nothing like the companionship of his warm and sensitive wife. But this was Jared's life now, and with a quick prayer, he left those thoughts behind and got to work.

Chapter Six

"But I want a real tree, real tree, real tree." Cassidy was in rare form. Last night had ignited her energy level and today she'd hit the ground running and hadn't stopped. Luckily, the patrons of Hand Me Ups had been in the Christmas spirit and fairly understanding. Although Maggie heard one older woman mutter something about *be good or else Santa won't...*

Cassidy either hadn't heard the prediction or had pretended not to hear. Sometimes Maggie couldn't tell.

"Real tree," Cassidy said yet again.

Maggie sat behind the counter and pushed a needle into an elf's hat. She'd promised to make fifty and was on number thirty-nine. They were easy, but fifty turned out to be more time consuming than she'd figured. Cassidy's chanting didn't help. Maggie ignored each and every pronouncement, even though they'd gotten louder each time. Things like money and convenience didn't really matter to Cassidy, yet. Someday they would. "I know, but our place isn't that big and real trees cost more."

"You need two trees," Cassidy decided, looking around the store. "We can get a little one, like you want, for upstairs, cuz you're right. It's small up there. But downstairs here in your shop, we can put up a real one, real one, real one."

Most of the shops had put up their Christmas trees the day after Thanksgiving. When Maggie and Cassidy got back from New York, the street had been transformed.

The bell above the door jangled as Beth Armstrong came in.

Cassidy took one look at the box in Beth's arms and said, "Yes, a big tree, and we can hang Miss Beth's soap like they're ornaments. That will help sell them."

"Not a bad idea," Beth said.

Maggie knew when she was outnumbered and wisely kept silent. A Christmas tree was just a tree, nothing else, no need to think it stood for anything but a decoration.

Still, Cassidy knew the exact moment she'd won the battle and ran for Beth, almost knocking over the woman. "I am so happy!" Turning to her mother, she asked, "When can we get them? Can they be real? Please."

"Maybe we'll go tonight, and we'll probably get them at Bob's Hardware. It's what we can afford."

Beth made a face. "Bob's Hardware. Ack."

"You know as well as I know that there are only two places in town selling imitation trees. I can't afford the novelty store. Bob's trees are reasonable."

"They're not even made at the North Pole," Beth muttered.

"Then where are they made?" Cassidy asked.

"We're changing the subject before I change my mind," Maggie said.

Luckily, a customer came through the door at that moment, and Maggie didn't have to say anything else. Cassidy was quite willing to take up the slack.

"Mommy doesn't have any new wedding dresses for you to look at."

"That's okay." Beth looked at Maggie. "Joel's got something to do tomorrow after church. I thought we could head to Fairfield and look at some of the antiques stores there. This close to Christmas, some of them stay open on Sundays. I've only a few weeks until the wedding. We need to find my dress, and soon."

"I want to go," Cassidy agreed.

"You could always attend ch—"

"I'm sorry," Maggie said. "I promised Sophia Totwell we'd come out to her house tomorrow afternoon. She called me this morning. She's been going through the basement and found suitcases full of old clothes. You could come with me. It's a long shot, but maybe we'd find a dress. Stranger things have happened."

"Can we do both?" Beth considered.

"We can try. Want me to pick you up at your house just after noon?"

"Sounds good," Beth agreed. Heading for one of the shelves next to the register, she added the handmade soap to her display and checked to see what had sold.

Maggie wished she could pay Beth early, but she cut the consignment checks once a month and now that it looked like the Tate women would be the proud owners of not one but two trees, Maggie needed to look again at her budget.

"It takes four years for a business to boast a profit," Maggie reminded herself.

"What?" Beth said.

"Just talking to myself."

"You're pretty good at talking," Beth commented. "You were holding your own last night with my future brother-in-law."

"We were talking kids."

"I figured that, but you got him talking and that's a feat. When Mandy died, he about crawled in a hole and stayed there." Beth's face was usually puppy-dog happy, but for a moment, a shadow crossed her features. "She was my best friend, you know."

Maggie knew. Beth was an open book.

"There wasn't a week I wasn't out there," Beth continued, "at Solitaire Farm, doing something with her family."

Maggie wasn't sure she wanted to know all this. From what she'd heard, Mandy McCreedy had died around four years ago and Jared still wasn't over her passing.

"He must have really loved her."

"Oh, he did." Beth took a notebook out of her purse, made a few notations, and then turned back to Maggie. "They started going out while she was still in junior high, too young to do anything but sit beside each other at youth-group events. He graduated before she did. Her parents said they couldn't be married until she got her high school diploma."

"Hometown favorites," Maggie said.

"Mandy was. Jared was always too grown-up to fit in with most of the high school boys. He was running the farm at sixteen."

"So," Maggie prompted, amazed by how curious she was, "the minute Mandy graduated, they got married."

"Yes and no," Beth said, leaning on the counter. "Mandy took night classes, computer classes and summer school. She graduated at midterm what should have been her junior year. If she'd have stayed, she'd have been captain of the cheerleaders and probably prom queen. Everyone loved her."

"But she loved Jared more."

"Yep. The day she got the passing grade for her final class, she told Jared even before she told her parents."

Beth wasn't done.

"That was a Friday. He proposed on Sunday. Probably the most romantic thing he'd done in his whole life."

"Proposing?"

"Yes, he did it in the foyer after church, right in front of everybody. Got down on one knee and everything. I was standing right next to Mandy's mother. No way could her parents talk to them about waiting and college after that."

"How old was Mandy?"

"Seventeen. Four years older than me."

"How'd you become best friends, then?"

Beth's cell phone sounded out a verse from "Going to the Chapel." "That's Joel. He promised to call." She punched a button, said, "I'm just on my way out of Maggie's store. Let me call you right back." Barely giving the man time to respond, she shut off the phone. "How'd we become best friends? Some things are just meant to be. Like you and me becoming friends." She closed her purse, pulled her scarf tighter around her neck and headed for the exit. "See you tomorrow."

The door banged shut behind her, but not before it let in a blast of cold air. Maggie was about to say "Brrrr," but already Beth was opening the door again.

"I'm glad you're helping him. He needs it more than you know."

Bam! Another slam of the door, another blast of cold air and then Beth was gone.

"She's pretty," Cassidy said, after the door closed. She added an afterthought, as if worried she had hurt her mother's feelings, "But not as pretty as you."

"Thank you," Maggie said. "I think."

When Maggie had opened Hand Me Ups, Beth had been her first customer. The next day, she'd brought both her sisters and a two-year-old niece. Soon Beth and Maggie were a team, always with Cassidy in tow, heading into the city and shopping. Maggie had an eye for retro and Beth had an eye for style.

Cassidy provided live entertainment.

On Saturdays and even a few evenings when Beth's fiancé was out of town, Beth had come to the shop and started sketching a mural across the back wall. In exchange, Maggie was giving Beth a discount on her wedding alterations. Beth was exactly what Maggie needed: upbeat and friendly.

Maybe, for the first time, Maggie had landed in a place where best friends did last forever. Beth was a beloved daughter, sister and town favorite all rolled up into one. She'd been born and raised here in Roanoke, only leaving to get her college degree. Maggie, on the other hand, had been an only child and army brat, spending time in Texas, Japan and Panama among other places.

When Maggie was twelve, they'd been in Hawaii. Christmas there was a bit different. Santa wore a flowered shirt for one thing, and everywhere you turned, people greeted you with *Mele Kalikimaka,* meaning Merry Christmas. While Maggie was at school, her mother had packed her belongings and walked out on the family.

She left behind presents under the tree, the last Maggie would get from her mother, and a note that said she couldn't take moving from place to place anymore.

The note hadn't explained why she couldn't take Maggie with her to just one place.

"She needs a tree."

Jared, just getting his brood rounded up for their outing, frowned at the phone. "What's keeping her from getting one?"

"Nothing," Beth said. "But, she's going to get two fake ones when two real ones would be better. Plus, since I know her finances, she'll go to Bob's Hardware in town. He only has three fake trees to choose from, and they're all lame. I know you're going tonight. You always go on the first Saturday of December. I know your schedule as well as I do my own. Call her up, and take her with you. The Deckers won't mind, and I'm sure they'll cut her a deal. I don't think she's ever had a real tree."

Jared shook his head, even though Beth couldn't see him on the other end. "There's nothing wrong with fake trees. Sometimes I think they'd be a whole lot easier."

"Then why aren't you getting one?"

She knew the answer to that. Paul Decker, his best friend from high school, owned a Christmas tree farm called Decker the Halls over in Indianola. It was a bit of a drive, but Paul and his family always made the night special for Jared's family even back when *special* didn't seem possible.

"Jared, this is her second Christmas without her husband."

"Then she's used to it." Even as the words exited his mouth, he wanted them back. They came from frustration, and yes, fear. He, more than anyone, understood the pain she was going through and it bothered him how much the idea of inviting her appealed to him.

"Call her," Beth ordered. "Or, I'll tell Joel to replace you as best man."

"Threaten me with something you'll really do."

"Ohhhh." She hung up on him.

"Dad, when are we going?" Matt, seven going on forty, stood at the bottom of the stairs. He was dressed, even to his shoes. He was Jared's little timekeeper and figured they were late.

"Thirty minutes."

"Do I have to go?" Ryan, nine but already acting like a teenager, didn't want to go, but the moment they got to the Deckers' place, Jared knew Ryan would be the one having the most fun.

Ryan stood at the top of the stairs, wearing shorts and socks, nothing else.

Paul Decker had a nine-year-old daughter who was just as good at video games as Ryan.

"Ryan!" Jared called, "Get dressed and find out what Caleb's doing."

Overhead, the sound of his oldest stomping his feet as he went from his bedroom to Caleb's echoed through the room. Ryan was a stomper.

The phone sounded.

"Hey, little bro," Jared answered.

"I can't believe you knew it was me. Did you finally break down and get call display?"

"No, but I know your fiancée quite well and I know exactly what she's thinking, which is why I can't call Maggie Tate. This time of year is just too personal. I've finally got my family back on track and, frankly, I want to enjoy the quality time with them. She just wouldn't fit."

"Maybe you need somebody who doesn't fit to shake you up a bit. And Christmas is the perfect time."

"I've had all the shaking up I need, believe me."

Jared turned down Joel's suggestion that he call Maggie Tate as easily as he'd turned down Beth's. And, like Beth, Joel hung up without a goodbye. Jared figured, judging by the indignant feminine noise coming through the connection that Beth had her hands on the phone.

What a difference a year makes. Jared could only shake his head. His little brother, the my-saddle-sits-still-for-no-one cowboy, was so over the moon about his future wife that he'd stooped to playing a second-fiddle matchmaker.

Jared had been that in love with his late wife—so in love that when she had died, he'd almost forgotten how to live. Luckily, he'd had a family to remind him.

He sat down on the couch and stared at the photo over the fireplace: his family. His late wife, Mandy, stood next to him, all smiles. He wasn't smiling, but then he'd never much cared for having his picture taken. Their three boys, stair-step brothers, were in front. Ryan held a squirming Caleb.

And Matt?

Matt, who looked exactly like Jared, was smiling.

Standing up, Jared went to the den and took the latest photograph album from a shelf. Grandpa Billy was a stickler for keeping them up-to-date.

This last year, there were more than fifty photos. The kids were in most of them. There were school photos, school activities, farm activities, church activities. There were even a few of the kids just being kids around the house.

Jared was in all of six. Hmmm, he had no excuse since Grandpa Billy was the camera man.

Matt didn't smile in any of them.

Neither did Jared.

Matt looked exactly like Jared, and maybe that wasn't a good thing.

But, it was hard to smile when your heart was broken. Jared put back the newest album and reached for last year's. It was much the same. The year before that was the same. They were all the same, clear until four years ago—the year Mandy died. Lord, he hadn't opened this one in a while, and it looked like, judging by the amount of dust, no one had. And there on the first page was the same family photograph—albeit smaller—as the one in the living room.

Matt smiling.

Mandy in her rightful place, head nestled against Jared's and a hand on the shoulder of each of her biggest boys.

He'd known the moment he had sat next to Mandy Jarrett at a church Bible Bowl practice that she was everything he'd wanted. It took him three months to work up the courage to ask if he could call. It took three phone calls—very short because he'd never been one for idle chitchat—before he finally asked her out. Their first date had been out to dinner with her parents.

He'd never been so uncomfortable in his life.

Their second date had been with his mom, Billy and Joel. It had gone a little easier because Joel carried the conversation.

Finally, after six months of parental supervision—okay, she'd been all of fifteen—they'd gone out for ice cream, just the two of them. He'd picked her up in his truck and they had a whole hour before he had to have her home.

He'd never been so comfortable in his life.

Not a chance that Maggie Tate would be a comfortable date. She'd be talking clothes and school and whether or not peanut butter could adequately stick a lunch box to a ceiling. She knew nothing about crops, football or weather cycles.

If he did invite her to come along to get a Christmas tree, what would they talk about in the truck?

Oh, Lordy, he remembered the last time she and her daughter were in the truck with him and the boys. One of the topics had been whether Jared liked girls.

No, little Miss Maggie could take care of her own tree.

She didn't need him to take her mind off a Christmas without a spouse.

"You going to sit there all night and think about calling her?" Billy came into the room, a paperback book tucked under his arm and Captain Rex at his feet. Only sixty, Billy had retired the year Mandy died. He'd taken over caring for the three boys when Jared had needed help. Today, thanks to Joel, he was more than a caregiver. He was whipping the house into shape for Joel and Beth's wedding. More than anyone, Billy knew how hard Jared worked, how hard Jared tried and how deeply Jared cared.

"Or," Billy continued, "are you going to go upstairs and round up the boys again. They've done gotten ready and now have forgotten what it is you promised them."

"No, we haven't!" Matt shouted.

"Yes, we have!" Ryan added.

"Wonder what Caleb is up to. I'll go check. Give you a little time to make the call."

"How did you—? Oh, never mind." Jared didn't want to know. "Tell them we leave in thirty minutes."

Billy nodded approvingly but said, "You're going to be late."

Jared hated being late. It took just a moment before Jared pulled out his calendar and the odds and ends of papers he collected there.

Maggie Tate's number was on top.

He'd call, but he really hoped she'd say no.

Chapter Seven

The reason Maggie said yes had to do with her daughter, sitting across the kitchen table all big-eyed, hopeful and promising to eat every last bite of her spaghetti. To Cassidy, going anywhere with kids was better than going anywhere alone and twenty times better than staying home, especially on a Saturday evening in December.

Maggie remembered feeling the same way. Only if her mother noticed, she didn't care. As for her father, if he noticed, he didn't have the time to oblige.

"We're only getting one tree," Maggie cautioned, "for downstairs. Your idea for hanging up Miss Beth's soap as ornaments was a good one."

"One tree," Cassidy agreed. The glint in her eyes said *we can renegotiate when we get wherever we're going.*

When Jared pulled up in front of their place, they were ready. Cassidy went flying, skidding on the slick sidewalk, and banging into the side of his truck.

Jared got out and steadied her. "You all right?"

"I always do that." Cassidy wasn't fazed. "It's fun."

Matt rolled down the window and frowned. Caleb, sitting in the back of Jared's extended cab, tried to climb over him, shouting, "I want to slide!"

By the opposite window, Ryan sat playing some sort of handheld device and didn't seem to notice.

"Am I in the front?" Cassidy asked. "Because I'd really rather sit in back with the boys."

"No," Matt said quickly.

"You can sit by me," Caleb offered.

"I'm not in the middle" was Ryan's only concern.

"Looks like you're in the front." Jared leaned down and in a loud whisper said, "But it's a lot warmer up there, and tonight's going to be plenty cold." He stepped back, appraising the Tate women and gave a nod.

Because of the snow, Maggie had added a red scarf to her cocoa leather and shearling coat. Her black boots weren't retro. Instead, they were inexpensive and warm. Maggie felt like she'd passed some sort of test.

Cassidy didn't seem to notice. Already she was scooting in the driver's seat, dripping bits of snow where Jared would be sitting. Maggie walked around to the passenger side, noting that very little traffic was out this cold Saturday evening. Good, maybe the small-town radar would miss this outing between two of its singles—one of whom was walking right behind Maggie, altogether too close. She was about to turn and ask him why when they reached her door. Without a word he opened it and held out a hand to help her up.

Wow.

Maggie couldn't remember the last time a gentleman opened a door for her.

After settling her in and closing her door, Jared got

behind the wheel, silently pulled out and headed for the outskirts of town.

"Tell me again where we're going," Maggie said.

"My friend Paul Decker's place. He has a Christmas tree farm over in Indianola. His family has operated it for the past fifty years."

"We've never been to a Christmas tree farm," Cassidy said. "Are there animals, too?"

"Lots of them," Caleb answered. "More than my daddy has even."

"I'm not much on livestock," Jared admitted. "Since Joel's moved home, we've doubled the number of animals."

"Have he and Beth decided what they're going to do after they get married?" Maggie knew this was a hot topic because at one time Joel had been half owner of Solitaire Farm. Since his return, Joel had worked shoulder to shoulder with Jared and profits were up, especially when it came to Solitaire's Market which, under Joel's care, had grown from a vegetable stand to a farm store.

"Not sure," was Jared's belated response.

Outside, the snow grew bigger and bolder. Inside the truck, it was dark and the smell of children and melting snow made for close quarters. Funny, Maggie usually was gripping the door handle by now. She never liked driving in snow. She never trusted anyone else driving in snow. But Jared seemed to know what he was doing and his truck, bigger than any she'd been in before, didn't seem to mind the outside conditions. Jared turned at the school and aimed his car to the emptiness of Iowa back roads.

"How long has the elementary school been at this location?" Maggie asked to break the silence.

"Since before I was born, though they've added on a time or two. This year I think they've had the highest enrollment. Billy says it's time to expand again."

"Billy?"

"Grandpa," Caleb supplied.

"You don't know Billy?" Ryan made it sound like a personality flaw.

"Watch your tone," Jared cautioned before adding, "Billy Staples. He's my stepfather and spent thirty plus years as principal of Roanoke Elementary. He helps at Solitaire Farm now. He takes care of the boys while I work."

Maggie watched as the school disappeared from view. Thirty-plus years? Imagine being in one place, one job, for that long. It was aged red brick, single level, with one class per grade.

"Was he at the Christmas party last night?"

"No." Jared turned on the high beams. "He's been fighting a cold and the cold's winning."

"I've met Grandpa Billy," Cassidy said. "He comes to school sometimes and helps. Right now he's helping with the Christmas program."

Aah, the Christmas program. Billy must be the older gentleman who sometimes helped with rehearsals.

"Any of you have parts in the play?" Maggie asked the backseat.

"Ryan has a lead," Jared said proudly.

"I give away presents," Matt answered.

"No, you don't," Caleb protested. "You just stand there."

A brief scuffle took place: Caleb whined for a moment, Matt apparently took exception to being tattled on and Ryan simply uttered, "Hey!"

"Stop" was Jared's response.

Maggie decided to try a safer discussion tactic. "I've not traveled this way."

"I've been down every road in this town it seems," Jared said. "Paul's place is about an hour away."

"And we caused you to get a late start."

"We were already running late," Ryan grumbled.

It looked like Jared was about to say something, and Maggie knew it wouldn't be something Ryan really wanted to hear.

"This is my best day ever," Cassidy said.

"Me, too," Caleb agreed.

Jared's fingers opened and closed, stretching over the steering wheel. He glanced at her and gave a tight smile.

He's as nervous as me, Maggie thought.

Paul raised an eyebrow but refrained from comment as Jared escorted Maggie and their brood into the living room. A fireplace big enough to cook in dominated the room. Two huge dogs were in front of it. Caleb and Cassidy headed for the dogs. Matt stayed by Jared's side. Surprisingly, Ryan was there, too.

"Wow," Maggie said. "This room is bigger than my whole apartment."

"My granddad was one of twelve kids. They needed a big place," Paul explained. "So, you want a tour and to pick out a tree before relaxing? Or do you want to relax before the tour and the tree?"

"Tree first!" Cassidy answered, without moving from

her location next to the dog. Caleb was trying to climb on board. His dog rolled to a standing position, dumped Caleb to the ground and came over to stand by Maggie, who quickly put a hand on the huge beast's head.

"Since my good friend here—" Paul nodded toward Jared "—seems to have forgotten his manners, I'll introduce myself. I'm Paul Decker and welcome to Decker the Halls."

"It's awesome," Maggie said. "I could see the lights for miles away. It made me think of what the shepherds must have seen when the star finally landed."

"The star landed?" Caleb asked. "Really, on the ground, by Jesus? Was everyone okay?"

"Everyone was fine," Ryan answered, rolling his eyes. Jared wasn't even tempted to talk about tone. "She means when they arrived to where the star stopped." Something was going on with his oldest son and Jared wasn't sure what. Granted, for the last two weeks, Caleb had been getting more than his fair share of attention, but Ryan hadn't been deprived.

"My wife and daughters are out helping the last few customers. Let's head over there before she shuts down. It's almost seven."

As they followed Paul out the door and past the trucks, Jared said, "Paul had all girls. I had all boys. Same ages and everything."

"Yes," Paul said, "but there might be a boy for me yet."

Jared stopped. "What? You're kidding."

"Just pretend I didn't tell you," Paul advised. "I know Wendy was itching to be the one to share the good news."

"Congratulations," Maggie said.

"A boy, huh." Jared's boots crunched in the snow as he walked alongside her. The Christmas trees flanked them. Maggie reached out a finger to touch a branch every now and then. Her cheeks were pink and her smile lit up her eyes.

"You ever go in the woods to get a tree?" he asked.

"Never. We always had a small fake one. After I married Dan, I bought a bigger one, but when we moved for the third time, I realized why my dad said, 'Never buy what you're not willing to pack.'"

"Huh?" Paul said.

"Military brat," Maggie explained. "Followed by military wife."

"But if you bought fresh trees, you'd not have to worry about packing."

"No, but you'd have to find the time to go and get..." Maggie stopped. "Let's just say that Christmas trees were never at the top of the list for things to do around Christmas time in my family."

A hunk of snow fell from the top of a tree and landed on her hat. Jared watched as she laughed while shaking it off. "I promise," she said, "they'll be a priority from now on."

She stopped in front of the tented area where Wendy, Paul's wife, and his girls were doing business. One of the neighbor boys was busy netting a purchase.

"Twenty-five for a small one," Maggie whispered. "Six dollars per foot for bigger ones."

"We're not typical customers," Jared whispered back. "Paul always sells me a tree that is somehow flawed. You know, it has too much of a gap between the branches or a crooked butt."

Caleb giggled, and Jared shot him a look.

"But you said the word b—" Caleb started.

"That's right," Jared interrupted. "I said the word, but you don't get to."

Caleb put his hands over his mouth, eyes dancing, looking like he was about to explode.

"What word does he want to say?" Cassidy asked.

"Never mind," Maggie said.

"You have a problem with her taking words out of context and being silly like this at home?" Jared asked.

"No, not really."

"I've always thought it was a boy thing," Jared agreed.

Maggie raised an eyebrow. Clearly, she wasn't convinced.

Jared looked at his three boys. Cassidy stood between Caleb and Matt. Caleb was as close to her as humanly possible without knocking her over. Matt was a good four inches away. Ryan was already talking to a girl who looked close to his age. He kept shooting glances Jared's way as if checking to make sure where he was.

"I can hardly wait to find out if that is a boy thing," Paul said.

"Yeah," Jared agreed. "Who can figure out women?"

Paul chuckled. "I was talking about girls. Guess you're thinking about women."

Jared shook his head.

This time, Paul outright laughed, almost choking as he said, "About time."

* * *

Once Wendy finished with her customer, she joined them, along with a little girl just Caleb's age named Grace. She escorted them through the rows. "We have Scotch Pine, Colorado Spruce, Frasier Fir and Balsam Fir."

"They all look the same," Cassidy noted. She looked at the little girl beside her, clearly expecting an answer, but not getting one.

"That's only because it's dark," Wendy said. "If it were daylight, you'd be able to see they have their own personality. Right, Grace?"

Grace nodded and shyly smiled. That was all the encouragement Cassidy needed. Soon the two little girls were holding hands.

The women easily left the men behind. Jared was telling Paul something about the Totwells and too many cows. That conversation was designed to make the kids scatter. Only Caleb seemed inclined to keep up with the girls. He was even willing to hold hands.

"Jared said you might have some trees on discount because of gaps or crooked butts." Maggie looked at Caleb and Cassidy. Both held mittened hands over their mouth to keep from responding.

"We do have some discounted trees. Jared and Mandy——" Wendy stopped, regrouped and said, "Jared's been bringing his family here to pick out their tree for more than a decade. It's tradition."

"How much?" Maggie asked. She had thirty-two dollars in her wallet. Hand Me Ups was closed tomorrow, so there'd be no money coming in. Plus, tomorrow they were heading to the Totwell place and Maggie might be purchasing vintage clothes. She preferred to outright buy rather than consign. She made more money that way, and right now, every dollar helped.

"We can probably find you the perfect tree for about fifteen."

"Like this one?" Cassidy stopped beside a tree double her height. "It's perfect."

"That's a Scotch Pine and definitely one of the most popular. When you get it home, and in the light, you'll see how beautiful the dark green foliage is."

"I can see that already," Cassidy said proudly.

"How old are you?" Wendy asked.

Cassidy proudly said, "Seven."

"Well, so is that tree. And, indeed, that tree is only fifteen dollars."

"Oh, Mom." Cassidy practically danced. "Can we keep it forever?"

"We'll keep it as long as we can," Maggie promised. Turning to Wendy she said, "I'm going to be putting it in my shop and hanging some of the merchandise on it."

"What kind of shop do you have?"

"Hand Me Ups, vintage clothes."

"Oh, I can't believe I didn't put two and two together. Beth talks about you all the time. I've been meaning to get into town and see what you have."

"You like vintage clothes?"

"I'm more a jeans and T-shirt kind of gal," Wendy confessed, "but I'm always looking for the perfect night-on-the-town outfit in case my husband surprises me."

"Come by. Since you're giving me a discount on the tree, I'll do the same in the store unless it's one of my consignment items."

Wendy looked back at Cassidy. "She your one and only?"

"Yes. My husband died in Afghanistan last year. We'd decided to wait until he got out of the service to have another baby."

Actually, Dan had decided that, and after Cassidy had been diagnosed with ADD, he'd stopped wanting to discuss a second child at all.

"That's tough. Jared knows how you feel. He and Mandy planned on five, same as me and Paul. She was more a jeans and T-shirt kind of gal, too. So, how long have you and Jared been going out?"

"We're not going out. Our kids are friends, and Beth pretty much convinced him that if he didn't bring me, I'd be buying a fake tree from Bob's Hardware."

Wendy shuddered. "I think Bob purchased a surplus of artificial trees back in the sixties and is still trying to foist them off on an unsuspecting public."

Maggie laughed. "An unsuspecting public would be me. Until this morning, I wasn't sure I'd even be getting a tree. Now it's going to be the centerpiece of my store."

"After you decorate the tree, call me. I'll take a picture and display it on the bulletin board in our store."

"You have a store, too?" Cassidy asked.

Grace answered, "The store has lots of candy canes."

"Among other things," Wendy said indignantly, "like tree stands, which you'll need, and wreaths, which you can buy a different year." As an aside to Maggie, she added, "Just about everyone in the area has some kind of side business, be it a store or something over the internet. We have to, in order to make ends meet." Louder, to include the kids, she said, "Let's get the men and show them your tree. It should be perfect. One thing about the Scotch Pine is the stiff branches. They'll hold up heavier items."

"Like Beth's soap," Maggie said.

"Like Beth's soap," Wendy agreed.

They led their followers back to where Jared was examining a tree even bigger than Maggie's.

Wendy said. "You guys can go ahead and cut, shake, wrap and load the trees. Jared, you bring enough blankets?"

"Matt and Ryan are fetching them now."

"Good. Maggie and I are going to go start the hot chocolate. Come to the kitchen after you've loaded everything up."

Wendy motioned for Maggie to follow. Cassidy didn't move. She stayed to make sure the men knew exactly which tree the Tate women wanted.

There was a part of Maggie that wanted to stay with the men, see what exactly happened when a Scotch Pine left the frozen ground and started its magical journey to the center of a little girl's Christmas.

Being pregnant hadn't slowed Wendy down one bit. She quickly led Maggie to a kitchen meant to feed a crowd. Soon, water was boiling and cups were set out. Wendy had a black marker—smart woman—to write names so cups didn't get mixed up.

"By the way," Wendy said, handing Maggie her hot chocolate. "Your comment about Jared bringing you because Beth convinced him to…"

Maggie took a long drink. "Yes."

"Jared doesn't do anything he doesn't want to do."

Maggie looked out the window and spotted Jared

holding one end of a giant tree. Jared did seem to know his own mind, but Maggie knew he was just doing Beth a favor by helping Maggie. That's all there was to it.

Chapter Eight

They'd stayed at the Deckers' longer than Jared intended. The boys had insisted on showing Cassidy the petting zoo. Paul was another farmer always thinking about earning an extra dollar in today's economy. Wendy had insisted on showing Maggie the store. Surprise—Maggie Tate was a woman who could enter a store and leave without purchases. Then, Paul insisted on a game of UNO that turned into five games. Everyone played except Caleb. Even Grace, who was five months younger than Caleb, knew how to play and played well.

Caleb partnered up with Maggie and made it through a game and a half before losing interest and heading off to chase the dogs.

It had been ten when Jared herded his sons out the door. Maggie and Cassidy were right behind.

Possibly because Matt fell asleep almost the minute they took off, Cassidy was quiet on the ride home and leaned against Maggie. Twice Cassidy asked for the candy cane Wendy Decker had given her on the way out. Twice Maggie said no. The second time, Maggie mentioned that if Cassidy asked again, the candy cane would be put away for an undisclosed amount of time.

Caleb's candy cane was long gone. The kid devoured it in two bites. Ryan didn't like candy canes, and Matt couldn't stay awake long enough to care about his.

How could three kids be so amazingly different?

It was eleven when Jared arrived at Maggie and Cassidy's place. Snow dripped from the eaves and the lights from the street made it, thanks to all the clothes on display, look like people were inside.

"Spooky," Caleb summed it up.

Cassidy seemed to think for a moment before saying, "But it's a good spooky."

"You need Christmas lights," Jared said.

"Next year."

Maggie and Cassidy climbed in the back of the truck and pushed, trying to unload their tree. To Jared, it looked like they laughed more than pushed. Jared, Ryan and Caleb pulled. Even with Caleb's help, or maybe because of Caleb's help, it took quite a few minutes to unload the tree.

Getting it through the door of the shop was another adventure. Once inside, it became clear that although Maggie had done well in choosing the spot—away from a heat vent—the space wasn't adequate. Jared coerced Ryan into moving a few things.

"I'll help you put it up," Jared offered.

"Dad!" Ryan's voice was a bit higher than usual. Jared's lips went together and his oldest son backed off.

"You guys are tired. It's almost midnight. I can do it," Maggie insisted.

Jared perused the room. If the tree fell, it would break things and tonight he'd realized that she was careful with her money. He respected that. Matt was sleeping on a couch Maggie had in the middle of the room. Caleb was tired, but busy with Cassidy. They were trying on old boots and dancing around. Ryan was yawning while inching toward the door. Hmm, he always begged to stay up late. Right now, the kid wasn't making much sense.

Come to think of it, neither was Jared. It was almost midnight. He'd need to get up in just another five hours. Yet, when he looked at Maggie and noted her hands, small and delicate, he shook his head. "I'll put the tree in its stand. It will only take a minute if we all work together."

"We have church in the morning." Ryan sounded just like Grandpa Billy.

"See, I don't want to keep you any longer." Maggie moved toward the front door as if to open it.

"Got an aspirin?" Jared asked.

Maggie stopped. "You have a headache?"

"No, but we need to put an aspirin in the water along with the Christmas tree food you purchased."

She smiled, no longer looking tired, but back to looking mischievous. "Are you telling me the tree has a headache?"

Jared could see Ryan shaking his head.

"No, but I'm telling you I've had real Christmas trees all my life and know what to do. Now, shall my boys and I stay a few minutes longer or do you really want to do this on your own?"

"I really want to go to church in the morning," Cassidy decided to add to the conversation, never mind she was off topic. "I haven't been in a long time."

Ryan stopped shaking his head and Jared noted the deer-in-the-headlights expression on his son's face.

"No, not this time," Maggie said. "We have things to do and—"

"She can come with us," Caleb volunteered. "We drive right by your shop every Sunday morning."

It was on the tip of Jared's tongue to say he could pick up both of them, but if he were to appear at church with both Maggie and Cassidy in tow, he might as well put an *I realize she's single and cute and I'm interested* sign on the back of his shirt.

He wasn't interested. But she was single and cute.

He wasn't looking for cute.

"We'd be glad to stop by and pick her up."

"Please, Mommy. I'll be good. I'll go to bed right now." Without waiting for an answer, Cassidy ran up the steps.

"Let's finish the tree," Maggie suggested softly. Jared noted that she hadn't given him a yes or no answer about Cassidy.

The minutes stretched into almost an hour until it was well after midnight when he finished. She'd tried—the whole time—to tell him it wasn't necessary, tried to convince him that either she could handle it herself or he could stop by tomorrow afternoon, but Jared had some thinking to do before church, during church and after church.

Some of it was about her and coming back tomorrow would only complicate matters.

His only son still awake was Ryan, and he was a

glum participant in cleaning up the pine needles that had fallen to the floor. He didn't look overjoyed when Maggie said that Cassidy could come to church with them, either.

Jared picked up Matt to carry him to the truck and Maggie headed upstairs to find Caleb. Jared was just coming back in the door when she came down. Ryan met her at the bottom of the stairs and held out his arms. Maggie handed over Caleb. Ryan headed for the truck.

When had Ryan gotten so tall?

Once everyone was buckled in, Jared got behind the wheel and with a yawn, headed home. Ryan, sitting on the passenger side, didn't say a word. Unusual? No. But tonight, there was just a bit more determination in his silence.

"You got something on your mind?" Jared finally asked.

For a moment, Ryan didn't say anything, then in a rush, "You're sure spending a lot of time with them."

"Maggie and her daughter?"

"Yes."

"And this is bothering you?"

"Yes, I like it the way it is, with Billy and Uncle Joel. We don't need anybody else in our life."

"Anybody else meaning a woman?"

Again Ryan didn't answer.

"There's nothing for you to worry about," Jared said. "Maggie's helping me figure out some things with Caleb. I'm not interested in anything else right now."

Even in the darkened cab of the truck, Jared could see the disbelief on Ryan's face.

Instead of saying anything else, Jared focused his

attention on the snowy road ahead because he didn't want to think about how *right now* had a bad habit of changing in the blink of an eye.

A light snow flaked the air Sunday morning. Maggie wished she'd have grabbed a warmer coat, but she just followed her daughter, who looked way too grown-up in her gray coat, blue velvet dress and black boots. Maggie garnered barely a wave as Cassidy exited the shop. That's how excited Cassidy was.

Maggie was of two minds as she watched her little girl, reddish-brown curls under a white winter hat, climb into Jared's truck. Jared helped her in before turning to wave at Maggie. He'd already offered to wait, had given her the chance to change her mind about coming with them, but no, this time Cassidy would have the front all to herself.

No, she wouldn't. Already Caleb, obviously ignoring his dad, was climbing in the front.

And Jared was moving him to the back where his car seat was.

Cassidy didn't need a car seat any longer. She was growing up, needing Maggie's guidance less and less, making good decisions, like *wanting to go to church.*

Maggie hoped that she, too, was making good decisions, like *letting Cassidy go to church.*

On one hand, Cassidy had been asking to go to church, and Maggie did want her daughter to know God. On the other hand, it opened a wound Maggie was trying to forget.

No, not trying to forget, a wound Maggie was trying to let heal.

Forget and forgive, two concepts Maggie seemed incapable of mastering. She'd never forget her late husband; she'd never forgive herself.

Heading back inside her shop, Maggie stopped before the Christmas tree. She'd promised Cassidy she wouldn't touch it. It hadn't looked so big back at Decker the Halls, but now it stood just to the left of her front entryway and looked huge, imposing, perfect. Ideas swirled. Christmas trees were really a shopkeeper's dream. There were so many products she could market. The tree was like a permanent salesman offering with outstretched boughs personal suggestions to anyone who walked through the door.

"Here, buy this soap. It smells like evergreen."

"Here, this hat is perfect for you. It will shelter your head."

"Here, try these socks. They'll keep your feet warm."

Maggie would carefully arrange the aged quilts right next to the new crochet blankets around the base. Doilies would be scattered like snowflakes. Scarves could be tied into bows and strategically placed.

Candy canes! Maggie needed candy canes!

Wanting to get started on those ideas practically made her fingers itch.

Heading upstairs, Maggie noted that a Sunday morning without Cassidy meant a different kind of silence than during the school week. The little apartment felt empty, wrong. Oh, evidence of her daughter was scattered across the room. A pair of shoes tried on and discarded—Cassidy was her mother's daughter. Two books her daughter had pretended to read this morning. Pretended, because Cassidy didn't like books. Maggie loved them. A half-full glass of milk was on the kitchen table. "It didn't taste good," Cassidy had said. Since she said it every time Maggie gave her milk, Maggie no longer listened. The glass went back into the fridge for later, and now Cassidy would have to drink double.

Leisurely, Maggie cleaned the apartment, taking extra care and even moving the couch to vacuum. The only thing she did in their bedroom was change the sheets. It was about time to remind Cassidy that any toys left on the floor might disappear, especially since Cassidy's bedroom was also Maggie's bedroom and Maggie didn't like stepping on tiny things.

Chores finished, Maggie went on to other items on her list, namely making sure her shop was ready for tomorrow's crowd.

Wouldn't it be wonderful if she had record sales just in time for Christmas? Only three presents were under the tree: the red boots, a book and a movie. The phone rang just as Maggie finished wrapping an empty box for under the Christmas tree downstairs. Checking the Caller ID, Maggie sighed and picked up the receiver.

"Hello, Kelly."

"I need to know when you'll be arriving. I'll arrange for someone to pick you up from the airport." If one were to look up *stubborn* in the dictionary, Dan's mother's photo was there. Kelly Tate was nearing sixty. She was a retired professor and used to handing out assignments and expecting their criteria to be met.

"We're not coming for Christmas." Maggie tried for patience, but it was the fourth time they'd had this conversation. "We came for Thanksgiving. I can't afford the travel and I don't want to close the shop. I'll make last-minute sales on Christmas Eve."

"Consider the airline tickets my present to you."

"It's just not possible this Christmas, Kelly. There's a lot of work to be done around the shop. I'm building a business."

Kelly Tate was silent. Maggie knew the woman was gripping the phone and trying to thinking of something to say that would assure a Christmas spent with her granddaughter. Finally, she mustered, "Why couldn't you have opened a shop here? I'd have helped with the finances."

She would have, too. Then, she would have pitched in—make that *tried to take over*—with raising Cassidy, and sending Cassidy to expensive private schools, and to join every dance class, karate class and soccer team that Cassidy merely indicated she was interested in. She'd have offered to pick out Cassidy's clothes and frowned at what Maggie served at the dinner table.

Control. She would have interfered with the control that Maggie so desperately needed to feel when it came to managing her life and Cassidy's life.

So far, Kelly was unaware that Cassidy had any trouble with focus. Anything her grandchild did was just fine. And, if she knew how careful Maggie was with food choices and structure, she'd have criticized.

"Are you still there?" Kelly finally asked.

"I do appreciate the offer," Maggie said, "but Cassidy and I have things to do. Maybe next Christmas."

"And then you won't come Thanksgiving."

Kelly was good, always one step ahead, and she was correct. Maggie also knew that Cassidy was an only grandchild and Maggie knew how precious family was, but sometimes her mother-in-law was like a steamroller.

When Dan was alive, they'd visited when they could, never staying more than a week. Dan admitted he'd joined the military to get away from his mom.

"You can always come here." Maggie felt safe making the offer. Kelly had clubs and commitments and a small town in Iowa just didn't offer the nightlife she was used to. Plus, there was no room at Maggie's little apartment and Kelly would go nuts stuck in one of the tiny rooms of the Roanoke Inn.

"May I speak with Cassidy?"

"She's at church."

"And you're not."

When Maggie didn't answer, Kelly backtracked. "I didn't mean for that to sound quite like it did. It's just, I'm glad she's at church. Did she go with a friend?"

"Yes."

"Did they invite you?"

"Yes."

"Oh, why don't you reconsider—"

"Kelly, Cassidy's going to be home real soon and we have an errand to run. I'll have her call you early this evening."

"All right. And remember, I'm praying for you."

After Kelly hung up, Maggie held the phone so tightly it hurt. Funny how those four little words *I'm praying for you* could pack such a punch. They erased every word Kelly spoke before and managed to end the conversation with an *I care about you* tone.

"You care about me because I'm raising your grand-daughter," Maggie muttered, pushing away the unwanted feeling she got every year around Christmas—a feeling that Dan and Cassidy had spread a blanket over until Maggie knew the warmth of a family's steady embrace. Unfortunately, Dan's deployments had worn the blanket thin in a few places. His death had unraveled many a thread.

Cassidy, however, was a master at mending the torn and tattered pieces of Maggie's heart.

Yet, Maggie couldn't completely shed the memory of feeling unwanted.

Sunday school had been easy. Jared simply dropped off Cassidy at the same classroom as Matt. He wasn't too happy about the fact that it looked like they had arrived together. Caleb had surprised Jared, though. Instead of begging to stay with Cassidy, Caleb had walked into his kindergarten class as big as could be. Of course, Beth was the teacher and Caleb would get to tell about bringing Cassidy, provided Joel hadn't already texted his fiancée.

Afterward, instead of looking for Beth, Cassidy sat next to Jared. She swung her feet, up and down, and asked him, "Do you like my shoes?"

Not once, in all his years of being a father, had one of his children asked him if he liked their shoes. Cassidy's shoes were black with silver buckles.

"They're nice."

"I like your shoes," Caleb said.

Cassidy beamed at him.

"Hey, look who's visiting."

Finally, Beth joined them. Jared expected Cassidy to change where she was sitting, but she didn't. If anything, she scooted closer as if Beth and Joel needed room. Caleb scooted closer, too. Matt scowled. Ryan was sitting with one of his friends.

"My mom said I could come."

"Next time," Beth said, "we'll get her to come, too."

"That would be fun," Cassidy agreed.

A loud "Ahem" into the microphone got everyone's attention. Soon, Cassidy and Caleb were singing. Well, Caleb was doing something like singing. He didn't know the words, just the tune. Every once in a while Cassidy glanced up at Jared as if looking for approval. He nodded and that seemed to make her happy.

Before he knew it, the singing ended, the offering took just a few minutes and then Children's Bible Hour was called. Caleb quite happily took Cassidy by the hand and tugged her to the aisle.

Matt gave a look of terror. Children's Bible Hour was for children three to eight. Matt was seven and had stopped going. He was straddling the fence between wanting to be like Ryan but also wanting to have fun. Clearly, he expected his dad to force him just to keep Cassidy happy.

But Cassidy didn't seem to notice. She let Caleb lead her along. Jared shrugged and Matt relaxed. In the moments before the sermon, Beth and Joel scooted down. Jared leaned over and whispered, "How does Cassidy know all the words to the songs?"

"Maggie sings all the time," Beth whispered back.

"Church songs?"

"They used to go to church before they moved here," Beth said softly. "Something happened right about the time her husband died. I'm not sure what, but I think Maggie is afraid of God now."

"Afraid of God?" Jared had stopped attending church after Mandy had died. He'd not been afraid of God. He'd been mad at God, furious, and glad to have somewhere to place his anger.

Make that misplace his anger.

Maggie'd said she saw no need for God. He'd interpreted that as a hole needing to be filled.

But afraid of God? Jared didn't know what to do with that information, but it sure made him want to help Maggie out.

Chapter Nine

The Totwell place was a farm so old that the once-white paint was now speckled gray. A living room window had boards nailed across it. Even to Maggie's untrained eye, it was easy to see that this was not an established *farm,* yet. There were chickens, some loose, and a barn that looked slightly better than the house.

"The Totwells have good ideas," Beth said, "but their money hasn't caught up to their ideas and they've probably bit off more than they can chew for beginners."

Sophia Totwell stepped out onto the porch. Two children quickly followed. In a heartbeat, Cassidy took off with her friend Lisa, from school, sliding across the snowy ground and heading for worlds unknown, namely the barn and all its animals. The little boy toddled behind. After a moment, everyone could hear Cassidy's squeal of joy.

Sophia shook her head. "They'll upset the chickens."

"I didn't know you could upset chickens," Maggie said.

"Neither did I," Sophia confided, "until we bought the farm."

"Let me go get her," Maggie said. "She doesn't need to scream."

"No, they'll be fine, and the kids are excited. We're so far away from everyone that playmates are few and far between. Lisa's been excited since we got home from church. She even cleaned her room. I'd rather have a clean room than calm chickens any day."

When the laughter finally ended, Beth looked toward the barn. "You do know," she asked Maggie, "that your daughter asked Santa for a pair of red boots, a puppy, a baby brother and a horse?"

"A horse! When did that get added?" Maggie shook her head. "I haven't even taken her to see Santa. I've been waiting for the perfect time to coach her."

"Coach her?" Sophia asked.

"Yes, I want to coach her to ask Santa for a few things that actually might appear under the tree. So far, the only thing she's getting from that list is the red boots."

"Santa came to the school on Friday," Beth said. "I was his helper for a while. Quite a few kids asked for horses."

Sophia led them into the house. "Lisa's got all four—red boots, a puppy or two, a baby brother and a horse. She'd rather move back to Omaha or at least live in town and have playmates."

"Living in town doesn't necessarily mean play-mates," Maggie said. "We live above the shop, not in a neighborhood, so there are no kids. Plus, we don't have a yard so she can't even invite friends over, not really. If I sat on Santa's knee, I'd be asking for a yard."

"I'd be asking for the perfect wedding dress," Beth put in.

"I'd be asking for a husband who's not always tired," Sophia said. "Speaking of which..."

The man entering the room had to be Kyle Totwell. Maggie hadn't met him before, but he shyly put out his hand for her to shake and then turned to Beth. "You think Joel'd have some time this afternoon to come out and help me put in a window?"

In answer, Beth whipped out her cell phone and sent a text. A moment later she nodded. "He says give him about an hour."

Sounding ever so much like an old cowboy, he said, "Much obliged," before heading back outside.

All three women giggled, and Sophia said, "Sometimes I think he thinks he's John Wayne."

It was enough to change the mood back to humor. Sophia started them on a tour, which began in the living room where the boarded-up window was.

"When we got home from church last Sunday, someone had broken the window, climbed in and taken the presents under the tree," Sophia said.

"Did they take anything else?" Beth asked.

Maggie followed Sophia's eyes as they swept the room.

"We didn't notice anything else missing," Sophia said, "and quite honestly, if I were the thief, I'd take one look around my house and think to myself 'I'm not going to waste my time.'"

"Your house isn't a waste of time," Maggie said. "It fits you and only you."

"True," Sophia agreed. "The couch belonged to my

grandmother, the kitchen table, too. All the utensils in my kitchen came from my mother and Kyle's. Even the quilt on our bed came from Grandma. Right now we live in a family cast-off melting pot of furniture and appliances."

"I didn't know my grandparents," Beth said. "I think you're lucky."

"I didn't know mine, either," Maggie added. "But I have a mother-in-law who takes up a lot of my time."

Both Sophia and Beth looked curious but neither ventured to ask. Maggie was glad. She didn't want to explain or complain about Kelly.

Sophia rubbed her hand on an old oak display cabinet. "This was Kyle's grandfather's. It's my favorite. We have antiques, but most are not in perfect condition like this one. Plus, they're not that easy to steal."

"Did they get all the kids' Christmas presents?" Maggie asked.

"No, I still have some hidden away to wrap but they got most."

"There's been a rash of break-ins," Beth said. "I know of at least four other families." For the next few minutes, they discussed the whens and wheres of the thefts. Seemed they only happened on Sunday morning while people were at church but didn't seem to be in a concentrated area.

Another reason for me not to go to church, Maggie thought but didn't say.

"Come see the rest of the house," Sophia finally said. "It will be cute when we finish. I'll tell you how we got here, too."

The farmhouse had two stories. Downstairs was a

living room and kitchen and bath. Upstairs were two bedrooms and a bath. Sophia led them to a bedroom that was smaller than the one Maggie shared with her daughter. About an hour later, Maggie knew that Kyle Totwell had been close to his grandfather who'd been an Iowa farmer in the fifties. That farm was long gone and Kyle's dad worked in Omaha, as far away from the farm as he could be, but Kyle had a dream and right now, the Totwells, albeit haltingly, were living that dream.

"Kyle didn't realize how hard farming really is," Sylvia confided.

Maggie remembered Jared saying something about buying too many cows too soon, but she didn't quite understand why that was a bad thing. Maybe it was a money thing.

"The previous owners, who've been gone forever, left a few things in the barn and down in the basement. I'm just now getting around to sorting through everything in the attic. That's why I called you. We thought it was pretty much empty except for rotting furniture, but then we moved an old bed frame and found the trunks.

In anticipation of their visit, Kyle had carried the trunks into their bedroom and Sophia had started to spread out the clothes. Because the room was small, she'd quickly consumed the space. Some items were rotted beyond repair, others were a yellow that Maggie couldn't begin to tackle, but a few had promise.

"The ugliest trunk actually had the nicest clothes," Sylvia said. "But, it smelled of mothballs."

"Mothballs? Now there's a smell I haven't missed," Beth said.

Maggie went down to her knees by the first trunk.

Sophia had half unpacked it. A quick look through what was left told Maggie everything she needed to know. "Mostly ladies' clothes from after the 1950s."

"How can you tell?" Sophia asked.

"By where the zippers are and the style." Maggie pulled a skirt from under a jacket. "Whoever owned these was very slim, probably a size four."

"I can't see a farmer's wife wearing that skirt," Sophia said.

Maggie nodded, her throat tightening a bit. She wasn't a size four, but this skirt was very much like the red velvet one she'd worn two Fridays ago when she'd paid Beth a visit at school. Not practical, but very stylish. And not the usual style of a farmer's wife. Probably not what Jared's wife would have worn to see her boys' teacher and certainly not to chase after her boys.

"Who says?" Beth challenged. "I think fifty years ago, maybe you were right, but today, a farmer's wife can wear anything she pleases."

"I wouldn't wear that skirt even if I was a size four. I'm happy in jeans," Sophia said.

"She wore jeans to church this morning," Beth told Maggie.

Sophia snapped, "It's the going to church that's important, not what you wear."

"Touché," Beth replied.

Twice Maggie went out to check on Cassidy. Both times Cassidy said this was the best day ever and the only thing that would possibly make it better was if she could take one of the horses home with her.

Sophia poured iced tea and brought cookies to the ladies as they went through the clothes. One pile was throwaways. One pile was giveaways. The last pile was Maggie's takeaways. Sophia gladly took the fifty dollars offered.

"But we didn't find a wedding dress," Beth said sadly.

"What kind of wedding dress do you want?" Sophia asked.

"We decided to go vintage." Ever the teacher, with her fingers Beth drew in the air. "Joel's wearing a turn-of-the-century black suit with bow tie and spats. I've even convinced him to wear a ruffled, maroon-front shirt."

"It's called a 'gambler' look," Maggie told Sophia.

"What are spats?"

"They go on the shoes," Maggie explained. "Have you ever seen a marching band? It's the material that covers the instep and ankle."

"Oh, I know what you're talking about. Why would you want him to wear spats?"

"I'm having the wedding of my dreams. After all, you only get married once."

Sophia nodded.

Maggie wanted to nod, wanted to agree, but she knew it wasn't always true. She was just twenty-seven and if she were to only be married once, her dreams for a bigger family, for someone to welcome home—a home with a yard and a puppy—at night, go for walks with, okay, *cuddle with,* were over. Instead she asked, "Have you convinced Jared to wear the spats?"

"No, not yet. I'm still working on him. I want everything to be authentic."

"So," Sophia said softly, "you want a turn-of-the-century wedding dress."

"Yes, but so far, we haven't found the right one."

"What size are you?"

Beth looked a bit surprised but wasn't shy. "I'm a twelve."

"I'm a ten, but it might work," Sophia said. "Follow me."

Back downstairs they went, to a storage area under the stairs. Sophia knew right where to look. After a minute of rearranging, grunting and a few interesting words like, "Well, shoot a monkey," she got hold of a good-sized cardboard box and dragged it into the living room. If Sophia weren't so far away, Maggie'd think about hiring her for the shop. She'd done everything right. She'd chosen an acid-free box and then she'd actually taken the time to fold whatever was inside accordion style with tissue paper between each fold. There was crumpled tissue everywhere.

"Oh, my," Beth said as Sophia held up the wedding dress.

"It was my great-grandmother's. She got married in 1936. My grandmother wore it in 1958. Mom skipped it and bought a new one, but I wore it just ten years ago. I'm saving it for Lisa, if she wants it, but it's too beautiful not to share. Would you like to borrow it?"

Beth managed a nod. Maggie doubted she could manage even that. She wasn't breathing. In all her years, she'd never seen, come across, anything so beautiful. And, obviously the women who'd worn it before Sophia had cared enough to preserve it. Maggie went to her knees, holding the material reverently in her hands and gently spreading it so Beth could see its true potential. "Rayon satin, net lace, a lace overcoat."

"Will it fit me?" Beth asked. "It looks small."

"It's a bias gown," Maggie said. "It's meant to hug your figure. You'll look awesome."

"I'm a size bigger than Sophia so there's more to hug. Are you sure?" Beth didn't look or sound near as excited as Maggie thought she should be.

"I'm sure, plus with the lace overcoat, you'll feel like a princess."

"You already look like one." A gust of cold air preceded Joel's entry. Immediately, Beth did look like a princess thanks to the expression on her face. Love did that to a gal. Maggie only hoped her face didn't look so much like an open book because right behind Joel came Jared, and Maggie's first instinct was to smile.

Jared shook the snow from his boots in the entryway. That's when he had noticed Maggie down on her hands and knees in the living room looking ever so much like a kid who'd just opened a much-wanted Christmas package.

"You going to stay here in the cold or go in?" Joel asked, tugging Jared forward. It was love, pure and simple, that had his little brother in a rush. Like a moth to a flame, Joel crossed the room to put his arm around Beth.

Kyle helped his wife to her feet, but Jared could tell that Maggie was happy right where she was.

"What do you have that out for?" Kyle looked at the wedding dress in Maggie's hands. "You buying it, too?"

Sophia almost let go of his hand and fell to the floor. "Are you kidding? No, I'd never sell it. But, I'm going to lend it to Beth for her wedding."

Jared studied the dress Maggie was holding and opened his mouth to say, "Looks small." The slightest shake of Maggie's chin told him that she knew what he was thinking and that she thought he should think twice.

Good advice.

Joel didn't need such assistance. "It will look great on you."

Yep, Joel wasn't just in love, he was besotted. Otherwise, he'd never have agreed to wear spats at his wedding.

Kyle was no dummy. He was helping his wife to her feet again and whispering something in her ear that had her smiling.

"How long have you two been married?" Joel asked.

"Going on ten years."

Jared closed his eyes. That's how long he'd been married. He opened his eyes and saw Maggie Tate watching him, an expression he couldn't read on her face.

"We got married in Omaha," Sophia said, "at a castle."

"A castle?" Beth was clearly intrigued. She, however, looked at Joel and said, "Don't worry. I'm quite happy that we'll be getting married at your place."

"No castles in Roanoke," Jared said.

"I'm surprised there's a castle in Omaha," Joel said. "I hear there's a shortage of moats there."

"It was built by a newspaper tycoon," Sophia said, "and it really looks like a castle." She practically flew from the room and after a moment returned with a white frilly photograph album. "See, turrets and everything."

Maggie gently lay the wedding dress back in its box and got to her feet. Looking at the pictures, the women oohed and aahed. Even Joel, peering over Beth's shoulder, looked vaguely interested. Kyle stood back aways. His face had that slightly embarrassed but proud look a man gets when his wife or kids have put him in an unwanted but favorable limelight.

Jared came a little farther in the room, not liking the cold against his back—a draft came through the broken window—and wanting to see the castle and feel a part of the conversation, even if it was about weddings. "Quincy didn't build a castle when he started the *Roanoke Times*."

"Hard to build much more than a shed with a once-a-month tabloid," Joel agreed. The brothers were the only Roanoke natives in the room.

"I had six bridesmaids," Sophia remembered.

"I'm just having my sisters. And Maggie's making their dresses. They'll be the same burgundy—"

"Dark maroon," Maggie corrected.

"—as the shirts Joel and Jared will be wearing."

"Cool," Sophia said approvingly. "I had pink, and I carried roses. Then the cake had roses—at least the first cake—on it. My cake was a five tier, and we ran out. My father ran to the nearest store and bought a big sheet cake. Otherwise, we wouldn't have had a piece to put in the fridge for our first anniversary."

"'Bout ran out of that one, too," Kyle contributed. "I thought her dad was going to faint."

Sophia chuckled. "Dad was more stressed by the wedding than either my mother or me. He found the place and he was actually more of a wedding planner than our actual wedding planner. I kept trying to calm him down and tell him the only thing he had to do was give me away."

"We're getting married in Joel's living room," Beth said. "Billy's giving me away."

It's my living room, Jared thought to himself. Immediately, he blocked the thought. It was Joel's home, too, and Billy's job was to give the bride away. Their stepfather had been honored when they had asked.

Beth was still speaking. "I won't need to decorate much because we're doing a Christmasy theme. The tree will still be up and there's a bunch of empty presents I've wrapped that will be placed around the room."

"Where did you get married, Maggie?" Sophia closed her album.

"I got married in Hawaii."

The oohs and aahs came again, but Maggie merely shook her head. "Dan was about to be deployed, and we didn't have much time, so we went to the courthouse and the Justice of the Peace married us."

"No bridesmaids," Sophia said.

"No cake," Beth added.

"No hassle," Joel said, earning him a punch.

Jared tried to imagine what Maggie must have looked like, what? Eight or nine years ago? Judging by her looks, she'd have just been barely twenty, only a little older than Mandy.

"You didn't want all the fuss?" he asked. "I mean, you like clothes so much."

"Clothes are easy—weddings are not."

Jared wondered what Maggie meant by *weddings are not.* Was it just the actual wedding day? Or, had she been thinking clothes are easy, and the wedding day and all the days after, the married days that followed, were not.

Chapter Ten

It took almost an hour for the men to replace the glass in the Totwells' living room window. The room went from cold, thanks to no glass in the frame, to freezing thanks to no glass in the frame *and* kids opening and closing the front door every two minutes. Cassidy was in her element, with everyone she loved nearby and lots of kids to play with. The yard, puppies and horses were just icing on the cake.

Finally, when it looked like one more door slam would send the men into anti-Santa mode, Beth headed outside to play with them. That's what the kids really wanted, an adult to play with them.

Maggie watched the men for a few minutes. "I might need to do this. The windows in my apartment are in wooden frames like this. I know I have some mold."

"We're grateful to be switching to double paned," said Kyle.

Maggie nodded. She'd be grateful, too. Maybe in a year or two. Leaving the men to their work, she sat next to Sophia and inch by inch they went over the dress. It was in great condition, considering its age, but the net lace needed stabilizing. Maggie could do that. There was also a bit of dirt along the hemline.

"Do you think this is the dress Beth really wants?" Sophia asked. "She acted excited for a moment and then nothing."

"She's overwhelmed. And, if it's not the dress for her, I can still do the repairs for you since you're thinking ahead to Lisa. I'll take it to the store and put it on one of my dress forms. Believe me, when she sees it, she'll fall over with joy."

"That would be great. I sew, quite a bit, but this is out of my league. Mom hired someone to go over it before my wedding."

"They did a pretty decent job." Not as good as Maggie would have done. She could tell repairs done by commission compared to repairs done by commitment. For her, working on a dress like this would be a labor of love.

"Mom wanted everything to be perfect."

"Will you and Kyle head to Omaha for Christmas?" Maggie asked, starting to carefully return the dress to the box.

"Yes, both sets of parents are there. We'll do Kyle's house in the morning, and mine in the afternoon. I'm not sure how we'll manage everything. Both sides are big gift givers. We spend the night, but Kyle wants an early start for home the day after Christmas. We can't leave the cows alone, and there's really no one else to pitch in."

"Did you ask Joel or Jared?"

"Joel's getting married just a week after Christmas,"

Sophia reminded. "And, Jared… Well, Kyle doesn't feel comfortable asking him. He's already so busy."

Maggie looked over to where Jared was doing something with a paintbrush near the window frame. He did look more serious than the other two men.

That serious look might make someone think twice about approaching him. Two weeks ago, Maggie would have thought the same thing, considered Jared McCreedy daunting, but now, not so much. If anything, it was just that he was so straightforward in everything he did. Standing around talking future wedding plans hadn't been something he *wanted* to do, but he'd done it and even asked a question or two. She thought back to their talk Friday night in the church nursery. For all his rough exterior, Jared actually just might have a true father's heart.

"Where are you going for Christmas?" Sophia asked.

"I'm looking forward to just staying home. We went to New York and my mother-in-law's for Thanksgiving. It was a whirlwind of activity. I'm ready for some downtime. Cassidy and I will eat, build a snowman, eat again and then watch a favorite Christmas movie."

"That actually sounds like fun." Sophia looked at the Christmas tree standing in the corner of her living room.

Maggie looked, too. She watched as the three men neared the end of installing the window. Once they'd started, Jared had relaxed. She admired how easily he worked as a team and followed Joel's instructions.

"We have to pack to go to Omaha," Sophia said. "Both sides of the family celebrate big. Then, coming back, we'll be bringing more stuff. Sometimes I don't know what to do with it all."

Kelly didn't quite get the concept of too much stuff. If she had her way, Maggie's apartment would be so crowded, there'd be no room to walk.

That was just one more reason why Maggie and Cassidy were taking care of themselves this Christmas.

The men finished about the time the children and Beth came in. Matt walked right next to her, talking more than Maggie had seen before. He had an earnest expression—quite like his dad's—on his face. Cassidy and Lisa were just behind, all red cheeked and laughing. Caleb and Lisa's little brother, David, skipped along behind them. They'd taken off their boots in the entryway, but Caleb's wet socks left soppy footprints across the room. David made it worse by purposely stepping wherever Caleb stepped.

"Where's Ryan?" Jared asked.

Lisa stopped, looking around. "Still in the barn, I think. He doesn't want to come in. We told him he had to but he laughed."

Jared shook his head.

"Where did you get married, Jared?" Maggie asked, taking them back to the earlier conversation. "Everyone else shared."

The paintbrush he held in his hand stilled. Joel almost seemed to settle back, as if anticipating the response.

Maggie wished the words back. It really hadn't been her place to ask.

He looked at Joel, a slow grin with a half smirk,

spreading across his face. "I got married at the church, like my dad before me and his dad before him."

"I should have guessed the church," Maggie said.

"I never would have guessed you for a Justice-of-the-Peace kind of gal." He nodded at the wedding gown. "You're so talented and creative. Seems you would have put together quite a show."

Maggie shook her head. "My dad was in North Korea and couldn't get back. Dan's mother told him not to get married. Then, she didn't come to the wedding because she thought if she refused, we wouldn't get married. By the time she realized we were serious, it was too late. We were married and she'd missed it."

"Why didn't she want you to get married?" Sophia was clearly puzzled.

"It wasn't that she didn't want us to get married, but more she wanted us to get married in New York so that she could plan it."

"What's wrong with that?"

"I didn't want a big wedding and neither did Dan. We just wanted to get married and get busy with life, have some fun, start a family. She wouldn't listen when he tried to tell her."

"What about your mother?" Beth asked. "You never talk about her. Did she come?"

Maggie stood up and busied herself putting away the wedding dress. She made sure each fold was protected with tissue paper. She wasn't going to cry, not with all these people around, not with Jared around.

"I haven't seen my mother since I was twelve. I have no idea where she is."

Sophia put a hand on Maggie's arm, staying Maggie's movements. "That's rough. I'm so sorry."

"It's life," Maggie said simply. "You deal with it, and go on. All you can do is make sure you don't make the same mistakes with your own children."

"Mothers make mistakes," Beth said gently.

Both McCreedy men were nodding. Joel was probably thinking about Beth's mother, who was currently serving time for embezzlement after trying to frame him. Jared was probably thinking of Mandy who wasn't around to help him raise three boys.

Not her mistake really, Maggie thought. Unlike Maggie's mother, Mandy McCreedy's leaving hadn't been desired, planned and executed by a woman who *chose* to leave behind a child.

Driving straight to church from the Totwells', Jared looked in the rearview window at his sons. Caleb was in the middle, happy as could be. He'd eaten two hot dogs—lately everybody seemed inclined to serve hot dogs—and had two of Matt's toy men and was doing battle. Matt was happy, too. He'd spent the entire dinnertime telling Beth everything he wanted for Christmas—skateboard, bike, scooter with sparks, etc.—and was now dreaming about getting them all.

Not a chance.

Ryan was the quiet one. He'd eaten half a hot dog.

Joel's eyes met Jared's.

So Joel saw it, too.

The church's parking lot was full. The Christmas season made people seek out hearth and home. There was no better hearth and home than church. Jared stopped in front of the door and let out the boys. No sense having them tramp through the snow and take more of it inside than necessary.

"You see Billy's car?" Joel asked.

"No, but I haven't looked yet. Ryan, you guys find Billy or go to our usual place and sit down. I'll be right behind."

"Yeah, Dad."

Jared expected Joel to exit but he didn't. The minute Ryan shut the door, Joel asked, "What's with Ryan?"

Jared thought about pretending ignorance but the truth always came out in the end. "He thinks I'm spending too much time with Maggie. He told me last night that he likes the way it is right now with just me and Billy taking care of them."

Joel whistled. "I didn't see that coming."

Jared pulled forward. Another car was behind him wanting to deposit people at the front entrance.

"Me, either. Especially since there's nothing between Maggie and me outside of having kids the same age."

"Are you sure about that?"

Jared nodded as he pulled into a parking spot. "If, and I do mean if, I date or get married again, I want someone who'll be happy as a farmer's wife. I don't see Maggie taking to that role. She likes fancy clothes and running her shop."

"You've spent the whole weekend tog—" Joel began.

"We happened to be at the same places at the same time. Saturday was Beth's fault."

"I hear you had a good time."

Jared opened the door and stepped into the snow. "I did have a good time. It's time I start getting out more."

Joel put his hands together as if in prayer. "About time. Please keep going out. And you couldn't find a nicer girl than Maggie."

"Who doesn't believe in God," Jared pointed out. "When you invited her to join us tonight, she didn't even hesitate in saying no."

"She believes in God," Joel said. "Beth and I think something happened when her husband died and that she's not been able to shake it."

Joel shut the truck's passenger side door and came around to join Jared. Putting one gloved hand on Jared's shoulder, he said, "I saw that happen to somebody else I know."

Jared made the phone call Monday morning. Monday before noon, he picked up Caleb from school and they went to Dr. Lazurus's office. Lazurus looked well past retirement, acted as if he knew everything—he did—and had the energy of someone just out of med school. He'd delivered all three of Jared's boys as well as Jared.

The front desk staff greeted Caleb by name and promised, "No shots." The nurse, who'd been in Jared's graduating class, weighed and measured Caleb, also promising, "No shots."

"Thanks, Patty. When did you move back?"

The Maynards were another farm family that had been around forever.

Patty chuckled. "Four months ago. I've been at church every time you have. I finished my degree and worked in an emergency room for six years, and finally realized why I wasn't happy."

"Why?"

"I missed my family, and I didn't like living where I could spit out the window and hit the house next door."

Jared grinned. She'd grown up with five brothers and could out-spit just about all of them.

Finally Jared and Caleb were sent to a room to wait for Dr. Lazurus. Once in the tiny observation room, Jared was at a loss. There were a few magazines, none interested Caleb. There were a few toys, all too young for Caleb, or maybe Caleb had already played with them when Billy brought him to the doctor's.

Caleb did exactly what he did at home. He explored, first everything on counters and then he lay on the floor and crawled under the table to see if anything was hidden under there. He went to the bathroom, again. He wandered out into the hall to watch the fish. Then, he wanted to wrestle.

"Not here, Caleb," Jared said.

"Why not?"

"This is a place of business."

Caleb looked around as if not convinced. Idly he stuck out his foot and kicked Jared gently in the shins and then grinned.

At home, Jared would have sent Caleb to his room, and if Caleb balked, Jared would have escorted him. Here at a doctor's office, Jared didn't have the same options, not unless he wanted the doctor to see a screaming kid when he finally showed up.

"Stop."

Caleb did, sort of. He stood by the door and kicked it instead of Jared.

Jared was in the process of pulling Caleb back to the bench to sit beside him when the door opened and Dr. Lazurus came in.

"Good to see you, Jared. Billy feeling all right?"

It was an innocent question but reminded Jared of who usually brought Caleb to the doctor, and who— now that Jared thought about it—usually made sure that a few toys and a drawing table came along.

"He's fine. I brought Caleb because I have a few questions."

Dr. Lazurus consulted a folder and then wrote something down before patting the observation table. Caleb climbed up easily. It took all of three minutes. Dr. Lazurus checked Caleb's ears, both with an instrument and then in a room with a machine. Jared didn't get to go to that test. Then, Dr. Lazurus did an eye test and listened to Caleb chatter about who got a gold star in class this morning. He also checked Caleb's reflexes and listened to Caleb talk about how many toys he had before checking Caleb's heart and listening to Caleb talk about having hot dogs last night at the Totwells'. Dr. Lazurus had patience. Checking the heart was a problem because Caleb needed to be quiet, and Caleb wasn't done telling Dr. Lazurus who was at dinner last night.

A few minutes later, Jared sat in Dr. Lazurus's office. It was full of toys and photos of his patients. Jared had no clue where his photo was in the collage, but he knew it was there. Caleb's was near the door.

Nothing wrong with Caleb's smile. Caleb could give half of it to Matt and no one would notice.

Jared suddenly wished he'd come to every single doctor's appointment with all his boys. He needed to know how they acted and what the doctor said firsthand. He needed to be involved in every facet.

Because Mandy wasn't here, and Billy was slowing down.

And because it was a father's job.

Maggie Tate had probably been to every appointment.

Caleb was up front with a nurse who also happened to have been his cradle roll teacher at church. Dr. Lazurus studied a chart before saying, "Caleb's teacher has good instincts. I'm glad we're looking into this now."

"I'm hoping it's just that he's an active little boy," Jared said. "I've been watching him all week at home, though. He runs roughshod over Matt, who takes it pretty well. He tries the same with Ryan. My older son's a little too willing to barricade himself in his bedroom."

Dr. Lazurus nodded.

"I've ordered a few books off the internet," Jared continued. "Maggie Tate recommended them."

"She's a good resource," Dr. Lazurus agreed. "Every child is different, though. What's working for Maggie might not work for Caleb."

"What happens if we wait until first grade, see how much he matures in a year? If we're having the same problems, I'll take action."

"It's an option," Dr. Lazurus agreed. "If you're right, nothing lost. However, if you're wrong, and Caleb does have Attention Deficit, then you've lost a whole year where he could have been getting help."

"What kind of help?"

"Some of it's diet."

Maggie had mentioned limiting sugar, watching dyes and something about fried chicken.

"I can work on his diet," Jared volunteered. "He gets way too much sugar."

"Some of it has to do with learning styles and getting him additional outside-the-classroom help—help that the state pays for."

"I can pay for what my son needs."

"It has nothing to do with what parents can and cannot pay. It has everything to do with the resources the school district is required by law to provide."

"I don't want him to be different."

"Every child is different. It would be boring if we were all the same."

Jared tried to smile. "That's one thing Caleb isn't. That kid's never boring."

Dr. Lazurus put the file on his desk and waited.

"Can you do the testing here?" Jared finally said.

"Some. Based on what you've told me and what his teachers say, I'd like you to see a pediatric allergist along with the developmental pediatrician. You'll need to go into Des Moines. Has the school already made a recommendation?"

"So, it could it be something besides Attention Deficit?"

"It could."

Dr. Lazurus's eyes were the same color as Maggie's, a dark liquid green. Both were wise when it came to children. Wiser than Jared, that's for sure.

Jared left the doctor, went to the front where the

receptionist handed him two business cards for some center in Des Moines and the allergy place. She also gave him a sheet of paper, some sort of behavioral list for Caleb's teacher, as well as the paperwork for Caleb's blood tests.

Blood tests?

"They'll be asking for these," the nurse said. "You might as well be prepared."

Somewhat in a daze, Jared guided his son to the truck. Suddenly, this whole focus issue seemed more than Jared expected.

Unaware of his dad's turmoil, Caleb opened his lunch box and took out his peanut butter and jelly sandwich. "You want half, Dad?"

"No, I'm good."

"You're always good."

Not always, Jared thought, turning on the ignition and heading back toward the elementary school. Ryan had play rehearsal right after school, and Jared had promised to help with the sets.

I'm not good at always making the right choices when it comes to my boys. That had been Mandy's job, with Jared sharing his thoughts. Making all these decisions alone was hard. But it had to be done. Jared thanked God for the doctor, for everyone trying to help, especially Maggie, and for the cold slapping against his cheeks.

What was it Maggie had said last Friday night while they were in the nursery?

This is nothing. It could be so much worse.

Maggie's words of wisdom played over and over in

his mind. She was right that it could be worse. Still, Jared couldn't grasp the concept of this being *nothing*. It was something. Something Jared didn't know how to deal with.

One more thing Jared didn't know how to deal with.

Chapter Eleven

Maggie stood on the stage of Roanoke Elementary and watched as the children who'd won the coveted lead roles practiced. Ryan McCreedy, without his handheld, was actually a pretty animated kid. Cassidy had been of two minds about trying out. She thought it would be great fun to be on stage but a great amount of work to memorize her lines.

In the end, Cassidy had won the role of lead elf, which is how Maggie wound up making fifty elf hats. Cassidy had no lines but got to stay by the giant Santa bag and hand out presents to all the elves who then went into the audience and distributed them randomly. Each present contained a candy cane.

"We really appreciate you helping out with the costumes," Cassidy's teacher said. Mrs. Youst was older, almost retirement age, and had been teaching second grade longer than Maggie had been alive. She had the patience of Job.

"I like to help."

"Used to be all the mothers knew how to sew. Now,

there's just a handful. You're the best thing to come along since Mandy McCreedy."

Maggie bristled about being compared to Mandy. From what everyone was saying, Maggie knew she was about as different from Mandy as different could be.

"My job is sewing. Beth said she'd help." Maggie nodded toward Beth, who was in front of the four students playing the leads. She had a script in one hand. Her other hand was like a conductor, up and down, as she gave instructions.

Maggie studied the students. Ryan's Santa costume was finished. Good thing because he looked to be in a grumpy mood lately. Maggie wasn't quite sure why, but whenever she came near him, to adjust a seam or check on a hem, he practically tripped over himself to get away. Mrs. Santa was a little lost in her costume. The pillow needed to be adjusted. The two Claus children were fine.

Glued to Beth's side was Matt. He wasn't a lead character, but an elf. Still, he liked to be where Beth was.

Caleb had shown up after rehearsal started. He followed behind his dad, waved at everybody like they were waiting for him and even managed to drive in a nail or two. Jared was standing right beside him, guiding every move. It looked like Jared was guiding everyone's moves. He barked orders, looking stressed the whole time and didn't give even a little encouragement to the crew he directed.

Okay, Maggie could cut him some slack. The scenery should have been finished a week ago, but the other dad who'd volunteered had wound up working overtime, so Jared and a few others had taken over and were now behind.

Jared looked up at one point, found her staring and gave her a smile. Then, just as quickly, he went back to what he was doing, leaving Maggie to wonder what the smile meant.

"Nothing, it meant nothing," she muttered.

"What did you say?" Mrs. Youst asked.

"I didn't say anything," Maggie said. After all, if she didn't say anything, that meant she'd said nothing which is exactly what she'd said.

Maggie looked around for Cassidy and finally located her inside the giant Santa sack that Maggie had finished just last week.

"There are no presents in there," Maggie shouted.

"I know!"

Comfortable that the costumes were fine, Maggie called Cassidy over, bundled her up and they started walking home. They'd not even crossed the street outside the school before Maggie realized everything wasn't fine. Cassidy's head was down. She seemed very interested in staring at exactly where her boots landed and how long they stayed in one spot before she stepped to another.

"You might as well tell me," Maggie encouraged.

"Well, I did throw Matt's lunch box today, but when the teacher asked me to stop, I did. Right away. And I even went and picked it up and gave it back to him."

"Why did you mess with his lunch box?"

"He had two candy bars. Two! I never even get one." Cassidy was very aware of the good things her friends got to eat that she didn't.

"Candy bars are treats, nothing more, and certainly nothing to throw a lunch box over."

"I told him I was sorry."

On one hand, Cassidy's teacher hadn't deemed it necessary to write a note. And, Cassidy had owned up to the misdeed. Granted, she thought that Maggie already knew.

Just another manic Monday.

"Anything else happen?" Maggie asked.

Her shoes still bore the lion's share of Cassidy's attention. "No," she squeaked.

Maggie knew something else had happened; she just wasn't sure what.

The walk home was quiet. Cassidy seemed determined to be good, as if being good now would remedy any past or future offenses.

As they neared Hand Me Ups, Maggie started walking faster. Even a block away she could see the door open to her shop. No one was entering or exiting.

The door shouldn't be open.

Maggie had put up her Be Back At… sign before leaving for Cassidy's school. She'd locked the door, no doubt. And she was definitely back before her specified time.

"Stay here!" she ordered Cassidy.

Running had never been her strong point. Today, this moment, changed all that. She sludged through the snow, her boots sinking momentarily but never for long and finally skidded to a stop by her front door, looked in and almost went to her knees. The once-proud Christmas tree was leaning toward the cash register. There were doilies on its branches, but that was about it.

"Mama, what's wrong?" Cassidy hadn't been able to obey, and for once, Maggie didn't blame her.

"It's all right. It's all right." Maggie didn't know what else to say. Her repetitious words didn't begin to soothe Cassidy.

"It's all right." Maggie felt inside her purse and pulled out her phone. She punched in 911. Even as the connection began, Henry Throxmorton from across the street hurried toward her. His old-fashioned gray coat flapped in the wind. "I've already called the chief of police," he shouted. "He's on his way."

Maggie stared at Hand Me Ups's door, noting the screwdriver stuck in the lock and the snow blowing in on her clean floor. "Did you see what happened?"

"No, but my wife was upstairs in our apartment and thought she heard a car backfire. When she looked out, she saw your door was open." He took Maggie by the arm, his red face grim as he looked at her shop and then up and down the street. "Come to my place. You don't want to touch anything. We can watch your building until the police get here."

"I don't want to leave the door open." She wanted to go inside, start inventorying, start cleaning, start screaming, but she couldn't do that last one until Cassidy was asleep or something.

Henry kicked the door shut and took her arm again. He turned her toward his shop and gave a little push. Cassidy ran ahead of her.

"I didn't think anything of it," Henry said, "until Tess said something about your door being open and you not being there and maybe I should head over to close it.

I'd seen you leave for the school play a good hour ago, so I knew something was wrong."

They were halfway across the street when Henry shared, "I've been broken into four times in the last ten years. Best to let the police go in first." Right there in the middle of the Main Street, he patted his head. Maggie imagined stitches and lumps.

"Mama, what's wrong?" Cassidy repeated.

"I think someone broke into our shop."

Think? She didn't think. She knew. She blinked back tears.

"Did they take my presents?" Cassidy's face turned white and she turned, taking three steps back the way they'd come. Maggie clutched her daughter close. There were only three presents under the tree, all for Cassidy.

"I'm not sure," Maggie said. "When the police come, we'll find out."

"Wait!" Cassidy said. "Did they take your money, Mama? Did they hurt your clothes?"

"I don't know about the money, but they didn't have time to hurt all the clothes. We'll be fine. The important thing is that we weren't home and so we're not hurt. God took care..."

She'd almost said *God took care of us.* But, at the moment, she didn't want to give God credit for that. Who knew what damage the half-fallen Christmas tree—a tree Maggie hadn't really wanted—had done. Most of the stuff underneath had been consignment. Maggie would now have to pay vendors for stock she'd collected nothing on.

And what about upstairs? Besides Cassidy's presents

there wasn't much else, not that a crook would want, but the computer…

If they took the computer, she'd be dead in the water. All her records, her contacts… Yes, she had the important stuff saved to a flash drive, but her hard drive contained so much more.

"It's odd they struck today. You've never been gone this long on a Monday afternoon," Henry said.

"It's getting closer to the day of the program. I wanted to see if everything was all right."

"Did you tell anyone you were going to close up your shop?"

Maggie thought for a moment. "I don't think it's a matter of who I told, but more a matter of who saw me arrive at the school and would be able to figure out why I was there and how long I might be."

"So, any parent picking up his or her child would know why you were at the school."

Maggie nodded. "Every parent who paid attention."

But wouldn't those same parents also know that Maggie was living hand to mouth? And that the only item of value she had was a sweet-faced seven-year-old girl?

For the first time since moving to Roanoke, Maggie felt her tentative hold on control slipping, as vulnerability took its place.

"Cassidy wanted to wrestle during recess and I got in trouble."

The recess incident resulted in a tiny scratch on Matt's shoulder. In Matt's mind, though, it was the size

of Iowa. Jared knew that one thing he and Matt shared
was the struggle with forgiveness.

"Why didn't you just walk away?" Jared asked.

Like Jared should be doing: walking, no, *running,*
away from Cassidy's mother.

"I tried, but she runs faster than me."

The tires on Jared's truck easily traveled over the
new snow on Main Street. The first hint of a gray twi-
light was beginning to fall in Roanoke, and Jared was
tired. The talk he'd had last night with his brother had
given him reason to lose sleep. Yes, he'd been with Maggie Tate Friday night, Saturday night and all Sunday
afternoon. No wonder Ryan thought they were dating.
All Jared needed to do was get through the Christmas
program and he could easily avoid Maggie.

"Hey," Caleb said, "I see a police car."

Jared slowed, fairly unconcerned. For the last few
months, ever since seeing an old episode of *Adam-12,*
Caleb had decided he wanted to be a policeman. On
drives to town, he looked for the chief's police car.
And, when possible, he went up to the chief of police
and said, "I'm going to be a cop someday."

Alex Farraday always said, "Good, then Roanoke
will have six cops instead of just five and I can spend
more time at home with Susan."

Susan was Beth's sister. Jared was just glad Caleb
hadn't been swayed by Joel into becoming a bull rider.

"It's in front of Cassidy's house," Matt noted, the
scratch the size of Iowa momentarily forgotten.

Jared didn't hesitate. He quickly traveled the remaining block and parked across the street in front of Roanoke Rummage. Leaning across the seat, he rolled down

the passenger-side window. Henry stood in the doorway, Cassidy right next to him, both looking out through the glass door like two kids denied access to candy.

"What happened?" Jared called. "Is Maggie all right?"

Henry opened his store's door a bit. "She got broken into while they were at the school. I heard a car pull away, and a minute later noticed her door was open. I called the police right away. I'm watching Cassidy but haven't seen or heard anything since Maggie and Farraday went inside."

"I think my presents got stolen," Cassidy complained.

Jared hurriedly rolled up the window, scooted his boys out of the backseat of the truck, and gave them to Henry. "I'll be over as soon as I know something."

Henry merely rolled his eyes good-naturedly and opened the door to his shop. For once, Ryan got with the program and moved. Matt even managed to look a little worried. Caleb's eyes lit up. Roanoke Rummage was full of junk and, as an added bonus, Cassidy was there, too.

The snow crunched underfoot as Jared made his way quickly toward Maggie's shop. It didn't escape him that just a few minutes ago he'd been congratulating himself for knowing enough to run away from her but now, here he was running toward her, as fast as he could. It also didn't escape him how worried he felt. After all, she was a friend, and he'd stop to help a stranger.

In his gut he knew he'd never felt this level of concern over a stranger.

When he stepped inside Hand Me Ups, the first thing he noticed was Farraday, a smile on his face, bent over, lifting fingerprints from the glass counter. "What's so funny?"

"I wish I had a surveillance camera on the thieves right now. Maggie says they took wrapped presents from under this tree and that all she'd done was wrap empty boxes for decoration. Picturing them opening empty box after empty box is something to smile about."

"Not everything they got was empty," Maggie said glumly.

"You all right?" Jared asked. He went to her and enveloped her in his arms, surprised when she let him. Gone was the Maggie Tate who was always in control, always seeing the glass half-full, and always ready with a smile or joke. He held a woman who wanted to hit something, but since there were no punching bags available, she let him hold her.

He liked that.

"Of course I'm all right, we're all right." Her voice shook with anger. "I was at school while this happened. But they took some of my inventory, some personal jewelry and Cassidy's presents."

Farraday sobered right up. "You're right, it wasn't just empty boxes they took, and I'm sorry. You're the tenth victim, and I have no idea who'd be so brash as to park in front of your shop in broad daylight, and break in. But, your break-in is a bit different as they didn't get much and they left behind a clue." Farraday held up a baggy, as proud as if he were showing off his firstborn. "A screwdriver."

"You going for prints?" Jared asked.

"No, can't get prints from a screwdriver, not really, especially one as small as this, but it's an unusual and very old screwdriver. It gives me something to trace."

"They left it in my door," Maggie said, backing out of Jared's embrace.

"It got stuck in the cylinder of the mortise lock," Farraday said.

"That's a pretty old lock." Jared looked at Maggie's door. "You need something newer, stronger."

"It was plenty strong. After all, the screwdriver got stuck," Maggie debated.

Jared didn't laugh.

"He's right," Farraday agreed. "Plus, a Christmas tree right by a window is an open invitation."

Jared watched as Maggie flinched. Her lips went together, and he wondered what she was thinking. After a moment, she said, "Every business on this street has a tree in their front window. It's called good marketing. We rely on our neighbors keeping watch and our police department doing its job to keep us safe. By the way, if you don't find my daughter's presents, she's not getting any. Is that clear enough, chief?"

Aah, the cat had claws.

"Henry says his wife heard a car," Jared put in.

"I planned on talking to him after I leave here. You mind if I go upstairs and look again? See if anything else is missing?" Maggie asked.

At Farraday's nod, Maggie went upstairs and Jared headed for the door. "Okay if I touch it?"

"Go ahead. I'm about done."

Jared studied the lock. "It's destroyed."

"The lock probably was worth more than what they got away with," Farraday said soberly.

"Maggie said jewelry."

"Most of it she claims she made herself. It was spread

out on the coffee table next to the tree. My guess is they saw it and made a sweep because it was convenient. The value comes from selling it for more than it cost to make. By her estimate, the only reason she's in the hole is because some items she had on consignment were taken and now she feels obligated to pay the vendors."

Together, Jared and Farraday righted the tree and secured it in the base. Soap ornaments fell at their feet. Once that was finished, Jared looked at the door. "Think Bob's Hardware will have a replacement?"

"He might, but you're going to be looking at more than two hundred dollars. Plus, for that kind of lock, you'll need a locksmith."

"I can do it."

"Looks easy, I know, but believe me, the mortise is not the easiest lock to mess with."

Jared headed to his truck. Thanks to what he was doing at school with the scenery, most of his tools were in his truck bed toolbox. No one was looking out the entryway of Roanoke Rummage. Either interest had died or Henry had his hands full supervising four children.

Jared got down the measurements and ascertained that it was a right-handed doorknob. Maggie came down the stairs. "No, everything is there. I'm going to get Cassidy and bring her home. She'll be worried."

"Grab my boys, too," Jared said. "If they can stick around a moment, I'll run to the hardware store and get you a lock."

Maggie stopped just short of her counter, took a breath, and said a soft "Thank you." Jared thought about going to her and wrapping his arms around her to tell her everything would be all right. If ever there was a woman who needed someone to hold her, it was Maggie, right now. If she'd been anybody else, he would have.

If she'd been anybody else, ulterior motives would not be questioned, especially by the man giving the hug.

But he didn't move.

And the moment vanished into regret before Jared had the wherewithal to realize a missed opportunity.

Plus, he wasn't sure who needed the hug more. Maggie or him. Maggie because she was scared. Jared because he was scared for her.

It had been a long time since he'd been scared for a woman.

Chapter Twelve

Maggie made homemade pizza for everyone. It was the only thing she had that would feed seven, since Henry had stayed. While she rolled out the dough, she tried to keep her eyes on Cassidy instead of the empty place under the tree. Someone had invaded her space, had taken things that didn't belong to them, and had made her feel like she was losing control.

Again.

Prayer would help. She knew it would, and if there was ever a day when she needed to talk to God, it was today. But when she tried to form the words, the thoughts, all she got was emptiness.

Having an apartment full of people was somewhat reassuring but it was also overwhelming. It had been just her and Cassidy for so long, even when Dan was alive because he was gone so often.

She wasn't quite sure how to respond to all this help.

Cassidy, of course, loved it and felt like she was a princess and everyone in the apartment was there to worship her. She and Matt did their homework at the kitchen table amid the smell of pizza sauce and garlic. Every once in a while, Cassidy leaned over to check what Matt was doing. Matt responded by shielding his work. After calling his wife, Tess, Henry sat with them. "She says she'll come over another time. Right now she's tired and just wants to go to bed."

Maggie wondered why she hadn't invited them over sooner. "I'll send a couple slices of pizza home with you."

Henry nodded as he admired Matt's handwriting and recommended that Cassidy start over.

"Help me," was Cassidy's suggestion.

And he did.

Ryan sat in the tiny living room watching television and watching Maggie.

"Want to help me spread the sauce?" Maggie asked.

"No."

"Put the pepperoni on?"

"No."

"Throw it up to the ceiling and see if it sticks?"

"Yes," shouted Cassidy, almost falling out of her chair. Caleb, on the floor surrounded by Cassidy's collection of toy horses nodded in agreement. Ever the boy, he had the ponies battling each other for control of a pretend base. Yes, if Cassidy were a princess, then Caleb was a prince.

"Don't be silly," Ryan said.

"Being silly is fun," Maggie said. "And on a day like today, it's better than crying."

"I'm the one who should be crying," Cassidy said. "It's my toys that got stolen. And, not just toys, but red boots probably. Do you know how important red boots are?"

"And how hard to find," Henry agreed.

All the boys looked bewildered. Even Caleb checked out his own boots as if to see if they'd turned red.

"I'm the one who should be crying." Jared walked into the room, a hammer in his hand and a scowl on his face. "That lock was a bear to replace."

"I can't thank you enough," Maggie said. "How much do I owe you?"

Jared took off his coat and gloves, folded them and put the hammer on top before coming into the kitchen and peering over her shoulder at the slightly round creations ready to go in the oven. "Two pizzas ought to cover it."

She could smell snow and something else, aftershave maybe, something definitely male.

Henry raised a hairy eyebrow but didn't say anything.

"No, really." Maggie brushed flour off her hands, stuck the pizzas in the oven and headed for her purse.

"I have the receipt in the truck," Jared said. "I'll bring it in when we're finished eating."

She left her purse where it was and got busy with drinks and napkins. She froze, two drinks in her hand and another on the counter, off to the side while Jared said a prayer. The boys and Henry bowed their heads automatically. Cassidy bowed, waited a moment, looked around at all the people bowing, bowed again, but was too interested in everyone else to understand she should be listening.

After the "Amen," Maggie started breathing again.

They weren't the best pizzas, but they weren't the worst, either. They were edible and hot, the only criteria in Maggie's kitchen. The kids gathered in the living room around the coffee table. Caleb and Cassidy ate everything handed to them. Matt ate one piece and complained about the sauce. Ryan complained about the sauce and went hungry. Good thing Jared thanked God before the meal because afterward might have been a different plea.

The adults were in the kitchen.

"I make my own sauce," explained Maggie. "That way I can control Cassidy's intake of Red Dye #40."

"That help?" Jared asked.

"It does, and luckily, since I'm not much of a cook, it's somewhat easy to make. I can send some home with you."

Jared hesitated a moment. "I took Caleb to the doctor today and came home with a bunch of paperwork, some of it just ideas, same as you mentioned to me before. We're going to see an allergy specialist tomorrow. Then, I'll need to call the Calcaw Center. I'm willing to try just about anything."

Seeing that both Matt and Cassidy were doing more listening than homework, Maggie turned to Henry and changed the subject, "Are there always some thefts around Christmas?"

"Some," Henry said. "But nothing like this year. And I don't remember presents being the target. Usually it was something like money from somebody ringing a bell for donations. One year someone broke into the church and stole the contributions."

"I remember that," Jared said. "You think it's the same person doing it now?"

"No." Henry didn't hesitate. "Both those times, it was one hit and over. This is a serial thief and they're targeting homes with children. I'm thinking it's someone new to town or someone from one of the neighboring towns."

"Someone from a neighboring town wouldn't know my schedule," Maggie pointed out.

"Maybe the thief didn't know your schedule but read the sign on the door and took a chance."

"So, you don't think they'll be back?" Maggie set down her pizza, half eaten.

"Not to your store," Henry said. "They got what they wanted."

"All the break-ins have been when the homeowners were gone," Jared reassured.

"Which is why I think it's someone local." Henry finished his pizza and then stared out the window. He took one finger and touched the center of the pane. "You need to replace this. You're losing good heat."

"I know," Maggie admitted. "It's on my list."

Henry took his plate to the sink and headed for the living room and his winter coat. Maggie didn't want Cassidy to think she had to worry about whoever had broken in coming back.

"I think it's someone local, too," she confided to Jared. "And I agree with Henry. They target people who have kids."

"So, toys are the goal?"

Maggie nodded. "They took my jewelry because it was convenient. I even had it lying on a towel. All they had to do was roll the towel closed. They took inventory that would make good Christmas presents."

"I think you might be right. You've been hit, the Totwells were hit. My neighbors, the McClanahans, were broken into a good three weeks ago while they were at church. I can't remember everyone else, but if we look, I'm sure kids and presents are the common denominator. Which is good, somewhat, because then you don't need to worry about them coming back."

"Dad! Caleb won't stop sticking his tongue out!" Matt hollered.

"It's time for us to go." Jared gathered up paper plates and napkins. He had his boys do the same. "We have homework and bedtime right around the corner. Thanks for feeding us."

"We enjoyed your company." It was true, too true. She was enjoying Jared's company more and more each time.

She didn't deserve it.

It wasn't until after everyone had left, Cassidy was in bed and Maggie was finishing up dishes, that she realized Jared hadn't returned with the receipt.

Sitting at her computer, she did a Google search for the lock but gave up. She couldn't remember what type Farraday had said it was, only that it was old.

Almost afraid, she went to her accounting software. She'd already giving Farraday a handwritten account of all that was missing downstairs. The thieves had hit the tree, grabbed presents and what she had nestled in that area, namely scarves, quilts and blankets, and had made off with more than five hundred dollars in handcrafted booty.

They'd taken the three presents under the tree. The boots had cost Maggie ten, the book three and the previously viewed DVD just under five. Eighteen dollars in all. At a time when eighteen might as well be a hundred.

The jewelry was nothing. She dabbled at jewelry making and someday wanted to do more with it. After all, she had a shop to sell it in. Right now, though, alterations paid the bills, homemade jewelry was just another impulse buy and a task she had little time to hone. Everything in her jewelry box had been homemade.

Her good jewelry was hidden. She'd already checked to make sure the Koa jewelry box Dan had given her the day they had married was still in the back of the closet inside her good suitcase.

Careful not to wake Cassidy, Maggie tiptoed into the bedroom and went into the closet, shutting the door behind her before she pulled the string to the light. It took a moment to move some quilts from on top of the suitcase, but then she held its contents in her hand. Of all the things Dan had given her, Cassidy excluded, this was Maggie's most cherished. At a time when money was tight, he'd spent all he had on a two-drawer, one-of-a-kind handcrafted box simply because she'd said she liked it.

He hadn't purchased the cheapest, either. He'd gotten her the one she'd wanted.

Settling cross-legged on the floor, she settled the Hawaiian jewelry box on her lap and tugged on one of the ebony handles. Inside was a necklace her mother had left behind. Maggie had no idea if it was worth anything or not. She also had no idea why she had kept it. There were at least a dozen earrings hanging in the tray back from her high school days and not her style any longer. Bracelets were crammed into the second drawer, not Maggie's favorites. Others had been left untouched on her dresser.

In the ring slot was just one offering.

She removed the ring from its black velvet resting place and rolled it between her fingers. It was yellow gold and not even a carat. Dan had purchased it online a month before getting the courage to ask her to marry him.

He'd loved her.

Made promises and kept them.

Maggie's tears came slowly at first. Guilt was a hard fist that didn't give way to emotions easily. But, after working all day, helping at the school, the break-in and then a whole household of people who called her friend, the guilt became an open wound. She was crying for Dan, but thinking of Jared.

She didn't deserve to have feelings for a man like Jared, a man who had loved his wife so much that if he ever married again, he wanted it to be to someone exactly like her.

Not exactly like Maggie.

When Dan had left for Afghanistan for his last tour, she'd waved goodbye at the airport and breathed a sigh of relief.

Because life was easier without him.

She was glad he was going. She prayed to God he'd be gone a little longer. She wanted to work on structure with Cassidy so that when Dan came back, there'd be no strife in the home.

She'd asked God to let Dan stay gone a little longer this time.

God had answered her prayer.

Dan was gone forever.

For the next couple of days, Jared made a point to drive by Hand Me Ups on his way to school and on his way from picking them up. A couple times he could see Maggie inside working, but she never noticed him.

At church on Wednesday evening, he sat in the auditorium class and for the first time, really looked around. For some reason the room looked brighter, the people more animated and more colorful. Everywhere there was a sense of happiness and togetherness.

Everywhere there were happy couples. Some were new couples, like his little brother and Beth. Some couples had been around a lot longer, like Henry Throxmorton and his wife, Tess. Jared knew exactly how long Henry and Tess had been together because right before Thanksgiving the church had thrown them a fiftieth wedding anniversary party.

Fifty years with one person. That was longer than Jared had been alive.

When Bible study ended, the kids filed into the auditorium for a short devotional. Matt liked to sit with Beth. Caleb moved from seat to seat, first sitting by Jared, then moving to Patty Maynard, the nurse who'd given him a sucker the other day. After a moment, and in a move that would do the NFL justice, he managed to quietly flip over the pew and sit next to the Totwells. He ended up crawling under the pew and leaning against

Billy, whispering in his grandpa's ear and drawing him a picture. Ryan sat next to Jared.

Wednesday nights were always hard.

After church, Jared and Billy helped the boys into their jackets. Patty even stooped down to assist Caleb as she was leaving.

"I like you," said Caleb. "You don't do shots."

"Not always," Patty agreed.

"Sometimes we have to have shots," Matt said, ever practical.

Both Ryan and Caleb frowned at him. Even Grandpa Billy looked at Matt with a touch of concern and said, "But we don't have to enjoy them."

Patty chuckled. "I thought the lesson was good to-night."

Ryan tugged on Jared's shirt. "Let's go. It's getting late. I'm tired."

Now he became the target of frowns.

"You're never tired," Matt accused.

Billy gathered all three in front of him and pushed toward the exit. Jared put on his hat and took one step to follow, then paused.

He'd noted the sense of togetherness in the church tonight, and, yes, lately he'd been feeling restless. He turned and looked at Patty. "Say, Patty, how you doing?"

She was the kind of woman he should be asking out. She'd grown up on a farm, knew the life. She was a great-looking woman.

She was slow in answering. "I'm fine. And you?"

"Good."

They stared at each other for a moment. Then, Patty

nodded before walking away as if understanding the question he hadn't asked.

The thought had crossed his mind to ask her out. A thought so obvious his oldest boy and stepfather had picked up on it.

But, if she was indeed the kind of woman Jared was looking for, he would have noticed before now.

By the time Jared got back to the farm with the family, it was after nine. Ryan and Matt got themselves to bed. Caleb was a bit more of a challenge. The later it got, the worse he behaved.

"He's tired," Billy said.

"So are the other boys." Jared actually had to fill the tub for Caleb's bath otherwise Caleb made the water too hot to step in. If he wasn't watched, he'd overflow the water, too.

"Every child is different."

Jared nodded. Caleb headed for the bath, all smiles, completely happy to be naked, completely happy to have help from Jared, because Caleb didn't remember Mandy at all.

Was that why Caleb was harder? Was it because he'd never had the feminine touch? After the bath, Jared helped dry off Caleb and put on his pajamas. Then, instead of rushing him to sleep, Jared sat on the edge of the bed and read a story from the Children's Bible, plus a Golden Book.

Caleb interrupted with questions, not about the stories. It took twice the time to read the books. Finally, Jared headed down the stairs, turned on the evening news and settled in his favorite chair.

"You want to talk?" Billy hit the remote so the television muted.

"Hey, I was watching that!"

"Really?" Billy asked. "Because the news ended ten minutes ago and you're watching a late-night talk show."

Jared looked at the television in disbelief. His stepfather was correct. Right now a parody on Santa made fun of the season. Not something Jared wanted to watch.

"So, where were your thoughts?"

After turning off the television, Billy sat down on the couch and waited. As an elementary-school principal, followed by taking over the raising of two rowdy boys, and now three rowdy grandsons, Billy was the epitome of patience. When Jared didn't volunteer to talk, Billy found something to say. "I guess Joel's still with Beth."

"He took her home from church."

"I know. That was about three hours ago. Guess they have a lot to talk about."

"He's in love."

"Not a bad thing," Billy said. "It certainly calmed Joel down, made him a happier person."

"Joel was always a happy person."

"No, he wasn't." Billy leaned forward and absently straightened the coffee table. His hair was fully gray now. It had been brown when he'd married Jared's mother. He was tall, taller than both Jared and Joel. He had a military walk but hadn't served. Instead of leading soldiers on the field, he'd lead in the school yard and at church.

"You should talk with your brother, really talk, find out why he left."

Jared felt the first touch of guilt. Joel had opened up

about why he'd left and it all had to do with not feeling like he had belonged. Jared couldn't begin to understand his little brother's feelings, couldn't imagine walking away from family, from the farm, from commitments. Yes, Joel was back now and all was forgiven, but there were consequences to every action. The worst one for Joel was no longer having any ownership of Solitaire Farm. He'd sold his portion to Jared, at a time when Jared could least afford the purchase. There'd been some lean years for Jared and Mandy, especially when Mandy got sick and they had the mortgage to pay.

It wouldn't have been quite so hard if Joel hadn't wanted his money right away. Or if Jared hadn't had to take out a mortgage at the exact time he lost the brother who was supposed to work alongside him.

"Think about Caleb," Billy said. "What if he does something to make Matt and Ryan mad and they turn on him."

"I didn't turn on Joel!"

"Yes, you did."

This conversation was taking a direction Jared wasn't prepared for. "What? I did not. I was always there for him."

"You were always there. That's different than being there for him." Billy leaned forward, glaring at Jared, as serious as he'd been in years.

Jared was willing to fight this out, but the exhaustion he saw on Billy's face stopped him.

"Do you feel all right?"

"It's just the cold, hanging on. I've finally stopped coughing but I'm tired, my bones hurt and I'm worried."

"You don't have to worry about me. Joel's the one

we worry about." Jared tried to make the words light, but they didn't sound light.

"Not anymore. Joel's a good guy and he's found his place. It's your turn."

Jared looked around the living room. How could Billy say Jared needed to find his place? His place had always been here. The portrait over the fireplace held Jared's family. Years ago, the portrait had been of Jared, Joel and his parents. His grandfather, grandmother and dad had been there at one time.

Where was that painting?

The curtains over the big window were fairly new. Mandy, with the help of her girlfriends, had made them. Back then, the house had been full of voices and giggles.

Well, it still was, but the voices and giggles were his kids—mostly Caleb.

"I made a big mistake," Billy said, "when I asked you if I could marry your mother."

Jared straightened. "You know, if I'd gone straight to bed, like I normally do, we wouldn't be having this conversation."

"Not tonight, but soon. I've been planning on it for some time now."

"A conversation telling me you did wrong marrying my mother?"

"No, not by marrying your mother. That was the smartest thing I ever did. The mistake was when I called you into my office and asked your permission. I called you in because you were the eldest son. I'd watched you. When your dad died, the three of you McCreedys banded together. Your mom was mom and dad both.

You took over the farm. I was amazed. You were just a teenager. You also took over raising Joel."

"He pretty much raised himself."

"No, he had you for an example."

"I'm not getting the mistake you're alluding to. Why was asking my permission a mistake?"

"Because I should have asked both you boys for permission. By asking just you, I left Joel out."

"He didn't feel..." Jared's words tapered off.

"Tell me," Billy asked. "When you proposed to Mandy and started getting ready to move her into the house, did you ever talk to Joel?"

"He was just a kid, still in high school. I don't remember. I don't think so. Why would I?"

"I think you might want to look at your own boys," Billy said. "Because change is coming, I can see it, and you need to talk to them, prepare them, and make sure they all feel included. Especially Ryan."

"If you're talking about Maggie Tate—"

"Maggie?" Billy's face had a look of fake surprise. "Isn't it Patty Maynard you asked out tonight?"

"Well," Jared stammered, "no, but almost...."

"It's not Maggie I'm talking about, although I wouldn't mind a bit should that happen. She'd make a fine wife for you."

"She's not—"

"Mandy? I noticed that, too. Neither is Patty Maynard. You've made Mandy a little too perfect in your memory. If you wait for another Mandy, you'll die alone."

"That's harsh."

Billy chuckled. "I'm not too worried. I think you're

working your way back to the land of the living, maybe even missing the soothing touch of a woman's hand, the sound of her laughter. The Bible says it in Proverbs 18. *He who finds a wife finds what is good and receives favor from the Lord.*"

Jared's throat tightened. The scripture was spot-on. It had been good with Mandy. His whole world had felt right. Billy was spot-on, too. Jared missed having a woman by his side. He wanted what he had with Mandy: someone who loved the farm, loved working side by side and loved him.

The only way he could have that was to find someone like Mandy.

Chapter Thirteen

There were shoppers and then there were hoppers.

Shoppers came to a store, strolled through the aisles, touched a few items, lingered for a caress or two, and then did it all again before finally settling on something to either try on or buy outright.

That's if the shopper was alone.

If the shopper came with a friend or friends, it was the same scenario, only because conversation took place between every step, the game took twice as long.

And usually resulted in twice the sales.

Hoppers were a different story. A hopper came to a store and meandered aimlessly through the aisles. Meandered was, in this case, a more frantic kind of walk. Aimlessly was a word shop owners avoided. Hoppers touched every item but didn't caress. Individual hoppers didn't repeat the process, mostly because they didn't want their hopper status recognized. Then, they'd leave the store with a *you don't have what I'm looking for* comment. Not true. A hopper wasn't really looking for anything but a way to kill time.

If hoppers came in a group, they were great fun. In a group, you had a chance for a sale because they might gang up on some real shoppers and speed up the process of making a choice. Or, one hopper might actually get guilted into making a purchase.

Maggie'd had a Thursday full of guilt-free hoppers and a cash register that was more register than cash. There were two weeks and two days until Christmas. Chief Farraday had been by twice to check up on her. He'd not found the thief.

Worry shadowed Maggie. A constant, sore reminder of how much she bore.

Alone.

Not just about replacing Cassidy's presents but also about paying rent and utilities. Christmas was supposed to increase sales, so what was going wrong?

"I'll take this."

Nothing like selling one scarf to boost morale.

After her customer left, Maggie typed in the keywords *Red Cowboys Boots* into her computer. She already knew what she'd find. The cheapest pair, before shipping, was twenty-five dollars. The pair that most resembled the ones stolen were seventy-five.

If she purchased the twenty-five dollar pair, that was it, all there was for Christmas.

It was her only choice.

Not her only choice.

Maggie slowly tugged her cell phone from the side pocket of her purse. The number she needed was on speed dial. This was absolutely *not* what she wanted to do.

Usually all she battled for was control, but now she

knew that alongside control was a battle for pride, and she was about to lose hers.

For Cassidy's sake.

She hit number two on the pad and listened as the connection made. Her fingers curled around the phone and her lips starting forming the words she needed to say. *Kelly, we had a break-in and we need help so that Cassidy will have a Christmas.*

In the back of her mind came the briefest beginning of a prayer. *Father, please help me make the right choice....* That's as far as she got. After all, really, Maggie had made the right choices. She'd worked hard and saved so that Cassidy would have a Christmas. She'd been frugal and diligent. She'd foregone things like going out to eat, and getting her nails done. Whatever was on free television was good enough for her. Some other lost soul had chosen the easy way—breaking into homes and taking what they hadn't worked for.

The words "This is Kelly Tate. I am unavailable. Please leave a message..." came on the recording at the exact moment Jared walked through the front door. Maggie wasn't sure which pleased her more—that she didn't have to talk to Kelly or that she did get to talk to Jared.

Only Jared wasn't walking through the front door. He was holding it open—letting the cold air in!—and examining the lock.

"It's working just fine?"

"Yes, and you forgot to give me the receipt so I can reimburse you."

Great, say the first thing that comes to mind when

it would have been smart to hope Jared's forgetfulness lasted until after Christmas.

Something that looked a lot like understanding flickered in his eyes and Maggie felt a strange tightening in her chest. "What?"

"I didn't say anything." Jared honestly looked confused.

"Well, you had this look in your eyes."

He closed the door behind him and came into the shop, stopping in front of her, almost as if sizing her up. "I would say that I didn't mean to have the look, but since I have no idea what look you're talking about, I'd be lying."

Maggie didn't blush often. Growing up with just a father and his crew of friends could harden a girl. Then, with Dan, there'd been more of the same.

So why was she blushing now?

"I was in town," Jared explained, "and thought I'd stop by to see if the lock worked and if everything was okay."

"The lock works. Everything is okay. Farraday's been by twice already."

He looked at the door, and not in a way that made her think he was checking out the lock again. More in a way that made her think he wanted to escape. She didn't blame him.

"How much do I owe you?" she repeated.

"Call it a Christmas gift."

So, the look had been real. "No, you barely know me."

"I owe you for offering me advice about Caleb and for the pizza sauce."

"I haven't given you any real concrete advice, and I gave you pizza sauce that two of your boys won't eat."

"I can take a rain check on the advice, and they'll eat if they're hungry enough." Jared looked at his watch. "I'm on my way to pick up Caleb. We're driving into Des Moines. I'm running early so thought I'd stop by here. I just keep thinking this is something I've done by not paying enough attention to him. Or maybe it's because he's only had men around."

"You want to be sure," Maggie said gently.

"Lately, I'm not sure about anything."

Boy, Maggie knew that feeling, especially today, especially about this man. He had no clue the emotions he aroused. But he was here to talk about Caleb. That she could handle.

Her phone sounded. Usually, she checked the ID before answering, but not this time.

"I see you called," Kelly Tate said.

"Yes, I did."

"Have you changed your mind about coming for Christmas? It's not too late. Of course, plane fare will be higher now, but I'm willing to pay."

"Hold on just a moment." Maggie smiled at Jared. "I'm going to run upstairs and take this call. It's really important."

"I think I'll look around."

"My shop?"

"Sure," he said easily. "I have time, and I still have a few presents to buy."

"Well, if a customer comes in, do your best to sell something." Maggie could only hope as she hurried up the stairs. He'd have to buy the whole shop or sell the whole shop in order to save her from what she was about to do.

Out of breath, Maggie sat at the kitchen table and pushed Cassidy's breakfast plate out of the way. Her daughter was supposed to put her dirty dishes in the sink. "Kelly, someone broke into the shop the other night and—"

"Is everyone all right?"

Maggie had to give Kelly credit. She'd asked if *everyone* was all right, not just Cassidy.

"We're fine. But, they took the Christmas presents. The police think it's someone targeting families and specifically toys."

"I'm so relieved you're all right."

"I've been on the computer all day. Cassidy wants a pair of red boots. I had them under the tree."

Silence.

"I can't afford to replace them."

"Just one pair of red boots?" Kelly's tone said it all. "Such a small request and you can't afford to replace them?"

Maggie started to sprout statistics about starting a business, being a single mom, but Kelly didn't let her finish.

"If you'd opened your shop here in New York, I'd have helped every step of the way. You could have lived with me and I'd—"

"Kelly, I always appreciated the offer, but Manhattan is not for me. I've always dreamed of living in a small town."

"Dreams don't pay bills."

Downstairs, someone pushed open the front door and a bell chimed.

Sometimes they do, Maggie mouthed the words. Aloud, she said, "I just need a loan. Two hundred dollars. I'll pay you fifty a month for four months."

"The boots cost two hundred dollars?"

"Nooo." Maggie knew full well Kelly knew the money was for boots and more.

"I can buy Cassidy the boots and send them. What size is she now? A three?"

Maggie cleared her throat, gave Kelly the brand and website address for the pair Cassidy really wanted and affirmed, "Yes, she's a three."

"Okay, then, that's settled."

Maggie nodded. She had the boots, but she didn't have the money to pay her customers what was owed them. And there'd not be much else under the tree.

Right now it was pretty hard living a dream.

A different woman came down the stairs. Maggie Tate, a woman who consistently seemed in control, had gone up. That's what he always noticed about her. She managed to conquer whatever obstacle life threw at her whether it be missing lunch boxes or missing Christmas presents. But the woman who came down the stairs was a lost soul.

"Are you okay?"

It didn't take a rocket scientist to realize that whatever the phone call had been about, she wasn't going to tell him and it obviously hadn't been good. It really wasn't his business. But he couldn't remember the last time he'd seen a woman look this…this tightly wound.

The closest was Beth, telling him that she thought something was wrong with Caleb's attention span.

No, not even close.

Lately, all Jared's strife was about his boys. Working Solitaire Farm had been easier since Joel's return. Two pairs of hands made twice the work and divided the time. Plus, Joel's ideas had brought in more money.

Whatever was bothering Maggie ran deep. Interfering was the last thing he should do but, at the moment, he'd do anything to put a smile back on her face. "I'm early picking up Caleb and have an hour to kill," he said. "I'm taking you to lunch."

She was shaking her head before he even finished speaking.

"I knew you'd say no. That's why I didn't ask. You need a break, and I'm hungry. When we come back, I'm finishing up my Christmas shopping. I found the perfect coat for Billy." To prove it, he pointed to the first coat on a rank of men's coats in the back of the store.

Her quest last month for a 1930s denim chore jacket for George Maynard had resulted in a few finds that didn't work for him. They were good coats, though, bargains, and Maggie simply hung them up and waited for the right buyer.

"Billy's a big man?"

Jared looked at the coat again. "Well, he's tall."

Walking over, Maggie took it off the rack and handed it to him. "I think it will fit you." Any other day, there'd have been a sparkle in her eye as she tried to sell him something as ridiculous as this old coat. But today, the very stillness, seriousness, of her actions made him careful in how he responded.

It was the first time he saw Maggie Tate as fragile.

The brown insulated parka he wore quickly left his shoulders. She helped him into the bluish striped chore jacket so big on him that the collar came up to his nose. The sleeves hung past his fingers. "If I zip it up, it could be a tent instead of a jacket."

Then, she giggled, and he knew he had her.

"Okay, it's not you. And, I doubt it's Grandpa Billy, either."

"Billy does need a work jacket, though," Jared said. "And you've got some that will work. You can show me one when we get back."

She had that look in her eyes, the I-gotta-get-out-of-here look that females sometimes get when the day has been too long, the kids too loud and the expectations too high.

Jared was glad he happened to be in the right place at the right time.

He wanted to rescue her.

"Who was at the door?" she asked.

"Henry wants you to run over when you have time."

Ten minutes later they were in the Red Barn Grille, the restaurant his family occasionally came to on Sundays after church. It was the nicest one in town, looked like a restaurant from the Wild West days and served home-style meals.

Jared stepped through the door expecting to feel instant guilt. After all, he'd brought Mandy here while they were dating, while they were engaged, as newlyweds and then with children. To his relief, it was like last night at church. The lights seemed a bit brighter, maybe due to the addition of Christmas bulbs and sparkling icicles. The people seemed just as animated, and he couldn't help but notice how many couples there were.

It was noon and the place was half-full.

It didn't escape his notice that he was with the prettiest woman in the room.

The hostess looked surprised. After they were seated, Jared saw that quite a few of the staff, both front and back, peeked out to see who he was with.

When his favorite waitress showed up, menus and water glasses in hand, and a way-too-happy smile on her face, he introduced Maggie as a friend, the mother of a student in Matt's class and someone working with him on the school's Christmas program.

Hillary, who'd been serving him chicken fried steak since he was ten, simply nodded and said, "Sure, honey. She's all that." Turning to Maggie, she said, "I don't think I've seen you in here before. Are you new in town?"

"Fairly new. We arrived in June. I purchased the building across from Roanoke Rummage. Maybe you've seen it. Hand Me Ups."

Hillary nodded. "Been meaning to come visit. I like old clothes."

"Every time I've driven by here, I've thought about coming in. We like good food."

"We?"

"I have a seven-year-old daughter."

"Glad you waited for a special occasion." Hillary patted Jared on the shoulder. "Next time bring the little girl."

Jared saved Maggie from having to answer. "We

need a few minutes." He set down his menu. He always got the same thing. Fried chicken. Billy couldn't make it so if the McCreedy men had it for dinner, it came from a box. Not the same as homemade.

Settling back, he enjoyed watching Maggie peruse the menu. She was still way too serious but no longer fragile-looking. He checked his watch. She wasn't in a hurry, either. "We've got maybe forty minutes before I need to pick up Caleb."

"Just enough time," she agreed and went back to the menu.

Okay. He looked out the window. It wasn't snowing, but what they'd had earlier in the week had turned to slush and mud. Alex Farraday, chief of police, drove by slowly.

Main Street didn't experience much of a rush hour on Thursday afternoons. Bob's Hardware Store had two or three people exiting its door. Jared only recognized one. Kyle Totwell. The other two people exiting the store were hidden behind a giant Christmas tree box.

Saps.

Roanoke Rummage was open, but Jared couldn't see anyone going in or coming out. The cold did that to people: inspired them to stay home. Christmas got them out, but it was still two weeks away. Plenty of time.

Jared flipped the menu to the back and skimmed the history of Roanoke again. He'd read it a few times before. He could read it again.

"I'm ready."

With the instincts of a seasoned waitress, Hillary knew right when to return and soon two salads appeared, plus a coffee and iced tea. Maggie picked up her fork and aimed it at the salad.

"You know," Jared said softly, "I usually say a prayer before eating. Would you join me? I promise to make it short."

"Go ahead," Maggie said softly. "Say your prayer." Jared kept his promise—short and simple. Yet, he noted that she didn't bow her head or close her eyes. She looked a little white knuckled.

Something about religion had turned off Maggie Tate, and since he wasn't sure what it was, he had to be careful.

Right after the *Amen* she started eating, slowly, delicately and deliberately.

"So, you want to tell me what upset you back there?" She raised one eyebrow. "I wasn't upset."

"Yes, you were."

She huffed a bit, looking cute and vulnerable at the same time. She stared out the window.

Great, if he wanted conversation to happen, with this usually very free-with-her-words female, he'd have to instigate.

"I have a lot of respect for you," he finally said. "I can't imagine what it's like to be a single mom and have to do everything. The way you handle Cassidy is amazing."

"I don't handle her, I guide her, but thanks. You're a single father, with three sons. You know exactly what I'm going through."

"I know the frustration and the time spent. I know the joys and feeling of accomplishment. But I don't have to do everything. When Mandy passed away, Billy stepped up to the plate. I never had to worry. My boys have both Billy and me to guide them, as you say. Now, Joel and Beth are in the mix, too."

"You're lucky."

"It's more than luck. God's been with me every step of the way even when I wasn't looking to Him or asking Him for help. Where's your family? Beth said you might have relatives here, but she wasn't sure."

"Beth's a good friend, and she listens." Maggie returned to her salad. End of story. Jared wasn't sure if it was the family references or the God reference that made her go silent so he switched topics. "Caleb and I have a four-o'clock appointment in Des Moines. We're going to the Calcaw Center and meeting with a developmental pediatrician. Beth filled out three pages of forms. So did I."

"The first visit is easy. They'll do pretty much what your primary physician did. Caleb will get weighed, measured and observed. They'll ask you some questions, too."

"Like?"

"I don't remember everything from the first visit. Dan was with me and he wanted there to be a cause for Cassidy's behavior. Someone told him she was allergic to food. He liked that idea because then there was a fix. She had every test under the sun. No allergies. Meeting with the developmental pediatrician meant there were questions about Cassidy's bedtime, what she ate and how often, and if she had a temper. What we did to redirect her behaviors. Things like that."

Hillary came, took away their dirty dishes and filled their drinks.

Jared nodded. "Caleb's my difficult child when it comes to bedtime. He's got thirty different things he wants to do before getting under the covers and then he wants to talk when it's story time."

"You're lucky to get an appointment this fast. It took me three months to schedule the first appointment."

"There was a cancellation and I was on the call list. Good thing it's winter. I can get away a lot easier."

"I've always wondered what farmers did in the winter."

"From May to November, we often work fifty to sixty hours, seven days a week. So, the first thing we do is recoup from all the hard work. Then, I play catchup on things like home and equipment maintenance. Of course, with Joel home, there's not so much to do. He fixes things the minute they break and he's fast. Me, I let them go until I have time and then it takes me forever to get them working again."

"Joel's a good guy."

"You're the second person to say that this week."

"Who was the first?"

"My stepfather. I wasted a lot of years being mad at Joel."

"Why?"

"After our father died, I pretty much took over the farm. The older Joel got, the more help I expected from him and the less he seemed to do."

"I'm an only child. I always wanted a brother or sister to do things with, to argue with."

Their main course arrived. Jared took a drumstick from his plate. Maggie took one from hers.

There'd been a time when Jared never figured to

have Joel back in his life. Now, every time Jared turned around, Joel was there, making some outrageous demand. Last year it had been, *let me move home and take care of me while I heal.*

Then, it was, *I'm staying, bro, and marrying Beth Armstrong. You can be my best man. Oh, and you get to wear spats. By the way, can I bring her here as my wife to live on Solitaire Farm? It's a big house.*

And recently, Joel's crowning achievement—*take Maggie Tate to buy a Christmas tree.*

Joel didn't always get what he wanted. Jared wasn't wearing spats.

And, lunch today was purely Jared's doing. Joel couldn't take credit at all.

Maggie finished her first piece, took a sip of her coffee and started a second. "So, are you going to sell Joel back a piece of property or what?"

Jared almost choked. Hillary had to stop and pat him on the back. "About time someone got him excited," she commented.

Jared gave both of them a dirty look. Lots of people asked what he intended to do. None were so explicit. "No."

"The wedding's in three weeks and two days," Maggie reminded. "You going to have them move in with you when they return from their honeymoon?"

"Joel will have to figure something out."

"Yes, there are apartments available in town," Maggie said brightly.

Jared scowled and changed the subject for the third time. "So, what had you so upset earlier?"

Maybe it was that her stomach was full, maybe it

was the adrenaline three cups of coffee provided, or maybe Maggie just needed someone to talk to. Jared didn't know, but Maggie finally slumped back and said, "I guess it doesn't matter—brothers, sisters, only children—we all have times when family drives us crazy."

Jared nodded.

"My mother-in-law," Maggie continued. "I called her today. She's the only family I have. We lived with Kelly in New York until six months ago. She didn't want us to move here, alone, so far away...."

"And?" Jared encouraged.

"I asked her if I could borrow money. I want to replace the cowboy boots that were stolen and have a bit more for Christmas."

"And?"

"She's sending boots but no money. She thinks if she doesn't send me money, eventually I'll have to move back in with her. That way she can be near her granddaughter. The only weapon she has is money."

"I'm sorry. I've been there. I purchased Joel's share of Solitaire Farm right after Ryan was born, and believe me, I wasn't making enough to pay the mortgage. Then," Jared's voice choked, "when Mandy got sick, if it weren't for Billy, we'd have lost everything."

"Well, I don't have a Billy, and my mother-in-law might win."

"No, you're a strong person and this is just a setback. We all have them. Some of us more than others. Don't give up hope. I know Alex Farraday. He's taking this personally. If anyone can find what's been stolen, it's him."

"Never give up hope," Hillary said bringing over the bill and gathering the dirty plates.

"I've been telling myself exactly that." Her voice sounded funny, sultry, and all Jared wanted to do was reach over, take her hands in his, and since he couldn't fix her problems, he wanted to pray. Automatically, he bowed his head.

"What are you doing?"

Her voice sounded funny again, but not strangled, more concerned.

He finished before answering, "I'm praying."

"For me?"

"For you."

"Oh, don't. Please. I can take care of myself."

He reached across the table and took her hand. Her fingers were warm to his touch. She'd painted the nails a bright pink. She had rings on her pinkies and one on her thumb. The area on her wedding-ring finger was no longer pale or indented.

He looked at his wedding-ring finger.

There'd never been an indentation or a pale circle. He'd been too afraid of losing it or of getting it caught on a piece of machinery to wear it. And, he was quite fond of his finger, more so than any wedding ring.

Hillary stopped at the table, picked up the bill and money and looked at him. "Need change?"

"It's all yours," he said.

She looked at Maggie. "Jared left me a pretty good tip. Now I'll give you one. Best place to learn about hope is church. Look up Romans 12:12."

Maggie's eyes followed Hillary's but her expression

didn't change even as she pulled her fingers from his. "What does Romans 12:12 say?"

"Rejoice in hope, be patient in tribulation, be constant in prayer."

"Sometimes I have a handle on the first two," Maggie said.

"The last one is the most necessary."

She gave the briefest shake of her head and said, "I need to get back to work."

He looked at the clock on the restaurant's wall. It was past time to pick up Caleb.

"You've made me late again," he accused, but he didn't care.

This time, it was worth it.

Chapter Fourteen

Maggie turned the Open sign so the public could see it. Lunch with Jared had been, well, interesting. She'd seen a side to him that surprised her. He'd been more open. He'd been not only sympathetic but empathetic, not something the men in her world excelled at, and he'd—typical male—offered concrete advice during their drive back to her shop.

Namely that she let him introduce her to the elders of the Main Street Church. They had a benevolent fund and he'd vouch for her.

Go to the church for money. Not a chance. She was still feeling a bit sensitive over the silent prayer he'd offered. She hoped it didn't backfire.

Maggie jogged up the stairs, grabbed a bottled water and came back down. There were still two hours before Cassidy got out of school. Hopefully there'd be a rush of customers. If not, she'd get some sewing done. Her goal: five elf hats and Mrs. Youst's sweaters. The elf hats were mindless. The sweaters, well, Cassidy's teacher loved sweaters but didn't like the size tag in the collar. Consequently, she pulled off the tags, managing to leave minute tears along the seam—tears that soon spread into unraveling big enough to put a fist through. Good thing for Maggie because they were quick and easy fixes. Too bad they didn't pay more.

Then, too, Maggie needed to do some of the final touches on Beth's wedding attire. Their final fitting was scheduled for Saturday at 9:00 a.m., an hour before the store opened.

Jared hadn't made it to the first fitting. It had been during the final harvest. Beth had measured him at the farm and then reported to Maggie.

The next hour passed with three customers and two very profitable phone calls. One from a bride needing alterations starting in January. Good, something to look forward to and weddings paid well. The other from a doctor wanting to know if she did custom shirts. She'd said yes but not until after the New Year. She could learn that quickly if she had to.

Just before three, she closed the shop and headed for the school. She needed to confirm she'd fulfilled her obligations, make sure Cassidy was doing what she was supposed to, and if she were lucky, there'd be some over-extended mom willing to pay to have a costume made. Maggie's fingers itched to get busy.

A few hours ago, they'd not itched. They'd been caressed. By Jared McCreedy. What was he thinking? Maybe he felt sorry for her. She hated that. Immediately, Maggie felt contrite. He'd been concerned, that's all. She'd been visibly upset after talking with Kelly.

Yes, that had to be it. She wondered how he was making out. About now, he'd be sitting on a sofa across from the developmental pediatrician and hearing what others—Beth and now the pediatrician—had written about his child.

It was never easy. Maggie didn't even want to think about her and Cassidy's next appointment at Calcaw. It wasn't for another three months.

Roanoke Elementary was bustling. Kids knew it was just a matter of days until no school and new toys. Cassidy wasn't the only kid flying.

Later, back at Hand Me Ups, Maggie settled Cassidy at the kitchen table with her homework before heading back down to work in the shop a little longer. She'd love a last-minute sale or two. She'd just settled behind the counter and picked up one of Mrs. Youst's sweaters when the door opened.

Henry, for the first time, had a smile that crossed his face. She saw the man he must have once been, young and vital. In his hands, he carried a stained and wrinkled brown grocery sack. "Cassidy around?" he said.

"I can get her."

"No." Furtively, he came to lean against the counter, checked the stairs, and then set down the bag.

Maggie felt the first stirring of surprise. "Did you bring me something?"

"Even better," Henry said.

Opening the bag, he tilted in toward her. She stood so she could peer in.

Red boots.

In even better condition than the ones that had been stolen.

"How? When?" Maggie felt like dancing, she felt like flying around the counter and giving Henry Throxmorton a hug. Instead, she hugged the bag containing the boots.

"I know every antiques and thrift shop in a five-city area. I emailed the owners, told them what I was looking for and the size. I got two responses this morning. This is the pair that worked."

"How did you get them so fast?"

"Just so happened one of the owners was coming into town to visit a friend. He dropped them off."

"How much do I owe you?" Maggie's voice didn't waver at the words, although she acknowledged she'd asked that question more than once today. Come to think of it, the first time, she'd not received an answer.

Henry looked a bit sheepish. That's when Maggie noticed a second brown bag, just as stained and wrinkled as the first, tucked under his arm. "There's five pairs of men's trousers in here. One of them has a pin indicating where they need to be hemmed. He wants them all the same. I said if you couldn't do it, I'd call to let him know."

Her fingers had been itching earlier. Looked like she had something to scratch.

"Henry, I can't thank you enough." She danced around the counter and gave him the hug he deserved.

"Well," Henry said humbly, "it just took a few minutes on the computer and a couple of prayers."

Maggie thought about Jared's prayer.

Too bad he hadn't prayed before she had called her mother-in-law.

"I hear you found a pair of boots."

It had been almost seventeen years since Jared Mc-Creedy had called a female on the pretense of small talk.

"I didn't. Henry did. They're wrapped and under the tree already." Maggie's voice lilted more like her old self but possibly a little guarded.

"I like Henry." Jared winced. He sounded a bit like his youngest son, not the image he was going for. This morning, he'd decided it was time. He'd driven by her shop, made sure all the windows looked intact, fretted a bit about the snow needing shoveling from her walk and realized that she was taking too much of his thinking time.

It was almost noon now, and he'd admitted to himself that he couldn't stop thinking about her. Maybe he'd survive if it were summer. Then, he'd be forced to shake the feeling that he needed to stop at Hand Me Ups just because he drove by. If it were summer, not only would he be bone tired—and happy—as he tilled, fertilized, planted and sprayed, but he'd not be driving through downtown Roanoke when the sun was shining.

"How did yesterday go?" Maggie asked.

Jared waited his turn at a four-way stop. One other car was in the intersection. Yesterday, he'd waited his turn amid a slew of parents. "I wasn't prepared for the waiting room. Everything else was pretty much as you predicted."

The guarded tone left her voice. "What do you mean about the waiting room?"

"Look," Jared said. "I just dropped off some things at school, and I'm a minute away. Can I take you to lunch today? I do need to talk."

"I can't afford to close my shop again. Sometimes I get people on their lunch break who stop in to take a quick look and actually buy."

"I'll bring lunch to you."

"You don't have to."

"You're right. I don't have to. I want to."

She was quiet for a moment, and he imagined her face. She was a smart woman, had already been married, had a child. He was no longer a concerned dad wanting advice. He was a concerned dad wanting advice and realizing that the most beautiful woman in Roanoke had the most to say.

Had the most to give.

"All right," she said, "but if a customer comes in, they're my priority."

"I know how to share." He hung up the phone, headed for the Red Barn Grille and soon had two to-go orders of meat loaf and mashed potatoes. Not the most romantic of offerings, but good enough for a man who'd taken an hour to actually get up the courage to make the phone call.

It sure felt like asking for a date.

She had customers when he entered the shop, a mother and daughter it looked like. Used to be, Jared knew everyone in Roanoke. He nodded at them and got out of the way by setting the food at the end of the counter and shrugging off his coat, then pulled out the stool Maggie usually sat on from behind the cash register.

"I like that coat," the mother said looking at Jared's parka instead of the merchandise.

Maggie looked at him, a slow smile spreading across her face. "He's attached to it himself. Unfortunately, it's not vintage so I don't have any in stock. But, I had him trying on this one yesterday."

Both customers made a face at the blue striped 1930s

denim chore jacket big enough to fit Santa Claus that Maggie pointed to.

"I want a coat for my husband. He keeps complaining he's cold." The woman spoke to Jared instead of Maggie. "We just bought the Calver farm. We want to try organic gardening."

"That's a good place," Jared said. "I've been there a few times back when Jack worked it. Right size if you don't add too many animals."

"We'll only do chickens," she said.

Jared stood and walked over to the women. "I was in here yesterday looking at coats. I'm going to buy my stepfather one. Here's the one I was thinking about."

He took a heavy jacket with John Deere stitched above the sleeve.

"Where do you work?" the mother asked. The daughter, realizing her mother was diverted, quickly sat on Maggie's stool and looked bored.

"I own Solitaire Farm." He stuck out his hand. "I'm Jared McCreedy."

"Oh! We've been there. Right, Celeste? We did the corn maze in October. We drove by a couple nights ago, thinking you'd have a Christmas maze going, but no. Why not?"

"My brother does Solitaire's Market. He's getting married in…"

"Twenty-three days," Maggie filled in.

"She's altering the wedding dress," Jared explained.

There was a bit more back and forth before the women left the store with a good used coat, a bunch of soap and a crocheted shawl in their bags.

"I'm sad now," Maggie said, "that I didn't get Cassidy over to your place to do the maze. She asked. I saw it as just one more thing to do on a busy schedule."

"When Joel first put it together, it seemed like a waste of time to me, too. But, it's making money."

"We'll have to try harder to get there next time." Maggie opened one of the take-out orders and nodded. "I'm running upstairs for drinks and extra napkins. I'll be right back."

While she was upstairs, Jared moved her stool and found a second so they could both sit at the counter. He'd just started to sit down when the front door opened again. Clearly this was not going to be a peaceful meal.

"Hey, Jared," Henry greeted. "Saw your truck. You here to see the boots I found?"

"More or less."

Henry looked at the two meals on the counter. "You look pretty comfortable. Something I should know?"

"The meat loaf is on special today over at the restaurant."

"I don't need to go over there. My wife makes the best meat loaf known to man. You going to Mandy's folks for Christmas?"

Christmas. The holiday where families get together. Last Christmas they'd gone for the day. Billy came, too. Joel had alrcady been courting Beth.

"I think they invited us."

"You think?" Henry smiled and shook his head. "You better find out for sure."

Maggie came down the steps, deposited what was in her arms on the counter and headed right for Henry. He got the kind of hug Jared had wanted when he'd walked in.

"Wife sent me over to see what you're doing for Christmas. It's just her and me, but we'd be proud if you and Cassidy came over."

"Henry, that's so sweet. Beth Armstrong already invited me to her sister's house."

"If you go to the Farradays'," Jared quipped, "at least your presents should be safe."

Neither Maggie nor Henry laughed.

"Did you hear about the preacher?" Henry asked, looking grave.

"No," Jared and Maggie answered together.

"Yesterday morning someone got in his house and took the present he'd wrapped for his grandson. They nabbed some cash, too, about fifty dollars."

"How many break-ins does that make?" Jared asked.

"We're up to eleven. And there's still just over two weeks until Christmas."

Henry left but not until accepting half of Maggie's meat loaf. She sat on her stool, one leg hooked over the other. How she managed to look comfortable was beyond Jared.

"Tell me about Calcaw," she said. "Especially what bothered you about the waiting room."

"First, I didn't like sitting there amid all those people I didn't know."

The waiting room had been about the size of Jared's living room and kitchen combined. He'd been given yet another form to fill out. Caleb was one of the youngest ones, but not by much. There'd been a sense of frantic motion in the room, but not from the kids. They were content to play their handheld video games or flit across the room from parent to aquarium to an activity corner and then do it all again.

"The seats were so close together." Jared had scrunched in a corner chair and again wrote down Caleb's age, address, school information.

After he'd turned in the chart, he listened to the parents around him. "These parents," Jared told Maggie, "were either seasoned professionals at doctor appointments or they were in shock."

"Which were you?"

"I didn't feel like either one. I felt like an imposter, like I didn't belong there."

"So what did you do?"

"Caleb was over by the aquarium, and I did the only thing I knew. I prayed."

"That this would all be a mistake." Maggie nodded.

"I won't deny that crossed my mind, big time. But mostly I prayed that every step I took would be the best step for helping him. I want him to do well in school, have friends, grow up to be successful."

"Then, why didn't you pray that what everyone's telling you is wrong? I know that's what I did." She finished her meat loaf, cleaned the counter around her and headed over to the trash can. She stood and looked at him, so serious.

"Between the books you recommended and Billy's advice, I just felt that I needed to offer up a different prayer."

"What did Billy say?"

"Billy said that most of us don't know what we ought to pray for, but that the spirit intercedes for us with groans that words cannot express."

Maggie blinked. "What exactly does that mean?"

"It's from Romans and means that God knows what is in our heart."

"God knows what's in our hearts," Maggie repeated. The thought didn't seem to make her happy.

"I've been reading those books you recommended," Jared said. "There's a chapter in one about kids who the parents thought had Attention Deficit but it turned out they didn't."

Maggie pressed her lips together. "You're on the chapter about autism."

"I'm praying that God watches me every step. He already knows my needs."

"But—" Maggie finally dropped everything in the trash and then wiped her hands against each other "—if you make a specific prayer request, God answers. Right?"

"Yes," Jared acknowledged, "but the answer isn't always what we think it should be."

"Got that right," Maggie muttered, finally headed back to her stool and close enough that he could see the dark brown flecks in her green eyes.

"What?"

"The book is more help, right now, than God."

Jared shook his head. "Without God, the book wouldn't even be in my hands."

"What do you mean?"

His voice broke. "If I were to have a specific prayer, for while I was sitting back there in Calcaw's waiting room, I'd have been praying for Mandy to be right beside me. She always made everything so much easier. But, that's not a prayer God would answer. You want the honest truth? I didn't know what to pray for. One, I wanted out of there. Not going to pray for that. I need to thank God for places like Calcaw where there are specialists who know more than I do. Two, I wished you were with me. That's a prayer that scares me. See, I've not noticed a woman since Mandy died. And, lately I'm noticing you a lot. Now do you see why I pretty much just prayed that God would watch my steps? He knows my heart. He knows all about the first two petitions."

"He knows your heart," she said softly. "Well, He knows mine, too. And my heart is not worthy of yours." She stood, picking up the empty container in front of him and throwing it in the trash.

"My prayers…" Her voice went to a whisper as she headed for the front door and opened it, unmindful of the cold and letting him know it was time to go. Louder, she said, "My prayers were answered. I don't want to pray anymore, ever again, and that pretty much tells you that I don't belong anywhere near your heart or prayers."

Chapter Fifteen

Friday night Beth made dinner for the McCreedy men. She brought over Christmas presents, too, arranging them under the tree next to the ones Billy had already placed there. The fake ones she'd wrapped for her wedding were all sparkling, solid shades of red, gold and silver. The ones for the children all had Santa wrapping paper.

Both Caleb and Matt still believed. Ryan wasn't picking a side. Jared figured Ryan feared that discrediting Santa might result in fewer presents.

The biggest gift was for Joel. "I still believe," he said. But, he wasn't looking at the tree or the present, he was looking at Beth.

"I want the decorations still in place," Beth reminded. "Since my sisters are wearing burgundy, the bulbs on the tree and all the Christmas decorations will match." She looked at Jared. "Will the tree last that long?"

"I'll go get a fresh one from Paul if it doesn't." It amazed Jared that Beth didn't want a big wedding. He figured it had something to do with her mother still being in prison.

"Did you hear about the preacher?" Jared asked as the family gathered at the table. The extra leaf stayed in now that Beth was a frequent guest.

Beth nodded, but no one else did. Jared caught them up on the break-in at Michael Russell's house. Beth knew a bit more, thanks to her sister being married to Chief Farraday. She knew the gifts had been for a four-year-old boy. "Mike had just gotten a train set in the mail."

"Someone must have seen the postman deliver it," Billy said. "Mike never put his tree in the window."

"We need to move our tree," Ryan said. "So it can't be seen from the road."

"We're already too far from the road for it to be seen," Jared reassured.

"Can he order another train?" Matt wanted to know. "And, will it get here in time?"

"Santa will bring it," Caleb predicted.

"How'd you hear about all this?" Billy said.

"I was at Hand Me Ups having lunch with Maggie. Henry stopped by. He always seems to know just about everything that goes on in town."

"You ate with Miss Maggie?" Caleb asked. "Again? Did you have spaghetti?"

Matt rolled his eyes.

Ryan just looked at his food.

"Everything all right with her?" Beth asked. "She seemed a little down when I stopped by after school."

Jared gave a brief shake of his head. He'd talk to Beth later, not when the boys were around.

"She going to be done with the dress in time?" Joel asked.

"I think so."

"You might want to find out. I'm leaving next week for Arkansas and the Elm Springs Rodeo. I'd like everything to be firmed up before I go."

"What's not firmed up, I'll take care of," Beth promised. "Just remember that our fitting," she said, then looked around the room, "everyone's fitting is tomorrow morning at nine. You do remember!"

Jared figured Billy was the only honest nodder.

"When's the next rodeo after Elm Springs?" Billy asked.

"New Year's Eve," Joel answered. "My wife and I will be attending together. Mr. and Mrs. Joel McCreedy."

Jared could only shake his head. Vagabond. That's what his brother was. And judging by the look in Joel's eyes, he was happier that he was taking his wife than getting to ride. Just wait until they had kids. He'd not be flitting here and there.

Of course, that's when he'd really be looking at Jared and talking about buying back, if not his share, then a few acres—enough to build a house and keep stock.

"Dad, Dad, I have a good idea. Can I give the preacher my train set from last Christmas?" Caleb asked.

Every adult paused, their eyes meeting across the table. Finally, Jared patted Caleb on the shoulder. The train set in question had been rode hard, put up wet and very loved. No way did Jared want to squash his son's giving nature. "We'll find out if that's needed when we go to church on Sunday."

The kids headed for the living room and the adults got busy. Joel went out to the barn to do animal duty. Billy settled down next to Caleb to work on letters. Ryan and Matt did their own homework.

Beth started gathering up the supper dishes. She didn't act surprised when Jared stood to work alongside her. "Why did Maggie stop going to church?"

"I don't know," Beth admitted. "It had something to do with the death of her husband. She's never really shared."

"He died in Afghanistan. Surely, she doesn't blame herself."

"I know how he died. I know she lived with his mother about six months and that she wasn't happy. I know she moved here because she always wondered if she might have family here. She found her mother's birth certificate. Her mother was born here. That's about all she's been willing to share."

"What was her mother's name?"

"Natalie Johnson. And her mother before that was Mary Johnson."

"There's two families at church named Johnson."

Beth nodded. "She spoke with them and with a few other families around town. We have plenty of Johnsons in Roanoke, just not the ones Maggie needs."

"How'd you meet Maggie?"

"That's your little brother's fault. She had hired Joel and I went along a few times. I was her first customer. Next thing I knew I'd made a friend. She knows more about clothes than anyone else. Plus, I love painting the murals on her walls."

"You're doing that in exchange for alterations."

"Yes," Beth said slowly, "but I pay her, too."

"Because she needs the money?" Jared guessed.

"She needs the money."

"I suggested yesterday that she go to our church and ask for help."

Maggie stopped wiping down the table and just stared at him. "I bet that went over well."

"Luckily, I suggested it while we were driving. She didn't answer, just stared out the window."

"That's typical Maggie. If she's uncomfortable with the subject, she gets quiet. It's how you know you struck a nerve. Anything else, she'll tell you what she thinks times two."

"So she never shares anything too deep?"

"I've heard about a few of the places that she's lived. And I know that Maggie was really hurt when her mom walked out on them."

"What kind of mom does that?"

Beth shook her head. "Maggie's one of the best moms I know. It's hard to believe she didn't have a good example."

Jared set the last of the dishes in the sink. "I pretty much told her that I was interested in her. And not because she's given me advice about Caleb and not because she has a child in my son's grade."

"Oh, Jared. I think that's wonderful. What did she say?"

"She said she didn't deserve my heart or my prayers. Then, she showed me the door."

"I told you she was afraid of God."

"Hmm," Jared said. "I think she's even more afraid of prayers."

"So, what are you going to do?"

"I'll fight fire with fire. I'll pray."

Saturday morning had Jared heading for his truck to make the group fitting appointment. He drove with Billy sitting next to him. Matt and Caleb were in the back. Ryan chose to ride with Joel in his truck.

"Three weeks until the wedding," Billy said. "Beth talk you into wearing those spats yet?"

"No. And there's two weeks until Christmas. Got all your baking done?"

Billy liked to cook but he hated to bake. Said it took up too much time. He was counting down to the wedding because when Beth moved in, she would take over making the sweets.

Once they got to Hand Me Ups, Maggie met Billy for the first time and let him flirt with her for all of a minute.

"So you're the one has my oldest boy coming to town often?"

She looked a bit stricken, at least to Jared's way of thinking, but she handled it well. "The way to a man's heart is through cooking, and he likes my pizza sauce."

Behind them both Matt and Ryan aimed their pointer fingers toward their mouths in a gagging motion.

Billy missed it. Jared and Beth did not. He licked his lips; she shrugged.

Then, Maggie became all businesslike. Not Cassidy. She served as greeter, information gatherer and general gopher. The men went into the dressing rooms downstairs. Beth and her sisters went upstairs to Maggie's apartment.

Maggie remained downstairs to start with the men's suits.

To Jared's chagrin, his jacket, vest and pants fit perfectly. Once he had them on, Maggie barely had to run a hand across his chest and over to his side to see if the arms moved loosely enough.

He grinned; she blushed.

Then, she tucked a hanky in his pocket and scowled at his shoes.

"Not wearing spats," he said.

Joel's clothes were a little tight. "Nerves," he said jokingly. "I keep eating."

"It's because Beth is a good cook," Billy said.

Heading back into the changing room, Joel hesitated while Maggie went upstairs. "Ryan had a few things to say on the drive over."

"About Maggie?" Jared guessed.

"He doesn't like her. I told him I was surprised. We talked a bit more, and it's not so much he doesn't like her. He's afraid she'll be around more."

Caleb came from upstairs with Cassidy by his side. You'd think he was her personal doll. He'd been the lone male allowed in their ranks. His tiny tux fit perfectly.

"Mandy would have loved this," Jared said to Billy.

"Since she's not here, it's a good thing you know enough to enjoy it." Billy's phone rang. Flipping it open, Billy said a curt, "Hello."

That was followed with, "You're kidding….No, I'll bring the boys….Who's in charge of the meeting?…

I'm with Maggie Tate now....Susan Farraday's here, too....I'll fill her in....I'm glad something's finally being done."

By the time Billy finished, all the bridesmaids were on the stairs, waiting. Only Beth couldn't come because she was in her wedding dress and Joel didn't get to see her in it yet. She hollered impatiently, "What's going on? It's cold up here. Who's on the phone?"

"What are you going to fill me in about?" Maggie carefully held the back of Susan's dress together. At eight months pregnant, Susan Farraday's prayer truly was that she'd lose weight by the time of her little sister's wedding: roughly eight pounds and six ounces.

Just in case she didn't, Maggie was dying a corset the exact same shade as the dress and adding part of it to each side of the zipper. She was also designing a wrap that would go perfectly.

"That was Mike Russell." To Maggie he added, "The minister at Main Street Church. There's a meeting tonight. The community is coming together to figure out what's been going on with the break-ins."

"Somebody else got hit?" Jared guessed.

"Your favorite waitress, Hillary. She got home from her shift last night and they'd taken everything under her tree. And she doesn't have the money to replace what was stolen by Christmastime. I think for the minister, Hillary was the final straw."

Jared heard Maggie's intake of breath and stepped closer to her. He put a hand on her shoulder. She didn't brush him off but she didn't give him any acknowledgment, either.

"Where's the meeting and what time?" she asked.

"Seven, and it's at the Main Street Church building."

"Why are they having it there instead of the school? Aren't most town meetings at the school?"

"This is last-minute. It's cheaper to heat the church, and the church offered," Billy said. "We were already having a prayer meeting."

"What can I do to help?" she asked next.

"What can we do to help?" came the sound of Beth and her sisters, all together.

"Call your husband and find out," Billy told Susan.

Susan took out the cell phone she'd tucked into the sleeve of her dress and made the call. When she hung up she said, "We need to spread the news."

"You need to do anything else on this dress?" Linda asked.

Jared had always liked Beth's oldest sister, Linda. She'd been in his class, and to his mind, she'd been the one to make sure little Beth was taken care of back when their mother had been way too strict.

Maggie shook her head.

"Then I need to get out of it and get busy. I'll make sure everyone who comes into my shop today for a hair appointment hears about the meeting tonight."

"Good," Susan said. "I'll head over to the police station and see if they've already made up flyers to hand out. I'll bring them over."

"No," both Beth and her older sister Linda said. "We can hand them out."

"I'm pregnant, not helpless."

"It's snowing and slippery," Billy toned. "You were always my best statistics student. Do the logic."

"Who invited him?" Susan grumped and turned to

flounce up the last two stairs. Jared noticed that being eight months pregnant didn't hinder her from abrupt movement.

The fitting was now over.

"Why would Hillary be the last straw?" Maggie asked Jared quietly. "I mean, I'm glad there's being more action taken, but it seems a little strange. After all, the minister's a victim, too."

"Hillary's a success story. She had a rough beginning. Her folks, well, let's just say they didn't deserve to be parents. Hillary made a couple mistakes but somewhere along the line, she found God. I think she's like the widow in the Bible who gave God a single mite but it was everything she had."

Maggie nodded, understanding.

"Also, and this isn't so well-known, Hillary used the benevolence fund at church a time or two. She's the only one, though, who's ever made sure to give back the money even when told not to."

"Pride and compassion," Maggie said.

"Pride and hope," Jared reminded. "Romans 12:12, remember?" He tightened his fingers on her shoulder and this time she looked up at him in a way that gave him hope.

"Dad, we need to leave," Ryan encouraged. "I want to go home."

"You never want to go home."

"I do today." It didn't escape Jared's notice that his oldest son was looking at Maggie while he asked.

As everyone began putting on their winter apparel, a cab pulled up in front of the shop.

Jared had been helping Maggie as she put jackets

back on soft hangers and carefully attached the bow ties to each collar. She turned, saw the cab and nearly sat down on the chair containing Billy's top hat.

"Someone you know?" Jared guessed.

"My mother-in-law."

Chapter Sixteen

Kelly Tate took in the crowded room, the cluttered stairs leading up to the apartment and calmly said, "Where shall I have him put my luggage?"

"Upstairs."

Instead of the cabbie, who'd never before driven his cab from Des Moines to Roanoke, the McCreedy men carried in the luggage. It went upstairs and into the bedroom Maggie shared with Cassidy.

Maggie would be sleeping on the couch tonight.

Everyone introduced themselves to Kelly, chattered about the wedding and about the Christmas thief, and then—too soon—started to leave. Joel and Beth were first. They were going on a wedding cake hunt. Billy and Jared took a moment to look at the window over Maggie's kitchen table.

"Needs replacing," Billy said.

"I'm getting good at windows," Jared said, taking a tape measure out of his back pocket.

"You carry tape measures with you?" Maggie asked.

"Not usually, but I remembered what Henry said the other night."

"Henry?" Kelly asked.

"He owns the shop across the street," Maggie answered, "and I'm not ready for a new window yet."

Once everyone left, Maggie showed Kelly the shop, mentioning the tree and what was missing and pointing out the mural Beth was working on.

"I didn't know you did weddings," Kelly said.

"I don't, usually. She's doing vintage, so we found the men's tuxes online. We found one of the bridesmaid's dresses and then I made the second. Beth borrowed the wedding dress from a friend."

"She doesn't like it."

"Huh?"

"Beth. She's not crazy about the dress."

Maggie blinked. Kelly had been here all of thirty minutes and already had an opinion that Maggie needed to pay attention to.

"What makes you think that?"

"Her sisters…"

"Susan and Linda."

"They kept looking in the mirror on your door. They couldn't stop looking. Beth glanced at it a couple times and then took off her dress."

"I like the dress, Grandma." Cassidy pranced from one side of the room to the other. "Did you see Matt? He's the second biggest boy. Isn't he cute? And Caleb, too. They have horses and a dog and—"

"And almost all the things on your Christmas list," Maggie finished.

Cassidy nodded. "Except for red cowboy boots.

Matt says red's a silly color for cowboy boots but Caleb thinks they'll be cool."

Maggie hadn't seen Cassidy's Christmas list in a few days, but Cassidy knew right where it was and fetched it. Knowing how small their apartment was and sensing that toys weren't going to flow down the chimney in unlimited numbers, Cassidy had kept her list small. After Thanksgiving, Maggie had suggested five items. Cassidy immediately wrote down two: red cowboy boots and a puppy. Of course, Maggie knew the list had grown. She'd seen the request for a baby brother. She'd heard about the addition of the horse.

"I'm at five now," Cassidy said proudly. "Mom says five is a reasonable number."

Kelly took the list. "Red cowboy boots, puppy, baby brother, horse, and," her voice faltered, "a daddy."

"Oh, my," said Maggie.

"Oh, my, indeed," said Kelly.

Kelly took Cassidy shopping. Since four of the items on the Santa list needed negotiating, Kelly felt the task necessary. The moment the door shut behind them, Maggie collapsed on her stool.

Without warning, her mother-in-law had decided to deliver the red cowboy boots in person and to stick around until after Christmas. At the moment, Maggie had no idea if the size of the apartment had changed Kelly's mind about staying. Based on how happy Kelly was to see Cassidy the answer was no.

Just wait until Kelly opened the refrigerator and saw how little food there was. Just wait until she saw the size of the shower in the minuscule bathroom. Just wait until Kelly heard that Cassidy had already picked out who she wanted for her next father.

There'd been a picture next to the words *a daddy*. Kelly might not have recognized the baseball cap and brown parka, but Maggie had. Cassidy had picked out Jared McCreedy.

Based on Thursday's lunch, he was willing to think about it.

Maggie let out a breath and looked up. The decorative tin ceiling was one of her favorite things about the shop. It was in great shape and even came complete with trim and borders. It had sheltered a hundred years of shop owners and their problems.

No, not it. God, really. He was in the little town and its people. He was with every person Maggie came in contact with lately. Everyone except Maggie.

"Thank You," Maggie mouthed then immediately felt guilty. Who was she thanking? No one. Because she didn't pray. Not even to say thank-you.

Things had been happening fast and furious since Thanksgiving, and really, she'd not had a chance to do anything but react.

"And if I prayed, I'd be praying right now."

Saturdays were usually the busiest day of the week, and today was no exception. As one customer after another came in the shop, some to buy and others to talk about tonight's meeting, Maggie was grateful for their patronage. Because she'd been tempted to pray and had she started, she might never have stopped.

Kelly and Cassidy came home with enough packages to require two trips up the stairs. They'd done the town and had even met Hillary at the Red Barn Grille.

"I've never seen her so happy," Kelly said, nodding at Cassidy. "We ran into at least three friends of hers from school. Then, all the men from that wedding party were at the restaurant."

"They bought our lunch," Cassidy said.

"We're going to put this stuff away and then go to the library. Cassidy says you both have overdue books."

Maggie almost fell off her stool. "Yes, we do. Cassidy, why didn't you remind me?"

"We've been busy, but Grandma has time to take me."

"I'm looking forward to it."

A customer came in, then another and another. Maggie started breathing a little easier. If she could keep this up, she'd have enough for a decent Christmas dinner. Kelly was a great cook, too.

Kelly and Cassidy came back down the stairs. Cassidy held on to her grandma's hand until she got to the bottom. She could see Henry shoveling his sidewalk across the street. "I've got to tell Henry that Grandma's here," Cassidy shouted. She turned to Kelly and asked, "Want to come with me?"

"I'll be over in just a minute."

"Look both ways before you cross the street," Maggie reminded.

Kelly, no stranger to winter, had on a fur coat, tights and knee boots. She walked over and looked in the pile Maggie was ringing up.

"Great Nehru jacket," she said. "Looks like it's actually from the 1960s."

"It is," Maggie affirmed.

The customer said something about making sure to

come back and then Kelly and Maggie were alone. They both looked out the window and across the street where Cassidy had taken over the shovel and Henry sat on a bench both advising and listening to her.

"I see why you like it here," Kelly said.

"Yeah, it's a pretty special place."

"He's wearing a brown parka," Kelly observed of Henry. "But I'm thinking he's not the man Cassidy was drawing on her Christmas list."

"No, he's not."

"Are you dating Jared McCreedy?" Kelly asked bluntly.

"No."

"Does he want to date you?"

"Yes."

"Then, what's wrong?"

Maggie's throat tightened. No way could she tell Kelly why she wasn't free to date a good man like Jared. Kelly wouldn't understand. Kelly wouldn't forgive.

Maggie didn't forgive herself.

Bob's Hardware Store carried plenty of windows. Jared paced back and forth trying to decide whether to keep Maggie's words in mind.

She'd said she wasn't ready for a new window. Meaning, she couldn't afford one right now. However, she needed a window. Not only was moisture a sign that cold air was getting it, but soon she'd have mold and decay.

If she didn't already.

He hated thinking about her up in that apartment, silent and cold.

Common sense told him the window could wait a month or two until they'd either entered a friendship, and he'd advise her; or they'd entered a relationship, and he could just do what he did best: take care of things.

She was too prickly now for him to buy and install without permission even though his gut told him that she needed a new window as a Christmas present more than she needed flowers or a candle.

"Not romantic enough," was Billy's input before heading off to the section stocked with kitchen supplies.

"You need a window?" Bob asked the obvious.

"Three foot tall by four foot wide."

"I've got Anderson, Pella and Marvin all in stock and in that size. Wait, I sold the last Anderson two weeks ago. Kyle Totwell's putting that old farm back together piece by piece."

"That he is," Jared said. "I helped him install his window. Why don't you go ahead and put together a price for me on both the Pella and Marvin. Let me know what I'll need and how much it is."

"I'll email it to you by Monday," Bob promised. "You going to the church tonight?"

"Wouldn't miss it."

Jared had already done what he could. They'd gone to the Red Barn Grille for lunch. No doubt, Hillary's tips were up, but that only solved one problem.

There were still two weeks until Christmas and whoever was committing the crimes was getting braver.

What if Maggie had been home when her place had been struck?

* * *

The Main Street Church was almost full when Maggie, Cassidy and Kelly walked in. Maggie wanted to slink in and find a spot in the back. Not Cassidy. She spotted Matt and took off like a magnet. Kelly wasn't far behind. Maggie didn't have much of a choice.

Next thing she knew she was in a full pew and sitting so close to Jared that her coat was unnecessary. Somebody had turned up the heat, or at least that's what Maggie hoped. Surely it couldn't be Jared's effect on her.

Kelly wound up next to Billy Staples. Maggie could see why Grandpa Billy was held in such high esteem. He had Caleb on one side with a dozen action movie figures doing battle.

"Are they saving the church?" Kelly asked Caleb.

"Maybe," Caleb answered.

Both Matt and Cassidy had taken notepaper from the back of the pew in front of them and were busy drawing. Matt had a near perfect Santa flying around the world. Cassidy had an all-pencil Santa who was more beard than belly.

Kelly and Billy chuckled companionably. Even though Jared separated her from her mother-in-law, Maggie could hear part of the conversation.

"I've been to Manhattan a time or two," Billy was telling Kelly. "It's been a while, though. I saw *42nd Street* back in the eighties. Jerry Orbach played Julian Marsh."

"I saw that one," Kelly breathed. "I was with my new husband. Dan wasn't born yet."

"I've often thought," Billy confided, "if I could do it all over, I'd act."

Both Joel and Jared's mouths dropped open.

"Your mother-in-law's nicer than I envisioned," Jared whispered.

"I'm not sure who this lady is," Maggie whispered back. "I think she's taken over Kelly's body. Be scared. Be very, very scared."

Mike Russell, who looked very much like a preacher even in jeans instead of his Sunday suit, took his place behind the podium. Alex Farraday stood, in full uniform, next to him. The auditorium's buzz increased instead of decreased. Tensions were high. Maggie used the time to look around. She had a vested interest in how tonight turned out. So did the minister. Jared pointed to his neighbors, the McClanahans. They'd been hit early on. "I don't see the Totwells," he whispered in Maggie's ear.

"I called them," Billy whispered back. "They said they'd try to make it. Their little boy's got a bad cold."

"Lisa had it earlier this week," Cassidy said. "She kept sneezing on me."

"Thanks for coming," the minister said loudly into the mike. "Let's go ahead and start with a prayer."

For once, Maggie wasn't the only one who didn't bow. But she listened to every word and felt the stirrings of something akin to comfort.

Hard to believe since Kelly Tate sat a few feet away.

"I'm Mike Russell, preacher here at the Main Street Church. Tonight we're going to hear some hard facts from the chief of police. We're also going to put our heads together and see if we can't figure out how to stop anyone else from losing their Christmas."

"We need more police," someone shouted.

Someone else said, "We need to watch the interstate. It has to be someone from out of town."

Mike moved aside and let Alex take the podium. "We don't think it's someone from the outside. In every instance the home owner was gone and people knew they'd be gone, whether it be for a church, school or work responsibility."

"That's right," the minister said. "I was here at church. At the same time, Hillary Phillips was at the restaurant and her two children were at the babysitter, like they are every Friday night."

"Not one of the break-ins appears random," Alex continued. "Plus, as most of you figured out already, the thief is targeting families and making off with toys while leaving items more valuable behind."

"Unless they happen to be easy to take and convenient," the minister added.

"Yes," Alex agreed. "What we want is for the community to band together. If you're going to be gone, ask a neighbor to keep an eye out. If there's a car in the neighborhood, even if it belongs to someone you know, write down the license number. That way we can see if there's a vehicle that happens to be in the area each and every time a theft occurs."

"We'll pray for whoever is taking our things, but we need to catch them and help them first."

"I'll help them," someone muttered in the back. "I'll help them right to jail."

Most people smiled and halfheartedly nodded. Down Maggie's pew, she could see Beth, a little white-faced. Maggie didn't know the whole story. She just knew that at one time Beth's mom had been the school secretary and that she'd embezzled for years in order to send her girls to college.

Looking at Kelly, Maggie realized she wouldn't need to do that. If it were for Cassidy, Kelly would be at the ready, checkbook open and pen in hand.

Maggie didn't want that much help. But she also didn't understand Beth's mother's choice.

Alex continued, "Please be sure to lock all doors and windows. Don't let anything valuable be seen from the windows, and yes, that might mean moving your Christmas tree. If you have time, go ahead and walk your neighborhoods. If you see anything suspicious, anything at all, give the police a call."

A few men went up and down the aisles and passed out papers. Maggie soon held a map of Roanoke. There were stars wherever a theft had taken place. No one area seemed targeted.

"Now that the police have done their thing," Mike Russell said, taking back the podium, "it's time for the church to step in. I've looked at the stars on this map. At least a third of the places hit belong to single parents."

"And single grandparents," Henry said loudly. "Don't forget your train."

"I won't," Michael promised. "There's not much time, but in the spirit of Christmas, the church would like to do something, maybe a quick donation or fundraiser."

The mood switched. Not everyone in the room was a church member. The word *donation* sent off a bit of a ripple throughout the crowd.

"What kind of donation?"

"I don't know," Michael said, "Maybe five dollars a family."

"What kind of fundraiser were you thinking?" Joel asked. "Something here at the church?"

"Could be."

"What did we do with the money from our winter program?" Henry asked.

"It went to the mission field, already mailed. How many would come to a second program if we could scramble and put it together?"

Caleb and Cassidy were among the few who raised their hands.

A woman up front raised her hand. Michael quieted the audience. She stood and turned around. "We just bought the Carver place this past summer."

Maggie recognized her. She'd been in Hand Me Ups Thursday.

"I normally wouldn't speak up, but my daughter and I were talking about this on the way here. See, we went to Solitaire Farm over Thanksgiving and went through that maze. We thought they'd do it for Christmas and drove all the way out there last week. It's just an idea, but I'd pay upward to twenty dollars if they did it up on a Christmas theme."

"That's an idea!" Michael said. "Jared, Billy, Joel, what do you think?"

Joel was already nodding, but Maggie noticed Billy and Jared exchange looks.

"All this and a wedding," Billy murmured.

"We'll divide the proceeds between the families who need it most," Michael said.

"Come on, Jared," a man Maggie didn't recognize

said. "We'll help you organize the maze and even do-nate more hay if you need it."

"McClanahan," Jared barbed, "you're real good about volunteering when it isn't your home."

"Hey, I get the traffic going to your place. Sometimes it even leaves the road and hits my fence."

"Once," Joel said. "It only happened once and I fixed the fence, remember."

"We've got the wedding," Jared said, "and we don't have anything to give people."

"Like what?" Kelly asked.

Beth had obviously been thinking. "Hot chocolate and baked goods. The church will help with the baked goods."

"I bake," Kelly said. "Just give me an oven."

Maggie doubted Kelly had seen the size of the oven in her apartment.

"When can you do it?" Michael asked.

"Next Friday," Joel volunteered.

"The day after the Christmas play at school." Billy now looked pale whereas Beth had gotten her color back.

"We'll string Christmas lights," Joel said.

"We'll use all the empty presents that I've wrapped," Beth add.

Caleb pulled on Billy's sleeve. "And you can be Santa."

"What!"

Kelly agreed, "You said you wished you could act. Here's your chance."

In front of the audience, Michael Russell said, "Let's pray."

Jared bowed his head. He nodded as he did it. And as he nodded, he looked at Maggie and took her hand. She knew he was thinking about her, helping her. She loved the way his hand felt, the roughness, the strength.

The window would have been easier.

Chapter Seventeen

It was late when Maggie put on her pajamas and put Cassidy to bed. She cleared off her side, getting it ready for Kelly, and wished she'd thought to change the sheets.

"I would have gotten a motel room but I couldn't bear the thought of being alone in a strange town," Kelly said. "I'm sleeping on the couch, you know that, right?"

"I want to sleep with Grandma," Cassidy murmured, half asleep and turning to face them.

"Guess that solves the problem," Maggie said. "You're the chosen one."

"No, I'll take the couch. It won't be the first time. Plus, I always get up early."

"So do I."

"I insist."

"It's my house," Maggie said.

"But—"

"My house," Maggie reminded, "and you're always welcome here as long as you're easy to get along with."

Kelly's lips twitched, and she paused before saying,

"I appreciate that. I think. I'll just get my pajamas on real quick."

Knowing that Kelly liked a cup of tea before bed, Maggie put on the water. She had tea, purchased by habit because of the months she'd lived with Kelly. While the water boiled, she turned the couch into a bed and, after checking on Cassidy, turned the television on low. An old Christmas movie with Jimmy Stewart played.

After the water boiled, Maggie brought Kelly her tea and settled into the easy chair right next to the sofa. She had her own cup of tea, too. It must be a mood thing. Picking up the box of elf hat material, Maggie started on yet one more.

"Do you have another needle?"

"Do birds sing?"

Over an hour later, they finished the last of the elf hats and made a couple extras for the maze.

"Why didn't we ever sit and visit like this when I was living with you?" Maggie asked.

"You were grieving, and I had my friends and meetings. We were too busy to enjoy each other. Plus, we were both angry. Not at each other, but at fate. A parent should not outlive her child. And, believe me, I know the void left when a husband dies. Now, tell me about your business and finances and young man. Don't leave anything out."

Maggie almost laughed. Who'd have guessed that telling her mother-in-law about Hand Me Ups business and finances would be easier than telling her about a male friend?

That's all Jared was: a friend.

* * *

It was time for bed. Joel took care of Matt, telling him all about his and Beth's plans come next week and how Matt could help. At a time when Matt had needed a friend, Beth had been there. They had a special relationship that extended to include Joel. Billy tackled Caleb, literally. Then, in respect to Billy's back, Joel carried Caleb up the stairs and into the bath.

By the time Jared put away the last of the popcorn dishes and turned off the kitchen light, Ryan was already in his room, under the covers, playing his hand-held game.

Stepping over clothes and some sports equipment, Jared made his way to the twin bed and sat down on the edge.

"I don't need to be tucked in," Ryan said, putting his game on the nightstand, turning so he faced the wall, and closing his eyes.

"Everyone needs to be tucked in."

Ryan turned his head frowned. "Are you going to talk to me about Maggie?"

"Why do you think that?"

"Last time you came in for a man-to-man talk was when I bumped into a girl at church and almost knocked her down. You said I had to apologize and be nice. You seem to come in the most when it has to do with girls."

Had it been that long? And was that the only reason? Usually, Jared was so busy making sure Caleb was in bed.

"I check on you every night."

"Not while I'm awake."

"You're right," Jared acknowledged. "I'll do better."

Ryan rolled over and faced his father. "So, are you here to talk about Maggie?"

"Yes."

"Great, just great." Typical nine-year-old, Ryan knew that tone was everything.

"Yes, it might be," Jared agreed. "But, then again, she and I might just be friends. Either way, you need to respect her."

"I don't want another mother. I liked the one I had."

"I liked the wife I had, too. When your mother died, I felt like someone took a scythe and cut my legs off at the knees. Sometimes it hurt to breathe, to walk, to try to go on."

Ryan turned so his face was in the pillow.

"We have it good here. I know," Jared said. "But, it could be better, and change is coming whether you want it or not. Another few weeks and Beth will be living here."

"I like Beth. I know her."

"Nothing's going to happen too fast or without you being part of the decision making. But, if Maggie lets me, I intend on asking her out again and again."

"Ew."

"Ew?"

"She's such a girly girl." Ryan sounded so much like an authority that Jared almost laughed. But, now was not the time. Reaching under the covers, Jared found Ryan's hand and held it. "From the time we brought you home, I've valued you, loved you and wanted what was best for you. You have to trust me now."

"I trust you."

Still holding on to his son's hand, Jared said a prayer.

"Father, help me do a better job each day of being a father to my sons, a worker in my fields and a giver at our church. Guide us all in our decisions. Amen."

Ryan didn't say anything, and Jared stood and retucked the quilt around his son's frame. Then, he went to the door and turned off the light. He'd already mostly shut the door behind him when he heard a soft, "I love you, Dad."

Ryan would be all right. It might take a while, but Ryan was really the one who remembered Mandy the most. No wonder he was scared.

Jared was scared, too.

Scared that he was falling in love with a woman who couldn't, wouldn't, love him back no matter how hard he prayed.

Kelly took Cassidy to church Sunday morning, casting a disappointed look in Maggie's direction. "It's past time," she said. For the second Sunday in a row, Maggie cleaned the apartment.

On Monday, Kelly worked in the shop, helping customers and baking while Maggie finished the costumes for Thursday's school program. A couple times Kelly started making suggestions, about a certain price, about the mural, or about the store's arrangement, but just a look from Maggie stilled any discussion about doing it Kelly's way. By the end of the day, Hand Me Ups smelled more like a bakery than a vintage clothes shop.

On Tuesday, right before lunchtime, Jared showed up at the door. He smiled at Kelly, making Maggie wonder what they'd talked about Sunday morning at church.

Kelly simply handed him a cookie. She'd been giving them out to customers, too, and sales were up.

Maggie had gone two days without seeing Jared. She'd parted company with him after the town meeting, about nine Saturday night, and now here it was eleven Tuesday morning.

Sixty-two hours.

Not that she'd been counting.

"Tonight," he asked, "would you like to drive around town and look at the Christmas lights?"

"I'll watch Cassidy," Kelly volunteered quickly.

"Oh, she'd like to come along—" Maggie started to say, and then she saw the expression in Jared's eye. He was asking her out on a date, a real honest-to-goodness date. Even though she'd told him straight out that she didn't belong anywhere near his heart or prayers.

Maggie looked at Kelly. She simply nodded and mouthed, "Go."

"I don't…"

Saying no was safe. Maggie could concentrate on keeping the store running, on keeping Cassidy running, on keeping hold of the precious control she needed in life.

Saying yes was chancy. Life had been a little out of control ever since Jared had appeared that awkward morning and cleaned up pancake batter spilled in her tiny kitchen. Seemed that since then, he'd been around so much she'd gotten used to him.

"Ahem," Kelly said, back to being the impatient mother-in-law. "You need to finish your answer. I suggest you say, 'I don't have any other plans and would love to.'"

"I'm sorry, Jared. My mother-in-law's here visiting, and I've got a lot of work to do. Maybe another time."

Jared nodded, his smile not diminishing a bit. "I'll ask again. For now, I'm back to the school and finishing up the stage. You'll be around later for practice, right?"

"Yeeess."

"Good, I look forward to seeing you."

He walked out the door and Maggie turned to Kelly. "I can't believe you're encouraging me to go out with him. Do you know how hard it is to tell him no?"

"And I can't believe you need encouragement. And why on earth would you tell him no? He's a good man who happens to be falling in love with you. He's the kind of man who'll take on Cassidy as his own. Maybe you'll even have more children. You're only twenty-seven. Life doesn't end just because a spouse dies."

"You never remarried," Maggie pointed out.

The last customer left, without buying anything, and Kelly walked to the door and turned the sign to Closed. Maggie let out a tiny protest.

"Five minutes," Kelly promised. "I just need five minutes to slap some sense into you."

To Maggie's amazement, the moment Kelly turned from locking the door, she burst into tears. Awkwardly, Maggie drew her mother-in-law into a hug noticing how ramrod straight she remained and how tense she was. They'd never done more than the get-close-and-pat-each-other-on-the-back kind of hug.

"If you're going to slap some sense into me, you'd better stop crying," Maggie advised.

"I'm so glad I came," Kelly blubbered.

"So that you can slap some sense into me?"

"No, so that I can stop thinking that my way is best, stop pressuring you to come back to Manhattan, and start realizing that my granddaughter can bloom without me."

"Okay, well, then I'm glad you came, too."

Almost as quickly as it started, Kelly's tears stopped. "I need a cup of tea," she said. "Give me a moment." Up the stairs she went. Maggie glanced at the Closed sign on the door, adjusted a few clothes racks, and followed her mother-in-law up the stairs.

The window by the kitchen table was frosted over. Kelly drew a tiny circle on it with her finger and looked out. "You're a really good mother," she said.

"What?" A comment about parenting skills was not what Maggie expected.

"You know enough to let her have wings. That was my problem with Dan. Because we had just one, I wanted to enjoy every moment and forgot that my son needed to enjoy every moment, too."

"You were a good parent. Dan turned out just fine."

"Dan couldn't wait to get away from home. That's why he joined the military."

Maggie wasn't going to lie because that's exactly what happened, but... "You did the best you knew how."

"You want to know why I didn't get remarried?" Kelly asked. "And, believe me, I had plenty of opportunities."

"Why?"

Kelly leaned in. "I never remarried because I wasn't willing to share Dan with another man. I wanted all control, and I got it. But the cost was high. In the end, the only thing I had control over was myself."

Control had always been an issue in Maggie's life, first battling her father who didn't understand a girl's needs, and then battling Dan over Cassidy's needs, and now maintaining control when there was no father or Dan in sight.

Well, Jared was in sight.

She'd given up a bit of control the day of the break-in. That little bit was like a door opening and letting Maggie see the potential in the world, potential being Henry Throxmorton who'd come across the street to help. Jared McCreedy who'd installed a new lock on her door within an hour. Alex Farraday who'd stopped by or called at least once a day with updates.

And now control was giving over, just a bit, to Kelly Tate who was turning out to be a natural storekeeper who gave cookies to customers and talked them into buying things they didn't need.

When Maggie didn't answer, Kelly said, "Really, the only one who should be in control is God. How I wished I'd understood that when Dan was young."

Oh, yeah, and God had been in control when Dan died.

That's what Maggie couldn't forget.

"I'm madder than spit," Beth said, holding a Christmas tree in place while Jared secured the bottom. Only two days until the Roanoke Elementary Christmas program and just about everything was in place.

"He forgot. That's all."

"Joel never forgets when it comes to his precious rodeo, and now we're doing all the work."

Jared stood, stretching his back. He'd placed a dozen

tiny fake trees, donated by Bob's Hardware, around the school's gymnasium. Right now, the older grades were putting out folding chairs. On stage, the kindergartners were practicing their song. Caleb's voice was loudest of all, which might be okay if he were singing the same song. Jared wasn't quite sure.

"We'll get the maze done, even without him. The McClanahans have been out every night."

"And my mother-in-law has made a thousand cookies." Maggie stepped up behind Beth. "We'll be coming on Friday after school to help."

"Friday's going to be ridiculously busy, and we'll be tired after Thursday night's program."

Beth walked away, shaking her head.

"It's not the maze that's bothering her," Maggie said. "It's that she's getting married in a little over two weeks and there's so much to do."

"And so little time to do it," Jared agreed. "I told them a Christmas wedding would be tough. Hey, I have something for you."

Reaching in his back pocket, he pulled out some papers. "I priced a new window for your apartment. Here are two cost comparisons. When Joel gets back in town, we'll do the work so you don't need to worry about labor."

"I'll pay for labor."

"Nah, putting in a window is easy, and we're pros. Remember, we did it at the Totwells'. Plus, you can give me some more advice about Caleb."

"Advice is free. Only with my mother-in-law does it come with a price."

"She seems fairly harmless."

"It's been an amazing visit so far," Maggie admitted, shrugging out of her coat and laying it on a chair. "When she first showed up, I just…"

"Just what?"

In a much quieter voice, Maggie said, "I wished she'd go away."

"We all wish our problems away at one time or another. By the way, speaking about problems, the allergy pediatrician called me yesterday," Jared said. "They think he's allergic to milk. All those questionnaires I filled out finally made sense to somebody. Caleb's complained about stomachaches since I can remember. We have to go back for more tests but, for the moment, the doctors are thinking it might be milk, eggs and cheese more than ADD."

Maggie shook her head. "And you're a farmer with an abundance of milk, eggs and cheese."

"I've got an abundance of a lot of things, and I'm always willing to share them with the right person."

"Jared, don't."

"Why, Maggie? Is it because it's Christmas and you're thinking about your late husband?"

"I need to go up on stage and check the costumes, see if they're in good condition. Kids tend to be rough during rehearsals."

"I'm a patient man. I didn't used to think so. But, thanks to you, I've learned quite a bit." He threw her words, from so many weeks ago, back at her. "Patience is a virtue, have it if you can. Seldom found in a woman. Never in a man."

Maggie looked away.

"Never in a man," he nudged gently. "Just give me a bit of hope. That's all I ask."

"It wouldn't be fair. You deserve someone—"

"I'm picky," Jared interrupted. "It's taken me a long time to find the person I want. I mean, deserve."

Before Maggie could answer, Beth came back, holding her cell phone for Jared to take. "It's Joel. He's got a few things to say, and I'm not talking to him."

"Hello, bro," Jared said. "I see I need to give marital counsel even before you're married."

"I'm half tempted to pack up and come home," Joel admitted. "I'm not in the mood to ride, and that never goes well. But I've paid the entry free."

"Yes." Jared looked at Beth. "The entry fee is non-refundable. I can see why you feel torn."

"Look," Joel said. "Can you make it over to Freeport today? Remember Jerry, the kid who wanted to be a bull rider and his dad owns Binky Burgers?"

Only Joel would throw that much information at Jared and think he might possibly remember. "No."

"Well, they've got a Santa sled they put in front of the fast-food restaurant every December. They're going to let us borrow it for Saturday night seeing as how it's a good cause. But, someone needs to go get it."

"That's perfect!"

"What?" said Beth. "What's perfect?"

"He found us a Santa sled to use Saturday night."

"Hmm, long-distance help still means we do the work," she sniffed.

"I heard that," Joel said. "Tell her I'll be back late Sunday and that I love her."

Jared relayed the message.

"Tell him," Beth said, "that he can stay gone."

Jared started to relay the message, but realized almost immediately that the only thing keeping Maggie upright was his hand under her arm. She looked about to faint.

"What's wrong with—" he started to say.

"Maggie, are you all right?" Beth asked.

Shaking her head, Maggie ran from the room, out the door, and to her car.

Without her coat.

It wasn't so much the coat that had Jared most worried, it was the words she flung back at Beth.

"Don't say that," she told Beth. "Don't ever say that."

Jared watched Maggie's ashen face as she jerked her vehicle into reverse and left the parking lot.

Beside him, Beth stood all confused. "What just happened? What did I say?"

"I don't know," Jared answered. "But whatever it was, you struck a nerve."

Beth thought for a moment. "I told you to tell Joel to stay gone."

Jared nodded.

"That must have been it. Me telling Joel to stay gone."

Jared agreed. Those words had Maggie looking like she'd seen a ghost, and from her words, Jared guessed she'd been haunted for a long time.

Chapter Eighteen

Beth couldn't leave. She had twenty-five singing kindergartners on stage. Jared didn't have such a dilemma. He was in his truck and on the lookout for Maggie within a minute.

What had just happened?

Don't say that, she'd told Beth. *Don't ever say that.*

What exactly had Beth said?

Tell him that he can stay gone.

Well, at least now Jared had some idea what was bothering Maggie, but not enough idea for him to do anything but gnaw at it.

He went to Maggie's shop. She wasn't there, but Kelly promised to call the minute she turned up. Her car wasn't at the library, the post office or the church.

Driving down Main Street, Jared saw one vehicle after another that he recognized, but not Maggie's van.

At Bob's Hardware, he watched as Kyle Totwell carried something to his truck. Kyle waved as he climbed in the driver's side.

Click.

Something flashed in Jared's brain. The window aisle. Bob saying they'd sold the last of the Anderson three-by-fours two weeks ago. The old screwdriver in the door and Kyle Totwell talking about his grandfather leaving him everything, everything old.

Great, just great.

Jared pulled out his cell phone and called Chief Alex Farraday.

"I'm in my truck and don't like using the cell. Do me a favor. Call Bob's Hardware and asked Bob when he sold Kyle Totwell the Anderson window."

Alex didn't hesitate, just said, "Will do," and hung up. A minute later, he returned the call. "December first."

"When did Kyle say the thief broke the window getting into his living room to steal the presents?"

After a moment, Alex came back with, "December third."

"You do know," Jared asked, "that Joel and I helped him install the new window on December 5."

"He purchased the window before the thief broke the window," Jared and Alex said together.

"I hope I'm wrong," Jared said, thinking of the two children and the woman who'd loaned Beth her wedding dress. Chances were she didn't know what Kyle had been up to.

It would be even worse if she did.

Right after Jared ended the call to Alex, Kelly Tate called. "Maggie stopped by. She's heading back to the school. She says she's got commitments to keep. She's been crying. You know anything about that?"

"I'll tell you when I figure it out," Jared promised.

Back at the school, however, Maggie became an expert at avoidance, and Jared didn't know how to approach her. But, the good thing about small towns was, she couldn't avoid him forever.

"Someone's ringing the doorbell," Kelly said.

"I'll get it," Cassidy offered. Because of the Christmas program and all, homework was not an issue this Tuesday night. The teachers were too busy to assign it.

"It's probably Beth wanting to talk again," Maggie said.

"She's your best friend. You need to talk to her," Kelly advised.

"I will, just not today."

"Then talk to me."

Maggie shook her head. Not a chance, not a chance.

Opening the window, she peered down at Jared Mc-Creedy. He held some presents in his arms. For a moment, the only emotion Maggie felt was annoyance. He'd brought her presents. She'd told him time and time again she wasn't interested.

Then, she recognized her own wrapping paper.

"You found Cassidy's presents!" she shouted down. For a moment happiness took over, pushing aside the guilt she'd been feeling.

"We found everything. Let me in."

Cassidy and Kelly were at her heels as she went down the stairs. Maggie opened the door and Jared breezed in. He gave the presents to Cassidy. "I believe these are yours."

In response, Cassidy ran upstairs to put them under the tree.

Maggie's jewelry was in a sack. She opened it,

checked the items and smiled. "I don't care about the jewelry, but the presents are greatly appreciated." She turned to Kelly. "Counting the red cowboy boots you bought her, she'll now have three pairs."

"Every girls needs a closetful of shoes," Kelly responded.

"Usually the police keep evidence, but with the evidence being Christmas presents and the thief confessing to everything, Alex decided that the good book had the best advice."

"What's that?" Maggie asked. "Thou shalt not steal?"

"Let the thief no longer steal," Kelly quoted from memory, "but rather let him labor, doing honest work with his own hands, so that he may have something to share with anyone in need."

"I think," Jared said, "that Alex was thinking more along the lines of 'Give and it will be given unto you.'"

"They all work." Kelly took a few steps up the stairs. "I'll check on Cassidy."

Maggie knew exactly what her mother-in-law was doing. She was leaving Maggie with Jared so they could talk.

"Who was the thief?"

"Kyle Totwell. He couldn't afford to buy gifts for his wife's family and he was ashamed. Apparently the first crime was spur of the moment. He saw an open door and an opportunity. I guess when Alex drove up the lane to their farm, Kyle started crying like a baby."

"What's going to happen to him?"

"I don't know. Everything was there, so the presents will be returned to their rightful owners and in time for Christmas. That will count as something."

"I'm glad for the other families. It was a worry." Maggie stepped to the door, reaching for the knob. "Are you going to cancel the maze now?"

"No, we've advertised it from Freeport to Des Moines. Even if I tried to cancel it, people would show up. I don't want to have to tell a hundred people they drove all the way out to Solitaire Farm for nothing."

"Kelly's baked again all day. She's also working on your Santa suit."

Jared rolled his eyes. "I can't believe Billy's back chose to go out now. The church has one, you know. I'll just wear it."

"Hmm, then I'm not sure what she's working on. It's red, white-fur lined, and she says it's for you."

Jared stepped toward the door, closer to her and bent his head. "There's still time to drive around tonight and look at the lights."

"No."

"You can tell me why you got upset today. After all, it's your fault we stumbled on to what Kyle Totwell was doing."

"What?"

"I was hunting for you when I put two and two together about the window he'd purchased." Quickly, Jared filled her in on the details.

When he finished, she still shook her head no. "I've got Kelly here and it's almost time to put Cassidy to bed."

"I can take care of myself," Kelly hollered from upstairs, "and Cassidy just put herself to bed!"

"Did not," Cassidy said calmly.

"I'm going to keep asking you," Jared promised.

"And I'm going to keep saying no," Maggie replied.

Jared tussled the top of her head. "Good, I like a challenge.'

Thursday night, the Roanoke Elementary Christmas program was a success, even though Caleb sang the wrong song and Cassidy got tangled up in the giant Santa bag while handing out presents to her elves.

Matt was so busy helping her that he forgot to be shy and actually did his part.

Ryan got a standing ovation.

Friday, Maggie closed Hand Me Ups early and piled everyone into her van and headed out to Solitaire Farm. "I've never been out here," she said, handing Kelly directions.

"You're kidding."

"No. We didn't make it to the Thanksgiving maze, and there's just no reason to come out this way."

"I can think of plenty of reasons," Kelly said.

Forty minutes later, Maggie saw the number two reason to visit a place like Solitaire Farm. On the rural road was Solitaire's Market. It looked like an old-time log cabin. There were rocking chairs, with price tags, on the front porch. Giant windows offered a peek at what was inside. This was where Joel sold produce and goods. It was beautiful.

Trucks were parked by the maze, and people—Maggie knew all of them—were stringing lights and putting up decorations.

"Wow," Cassidy said.

Maggie would need more than "wow" to describe what she saw next. The market didn't compare to the number one reason to visit Solitaire Farm. That would be the actual farm, past the trees, a good quarter mile down the gravel drive.

As dusk settled, lights glowed yellow in the windows. The farmhouse was white clapboard, two-storied and came with a wraparound front porch all draped in wintery white and dripping icicles. The yard went on forever, and a dog ran through the snow toward them.

"Captain Rex!" Cassidy shouted.

"What happened to normal names like Butch and Tiger?" Kelly asked.

As Maggie parked, Jared came to the porch and hurried down to open the van's door. Behind him came the others, all grabbing boxes of baked goods and helping in the ladies.

The house was full of people.

The minister was wrapping presents. The McClanahans were lettering signs. Kelly headed right to the kitchen to stand alongside Billy as he decided which cookies would be served first and how much hot chocolate they'd need.

Beth was on the phone. "Everything's going fine. You be careful today. Don't get hurt. Go ahead and place."

She'd had time to retract her wish.

Jared took Maggie by the hand and led her in and out of rooms, up and down stairs, showing off his home. He pointed out the family portrait which included Mandy.

"She's beautiful," Maggie said, disengaging her hand.

"Yes, she was. And she would have liked you."

Last, he made her get back into her winter coat and took her out to the barn. "This is my favorite place."

There were three pens, each containing a horse. Hay bales were against one wall. A tractor took up most of the room. "I come out here whenever I need to think. For a long time, after Mandy died, I came out here every evening for hours at a time. Lately, I've gone a whole week without coming here except for chores."

"That's good."

Someone shouted Jared's name and they headed back inside. Beth was busy giving people jobs for Saturday's maze day. Maggie wound up being assigned Solitaire Market duty. After all, people would be browsing both before and after their turn at the maze. There was no produce, but there were jars of honey, homemade soap and as Jared suggested, "Why don't you bring some of your shawls, mittens and stuff tomorrow to sell? We're in this together."

At seven, everyone gathered in the living room and Mike Russell, the minister, asked if there were any prayer requests before he offered thanks for the chili Billy and Kelly had whipped up. Soon, he had a list. He was praying for Tess Throxmorton's health. He was praying for winter to be over, for out-of-town travelers over the holidays, and especially—per Beth—for Joel's safety both on the bull and on the road.

Someone even suggested they pray for the Totwells. Every head, including Maggie's nodded. Soon, even though her eyes were open, she bowed her head.

"Father," the minister said, "we thank You for all You've done for us. Please be with those traveling over the holidays and those with health issues. We thank You for the McCreedys who've opened their home and land for good works. We pray that tomorrow night's activities will honor thy name. Amen."

Maggie settled on the bottom step of the stairs and looked around for Cassidy. She was in the kitchen with Billy and Kelly and the boys. Captain Rex was with them and helpfully lapped up the food that fell.

Jared soon nudged her over. "Room for me?"

There was nowhere else for him to sit, really.

"This is great. I love that we prayed for the Totwells."

"We prayed?" His smile widened.

Maggie tried to scoot over more, but there was no room. She was pressed right against him. She wasn't sure if she should be annoyed—and, really, being annoyed all the time was just bothersome—or just enjoy the contact. "Yes, I prayed."

"The Totwells have been on a lot of hearts today," Jared said. "Mike has been calling the people who had their presents stolen to see how much each of them needed from tonight's fundraiser. Very few needed any money. He started querying where our proceeds should go. Guess what we're doing with the lion's share of the money?"

"The church?"

"Not a cent."

"Salvation Army?"

"That was suggested. No, we're giving most of it to Sophia Totwell. With her husband in jail, she's going to need all the help she can get."

"Wow."

"It was Beth and Joel's idea."

"Because of Beth's mother," Maggie guessed.

"We all make mistakes. Nearly every family the preacher spoke with thought the same things."

Jared had no idea how true his words were and how they made Maggie feel. Words had gotten her into this mess.

"We invited the Totwells tonight, but Sophia couldn't bear to come. If it weren't for the farm, she'd go home to her parents. When Joel gets back, she'll do just that and he's going to stay there for a while. Then, after he and Beth get married, she'll stay there, too, until Kyle figures out what he's going to do."

"That's nice of them."

"Yes." Jared turned to Maggie. "What do you think I should do? Should I offer to sell Joel back his portion of the farm? After all, he runs the market and does much of the work."

"Does he want his portion back?"

"He wants to live here."

"But does he want his portion back? What does he want?"

Jared shook his head. "He doesn't want all this land. He wants just enough for the animals, a workshop for his craft and the market. He's not a farmer."

"Have you gotten him a wedding present yet?" Maggie asked.

"No."

"Well, he's your brother. Give him just enough for the animals, a workshop and the market."

"I can't make ends meet without proceeds from the market."

"He gets the market, but you get to sell produce in it, too. After all, it's on your land."

Jared looked around the room until he spotted Beth. She, of course, was on the phone. "You talking to Joel?"

She nodded, and soon Jared was talking to Joel and Beth was sitting next to Maggie.

"Are you okay?" Beth asked.

"I'm fine. Sorry I wigged out on you the other day."

"It's the Christmas season." Beth wrapped her arm around Maggie. "It's hard on those of us who've suffered loss in the last year."

If just loss were the only thing Maggie suffered. In some ways, loss was easier than guilt.

Jared usually woke up before the alarm but not this Saturday. There'd been cleanup last night and excited kids and even an excited Billy.

"That woman knows how to bake a cookie," Billy said about Kelly.

"We all have our gifts," Jared agreed.

After breakfast, Billy and the boys got into the van and went out to put up signs pointing the way to the Christmas maze. Jared took care of the animals and general maintenance before heading to Solitaire's Market to make sure all was well there.

It was.

His next job was to start taking tables out of storage and put them where the lines would be.

Hot chocolate was fifty cents a cup. Cookies a dollar for two. There were also the usual cakes and brownies and such. The people from the Main Street Church and even a few non-church people had stepped up to the plate.

At five, helpers started arriving.

Jared only had eyes for one and she was taking her sweet time it looked like. Maggie Tate was always late. And he was quite willing to wait.

"She'll be here," Billy said.

At six, Jared went in to put on the Santa suit. "Really, Billy, you should be Santa."

"I can't take the weight of all those children. You know that."

"Then the minister."

"He'll be busy being the photographer and spreading the word while he does it. What an opportunity tonight is for him."

Looking in the mirror, Jared could only shake his head. He was too thin to look like the real thing. Plus, his dark hair showed through the scraggly white hair of the church's Santa suit. It had been worn often and Jared wished he'd have asked Billy to throw it in the wash. Too late now.

Maggie's van finally pulled in the driveway. He hurried to help her with the clothes and stuff she'd brought from Hand Me Ups.

"Thanks for letting me do this," she said.

"When we open for the season, you can stock some items for us to sell."

She smiled but made no promise.

Quickly, the volunteers got into place. All except for Kelly, who looked at Billy, a comical perplexed look on her face as she said, "It's just too cold for me to help with the hot chocolate and sweets outside. I think I'll work in the market."

"I could always use the help," Maggie agreed.

"That would make it too crowded." Kelly looked thoughtful for a moment, before saying, "Billy, bring me the quilted bag I left by the door."

In a moment Billy was back and Kelly was unloading the Santa outfit she'd been furtively working on for the last few days. She fluffed it out.

Jared saw Maggie's eyebrows raise. "Not Santa!" she breathed.

"Mrs. Claus!" the kids yelled.

Jared watched Maggie back up as the outfit was handed from kid to kid until it made its way to her. She held it up. A long-sleeved red dress with white marabou trim was just her size. It looked like it would fall to right above her knees. Kelly handed over a package of new red tights. "Here's the hat, too."

"I can't be Mrs. Claus. I have a shop to run."

"I've done fine all week without you. You help Jared."

"Please, Mom."

"Mom? I like that. Oh, and here's one more thing, an early Christmas present for you to unwrap."

Maggie shot Kelly a look that made Jared glad he had nothing to do with this plan.

Where Kelly got the package, Jared didn't see. Maggie quickly opened it and pulled out...red cowboy boots.

"They were Cassidy's idea," Kelly said. "I added the white fur. You can take it off later."

"You do know," Jared said, "Mrs. Claus always sits on Mr. Claus's lap for the first picture."

The look in Maggie's eyes told him that he'd better stay out of kicking range of her boots.

Mike Russell didn't even suggest that Maggie climb on Jared's lap. He just grinned and said, "The Lord works in mysterious ways."

"More like my mother-in-law works in mysterious ways," Maggie muttered.

From six-thirty on, there was a continuous line. The McClanahans and Jared's boys were elves leading people through the maze. Beth was the helper who organized the line. Maggie led children to Santa and arranged them for their picture.

First, though, Santa always asked what they wanted for Christmas.

For the most part, the requests were the same. "I want a new video game."

"I want a doll."

"I want a skateboard."

"I want a horse."

At least Cassidy wasn't the only one.

One little boy broke Maggie's heart. "I want my granddaddy to go away," he whispered in Santa's ear. "I prayed about it. Can you take him to the North Pole? He likes toys." Only Maggie and Mike Russell were close enough to hear.

Mike took over. "Why is that?"

"He makes my mommy cry."

Jared's eyes met Maggie's over the little boy's head. Mike gave a quick shake of his head.

"Can I put something under the tree for you?" Jared, er, Santa, asked.

"A puzzle. Granddaddy will help me put it together."

A few minutes later, there was finally a lull and Maggie said to Mike, "Did you know that little boy?"

"That was Joshua Phillips. Hillary's youngest son."

Maggie remembered what Jared had said, about Hillary's hard beginnings, who she was today, and parents who didn't deserve to be parents.

"Can we contact someone?" Maggie asked. "Social services or something?"

"Abe Phillips is just a strange old man," Mike said. "He makes Hillary cry because she's the sole breadwinner. He's never worked a day in his life. But, it's his house she lives in, and he watches the boys while she works. He does play with them. He's the kind of guy who never grew up. They wouldn't be better off, at least right now, without him."

"That's sad."

"It is, but if you knew the situation five years ago, you'd know how much better it is now and how much hope both Hillary and her dad have."

"But," Maggie said, "that little boy is praying that his grandpa goes away. That can't be good."

"Have you ever heard of First Chronicles 28:9?"

Maggie shook her head. Thanks to her short marriage to Dan, she knew the stories of the Bible, the lessons therein, but she'd not had the opportunity or teachings to put many verses to memory.

"For the Lord searches every heart and understands every motive behind the thoughts."

Maggie let out a breath, loud enough for Jared to hear. He looked at her. Tears, quickly stopped by the cold, brimmed just beyond her cheeks. "Oh, oh."

"Maggie, are you okay?"

"Is that scripture for real?"

"Yes, and it's one of my favorites," Mike said. "If God answered some of the prayers I've uttered in haste, I'd be in trouble."

"Ohhhh." Maggie felt her body relax, like something escaping—guilt?—to let something else take its place—joy?

An elf came through the maze right in front of more kids. Maggie wiped her eyes and got back to business. This time, there was a lightness to her step and the joy of the season followed her every movement. Between children, she looked at Jared.

He looked back and she nodded yes to the questions in his eyes.

Then, suddenly, it was her own daughter's turn on Santa's lap.

Cassidy didn't seem to remember that Santa was really Jared. She crawled up on his lap, not needing Maggie's assistance, and reached into her pocket.

"I brought my list."

"Let me see it."

Maggie peered over Jared's shoulder and read aloud, "Red cowboy boots, puppy, baby brother, horse and a daddy."

"Hmm." Jared looked at Maggie and said, "I think I can help with most of those. Do you want me to…?"

Mike Russell just barely got the camera ready in time to photograph the kiss Maggie Tate gave Jared as she joined her daughter on Santa's lap and said, "I do."

Epilogue

"It's perfect," Maggie said.

Beth looked in the mirror, first front and then back before finally going sideways just to do it all again.

Maggie smiled. Everything about the light, ivory-colored organza-over-satin dress suited the artistic Beth, from the embroidered tulips, looking three dimensional, to the attached double sash that attached to the train also embroidered with tulips. The nipped waistline to the princess-seamed bust molded perfectly to Beth's body.

"Mrs. Tate, can I really wear it?"

"Call me Kelly and absolutely. That's why I had it sent. I knew when I saw the McCreedy's living room and realized the Christmas theme for your wedding, that my old wedding dress was perfect."

Beth looked at Maggie. "And you don't mind that I'm not wearing the one you've been repairing?"

"Oh," Maggie said slowly, "I think somebody else might get to wear that dress." Walking over, she took it down and admired it.

"Try it on," Beth urged.

"She has," Kelly said. "Twice that I'm aware of."

"Just to make sure the alterations were smooth."

Beth and Kelly exchanged a look that clearly communicated "Yeah, right."

"I'll just put on the lace overcoat so you can see how it looks now that I've repaired it."

Gently, Maggie took it from the soft hanger. It fell to her shoulders perfectly. The sleeves tapered at her wrists.

"Wow," Beth said.

Kelly nodded.

Downstairs, the bell above the door sounded and kids' voices filled the shop. Cassidy and Caleb's volume were always on high.

"Well," came a shout, "did you find the perfect dress?"

"Joel, don't come up!" Beth shouted.

"Can I come up?" Jared's voice, deep and rich, questioned.

"You can't come up, either!" Beth shouted. "You can't see the bride." Quietly, she added, "And I'm not talking about me."

Maggie took off the overcoat and returned it to the hanger.

"I'll step down and see how the men are doing."

Beth chuckled. "Men, right. You mean the *man*."

"I guess I do." Maggie opened the door to her shop and took a few steps down, only to meet Jared who was already more than halfway up. As he caught her to him in a tight embrace, she shouted up to Beth, "Oh, and I like spats, too. I've already told Jared to consider wearing them at your wedding as practice."

"So he's wearing them?" Beth sounded excited.

"You should see how quickly I put them on," Jared answered right before he bent down to kiss his future wife.

* * * * *

HARLEQUIN
PLUS

Announcing a **BRAND-NEW** multimedia subscription service for romance fans like you!

Read, Watch and Play.

Experience the easiest way to get the romance content you crave.

Start your **FREE 7 DAY TRIAL** at
<u>www.harlequinplus.com/freetrial</u>.

"Oh, no," Mike whispered. "Not here, too."

A heavy stone of foreboding dropped in Julia's stomach as she slowly rose and pivoted to look at whatever Mike had just seen.

A fire was beginning to curl up the side of the cabin next door. It was maybe thirty yards away, separated by a dozen trees—and a pile of chopped wood that stretched between the cabins like one long dynamite fuse.

How could this have happened? There'd been no lightning. No one was staying in the other cabins. There was no reason a fire could spontaneously begin next door. There was only one answer—

The evil that had been setting Crooked Valley on fire had followed them here. Why?

"Daddy! There's a fire!" Ginny pointed at the orange flames eagerly running up the wooden siding of the cabin next door, inches away from the woodpile. Any hope Julia had that her eyes were deceiving her disappeared. The house next door was on fire, and their lives were suddenly in very real danger.

"We need to get out of here. Now." Mike grabbed Ginny's coat and started helping her arms into the sleeves. Julia bent down beside him and fastened the zipper, then grabbed Ginny's hat and tugged it on her head as Mike pulled back on his boots. Julia grabbed her coat just in time to see the flames leap to the pile of dried wood and race across the top like a hungry animal.

Heading straight for their cabin.

"Get in my car!" Mike shouted.

They ran for the SUV, but Julia stopped short just as Mike opened the passenger-side door. "Mike, look." The two front tires had been slashed. Julia spun to the right and saw the same thing had been done to her car. "Someone doesn't want us leaving," she said under her breath. Fear curled a tight fist inside her chest.

Mike quickly scanned the area. "He's out there. Somewhere."

Oh, God. Why would the arsonist follow them? Why would he target Mike and Ginny? Or Julia, for that matter?

A chill snaked up her spine as she realized the arsonist must have *watched* them stringing lights, singing Christmas carols. He'd watched them—and still decided to take the lives of two adults and a small child. What kind of evil person did that?

"Come on. We have to go on foot." Mike took Julia's hand in one hand, then scooped up Ginny with the other.

Even as he said the words, she could see the fire overtaking the small cabin, eagerly devouring the Christmas lights they had just hung. The sweet moment the three of them had was being erased.

It was a two-mile trip down the mountain. Another two miles back to town. On foot, they'd never make it before dark. How were they going to get back to safety?

Don't miss
Refuge Up in Flames *by Shirley Jump,*
available December 2022 wherever
Love Inspired books and ebooks are sold.

LoveInspired.com

LIMREXP1022

LOVE INSPIRED

Stories to uplift and inspire

Fall in love with Love Inspired—
inspirational and uplifting stories of faith
and hope. Find strength and comfort in
the bonds of friendship and community.
Revel in the warmth of possibility and the
promise of new beginnings.

Sign up for the Love Inspired newsletter
at **LoveInspired.com** to be the first
to find out about upcoming titles,
special promotions and exclusive content.

CONNECT WITH US AT:

 Facebook.com/LoveInspiredBooks

Twitter.com/LoveInspiredBks

IF YOU ENJOYED THIS BOOK, DON'T MISS NEW EXTENDED-LENGTH NOVELS FROM LOVE INSPIRED!

In addition to the Love Inspired books you know and love, we're excited to introduce even more uplifting stories in a longer format, with more inspiring fresh starts and page-turning thrills!

LOVE INSPIRED

Stories to uplift and inspire.

Fall in love with Love Inspired—inspirational and uplifting stories of faith and hope. Find strength and comfort in the bonds of friendship and community. Revel in the warmth of possibility, and the promise of new beginnings.

LOOK FOR THESE LOVE INSPIRED TITLES ONLINE AND IN THE BOOK DEPARTMENT OF YOUR FAVORITE RETAILER!

If you like **THE RESCUE,** you'll love
THE HURRICANE
by J.B. Watson

"Fast-moving. . . . well-written. . . . with harrow-ing moments likely to get the reader's heart beating faster. . . . "

—*Publishers Weekly*

And don't miss these other exciting **SURVIVE!** stories:

THE BLIZZARD
by Jim O'Connor

THE HOSTAGE
by Larry Weinberg

THE RESCUE

THE RESCUE

By Jeff Morgan

Grosset & Dunlap
New York

Cover illustration by Chris Cocozza

*For all those who respect, enjoy, and preserve
the wild places —J.M.*

I saw Alex fall. I watched the whole thing. When he stopped climbing near the top of the cliff, I knew he was stuck. He wasn't the kind of guy who would stop to rest so close to the top, and the way he kept reaching out and trying for a toehold with his foot told me that he couldn't find a way to go up or down, couldn't move at all. But he kept trying for a long time, long enough that I became worried and thought how afraid I would be if I were the one clinging to the cliff. I would have turned and looked down at the person on the ground with a *help-me* look, but Alex never did.

He finally tried something desperate. It looked like he lunged upward and grabbed at something I couldn't see, and then he was falling. His body twisted, skidded, and

1

bounced off the cliff.

He never uttered a sound, but I heard the ripping, crashing noise as he fell through the dead spruce tree that stuck out from a crack in the cliff. Its thin trunk snapped so that Alex and the trunk and pieces of scraggly broken branches fell together and landed in the rocks below. I expected to hear a cry or scream, and it scared me when none came. Except for the clatter of the tree coming down, I heard nothing but my own gasping breath and the pounding of my feet as I ran to where he fell. Everything else was as silent as death.

Maybe I was already running toward him before he hit. Or maybe I watched the whole awful fall without moving. I don't really remember that part. I only remember running through the woody bushes from the lakeshore and racing over the rough rock near the foot of the cliff to get to him. I ran thinking he was dead, that he had to be dead, and I wondered what I would see when I got to him, whether he would still be whole, or splattered like a bug on a windshield.

But when I got there he wasn't dead. At first I was glad, but then for a second I thought that was even worse, that it would be better if he were already dead. I couldn't stand to watch him die.

He'd landed on the sloping ground among the boulders in a kind of sitting position, leaning back with his legs stretched, as if in a reclining chair. His shoulders were twisted one way, his hips the other. Broken bits of the tree were everywhere. I crouched over him, then stood and looked down. I was very scared and nearly crying. I felt the way I did when I was a little kid and something scared me and I wanted to run but didn't know which way to go.

Alex's shirt was almost all torn away. Cuts and scratches covered his chest, arms, and one side of his face. The other side looked like it had been scraped off. All I could see was oozing blood and raw flesh. If I hadn't been so scared and pumped up, it would have made me sick. His left arm looked like it had an extra joint in it between the wrist and elbow, and his legs were twisted. His

body didn't line up right. It looked like some of his bones vaporized during the fall, leaving nothing behind to hold parts of him in place.

I wondered if his neck was broken and I thought again that he was dying, that I was watching him die, or that he might already now be dead. And I thought how awful it would be for his parents, who'd already seen their only daughter die just a few years ago. If Alex . . .

Then he slowly turned his head toward me and moaned. A moment later he was whimpering softly like a baby animal and weakly, blindly, reaching for something with his right hand. I suddenly felt like I had to do something to help him, that I shouldn't be just kneeling there, crying and quivering. As fast as I could, I ran back to the lake to get water. I wasn't sure what I would use it for, but it was the only thing I could think to do. I put one foot in the canoe, yanked at the straps on the big pack that held our cooking gear, and pulled out two small pots. I dipped them into the lake, filling each to the brim,

and headed back to Alex.

When I got to him this time, he was moving his head in little circles and babbling to himself, just making sounds that didn't mean anything. I plunged my bandana into one of the pots and pulled it out, dripping wet. Holding it over Alex's head, I wrung it so the water ran down the side of his face that wasn't as badly hurt. I did that because they are always throwing water on people to revive them in those old movies on TV. It didn't work on Alex. I did it again. Nothing changed. My hand trembled as I dabbed the cuts and scrapes on his upper arm, shoulder, and chest. As I cleaned the smeared blood, I saw that he was more poked and gouged than cut. After a few minutes, I got braver about touching him. I soaked the bandana and wiped it across his forehead. He tried to raise his broken arm, then stopped and moaned.

"Alex," I said, "it's Hobie. Can you hear me? Alex!"

"Huh?" he said softly.

I was sure it was an answer and not just a

nonsense noise. I felt a surge of joy. Maybe he wouldn't die. "Alex!" I yelled. "You fell! You're hurt! Don't move. Don't even try!" I wiped his forehead again and a little water trickled across the scraped side of his face. He flinched and tried to pull away. "Don't move," I said again.

His eyes fluttered, blinked open, then closed. "Hurt," he said. I don't think I'll ever hear a word that sounds better. It meant that he could make sense, that he was still with me. Having him crumpled at the bottom of the cliff made me afraid, for his sake and mine. It made me feel very alone. We were days from help and no one knew where we were.

I cleaned up the scraped side of his face last. It wasn't as bad as it had first looked, but it was bad enough. He looked like he'd shot off his bike, landed on the side of his head, and slid on rough pavement. Even his ear was raw and mangled. A bad gash ran from above his eye back into his hair.

Alex grew more and more conscious as I washed that side of his face, maybe because

the bandana hurt him so much, though I dabbed as gently as I could. As he became more conscious, he trembled like someone who was really cold. Two or three times he tried to move, only to stop and gasp with pain. Once after he moved, he turned his head to the side and threw up. I think he was crying, but it was like crying and moaning and trying to talk all at once. All this time a panicked voice deep in my brain screamed over and over, *What am I going to do? What am I going to do?*

In the time it took Alex to fall, everything changed. He had always been the strong one, the leader, the one who made decisions, the one who had ideas and got others to go along with them. Now I was on my own. Even though Alex was moving a little and talking, I didn't know if he'd make it. His bones were broken. The injuries that I could see on the outside of his body didn't look like the kind that kill people, but when he threw up it made me think that he might be hurt real badly inside, so badly he could die. And even if he got a little better, he wasn't going

to just rest for a while, get up, dust himself off, say, "Whew, man, that was a close one!" and walk back to the canoe. I was the one who would have to decide things and do things now.

I wished we'd never seen the cliff, but wishing wouldn't change anything. Alex had climbed it because it was a challenge. To him the word "challenge" meant fun.

He'd always been like that, at least ever since I first met him. He liked to be the best at sports and games. He wasn't the kind of person who had to be the best to be happy, but he always tried to beat his own record. That kind of drive, combined with his natural ability, made him one of the best athletes in our school. He was also one of the biggest kids and one of the strongest and best looking. And all of those things, being fun and big and handsome and strong, also made him one of the most popular. But I think that people liked him because he had something that most kids our age don't—confidence. Alex *always* acted confident, too confident, about his ability to do things, and

the kids in our class flocked to him. Especially the girls.

He didn't see things as fun *because* they were dangerous. He saw them as different ways to do something new and then be able to say, "I did it!" But he sure didn't back away from danger. Lots of times he tried to talk me into doing things with him, kind of like contests. Sometimes I went along but, more often, I held back.

I just wasn't like Alex. I didn't like to take risks. Maybe I was scared, but I'd seen what happened to Alex in the past when he tried too hard. He'd paid a price for his daring. He'd suffered a lot of minor injuries, even some broken bones. But nothing like this. Now he lay broken and bleeding in the wilderness with only me to help him.

I had thought that climbing the cliff would be too scary and risky. "We shouldn't do this," I'd said. "If one of us slips and breaks his butt there's nowhere to go for help. We're miles away from anyone."

"It'll be great," Alex had said.

"This isn't smart. Think about it. We're

alone in the woods. What if . . ."

"Piece of cake," Alex had said. "Besides, part of the reason for being here is doing stuff like this. I'm going."

"Good luck." I watched him start up the steep, rough rock. Then I went back to the canoe at the edge of the lake.

At first it looked like it might *be* a piece of cake. With his way of making something hard look easy, Alex went up the lower section like Spiderman. The cliff was solid rock. It wasn't straight up. It had a slight slope to it, and its surface was rough enough and broken enough to give handholds and footholds. But as he got higher, maybe because the rock was weathered smoother there, Alex had to pause and feel for a small crack or a little hint of a ledge that he could get his fingers or toes into. At the steepest places he pressed against the rock so tightly that he must have been tasting it, breathing it, feeling its damp, gritty surface against his face. I don't know if he was ever scared. I know I would have been, but I doubt that he was. Probably, knowing him, at the very last in-

stant before he fell, he thought, *If I try hard enough, I'll make it.* But he didn't make it, and he broke a lot more than his butt when he failed.

"Alex, can you hear me?" I said. I'd forced myself to stop crying but my voice still sounded like a whimper.

He nodded, his eyes closed.

"What are we going to do?"

"Don't know," he whispered.

"How badly do you think you're hurt?"

"Don't know. Bad."

"Can you move?"

"No. Hurts."

My dad, a dentist, had made our first aid kit, and I now used the medicines for cuts and scrapes on Alex. He stood it pretty well, but I could tell it hurt. Then I covered the really bad places with bandages. But the best thing I had was pain pills, ones that you have to be a doctor or dentist to get. I gave Alex two pills, the max dose, and within thirty minutes he felt better. I also had antibiotics for fighting infection and gave him the max dose of those, too. These were all I had and they helped, but Alex needed more than a first aid kit. He needed a hospital. At the broken places, his arm and legs swelled as big as footballs.

I got more and more scared. It was a different kind of fear from the first panicked jolt. It was a fear that came down on me like

a huge, crushing weight. The endless lakes and woods, being alone in the wilderness, the whole trip had always been a little scary to me, but just scary enough to be fun. When Alex fell, the fun vanished. Only the scariness remained, and it went all the way to the bone. I had this strange feeling, like someone was going to show up to help me. But there was no one around—no mom or dad, no neighbor lady, no teacher or coach, no cop. I had only the forest and lakes and rocky shores. I felt surrounded by something awful. Alex's life depended on me.

The first decision was the hardest. Alex needed to be moved to a hospital as fast as possible and I couldn't move him. I had to get someone to come to him. But how? I could think only of two things.

I could signal for help. I could build a big, smoky fire and hope that someone would notice the smoke and come to see what caused it. That way I could stay with Alex and try to take care of him. Or I could leave Alex and go get help at the ranger's cabin where we began our trip. I didn't like this.

What if something happened to Alex while I was gone? What if something happened to *me*? If I didn't make it, Alex would die a slow, terrible death. This was reason enough not to leave him, but there was something else holding me back. I didn't want to go off by myself. Even though Alex was helpless, I liked the idea of being with him better than the idea of being alone. But the signal fire idea had one big problem—its success depended totally upon chance.

A plane passing nearby was the only hope of anyone noticing the smoke. We had been traveling through the wilderness for two and a half days and hadn't seen a plane or even heard one. Maybe one would come by sooner or later and maybe it wouldn't. But we couldn't wait—Alex needed the help now. And the surest way to get help was for me to go to where I knew I could find it—the ranger's cabin. Fear squeezed my guts. I half ran, half staggered a short way into the woods, yanked at my belt, and pushed my pants to my knees. Everything inside me was like water.

After that I began going through our packs and started organizing gear I'd need if I went. I didn't want to leave Alex yet. It was too soon to know if he could be left and besides, I hadn't yet screwed up the courage to go. But a voice in my head kept saying, *Don't waste time!* At first I just looked at our gear. My hands shook. I was panicky and sick and didn't know what to do. I started pulling out only the things I couldn't do without: map, flashlight, rope, tent, sleeping bag, insect repellent. In my pockets I had my knife, compass, and my waterproof match holder full of wooden matches.

Every few minutes I ran back to the cliff to check on Alex. He lay in the same position, on his back with his good arm draped over his eyes, his legs sprawled helplessly. Sometimes he turned to look at me, sometimes he didn't. And a few times he was so still I thought he might be dead. Once, when he seemed not to notice me, I stopped a few yards off and looked at him. I realized that the big problem wasn't organizing gear for my trip, but getting together stuff for him to

survive with on his own. Everything he needed would have to be within reach of his right hand. Maybe leaving him was wrong. It wasn't good to go and it wasn't good to stay.

Food! How would Alex eat? All of our food was in a pack by itself. I emptied it and stacked everything on the big flat rocks at the water's edge, then sorted everything into two groups, one of ready-to-eats and one of things that needed to be cooked. We began the trip with plenty of food for seven days. Two days were gone. I had a pretty big pile of ready-to-eats, enough to last for . . . for what?

If I went back the way we came, how long would it take—three days? Four? How fast could I make the canoe go by myself? But it wasn't just canoeing I was worried about. Every time I came to land, I'd have to take my canoe out of the water, and carry it down a trail to the next lake. These trails, called portages, could be pretty difficult. And I'd never "portaged" a canoe on my own. How hard would it be? I looked at the map. We'd planned to follow a loop route that began and ended at the ranger's cabin without

backtracking. I could either go back the way we'd come or continue on the way we'd planned to go. Going back was familiar. Going on looked shorter. I guessed it would take two or three days. I decided to figure on three just to be safe. We had enough ready-to-eat food for both Alex and me to get by for that long. I didn't have to worry about water. We drank it straight from the pure northern lakes.

But Alex needed water! The thought hit me like a fist. He couldn't just dip his cup in a lake where he was. How much would he need? We had a collapsible plastic water carrier that held a gallon. Our cooking kit contained only a small frying pan, a small coffeepot, and a small saucepan. We each had a Sierra cup. That wouldn't be enough. I felt panicky again. I wasn't thinking straight. My plan to go for help was no good.

Think! Think! All our food came packaged in plastic bags and foil pouches. I could take everything I hadn't planned for Alex or me to eat, dump out the food, and refill the containers with water. I could seal the bags with

their twisty wires. I'd have to find some way to get the foil pouches to stand up straight within Alex's reach. It still didn't look like enough water. Food he could go without for a while and be okay, but without water, especially the way he'd bled, he'd die.

Think! The tackle box! We carried our fishing gear in a big plastic tackle box, so big the outfitter had made fun of it when he saw it. It would hold at least two or three gallons, maybe more. I grabbed it out of the canoe and dumped all the bright lures and gadgets into the empty food pack. I dipped the tackle box in the lake, rinsed it, then washed it with a bandana, then rinsed it again. With it full of water, I could barely lift it.

I set all the filled containers beside Alex. He watched me. "Water," I said. I didn't want to tell him my plan. I could feel the knots in my stomach tighten when I thought about what I had to do. I didn't want to leave Alex, didn't want to go into the woods alone.

"I'm going for help," I said. "Back to the ranger's cabin."

He nodded and closed his eyes, but then

opened them again. He looked right at me and whispered, "Don't go. I need you here."

All the fear and doubt rose again within me. I felt the lump in my throat that comes right before tears. My eyes burned. I fought it off. "I have to," I said.

"No, Hobie," he said. "I can't even move."

"Listen, I've figured this out." My voice was shaky. "If I stay, help might never come. You could die. It's like trusting luck. Going is the surest way."

I saw the deep fear in his eyes, fear that matched my own. He was helpless, and we both knew it. "It'll take too long," he said. "I could die alone. I could . . ."

"I'm fixing it so you'll be okay," I said. "Water, food, medicine, some kind of tent. And I'll get help as fast as I can, a plane, doctors." He looked at me with pleading eyes. "I don't want to go," I said. "But I don't have any choice."

I put the food and water on his right side within easy reach of his good arm. It took several trips back and forth to the canoe and on one of them I stopped and looked at Alex

through the trees and bushes and imagined that that was how an animal would see him. What if an animal smelled the food or Alex's blood? I got the folding saw from the gear pack and cut a sturdy club from the trunk of a small tree. I set it beside the food.

I got our bright blue plastic tarp and Alex's sleeping bag from the canoe. I wanted to get some cover over him to keep him out of bad weather, and also try to get some padding under him, so he'd be more comfortable. The tarp was a problem, because on one side of Alex there was nothing but the cliff and some boulders. I cut the rest of the small tree trunk into two lengths. I wedged these between and behind the boulders, weighted them down with rocks, then tied the tarp to them. I pulled on it hard. It held. Small trees on the other side made finishing the job easier. The sleeping bag was also a problem. I could only get it under Alex's back, shoulders, and head, and even that hurt him. When I tried to help him move his hips and legs to get the sleeping bag under them, he screamed so hard that I didn't try again.

I put all our extra clothes and both towels in a pack and laid it beside him. That way he could get things out to make pillows and pads. I put the pain pills, antibiotics, other medicines, and a bottle of insect repellent in the outside pocket of the pack where they couldn't roll away from him. With a lot of trouble for me and pain for Alex, I got him into his light, loose rain parka to cover his half-naked chest and back.

During all this time I thought about whether I would go back the way we came or finish the circle we'd started. The first portage we'd crossed coming in, the one from the ranger's lake to the first wilderness lake, was a killer. It was long and hard, steep, rocky, and wet, so bad that it was one of the two reasons why this part of the lake country was so remote, so untraveled. We had come this way in the first place because of it, to be on our own. I didn't want to face it again alone. The other reason no one came here was the last portage on the route. I'd cross it if I finished the circle. It was supposed to be just as bad, but I didn't see how

it could be and it was shorter. I decided to go with the shortest way back—I'd finish the loop route we had started.

I got more scared as the time for leaving drew closer. I thought I might throw up. I think Alex felt the same way. He looked like a captured animal waiting for the final, terrible result of being caught. I crouched beside him and replaced his bandages with the last fresh ones. I showed him where the pills were and told him how often and how many he should take. He listened to me now like he never had before. "Don't take the pain pills unless you just can't stand it," I said. "When they're gone, they're gone." I showed him what all the different foods were. I showed him the club.

That was all. There wasn't anything else for me to do, but I stayed there squatting beside him for a while. Neither of us talked. I felt all torn apart inside. Finally I said, "Time to go," forcing myself to be brave.

Alex nodded. "Hurry," he said weakly.

I nodded. I couldn't talk anymore without crying. I was afraid for Alex and afraid for

myself. I looked at the lake and the dark forest all around it. I had miles and miles of lakes and forest to cross. I didn't have any choice.

I slid the canoe into the lake and pulled her straight alongside the rocky shore. I felt like all my insides had turned into some kind of sickening jelly. I set both paddles in the stern and struggled to hoist my pack in. Then I squatted on the rocks, hugging my knees, trying to pull myself together.

I strapped on my life jacket, stepped into the canoe, settled on the stern seat, and pushed against the shore with my paddle. The canoe moved slowly toward deeper water. With trembling hands and a mouth as dry as a desert, I took the first stroke on the scariest and most important trip I'd probably ever make in all my life.

I didn't even get out of the bay before I knew I had a problem. The canoe crept forward as if dragging an anchor behind her.

24

And she felt tippy. I strained at the paddle. It was like one of those dreams in which you have to run but can't. Everything in me wanted to make the canoe go fast to get help for Alex. But I couldn't do it.

It took a long time to reach the mouth of the bay. When I did, I left the shelter of its shores and entered the channel between it and the island. The canoe suddenly turned to the left in the breeze and I had to paddle harder to keep her going straight. I reached out farther with the paddle to get a bigger sweep in the water, leaning out to do it, and she tipped so sharply it nearly dumped me in the lake. Scared me.

Something was wrong. The canoe never acted like this before. It was like a jinx. At the one time in my life when I really needed to move fast, I could barely move at all. I started to cry again and felt mad, like I wanted to kick something. Alex depended upon me. He probably thought I was halfway across the lake by now, racing for help, and I hadn't gone more than three football fields from where I started.

Then it hit me. When you're in a canoe alone, you need to be in the middle. That was it. The canoe was out of balance—too much weight in the stern. The bow rode too high and turned in the light breeze like a weather vane. I was screwed up, rattled by all that had happened. I wasn't thinking.

But I couldn't paddle from the middle. I tried. There was no seat there. I had to kneel and reach out too far with the paddle. The long reach made the canoe tip and kept me from getting a strong stroke in the water. I felt like I was trying to paddle from the bottom of a bathtub. I needed to be on the stern seat. But with me in the stern the canoe needed a person in the bow . . . or at least the *weight* of a person.

I paddled to shore and got out to look for rocks. I found four good-sized ones that each weighed fifteen or twenty pounds. I put them under the bow seat and leaned the pack against them.

When I got in the stern and again pushed away from the shore with my paddle, the load felt good. It was the right amount of

weight and it was low in the canoe. This would help keep the canoe steady. I pushed once more against the bottom, shoving backward, then let my paddle drag on the left side to turn back into the channel. I took a few strokes on the right, and the canoe moved sluggishly forward. She still veered to the left, but not as much as before, and the weight in the bow held it down so the wind didn't bother it as much. I was back on the stern seat in a comfortable paddling position. I thought this was probably about as good as I could do.

I took two hard strokes on the right, then a couple easy ones on the left to stop the turn and get the canoe going straight. I switched back to the right side and tried to get into a rhythm of steady strokes. *Hurry!* I thought to myself, and as I did I could hear Alex's voice saying "Hurry!" when I left him. But the canoe did not hurry. She rode better, but she didn't speed ahead. I felt like I was trying to paddle a parked car through mud. "C'mon! C'mon!" I pleaded out loud. "Please!" The rocks added the weight of a

passenger who rode without paddling.

When I reached the end of the island, I paddled out of the channel and into the big water of the open lake. I felt the breeze pick up right away. It tried to turn the canoe to the right and I had to paddle harder on that side to keep her course true. That worked out okay because I'm stronger on my right side, and with the breeze making me paddle harder, the canoe moved a little faster.

I needed to cross the end of the lake to its east shore. Then, according to the map, almost exactly halfway down that shore at the point where it reached farthest to the east, I'd find the portage trail to the next lake.

I could look all the way down the lake now. Its whole length lay to the south off my right. This was a small lake, far smaller than some, but still big enough to make me feel how very, very small the canoe and I were. Then I thought that beyond this lake's forested shores there were more lakes, some much, much bigger, and beyond them more forest and still more lakes in a wilderness

that went on and on. I stopped paddling and looked all around. It looked the same in every direction—water, rock, trees, sky— endless.

When Alex and I began the trip, this wild place seemed like a kind of amusement park. But now everything about it seemed to be ganging up on me, standing between me and what I needed. It was like an enemy, not because it would try to hurt me, but because it wouldn't help me. I was afraid and tired. How would I do it? So far to go. What if I couldn't do it? Why did I have to be the one to try? For the first time I felt mad at Alex. This was really all his fault. Then I felt ashamed. Alex was not only as alone as I was, but helpless and suffering, with nothing to do but wait and hope. Besides, he had sort of saved *me* once. Now I could return the favor.

Ganging up on me. Being alone and feeling surrounded and afraid made me think of how I first met Alex.

I was the new kid at school. When my family moved, I had to come in late in the school year to a new junior high in Minneapolis, where I didn't know anyone. My mom took me in on that first morning and did some enrollment stuff in the principal's office. When she left, the assistant principal walked me down the strange hallway to my classroom. He interrupted the class to take me in, and I had to stand at the front of the room while he and the teacher whispered about me. All the kids stared at me like I was some geek from a different planet. I didn't know what to do, didn't know if I should look back at them or try to smile or what. I

only wanted them to like me. They all knew each other and I was all alone.

That afternoon I had to take the bus home. There were two groups of buses. The first group loaded up and left, and then the second group came. My bus was in the second group, so, standing by myself, I had to wait for it.

A bunch of tough-punk guys started picking on me—I guess just because I was new and alone. They made a loose circle with me and the biggest one of them, a sneering, bony kid, in the middle. He made fun of me and pushed me and tried to get me to fight. He'd push me to the edge of the circle and then one of the guys there would push me back in. I knew if I tried to fight back they'd beat me up for trying and if I didn't try they'd beat me up for being a wimp. All the other kids were watching to see what would happen.

Suddenly there was another kid in the circle, a big kid from my class who had said hi to me for no reason earlier in the day. He shoved his way in, grabbed the kid who was

bullying me by the shoulders, and said, "Hey, Ricky, you want to pick on somebody, pick on me!" Then he spun Ricky into the side of a parked bus so hard he left a little dent. The other guys backed off and watched Ricky stagger away.

The big kid who helped me was Alex. After that, of course, I hung around him at school. He was good at everything and seemed to like all sorts of things, including computers. I had a really cool setup at home that was kind of mine and kind of my dad's. I invited Alex to come over to see it. And we both had minibikes. Soon we began eating lunch together at school and then doing things together after school and on weekends. We got to be best friends.

The idea for our trip came from a great story I'd read about two teenagers who went on a wilderness canoe trip in Canada. They traveled a huge distance on their own and finished it feeling ready for whatever the future would bring.

I gave the story to Alex. He liked it even more than I did. We wanted to go on a canoe

trip and it seemed possible. We lived only a few hours from some of the world's best canoe country.

We wanted to go alone like the two guys in the story and tried hard to talk our parents into it, but they said we were too young to be alone in the woods for that long. Then my dad talked to Alex's dad and they made a plan for us to go on a canoe trip the next summer with a group of other kids, led by guides. It was less than we wanted. Alex called it wimpy, but it was better than no trip at all, and we both thought our parents were pretty cool for working it out. Then my grandpa gave me his canoe. I didn't even know he had it until he took me out behind his shop. He showed it to me and said, "Hobie, this thing's been stored here since before you were born. It's been waiting for someone to put it to good use. It's yours if you want it."

I wanted it.

"She needs a little work," he added, "but I bet you can handle it."

I handled it. And after spending hours and

hours that winter in the cold garage, when all the dents were tapped out and all the scrapes were buffed smooth, I felt like the canoe was really mine, more completely mine than a canoe bought new ever could be. I named it SilverWolf.

Many nights I fell asleep reading about canoeing or canoe country. I got the books from the library and passed some of them, the ones I knew he'd like, on to Alex. We learned about the area where our guided trip would go. We learned that just north of it was a wilderness area that was pretty isolated because the portages were so long and hard. It wasn't a secret, of course. It was in the books and people knew about it, but we imagined it as being a secret place because almost no one went there.

When summer came, we took the water safety and canoe classes that were part of the deal with our parents. But after all that— the hours spent on SilverWolf, the lessons, the reading, and the endless waiting—our trip almost ended before it began.

On the day that Alex's dad was supposed

to drive us up north, Alex's little brother had to have an emergency operation. It was his appendix, but by the time the people in the emergency room and Alex's family doctor got it figured out and wheeled the poor kid into the operating room, the day was more than half gone and Alex's parents were too frazzled to drive anyone anywhere. Alex's older sister had died when Alex was a tiny kid. He could just barely remember her, but his parents never really got over it. It made them especially nervous about their other kids' health and safety. My dad was at a convention in Seattle. My mom had my little sister to take care of and out-of-town guests coming that night. I'd never felt more disappointed. It was like being ready to step into a dream come true only to have it vanish.

That evening Alex's dad called the outfitter, the guy who organized all the canoe trips, and made new arrangements. We would come the next day, one day behind the rest of the group, and catch up with them at the first campsite, which was a short, easy paddle from the ranger's cabin. And that's

what we did—or started to do. At the time he called, Alex's dad was still unsure about leaving. He told the outfitter that he would bring us if he could get away and that if he couldn't, we wouldn't be there at all. The guides went into the woods thinking maybe two kids would come late and maybe they wouldn't.

We left Minneapolis early the next morning with SilverWolf gleaming on top of the car, and got to the outfitter's lakeside lodge before lunch. The outfitter, an old, wiry, rugged-looking man who was nice without smiling much, gave us a map and pointed out the ranger's cabin where we would start paddling, and the campsite where we would meet the rest of the group. It was a short, simple route. "There's nothing to it," he said to Alex's dad. "It's right down this one lake. They can't miss it."

We loaded our stuff into a big open motor-boat with a high rack on it for SilverWolf, and sped down the lake to a dock where two floatplanes waited. One of them carried us to the ranger's cabin. We flew high enough to

see the whole spread of the country, and low enough to see its detail: the individual trees, the pattern of waves on the lakes. It felt like our map had sprung to life beneath us. We had our faces pressed against the windows the whole way, watching the shadow of our plane, with SilverWolf under one wing, glide over the deep greens of the dense woods and the sparkling blue of the shining lakes. There were no houses, no cabins, no roads, no power lines. It looked as it must have looked before there were people to see it.

We helped the pilot unload our gear on the ranger's dock. The ranger came out to meet us and chat with the pilot. He took us into his three-room cabin where we registered as park visitors. "The crew that came through yesterday told me you might be coming," he said. "And then I got a call from Ben," he nodded at his radio, "saying you were on your way and that you know what you're doing and where you're going." Ben was the outfitter. "It's an easy paddle and the weather's good. You'll be there before supper, no problem."

By car, by boat, by plane and, finally, by canoe. We were underway in SilverWolf on a remote Northwoods lake at last. The ranger's cabin fell farther behind us with each paddle stroke. It was a perfect summer day, warm and still. The lake gleamed in the afternoon sun. SilverWolf moved easily. Alex, in the stern, did the steering. He had the map in his lap and looked at it often. After a long while, he turned SilverWolf to the north. But the group was supposed to be straight down the lake to the east. I turned and looked at him. "What are you doing?" I asked, pointing to the east. "It's still that way."

"It's a secret," he said mysteriously.

"What?"

"Something I thought of."

"Well, what?" I asked.

"You'll like it."

I turned around and paddled. He kept us going north. After a few more minutes I looked at him again. "C'mon, man, what are you doing?" I asked.

He gave me one of his fun, *something's-up* looks. "Straight ahead is that hard trail to the

wilderness area we read about. You know, the one where no one goes."

"So?"

"So, that's where we're going."

He wasn't kidding. I didn't like it. We had the longest and worst argument we'd ever had. I didn't want to double-cross our parents. They'd been good to let us have any trip at all. But Alex said, "This is our chance to take the trip we always wanted, to go alone. The guides aren't sure we're coming. If we don't show, no one will panic and look for us. And when we get back we'll just say that we got lost and couldn't find the group or something. We can't pass this up."

I stood up to Alex more than I ever had before, but he was stronger and more self-confident than I was. Besides, deep down it sounded fun and exciting to me, too. It was what we'd dreamed of and there it was for the taking. The more Alex talked in that way of his, the better it sounded.

"C'mon, Hobe," he said. "Think what an adventure it will be. Don't wimp out on

this one." The temptation was too great. I did it Alex's way.

We made camp on the shore of the bay that leads to the tough portage. Alex went for a swim. He teased me about my fear of swimming in lakes where I can't see the bottom and jokingly threatened to throw me in. I said, "Don't even kid about it. It's too serious." And he stopped because he knew it was.

That night we studied our map by flashlight in the tent. We would have a little wild part of the world all to ourselves. Excitement kept us awake and talking too late. The night outside our faintly lit tent was completely dark and silent.

I don't know what Alex would have done if I'd just refused to go along with his idea. Now, paddling by myself with the unknown wilderness in front of me and Alex's broken body behind me, I knew what a bad choice I'd made.

I turned toward the portage, angling south-east across the lake. Right away I got an advantage I hadn't considered. The breeze came from behind me after I turned. As long as it isn't too strong, a tail wind is great. I dug into the lake with the paddle. SilverWolf pulled forward, still not like she would with two people paddling, but pretty good. *Doing it,* I said to myself, pretending to be less scared than I was. *I'm doing it!*

I could see the entire shore ahead of me, one long stretch of tree-lined water, but I couldn't make out any detail. All of the little ins and outs of the shore that my map showed were blurred by distance into the sameness of lakeside forest. Even close up, things that showed with a sharp, hard line on the map faded into blurry, brushy softness

on the real lakeshore.

I could see where the portage was on the map, but across the distance I had to guess where that spot was on the shore. I didn't have to be exactly right, just close. Then I'd paddle right next to the shore until I spotted the trail.

I wanted to get to the portage, but I dreaded getting there almost as much. On that first hard portage and at tricky places on the others, Alex and I had carried SilverWolf together. Most of the rest of the time Alex carried her. When I took her, Alex had to help me get her on my shoulders and then she was almost too much for me, even in the easy places. I didn't want to have to do it all alone. I knew it would hurt and was afraid that I wouldn't be able to handle it.

Finally the shore ahead opened into a wide shallow bay. The map showed the portage at the end of this bay. On the map the bay looked like a wide arrowhead with the portage at the very point, but in the real world of the real lake there wasn't any point, just a rough curving shore.

I looked and looked and couldn't find the trail. My stomach clenched up and I felt that sick feeling again in the pit of my gut. Was I in the wrong place? I studied the map hard enough to burn holes in it, then looked at the lake, trying to make it fit the map. I couldn't really tell where the portage should be. Alex and I had learned that sometimes the map was not always exactly right. But I couldn't find any portage here at all. "Not fair!" I wanted to scream. My eyes burned again. I had to be in the right place. On this small lake with its simple shoreline, I just *couldn't* be far off.

A miniature forest of high reeds grew in the shallower water toward the end of the bay. On either side of it, the land rose slightly into the uneven granite forms and stunted evergreens of the Northwoods. But no portage. Not knowing what to do, I let SilverWolf drift. Could the map be completely wrong? I began to feel sweaty, desperate. What would Alex do if he were here? I knew one thing he wouldn't do. He wouldn't sit in the canoe and worry. He'd explore.

I forced SilverWolf into the reeds. It was like going through a curtain. She moved like a slow, heavy knife, the reeds parting before her. They dragged along her hull with light scraping sounds.

They opened into a channel, a kind of roofless tunnel of reeds. SilverWolf floated here on less than a foot of water over a layer of loose, dark silt that rose and swirled with every paddle stroke. The channel wandered, turning a little this way, a little that way, and narrowed and got deeper the farther I went. I couldn't see much through the curtain of reeds, but I could see above it that I was getting closer to the edge of the woods. And I heard the soft gurgle of running water. A forest stream flowing into the lake made a channel through the marsh. A big tangle of dead drifted logs blocked it, but to the right side, rising from the lake and disappearing into the dark woods, was a narrow trail—the portage. "Thank you! Thank you!" I said to the lake and trees.

I got SilverWolf as close to solid ground as I could and stepped out, sinking halfway to

my knees in the silty muck. I slogged to dry land towing SilverWolf behind me with the rope we kept tied to her bow. I swung my pack onto the shore, heaved my ballast rocks out, and then dragged SilverWolf out of the water and tied her to a bush. She felt heavy.

I was hungry and really tired, like my insides had been drained dry of energy. I ate a couple handfuls of gorp mix my mom had made us, and promised myself something more and better to eat when I finished the portage. I looked at the trail. It climbed away from the lake and disappeared into the trees. I didn't want to go down it alone, even without carrying anything, but I had to—had to go, had to carry the stuff. *Don't waste time!* I decided to take the easy stuff first. Then I'd come back for SilverWolf. Shouldering the pack, I picked up the paddles and set off.

As I left sight of the lake, I felt kind of scared and kind of proud. I'd paddled the lake and found the portage alone. I'd made a slow start, but I was doing okay. I thought about Alex and how he'd said, "Don't go." I walked as fast as I could.

In some places I couldn't go very fast. Like other wilderness portage trials, this one was a stumble course of roots and rocks with low places mired in mud and boggy muck. And in those low places, back in the woods out of the wind, with the mud and muck came mosquitos, little ones the size of gnats. They made a haze in the air and attacked like kamikazes, biting and sucking my blood—or die trying. Many died. I swatted until my hands were sore. I waved my hands and arms in front of my face as if trying to fan away some deadly gas.

The mosquitos came at two places. The trail rose from the marsh and then dropped to follow the stream for a while, then veered away from the stream and climbed uphill again, then went downhill into a really sloppy, mucky area. Here, deep in the still forest, with my boots squishing in ooze, the bugs were the worst.

From there the trail made a long steep climb. The middle of it, the steepest part, was solid granite for twenty or thirty yards. It was slick. There were two ways to go. One

went up and across the granite at a steep
angle. The other went around the granite by
making a long curve below it. It was the
longest way, and I thought it had probably
been made by people who were afraid of the
steep rock. I could see why. It looked dangerous. I hesitated. What would Alex do?

He'd go for the rock. Stepping carefully
and using one paddle as a brace on the
downhill side, I crossed it without slipping
and made the top of the climb, out of breath
and sweat-soaked. I wondered if I would
make it with SilverWolf. The way that
bypassed the granite did not look much easier; it was less dangerous, but longer.

The trail curved to the left now, back
toward the stream. When I'd crossed the
mosquito ooze, I could hear the stream rushing like rapids. If I'd heard it when I climbed
the steep granite, I didn't notice. I had too
much else on my mind there, but I could
hear it now. The same big hill that I had just
climbed turned the stream into a long waterfall. It fell to a pool of swirling water, white
and green, and in it, rolling and turning

slowly in the current, was a dead animal. I couldn't tell what kind. It was all puffed up and bloated, and its legs stuck straight out. I wondered if it had gone over the falls and, if so, dead or alive? And I wondered what my chances in the wilderness were if the animals born in this place couldn't handle it.

I followed a long, more or less level route now as the trail followed the stream. The pack straps cut into my shoulders. I put my thumbs between them and my collarbone to take some of the weight. Still it hurt. While I thought of that and looked down the trail, I saw the silvery flash of water through the tunnel of trees. The end of the portage. The next lake.

I dumped the pack on the shore at the water's edge, knelt, and dipped my cup into the lake. I thought about that dead animal back in the stream, but I drank anyway. I knew from the map, and could tell now by looking, that this was a big lake. Straight out from me, blocking my view dead ahead, was a huge island, the biggest I'd seen so far. I could also see a small one not far from shore,

and several others. I wanted to lie down and rest but thought that if I did, I wouldn't be able to get back up. I drank again, then forced myself to head back for SilverWolf.

The idea of carrying her made me feel like I did when I first paddled away from Alex— nervous, like knowing that someone who can beat you up is waiting for you. I wanted Alex there to help me.

I heaved and pulled SilverWolf farther up the shore until she lay across the beginning of the trail. Alex could lift her up and set her on his shoulders by himself. I couldn't.

I could lift one end. I lifted the bow, and held it up while I worked my way to the middle of the canoe and got under the carrying yoke. Then I let SilverWolf down. She balanced upside-down on my shoulders. It was a crushing weight. My heart raced. My mouth went dry. My knees felt weak.

Once I got going with her, she had a momentum of her own. It was hard to stop, hard to turn, hard to do anything except keep going and try to stand the pain. By the time I got to the mosquito muck I was sticky

with sweat and really hurting. It felt like SilverWolf's weight was slowly pulling apart all the bones and muscles and tendons of my shoulders and neck. The mosquitos took my mind off that for a few minutes. Now I had no defense against them. I couldn't even walk fast. Staggering forward ankle-deep in ooze, I could only shake my head and try not to inhale them.

Then I started the steep climb. I breathed harder. My legs throbbed with every step. When I reached the intersection of the two trails, the one that crossed the granite and the one around it, I stopped. I had decided that I would go up the granite again, but now I felt chicken. Even just standing there balancing the weight hurt so badly that I wanted to shriek. I'd never had to do anything so hard. I wanted to throw SilverWolf down, do anything to get out from under the huge weight, but I was afraid I'd never get her up again.

Alex's fault, I thought. *His fault that I have to do this. What a bogus show-off jerk!* Standing still just meant more time and more pain

under the weight. The way around the granite was longer. Besides, I knew what Alex would do, and even though I was mad at him, I wished I were more like him. He'd tough it out and power through.

Baby steps. Up the steep, slick rock. Slow steps. Not because I wanted to but because I had to. I felt like I was climbing Mount Everest carrying a battleship. I gasped for breath and the slowness gave the weight more time to tear me down. I would have run up the hill if I could have, just to get it over with.

I almost made it. I got all the way to the top of the granite when suddenly I was sliding and rolling down it, the forest spinning and tumbling, SilverWolf bouncing behind me. In my mind I saw Alex falling down the cliff. I tried to stop myself and couldn't. Rough things grabbed at my hands and scraped my face. SilverWolf's booming, grinding noise filled the woods and her huge shape loomed above me. That's all I remember—then I was lying on the soft forest floor at the bottom of the hill. SilverWolf hit some

trees and stopped before I did. I just lay there waiting for the pain to start. *Dead or crippled*, I thought. *Just like Alex.*

The side of my face burned and seeped blood. My hands were scraped. That was all. I wasn't crippled. But I felt crushed, lost, and helpless. The tears came not from pain but from feeling alone and beaten. I had that crazy feeling again that someone would come and help me. Someone always had before.

But no one came. No one saw. No one knew.

For a little while I didn't move at all. I imagined my body lying there with the life draining out of it. I'd been scared all day— scared of being alone, scared of getting lost, scared of not being able to do what I had to do. Now, for the first time, the idea that I could die became real. I thought of the dead animal at the foot of the falls. What slip or

mistake had it made? So much for imitating Alex's showy, hard-charging style. If I'd crippled myself or wrecked the canoe, we'd both die slow deaths in the woods. His way caused him to fall and start all this trouble, and now trying to be like him made me fall, too.

SilverWolf was okay. She had some scrapes, but no big dents. I felt bad because I'd screwed up and hurt her. I don't know how she got off so easy, but she did. We were both lucky.

I landed close to the safer, longer trail. SilverWolf was on the steep hillside lying against the trees that stopped her from falling farther. Lifting her again and putting that weight back on my sore shoulders was almost more than I could think about, let alone do. But I had to do it. Weak and whipped as I felt, I was the only one there. The lifting wasn't so bad. The steepness of the hill helped me, but carrying her downhill through the trees, with the stern dragging and snagging on the high ground behind me, was torture. And trying to turn

her in the trees to get lined up with the trail when we reached it was worse. But somehow, by jockeying around with tiny steps and forcing myself to stand the hurt and be patient, I did it.

This time when I saw the lake gleaming at the end of the trail, it was like seeing heaven through the gates of hell. With SilverWolf off my back, I drank again from the lake, then rinsed my face and arms. The cold water stung my face.

I rested. I never before needed to rest so much. I sat on the ground, leaned against SilverWolf, and looked at the lake. I reached around and patted her and said, "It's okay. You carry me on water and I'll carry you on land. I'll try to do better. I have to do better."

It was dusk, and the wind had picked up. Both things surprised me. I had to learn to pay attention if I hoped to get by on my own. I had to know how the day was passing, what the weather was doing, and what I was going to do next. I had to be on top of things. I couldn't live with surprises.

What to do next? "Eat," I said. "Eat and

rest." I didn't want to move. I felt like I could just become part of the shore, like a rock, motionless forever. I watched the dark come down, then dug in the pack for my flashlight and my supper—some bread, peanut butter, gorp, cookies. I was so tired that I fell asleep with a cookie in my hand and woke up with it still there. I don't know how long I slept, a few minutes or an hour or more. The moon was up and I could see okay. I listened. Not a sound except the wind. I thought of Alex lying in the dark, listening to the night around him. I hoped that he heard nothing moving but wind. I hoped he was asleep.

I hadn't thought about being in the dark and it scared me a bit. Thinking of Alex made me wonder if I should push on. The night was clear. I could cross this lake in the dark, sleep on its far shore, and be that much farther along by morning. That would make best use of the time—and time was everything. Besides, I knew that was what Alex would do if I were the injured one lying in the dark.

But hadn't I just learned that Alex's way

led to trouble? The other choice was to sleep now and start fresh in the morning. But the woods were dark and moon-shadowed, like haunted forests in fairy tales. The open moonlit lake looked friendlier.

Using my flashlight, I found some new rocks, smaller and lighter than the old ones. I put them in the canoe and set off again. The paddle hurt my skinned hands. Trying to ignore the soreness was about all I could do. Right in front of me, the big island lay in the water like a sleeping giant. I paddled toward it and then turned south down the channel between the island and the mainland. The wind gusted behind me. All I wanted to do was cross the lake and find a campsite. The night was beautiful, the moonlight silver on the water. As exhausted as I was, I still noticed it. I remembered my grandpa saying that it takes a long time to learn the worth of the simplest things. I wished he were with me now.

The smaller island I had noticed earlier lay off the south end of the big one; it was closer to the mainland. I turned between

the islands, looming black shapes on the gleaming water, to cross the lake. I aimed SilverWolf straight across. In the dark I wanted to get as close to the far shore as soon as I could. Already my old fear of deep water came back to me. I imagined something rising from the bottom of this big lake and surfacing, huge and shapeless, near me.

Wind ambushed me as soon as SilverWolf pulled clear of the island and into open water. Gusting hard, it came down the lake and gave me a bigger dose of the same problems I'd had when I first left Alex. It knew I was tired. Maybe it was trying to show me how tired I was. It also knew that I didn't have enough weight in the bow. It turned SilverWolf, trying to force her down the length of the lake instead of across it. I tried to hold my course, but couldn't. My arms quivered like limp noodles that could barely pull the paddle through the water. A stronger gust blasted SilverWolf and nearly yanked the paddle away. I stopped. I didn't have enough strength or will left to fight it. I didn't have anything left at all. I thought about how

I'd pushed myself too hard and had fallen on the granite.

I let the wind help turn SilverWolf around, then paddled back toward the end of the big island. It had a high, steep shore and was thickly wooded. I was glad to get behind it again. The wind gusted even stronger and stirred the moonlight on the water. The little island, the one close to shore, looked safe. It was low, fairly flat, and open; too small to hide anything. As I got closer, I saw a good place to land SilverWolf and nosed her into it.

When I stepped onto the shore, I was so tired that I stumbled and nearly fell lifting my pack from the canoe. I was too tired to think. I groped in the pack for my flashlight. Beyond the shore bushes I found a clearing. It was kind of rocky but an okay campsite, especially since I didn't think I could go two more steps. But I found the strength to put up the tent. It seemed like a kind of protection. I threw the sleeping bag in and crawled in after it. I'd never been this tired—too tired even to be afraid of being alone in the night.

I thought of Alex. I heard the wind still gaining strength, whooshing through the trees. I fell asleep.

I awoke to bright light. I closed my eyes again to doze as I would at home, then jerked awake, wide-awake, thinking of Alex. Bright light. I'd hoped to make an early start. I was already late, already frustrated even before I got out of the sleeping bag. *Late! Time is everything! Alex!*

At the edge of the clearing I peed, squinting in the dazzling light. Through the trees I could see the mainland in one direction, the big island in another. Things that looked threatening in the dark looked harmless now. The sun felt good on my back.

My stomach was shriveled up—I was hungry, not the *I-guess-it's-time-to-eat* hungry of home, but real hunger, the feeling that my body *needed* food. I got out three slices of bread, some peanut butter, four cookies, and

an apple from the pack, and ate while quickly breaking camp. Then I hauled the pack to the lake. I was a little nervous about the long paddle ahead, but the weather was good and the route looked pretty easy. I wondered if I could find better rocks for weight on the island. I was thinking of that when I reached the shore. Where was SilverWolf? I thought I'd walked straight to where I left her, but the difference between dark and daylight made it hard to tell. Everything looked different.

Then I remembered the good canoe landing I'd found in the night. I was standing at a good landing now. Could there be another one nearby? The island wasn't that big. The muscles tightened in my neck and my gut clenched up. I started to feel hot. I walked fast along the shore, pushing through the brush and stumbling on the rock until I reached the end of the island opposite the big island. There was no other good landing that way, no sign of Silverwolf. I turned and went the other way, backtracking to where I'd first stopped and then on beyond it.

I began to realize that something was terribly wrong. I dropped the pack and ran, crashing through the brush. Twigs and branches whipped and snatched at my clothes and skin. No SilverWolf. No landings. I ran until I knew I was much farther from the campsite than when I'd landed in the night, until I could see the other end of the island. I turned and ran back the way I'd just come.

I *knew* I'd landed on that side of the island. SilverWolf had to be there. Then, with the most awful sinking feeling, like all of my insides were collapsing, I remembered. I hadn't dragged her onto shore. I'd left her in the water. I couldn't remember tying her. I'd meant to go back but forgot. I felt like I'd been kicked in the stomach. Gone!

I stopped running when I got back to the good landing. Now I knew this was where SilverWolf had been. I could see the big island and the huge sweep of the lake in the clear bright morning. No canoe. I stared at the water where I'd left her as if I could make her appear by concentrating hard

enough. She *had* to be there.

Suddenly I turned and bolted across the island, running right through my campsite, dodging trees, ignoring bushes. Maybe she was on the other side of the island. Maybe I was confused and actually left her there or maybe she'd drifted there. I knew it didn't make sense, but I also knew that she wasn't where she should be and I was willing to run toward any hope. "Please!" I gasped as I ran up to that edge of the island. Nothing.

I was near the top of the island, the north end, and could see the channel and mainland shore to the north. I staggered, running to the south along the edge of the island, spitting out words and parts of thoughts as I went. "No . . . can't be . . . never get out . . . Alex . . ." I looked at everything—the channel, the shore, the trees, and the bushes, as if SilverWolf could have climbed out of the lake during the night. I stopped at the very southern tip of land, with my heart pounding in my throat and a desperate, pleading hope filling my brain. I had seen everything far and near that could be seen from

the island. No canoe.

I ran north along the lakeside shore over ground I'd just covered minutes earlier. I ran blindly now, not looking for or seeing much of anything until I came to the pack that I'd dropped earlier. I'd forgotten about it and it surprised me when I saw it. I stopped there and looked out at the wide empty lake that seemed as big as an ocean. And then I collapsed as if my legs had been shot out from under me. "Alex!" I cried. "Alex will die."

I lay on my side with my knees pulled up to my chest and my arms clasped around them. I panted, sobbed. Tears and sweat slid down my scratched-up face. Grim, wild images streaked through my head: Alex's bones picked clean and scattered before being found . . . mine never being found at all. I remembered Alex's scared and desperate voice saying, "Don't go." I thought of our parents, trusting us—letting us come here, thinking we were safe. Of all the things that could happen, what could be worse than this? And it was my fault, my own fault, all my fault. Stupid. My stupid fault. *I deserve it,*

I thought. *I deserve it, but not Alex. Not his fault.* Then I thought, *Yes, his fault. He climbed and fell and caused everything. Caused me to be here by myself. Caused SilverWolf to be lost.* I wanted to kick him, shout in his face until he understood what he'd done. Killed us both. Fallen to his slow death and sent me alone to mine.

Under the guilt and anger, I felt so alone, like my last friend had been stolen in the night. Together, SilverWolf and I could have made it. Alone, I'd never get out of these woods. I would die from starvation, exposure, injury, whatever; SilverWolf would drift until winter froze the lake and crushed her in the ice.

With my eyes closed and burning, I tried to picture the map. Could I hike and swim my way to help? I would have to walk around the shores of the lakes, lake after lake, and through the pathless forest that looked forever the same no matter where you were. I might get through, but not in time to save Alex, and the picture I saw in my mind of my body lying in some isolated,

wooded place seemed too strong and clear to be anything but true. And then there was the swim from island to island to worry about. The distance wasn't that great, but still . . .

Then I thought of something else and jerked like I'd been shocked. I didn't have the map! It was under my seat in the canoe, weighted with a rock. I didn't remember getting it out, didn't remember seeing it with my other stuff. I got on my knees and grabbed the pack, snatched its buckles open, flipped it over, and dumped everything out on the ground. No map! I untied and unrolled the tent, pulled its zipper open, and climbed in as if it were a big flat bag. No map! No map meant no hope.

Then I just sat in the midst of the clutter and held my head in my hands. I didn't feel like crying anymore. *Wimp*, I thought. *Stupid little wimp! You read some books and took some lessons and came into the woods with a kid who doesn't have enough sense not to cripple himself. He was stupid enough to take a chance in a place that doesn't give chances and doesn't tolerate stupid, and you were stupid enough to*

break a basic rule of canoe camping—always tie up your canoe. Now both of you get to pay.

Slowly a big thirst came over me, as if the morning had sucked me dry. I stood weakly, without any energy or hope. My Sierra cup still hung from my belt and I walked to the landing and dipped it in the water. I looked again at the lake. I missed SilverWolf like I missed Alex, maybe like he missed me. I was his friend and his only hope for being saved. SilverWolf was my friend and my only hope.

Except for a loon drifting close to the island, the lake, the forest—the whole world around me—seemed empty. *Nothing here to help me*, I thought again. *No parents, no teachers, no telephone.*

I watched the drifting loon, the bird of amazing voices, the bird of the Northwoods. Its body rode so low in the water that its black head looked like a periscope, keeping a wary, shining eye on me as it drifted along. The eye stood out like a beacon in the morning sun.

Shining. Drifting. The words, the ideas, seemed important. Somewhere on the lake

SilverWolf floated freely. A canoe like her wouldn't sink. Even if filled with water, she would float a little. And if she was floating she could be found. If a loon's eye shone in the sunshine, SilverWolf should stand out like a lighthouse. I had to find her.

But how? Get off the island. If I could get to the mainland, I could hike the lakeshore and hope to see SilverWolf somewhere on the lake. It was a big lake, but long and narrow. If SilverWolf was out there and I was looking from the right spot, I should be able to see her.

I'd have to swim to the mainland. The idea made me cringe. It was a short swim, about twice as long as my school's pool, but I feared it for the old reason—the lake water, the unknown depth, the things that might be watching me from the bottom. I'd just have to do it. It was better than staying on the island, waiting to die. Besides, I told myself, in such a narrow channel the water probably wasn't very deep.

The pack was a problem. I couldn't swim with it. Maybe I could take just enough stuff

to get me through the night, stuff that water wouldn't wreck. That way if I couldn't come back to the island, I could get by. Then I thought I should take enough food for all of the next day. I didn't know how far I would have to go. I might have to hike around the whole lake. How long would that take? A day? Three days? I didn't know.

My decisions were very important. I had to take just what I needed to survive, and no more. I took everything out of my pockets and put it with the other stuff on the ground. Then I made two piles, takers and leavers. The taker pile had my knife, my waterproof container of matches, the flashlight, insect repellent, jacket, cup, and most of my remaining ready-to-eat food. The food couldn't get wet. I needed some way to keep it dry while swimming.

I put the leavers—the stove and tent and the rest—back in the pack. I picked up the sleeping bag. The nylon bag it was stowed in could be my pack. It wasn't waterproof, but it was at least a way to carry things. If I could hold it up out of the water and swim at the

same time, I could keep things dry.

All the time, the channel swim loomed in my mind like a monster I had to face. I tried to keep it out of my thoughts, but I knew that carrying the sack meant a slow swim, more time in the water for . . . "Stop!" I said out loud. "You've just got to do it."

What to do with the big pack? I didn't want to leave it on the ground. Animals could get into it, maybe a bear. I knew from reading that being on an island was no insurance against bears. They swim better than dogs. I got the rope out of the pack, tied it around the straps, found a sturdy limb, and hoisted the pack. *Ten feet off the ground, five feet from the trunk*. I remembered this from all the books I'd read about hiking in the woods. The feeling that I was wasting time came back to me. I knew Alex wouldn't screw around with the pack like this. He'd just go. But I didn't want to come back to the island and no pack.

The time to swim had come. The point of the island closest to the main shore was steep and rough. To get into the water there,

I'd have to jump. I wanted a spot where I could wade out, and I found one where the island rose from the lake like a rocky ramp. Standing at its edge I discovered a new problem—my clothes. I could carry my shoes and socks with the sack, but I'd have to wear my pants and shirt.

The ramp disappeared into the shadowy water. I could see the bottom fairly far out, until the water got about ten feet deep or so. *That's okay*, I thought. *That's fine, but what's beyond that?* I looked for too long. "Staring and waiting won't change anything," I said. "Think of Alex."

I did not do it bravely, but I stepped in. The water was so cold it stung. The ramp was hard and slick. With the water waist-deep, I lifted the sack above my head with my left hand. When the water was up to my ribs, I let myself fall gently forward and pushed off with my feet. I swam sidestroke with the sack riding safe and dry. My body tensed with fear and cold. I swam as fast as I could, but that wasn't very fast. *It's not far*, I told myself, *and this channel isn't deep* . . .

*that's why there's an island . . . shallow . . . still,
when you can't see, you don't know what might
be . . .*

My clothes didn't help. They felt heavy, a
force pulling me down, and they kept me
from moving freely. I swam like I was
wrapped in a wet rug. My breath came in
gasps from the shock of such cold water.

I needed to find a good place to land, a
place where I could climb out with only one
free hand. I saw one that looked okay, not
too steep. I went for it and as I got near, something huge and heavy and rough dragged
against me in the water. I yelled out some
wordless grunt and nearly plunged the sack
into the lake as I whirled and kicked to get
away. It was just a tree trunk angling down
into the water from where it had fallen on
the shore, but it almost scared me senseless.

I began feeling for the bottom with my
feet. When I found it, I stood up and struggled to reach the rocky shore. I pulled
myself out with a shudder as if I'd barely
slipped past the slimy grip of something
unknown in the deep dark. But I'd made it.

Within minutes I was shivering out of control with cold. The clothes were a mistake. Even on this summer morning I just about froze. And wet clothes weighed a ton. I took them off and wrung them out. I could either put them back on and wear them wet or go naked and carry them. I put them on.

At least my sack worked great. There was hardly a splash of water on the outside, and everything in the pack was as dry as when I'd put it in.

I felt less safe on the mainland than I had on the island. Being so alone in such a vast, wild place brought out all those little-kid fears I used to have. And I was *alone*. Not like when I was in my room at night or home when my parents were out, but something much scarier. The island was small and sim-

ple and set apart. The mainland seemed huge and complicated. If anything had been on the island with me, I would have known it. On the mainland I couldn't be so sure. The wilderness went on for miles in every direction, and there was just me now to deal with it.

I closed my eyes and strained to remember what this lake looked like on the map. It was big, the biggest I'd been on except for the ranger's lake. It was much longer than it was wide, had a lot of islands, and two or three big bays. I was about at the middle of the west shore. I could only start walking and looking.

Without really thinking about it, I started out to the north. I guess I did that because when I was on the little island I could see a long way to the south, but the big island had blocked my view to the north, so it seemed like SilverWolf could be closer that way.

I had no idea how long it would take to find SilverWolf or even if I ever would find her. And I had no idea how long it would take me to hike around the lake, if I could do

it at all. Starting in the right direction could be the difference between a happy ending and a newspaper headline that read BOYS MISSING. But I didn't know the right direction. I could only guess.

The big island blocked my view of the lake. I wanted to get past it so I could look for SilverWolf across open water. I felt frustrated again from wanting to go fast and having to go slow. In many places I could walk fast, but my route zigzagged so much that I made slow progress. As I walked I came to a large bay. It was directly opposite the big island. And then I stopped walking. I'd come upon a trail. Finding a trail here surprised me until I realized it was the portage trail to the lake where Alex lay hurt. Coming to a scrap of familiar ground made me feel better, like finding someone you recognize in a crowd of faces you don't know. But it also made me think how close I was to Alex, maybe closer to him than to SilverWolf. How little distance I'd gone on my mission to get help. I felt ashamed. I was glad he didn't know where I was. I started walking again.

When I got even with the end of the big island, I found more islands, a bunch of them, scattered like a fleet of green ships across that part of the lake. I could see a lot of open water too, not the whole end of the lake, but some of it. No SilverWolf. I thought she might be floating out there behind one of the islands where I couldn't see her. Then a thought came to me that I didn't like. When I started, I'd hoped that she'd drifted to shore, got hung up in rocks or something, and that I'd find her and be able to walk right up to her. What if that had happened, but on one of the islands instead of the main shore? I might never find her.

The land began to rise away from the lake, making a long, wide hillside, not very steep. At one place a wide stretch of smooth, bare granite sloped into the water like a solid rock beach. An odd-looking, dark, shiny streak ran down it, widest near the water and tapering off as it got higher, like a long, narrow, upside-down V.

It looked like a stain or a vein of something in the rock, but when I got to it I found

that it was water. A ragged wet streak ran across the granite from the lake to the woods. I was too worried about SilverWolf to think much of it until I saw the clamshells. Broken shells covered the edge of rock just above the water and the shallows below it. A wet trail leading to a scattered heap of broken clamshells? For a minute I was blank, but I stopped because some deep, voiceless part of me knew that this needed to be understood.

Something had come out of the lake here. I shuddered. This was my old fear come to life—something rising from the water. I whirled and looked behind me. Nothing. The silent, wet stain pointed to the forest. Had what made it walked, crawled, slithered? Step by slow, frightened step I followed it for a few yards, stopping when I saw the footprint. It was a little shorter than mine, but much wider, the five toes clear on the rock. Whatever made it was as big or bigger than I. *Something awful,* I thought, *something from the deep lake.* But the clamshells? Then it hit me like lightning. A bear! A bear waded in

the lake for clams and left the wet streak as it walked back to the woods.

A bear was better than a creature from the deep, but this bear was a little too close for comfort. I didn't need to be a detective to know that for the rock to still be this wet, the bear had to have been there just minutes before. I shuddered again. Everything I knew about black bears—the most common type in America—said that they were shy and wouldn't attack unless threatened. But what would one do if it saw a kid my size walking alone on a lakeshore? Maybe it was watching me right now.

I wanted to go up the hillside to get an overview of the lake, but that's where the bear had gone. Ever since Alex fell, the things I felt I had to do were things I was afraid to do. I walked farther along the shore and then turned uphill. Something I'd read said it was good to make noise in bear country. Bears will avoid people if they can, but if you startle one it might attack. I began to sing and talk, babbling anything that came to mind.

I climbed high enough to get a good view and found a slightly elevated dome that made a decent lookout. I was scared to turn my back to the woods, but I had to. The lake glistened in the sun, bigger than I expected. I thought I might be near its north end, but even from here the water went on beyond my sight. And to the south it went on forever. Across all that water, I couldn't see anything that looked like SilverWolf.

I felt defeated. A cold clammy sweat came over me. The lake was just too big. It would take too long to search. Alex's water could run out before I walked the whole lake and I still might not find SilverWolf. I cursed myself again for being too stupid to tie my canoe. But the punishment seemed too great. It wasn't fair. I made one mistake and now . . .

Something moved behind me in the woods. I almost jumped off the edge of the overlook. I whirled around expecting the bear, but saw nothing. Then a flash of red fur shot up a tree trunk. A squirrel. My heart beat so fast I felt dizzy. I sat down and felt a

cool breeze on my face and neck. I looked back at the lake. The breeze stirred again. I thought how great it would be if SilverWolf was drifting behind one of the closer islands and the breeze pushed her into sight. The breeze *could* be moving her. Any instant she might appear.

And then I thought of something that changed the whole day, something I should have thought of before I started—the wind!

I jumped to my feet. The wind! The wind! The wind! During the night it had come from the northeast, blowing toward the southwest. I tried to paddle across the lake and couldn't because of that wind. I closed my eyes to remember it, to feel it on my face when it turned SilverWolf, how I strained to fight it, how I listened to it as I fell asleep. I was looking in the wrong place. I'd gone the wrong way. The wind last night would have pushed SilverWolf to the south.

I didn't know whether to be happy with myself for remembering or furious for wasting time by not thinking of it sooner. I still hadn't learned the lesson about doing with-

out thinking. I still hadn't learned to pay attention to the things that could help me. I began scrambling downhill toward the shore. I still didn't know if I would find SilverWolf, but I knew that the search area was half as big as it was two minutes ago. She had to be somewhere south of my little island.

I backtracked now as fast as I could. But I hadn't forgotten the bear. I looked for it and saw it in every dark boulder and distant shadow. I knew all along that bears live in the woods, but the wet footprint on the shore made them real—not something somewhere in the woods, but something in the same place at the same time as me.

At the place where I'd ended my swim and pulled myself out of the lake, I found no sign that I'd ever been there. The spot where I stood dripping and wringing my clothes was now dry. My passing hadn't left a mark. This place, this wilderness, looked exactly as it had before I came, exactly as it would after I left. I didn't matter to it. It was not my enemy. It was not my friend. It just *was*.

Now I started into the area I hadn't seen

before. The hope of finding SilverWolf on the shore came back to me. The wind had been blowing toward this shore and there were far fewer islands here. Maybe I'd find her blown aground toward the south end of the lake. But the south end was a long way off.

It was tough going. Alex and I learned to canoe on a city lake with a smooth, even shore. Walking along it was like walking across a wide lawn. It was a tame lake. This one was wild. I scrambled more than walked. I climbed, crawled, tripped, stumbled. In a few places I had to give up my view of the lake and cut inland to get past some barrier—trees crowding the shore, thickets, steep rock, bogs. And inland I met other obstacles—rows of deadfall trees pushed down by some monster wind like so many shattered and scattered pencils. And mosquitos. As soon as I left the breeze of the shore and stepped into the stiller air of the trees, mosquitos appeared as if my footsteps created them from the forest floor. The insect repellent kept them from biting, but they hovered and whined an inch away from

my skin and clothes, an inch from my eyes, nose, and mouth.

My hands, still sore, started to bleed from grabbing rough bark and pressing against sharp rock as I pulled and pushed myself along. But each time I came back to the water, I hoped to see SilverWolf. And each time a little hope slipped away. Sometimes I cried a little because I felt so hopeless and alone.

I stopped only to drink and two or three times to rest when I couldn't take another step. I never sat down, just stood staring at the lake until I gathered some strength, then forced myself to go on. "I'm going to find her," I whispered to myself. I ate some gorp while I walked.

The day slipped away with my footsteps and my hope. I thought I could make the south end of the lake before dark. What would it mean if SilverWolf wasn't there? Could she be drifting as I walked so that she would always be just out of sight? Would I walk until I died? My feet hurt so much I worried that I would start to limp and go

even slower. My ankles were gouged and bruised. The backs of my hands and arms were scraped and scratched. I thought about what it would be like to be caught by darkness and have to find a spot in the woods to curl up and sleep.

"All up to me," I said aloud. And as I did I crossed the top of a low ridge and looked out at the big lake for the thousandth time. Far out on the water something flashed in the sun, vanished, then flashed again. I shaded my eyes and squinted. It was SilverWolf!

SilverWolf! The name rang in my head like a cheer. Stepping on that ridge top and seeing the canoe changed everything. I wanted to laugh and yell. I'd been smart! Thinking of the wind made all the difference. If I hadn't, I'd still be going in the wrong direction at the north end of the lake, maybe days away from finding SilverWolf, maybe never finding her at all. I found her because I thought of the right thing. It wasn't just luck. It took too long. I wasted time. But I did it!

As I stood there feeling happy for the first time since Alex fell, a voice at the back of my head said, *Nobody's safe yet. You've found your canoe, but you aren't in it.* She'd drifted far out on the lake, at least halfway across, maybe farther. The urge to laugh and shout slipped away. How would I get her?

It looked too far to swim. Too far and too scary. I could hardly bring myself to think of it. *She'll drift to shore,* I thought. *She has to sooner or later. I just need to keep her in sight.* But what if it wasn't sooner? What if it was later, much later? She'd drifted most of the night and most of the day and she wasn't to shore yet.

Two voices inside me said opposite things. The familiar, fearful voice I'd known all my life told me I couldn't swim that far and a new voice told me I had to. I knew what Alex would do. He'd be swimming already. But he wasn't swimming. He was waiting and hurting, trusting me to get help.

Why did it have to be my worst fear? The surface of the lake looked like the shining top of a secret world where things lived and moved silently. How deep could it be? Hundreds of feet? Who could know for sure what life forms hung in its dark depths or rested in the lightless openings of underwater caves? There could be things from long ago ages of the earth, things that don't often rise near the surface or come near the

shore. Who could say what bulging eyes and hungry mouths hunted the deep?

The swim from the island to the mainland seemed like child's play now. The water was shallow there and I'd only been in it for a few minutes. This water was deep—deep enough to hide all kinds of things and I'd have to be in it for a long time.

While all these thoughts whirled around, I started to take off my shirt. My hands knew what I was going to do before I really decided to do it. I'd learned the lesson about clothes—I couldn't swim with them on. But as I stripped them off I trembled with fear. I still wasn't sure I could do this.

I put my sack on top of my clothes right there on the rock crest of the little ridge. Then I eased myself down the short slope and stopped with my toes at the water's edge. The old Hobie didn't want to go in. The new Hobie knew this was the only choice—I couldn't waste time. Naked and still trembling, I stepped in. Needles of cold shot into my feet and ankles, bone-aching cold. When the water got about knee-deep, I felt some-

thing mossy between my toes, something slimy and alive. I began to slip and, half lunging, half diving, I thrust myself into the lake. The cold jolted my body like a bad shock.

Right away I was out of breath, gasping for air, my arms flailing at the water. I was trying to fight off the cold more than I was trying to swim. I knew I was working too hard, wearing myself out. I remembered what our gym teacher had said about going the distance. You have to set a pace that will get you through. You can't use all your energy at the beginning. Using it up at the beginning of this distance would mean drowning.

I'm not a great swimmer. I'm okay at it. But I had never tried to swim any distance, really, and it scared me. I feared the distance more than what might be below me.

Within about ten minutes my body began to get used to the water. But I still felt cold. When your body runs out of energy and can't keep itself afloat, you die. I was burning energy to stay warm and swim, too. How long could I do it? Left arm, right arm. I took

big gulps of air. My legs beat against the lake, kicking and splashing. How long 'til I reached her? *Keep swimming!* I told myself.

After a while I realized I had to spot SilverWolf and make sure I was going in the right direction. I raised my head out of the water but couldn't see her. I stopped swimming and treaded water, trying to get my head as high above the lake as I could. No SilverWolf. I turned completely around. Nothing. I felt the choking grip of panic. Had I somehow veered in the wrong direction? Were the lake's reflections hiding her from me? If I didn't find her, could I swim all the way across the lake to safety or would I drown trying?

After turning around, I lost track of the direction I'd been going. Everything looked the same. I turned again, recognized the shore I'd left, and tried to remember the angle I'd gone from it. *Keep swimming!*

I tried to be smart by keeping an easy, steady pace. To do this I had to beat down the part of me that wanted to flail at the water in a wild fit of fear. I was getting tired.

The cold water had lost its sharpness and had become a dull ache—I wondered if that was good or bad. *Keep swimming!*

Every few strokes I raised my head as high as I could, straining to see SilverWolf. Why couldn't I see her? I should be getting close enough. Something stabbed into my thoughts like a long, sharp blade. Wind. I didn't know if there was any breeze, or what direction or how strong it was blowing. I hadn't checked it before I started to swim and in the water I couldn't feel it. All I felt was cold, tired, and scared. If the breeze was up, I might as well be swimming across the sky after a loose kite. What if I did see her but the breeze pushed her steadily away from me? I could swim after her until I sank. But it could just as easily push her toward me. I couldn't give up. *Keep swimming!*

My mind raced from one threat to another as my arms churned. I imagined finally reaching the canoe and finding her without a paddle. What had I done with the paddles last night? I couldn't remember. I tried to picture them lying in the canoe or leaning

against a tree on shore. No picture came. I knew I hadn't seen them that morning. Being in a canoe without a paddle on this big lake was hardly better than not finding the canoe at all. *Keep swimming!*

I swam farther and farther into the lake. My arms felt rubbery tired, like there wasn't any strength left in them at all. They just kept going through the water on their own. I couldn't tell whether my feet were still kicking or just dragging. I took huge breaths. *Keep swimming!*

And then when I was so far out on the water that I didn't even know where the closest land was, the old fear came back to me. I couldn't shut it out. It took the form of a huge, dull-colored thing stirring sluggishly at the dark bottom of the lake. I couldn't picture its gloomy shape, but it was big, all mouth and muscle. It was something never seen by human eyes, something from the time when ice covered the world and glaciers gouged these lakes from the frozen earth. When the ice slowly melted it was left behind in the cold dim depths, waiting,

snatching the great fish that swam too deep. And now it rose, slowly at first, gaining speed, coming up from the dark, tracking me. I imagined what I looked like from below—stretched out and splashing on the surface like the lures fishermen use to bring big fish to the surface. I expected to feel my toes brush against a hard, gristly mouth just before it closed around my legs and pulled me under.

Kid stuff! the new voice shouted in my brain. *Stop it!* I'd worked myself into a frenzy of wild swimming when I had no energy to spare. The real danger was not the monsters of my imagination, but exhausting myself and drowning. *Keep swimming!*

Now I looked for SilverWolf again. I kicked up as high as I could above the water. I saw her! She floated calmly about one hundred yards from me as if she had landed on the water like a bird while I wasn't looking.

A new kind of energy surged through me. I knew that I'd make it, that I'd done it, that I'd won. I finished the distance quickly. I grabbed the bow and hung on. The light rope

that I'd forgotten to tie the night before dangled in the water beside me. I hung there as limp as the rope, breathing like a marathon runner at the finish line. Aching with fatigue and cold, I patted SilverWolf on her side.

In our class Alex and I had learned how to get into a canoe from the water. I pulled myself along the side to the middle where she was most stable. I made a weak try to get in. SilverWolf rocked sharply, but I didn't come close to getting in. I wondered if I had the strength left to do it. Holding on tightly, I pushed myself down in the water as far as I could, then kicked and pulled upward. SilverWolf rolled on her side and I got one knee hooked into her. I wriggled and squirmed the rest of the way in.

She took in water ankle-deep when I pulled her down to climb aboard. My life jacket and Alex's paddle floated in her. My map lay anchored by its rock beneath the stern seat and my paddle leaned against the bow seat. I grabbed my paddle and stood up. Naked and dripping, I raised it above my head and yelled "YES!" as loud as I could into

the great silence of forests and lakes. From the distant shore a clear echo came back— "YES!"—as if all nature agreed with me.

My bones still ached from the lake's deep cold. I put on my life jacket, and the wet fabric against my bare skin made me colder. I turned toward the sun, closed my eyes, and raised my face to soak up the warmth. It made me think about coming into my house on cold winter nights and how great it is to be comfortable and warm and part of a family.

Having SilverWolf back was almost as good as being home. She seemed like my own personal island of safety and hope. It was like finding a part of myself that I couldn't live without. I was complete again, fully equipped and back in the game. "It was all my fault," I said to her. "I'll do better now."

I studied the west shore. I was too far out to see much detail and I could only guess at

where I'd left my pack and clothes, but I knew the general direction. The weight of water in SilverWolf was like the rocks. It made my weight in the stern less of a problem and I could paddle by kneeling just in front of the stern seat. It was slow going, but at least it was going—SilverWolf and I, back together and on the move again.

Though I didn't feel so strong, I wasn't totally wiped out, either. I felt like I'd won a hard contest and that SilverWolf and another chance were the prizes. Bordered by the bright trees and blue sky, the lake was dazzlingly beautiful. SilverWolf and I seemed to float on the surface of a liquid jewel. It made me remember how great Alex and I thought it was being among these lakes and woods before he fell.

Thinking of Alex reminded me that I needed to hurry. Finding SilverWolf and getting her back was not the victory. My real mission waited, unfinished. I drove the paddle harder into the lake.

I had trouble finding the place where I had left my clothes and sack. I had no idea what

it looked like from the water. If I'd been smart, I would have tied my shirt or something in a tree, like a flag. I had to remind myself I was still learning.

Finally, I saw the blue sack. I hauled SilverWolf onto the shore as best I could and rolled her over to get the water out. As I pulled on my clothes, I noticed the time. The sun shone from low in the sky. I only had a couple hours of daylight left.

I paddled back to my little island. I didn't need to look at the map. For the first time I had a sense of where I was and where I was going. The shore glided by me in the bright sun and still air. It seemed familiar and friendly. This was the same shore, the same trees, rock, and water that seemed so threatening when I hiked by them earlier. What had happened? I knew that if there had been a change it was a change in me.

I paddled back to the same landing I used the night before. I dragged SilverWolf up the easy slope and completely out of the water, turned her upside-down, and tied her to a tree trunk.

I needed to rest. While I was paddling I knew it was just a matter of time before exhaustion and hunger hit me, and once I reached the island I was overcome by the desire to eat and sleep. My body knew it was okay now to give in to this need. I'd hardly eaten anything all day, hadn't eaten much since Alex fell. I needed food.

The pack hung untouched where I'd left it. I got out one of the freeze-dried dinners—something with chicken and noodles, just add water—and the little one-burner stove. As I got water from the lake, I looked at the setting sun. Evenings like this one had filled my winter dreams of canoe camping, but being alone and desperate hadn't been part of those dreams.

Cooking freeze-dried food is mostly soaking it in hot water. It's almost impossible to overdo it. I thought that after eating I might not have energy to do anything but collapse into my sleeping bag, so while the chicken noodle stuff cooked I made my bed. I used the tent's light nylon rain cover as a ground cover and put my sleeping bag on top. I

couldn't face the work of setting up the tent and I didn't think I'd need it. The night was clear, warm and still. I remembered the bear track and the clamshells but figured the paper-thin tent fabric wouldn't make any difference to a bear. The night before, I'd pitched the tent when I was nearly too tired to walk. Now I felt like I could get by without it.

I ate my dinner on the lakeshore by SilverWolf. The package said it made four servings, but whoever wrote that hadn't walked through the woods all day and swum halfway across a big lake.

A few mosquitos buzzed around my face in the evening stillness. I brushed them away and thought of Alex. I felt guilty about having so much hot food when he had none. But I needed the food. The best thing I could do for Alex was refuel and rest and be strong enough in the morning to make a new start. He had water and food—not the greatest food, but enough. I thought again of the bear. If a bear smelled his food and came for it, could Alex scare it off? Should he even

try? I didn't know, didn't even want to think about it.

Thinking of myself sleeping in the open, I was glad to have no leftover food as bear bait. Staggering and fumbling now and working by flashlight, I forced myself to carefully wash my dishes and the foil pouch the chicken noodle stuff came in to get rid of the smell of food.

I rolled my shirt and pants into a pillow. As I climbed into the bag, a loon raised its wild, sad, musical voice far away on the dark lake. It marked the end of the hardest day of my life. I'd brought it on myself with a brainless mistake. It cost Alex and me a needless day of suffering.

I rolled on my back and opened my eyes for the last time that day. A quad-jillion stars hung above the treetops. They reminded me of the screen of one of Alex's and my favorite computer games. Then I thought, *No. This is real.* The loon called. The stars glittered. The lake lapped at the island. Something inside of me said, *These are the real powers that make everything else possible.* What a big

mysterious place the universe is. I was exhausted and alone, but for the first time in my life I thought, *I belong here. I can get by.*

I opened my eyes to gray light. Dawn. I forced myself to unzip my sleeping bag and get out. Without dressing, I walked barefoot in the cool air to check SilverWolf. She rested right where I'd left her. Wisps of mist rose from the lake like ghosts, rising and disappearing in the still air.

I pulled on my clothes, got the pack down from the tree, and started heating water for instant oatmeal. While it heated, I stowed my bag and tent cover and thought what it would be like to find bear tracks around my sleeping spot. There weren't any—I looked.

I sat by SilverWolf, eating the sticky oatmeal and drinking instant hot chocolate, studying the map, and looking at the lake. Then I got SilverWolf into the lake, loaded in my gear and rocks, and set out on the glass-

smooth water. From the time I woke up until the time I shoved off from the island, it was no more than forty minutes.

My course across the lake was southeast to the mouth of a long bay. The next portage waited at the far end of that bay. As the sun climbed higher, a slight breeze came from directly behind me. I fell into the rhythm of paddling, now on the right, now on the left, watching the drops come off the paddle like diamonds scattered on the lake. SilverWolf moved slowly—I just couldn't get up any speed by myself—but she moved steadily.

The map showed an island right where the bay opened into the lake. When I could finally see the island against the distant shore, I steered for it and then turned into the bay. Stroke after stroke after stroke, time slipped by with the cedars, spruces, and pines, grasses, lily pads, driftwood, and rocks. The air grew warm. I grew tired. My arms and shoulders were weak from the endless paddling. My hands throbbed. My body felt achy and stiff from its unchanging position. But I kept going. I'd thought about rest-

ing on the island at the mouth of the bay, but pushed myself onward for Alex's sake.

Somewhere at the end of the bay was the next portage, about the same length as the last one. I knew now that I could portage alone, but I wondered how tough a go this one would be. I dreaded it the way a boxer might dread a tough fight he thinks he can win.

I found the portage by spotting the faint silver streaks where aluminum canoes had been run aground on the rocks over the years. I decided to take SilverWolf first, when I would be strongest, and the much easier pack, paddles, and life jacket on the second trip. "You're learning," I said to myself. I also told myself that when I finished both trips I would have some lunch and a short rest as a reward.

Rolling her over and going through the struggle of getting her onto my shoulders, I treated SilverWolf as gently as I could. She had become like a living thing to me, my helper and only friend. But carrying her just about killed me. It hurt so badly that I won-

dered if I were wrecking my body, if I would be twisted and crippled when I grew up.

The air was warm, heavy and sticky, like what my dad calls tornado weather. Rivers of sweat ran down my face and neck, and the bugs were bad in some places. Finally I saw the next lake glistening through the trees.

I tied up SilverWolf and went back for the other gear. Hauling it across the portage, I heard the sound of wind in the treetops, not much wind, just a breeze. I couldn't feel it in the woods and couldn't judge its direction, but I tried. *Learning.*

I studied the map while I ate another snack-food lunch and drank about a gallon of water. My course would be to cut across the lower end of this lake. I could tell now, the wind would be behind me.

I was paddling again. I passed between a big island and a tiny island. After that it was all open water. I steered for the southeast corner of the lake and the next portage, a long one. I paddled until my arms felt like marshmallows. The breeze helped me. It came across the lake from straight behind,

strong enough to give me a boost, but not strong enough to cause trouble. It probably moved SilverWolf forward as much as my tired arms did.

More than halfway across I got a weird feeling that something was behind me. I thought it came from being chased by the breeze, but then a strong, cold gust hit the back of my neck and a dark shadow suddenly fell across the lake. I turned around to look. A towering wall of rolling black clouds filled the western sky. It was a big storm, coming right down on me.

A gusting, rising wind kicked up a chop on the lake. Thunder rumbled in the distance behind me. I had no shore, no island for shelter. I was as close to the portage shore as to anything and now the wind was driving me straight at it. I paddled furiously, trying to beat the storm.

But it moved faster than I did. Thunder rumbled closer and more often. *Too close,* I thought. In class we'd learned to clear off the water at the first hint of lightning. The teacher told us that she had seen a woman

who'd been struck in a canoe, right next to shore. It turned her whole body grayish-blue. *This isn't wimpy kid fear,* I thought. *This is real trouble.*

I was afraid for myself, afraid of having my skin fried by lightning. I carried Alex's life with mine. If lightning got me, I'd at least die fast, but Alex's death would be slow, hour by hour, day by day.

I had no decisions to make, no choices in front of me. All I could do was paddle like crazy for the shore. SilverWolf bucked and rolled on the swollen waves that caught us from behind. The wind tried to turn her broadside, but I held her straight, paddling for all I was worth. Hard rain pinged on the aluminum like BBs and stung the back of my neck.

The wind dropped for a minute as if to catch its breath, just long enough for me to wonder if the worst was over. Then lightning, a real boomer, struck close and the wind hit again with new force. It nearly knocked me out of the canoe. Shuddering, the canoe spun around, sloshing sideways

before the wind, as if hit by a bulldozer blade. SilverWolf rolled hard. The right gunwale dipped into the lake and water poured in. I threw my weight on the high side. She righted and I slid down into the bottom—in two or three inches of water—to keep my weight low and steady her. Rain shrieked over and by us, not falling rain, but wind-driven rain blown sideways.

When I looked again at the dark shore, it was much closer than I expected and seemed to loom up in front of me. New problem. How would I land SilverWolf? We could be smashed against the rocky shore by the waves. I couldn't control her, couldn't turn her. Control belonged to the storm now. All I could do was try to spot the best landing, line her up with it, and let the wind and waves drive us to it. I strained to read the shore. Another close lightning blast lit it up like a camera flash. It showed me a miracle almost beyond hoping for. A little strip of flat beach wasn't far off. If I could just get SilverWolf lined up with it, maybe we wouldn't get thrown against the rocks.

But there was something else, too. In the nanosecond of light, I thought I saw part of a roof among the wildly dancing trees behind the beach. I couldn't believe it. Then I saw it again without lightning. Then it was gone. Another streak of lightning hit so close I could feel the charged and tingling air, and the thunder nearly blasted me out of the canoe. I saw the roof again. It was real. It spooked me. What could it be?

I paddled with all I had to get SilverWolf lined up with the beach. She tossed and rolled so much that some of my strokes missed the water and others drove the paddle in up to my elbow. A few yards before the sand—WHAM!—she hit a rock in the shallow water and rolled completely on her side. I don't know if I jumped out or got dumped, but all of a sudden I was in thigh-deep water with one hand holding SilverWolf's stern. Waves helped me haul her onto the wet sand. I yanked the pack and paddles out and rolled her over to dump the water. Then I dragged her across the narrow beach, turned her over, and carefully tied

her to a tree. After all this, I went back for the pack, paddles, and life jacket and ran with the stuff toward the roof I'd seen from the water.

It was a tiny trapper's cabin that, with its door and window missing, looked like a miniature haunted house. I stepped through the doorway out of the rain and groped in the pack for my flashlight. There was just one small room. Something had knocked a big hole in one side of the low roof. Rain streamed through it, and the floor under it had rotted away. But the other side of the room seemed okay—except for being filthy. The cabin was damp, dark, rotting, and probably rodent-infested. It smelled bad. Moss grew on the inside of the log walls. But its good half, creepy as it was, gave shelter from the wind and rain.

The real creepiness, the spookiness, came not from what mice and squirrels and weather had done, but from what the trapper had left behind. It looked like he'd left everything. His things stood out in my flashlight beam like museum pieces set just where

he'd left them—I felt like a trespasser. The big things like the wood stove and handmade bed frame didn't bother me. You'd expect someone to leave those. But why would he have left the little things? A rotting shirt and a pair of suspenders hung from nails on one wall. A metal coffeepot and cup sat side by side on the wood stove and a few metal dishes still lay on the table. An old-fashioned tobacco can rested near them. Some tools hung on one wall and a lantern hung from a nail at one end of the bed frame. It all looked like whoever had left it planned to come back but never did. Not far from the lantern, some little shiny, wiry thing hung on the wall within easy reach of the bed. I looked closer. It was a pair of glasses.

I was shaking with cold. My clothes were as wet as the day I swam in them. Was it just yesterday? It seemed longer. I'd spent a lot of time since Alex fell being scared, wet, and cold.

Using one of the paddles like a broom, I cleared a place on the floor under the good part of the roof. Only one corner of my

sleeping bag was wet from the water in the bottom of the canoe. I put the bag on the floor, stripped off my dripping clothes and hung them on the wall, climbed in the bag, and pulled it over my head. I didn't want any part of me touching that creepy floor.

I thought of Alex again. I kept thinking of how helpless he looked when I left, how he'd said, "Don't go." Had the tarp held? Was he dry and warm enough or soaked and cold? I'd done the best I could for him. I hoped it was good enough.

When I warmed up, I reached out and pulled the pack over beside me and dug in it for food—more bread, peanut butter, and cookies. I ate sitting up, with the bag pulled around me.

I couldn't tell whether it was dark because of the storm or because it was nighttime now. I lay down and pulled the bag over my head again. I thought of the trapper. He wouldn't have just left his glasses on the wall like that. What happened? Maybe he was an old guy who died. Or maybe he had an accident in the wilderness and couldn't get help.

Could he have been murdered? How long ago? The tobacco can and glasses looked old. Maybe he was one of those people who goes crazy from being in the woods all alone. I shuddered and wriggled deeper into the bag.

Morning. Gray light again. Drizzly rain drummed on the cabin roof and dripped on the rotted floor a few feet from my head. Through the hole in the roof I saw thick, low clouds. I couldn't tell what time it was. Early, I hoped.

My clothes were still wet. Pulling them on made me shiver. I wondered if Alex was warm enough. And if he had any pain pills left.

While pulling on my shirt, I walked quickly to the line of trees where I'd left SilverWolf. She was fine. The wind hadn't moved her. Nothing had fallen on her. She had a slight dent and rough scrape from the rock we'd hit, but that wouldn't bother her much. I patted her cold, hard side. Walking back to the cabin, I discovered it was on a

trail that led off into the woods. Could it be the portage?

I was hungry and cold. I ate two packages of instant oatmeal, some more bread, my last apple, and my last cup of hot cocoa.

I packed my gear and took the map outside to look at the trail. The map showed the portage running east and west. My compass said that this trail ran east and west. But how could I tell for sure it was the right one? Starting down it with a load and finding out it wasn't right would waste time and energy. The storm brought me to the beach and cabin almost by luck. The portage trail might be somewhere else and I might have to get SilverWolf back on the lake to find it. But if it was somewhere else, it couldn't be very far from here. The map showed the trail at this part of the lakeshore. I didn't know exactly where on the shore I was and there were no landmarks, like an island, to help me figure it out.

With just the compass and map, I walked the trail for a few minutes, long enough to see that it kept going more or less east. It had

to be right. The map showed only one trail. This one was going the right direction. The beach made a perfect canoe landing. And the trapper probably built his cabin in a place where he could go easily from one lake to the next.

As I started back toward the cabin, something moved in the woods and startled me. It was probably a rain-heavy limb falling or maybe a squirrel, but the creepy cabin nearby made me imagine someone watching me from the woods.

Again, I decided to take SilverWolf down the portage first. I left the pack just inside the cabin door out of the rain. The map showed this portage as longer than the others. I hated the thought of it, and wished I had a magic way to float a canoe across a portage in the air. Carrying SilverWolf hurt so much that thinking of it ahead of time made me feel kind of sick. But it was another case of no choice but to do it. At least it might warm me up. In my wet clothes in the drizzly, chilly morning, I was so cold I couldn't stop shaking.

The portage was hard because of the trail's length. The longer the distance, the longer the time the canoe was on my shoulders. Toward the end each step jarred my whole upper body with pain. But luckily it was mostly flat and open, following the edge of a wide marsh with no trees. In some places I slogged through silty muck or a few inches of water, but being wet meant nothing to me now. I hardly felt wetter when I finished wading than I had before I started.

Hiking back to the cabin after I left the canoe, I came to a place where I could look down the tunnel of trees and see the cabin and lake. Just as I did, something big moved around the far corner of the cabin and out of my sight. I stopped cold. I couldn't tell what it was, something dark, maybe a shadow. All I really saw was movement. For a minute I just stood and looked. Who or what? Could it be that someone . . . could it be the trapper?

I wheeled around where I stood trying to take in all of the forest and trail in one instant, to see if anyone or anything else was

there, like maybe some crazy guy with an axe. Nothing. I didn't know whether to run to the cabin or stay back and watch for a while. What had I seen? Nothing else moved. Everything looked fine. I walked slowly ahead, kind of crouching, and stopped again in the trees just before the trail entered the clearing. I stood stock-still and listened. Just drizzle and breeze. The cabin looked different, like something was missing. My pack was gone!

I took a few steps back. My heart beat like it might tear loose inside me. I felt chilled to the core. Someone had taken my pack. I couldn't remember exactly what I'd seen. Maybe the movement was someone going into the cabin.

I crept up on the corner closest to me. I could see down the side wall and down the front wall with the window and door in it. My hands were clenched in tight fists. I inched my way toward the window and peeked in. I could see most of the tiny room. Nothing. Nobody. No pack. I edged over to the door. Empty.

Now, trembling, I went slowly along the front wall to the far corner where I first thought I saw movement. Someone could be waiting just around it. I moved out from the front wall so I would be out of reach and then looked around the corner. Nothing. I crept down the side wall to the back corner and looked around it the same way. There was nothing there but a trash heap, mostly old rusted cans. Beyond it stood a dense, brushy thicket of saplings. Then a noise came from the thicket. I froze in mid-step and listened. It was a soft popping, tearing noise. I heard it again, not loud, slightly different. Something was there, but I couldn't tell what it was or what it was doing.

Holding my breath and stepping as slowly and quietly as I could, I followed the noise. Cold sweat seeped all over me. I could be walking into something awful. Maybe I shouldn't. Maybe I should turn and grab the paddles and run to SilverWolf and take off. But whatever it was, it had taken some of the things I needed.

When I reached the edge of the thicket,

I snaked my way through the thin, close trunks, pausing, listening, stepping quietly. I came closer to the noise. One instant it sounded like the grunt-thump of a football play. Then silence. Then a kind of wet smacking sound.

The little trees were so thick that, with hardly any warning, they stopped and gave way to a clearing. I stopped and stood just behind the last row of them—looking at a bear!

It was on all fours. I was behind it and to one side and could see along the side of its body to its head. It was eating from my pack. Black and roundish, it didn't look much larger than a really big dog. It wasn't the towering monster of nightmares, but it was still a bear.

I had to get away. I'd come back later to see if I could save anything from the pack. I stepped back and tripped. Starting to fall backward, I lurched forward to save myself and then fell forward, going down at the edge of the thicket with a crash. I was back on my feet so fast that I barely touched the

ground, so fast that the bear had not yet finished spinning around and standing up to see what made the noise. Now it looked *big*. Its small eyes locked onto mine like dark lasers. I just had time to wonder if I should run or drop to the ground and curl up when the bear turned around, streaked across the clearing, and went crashing through the woods as fast as it could go.

It took me a minute to figure out what happened. Then I started laughing, partly glad to be alive and partly in surprise. The bear was afraid of me, *really* afraid. I looked down at my still-clenched hands. I never would have thought that a bear would run from me.

I didn't laugh for long. My food was gone, all of it. The bear had even ripped into the sealed foil packets. The pack was shredded, my life jacket torn to pieces, and much of my other gear, including the map, damaged. Then I thought, *What if the bear comes back to see if it left any food?* I moved fast. I put everything in the ruined pack, grabbed the paddles, and walked quickly, nearly run-

ning, away from the cabin and toward SilverWolf. I kept looking back over my shoulder as I went.

The bear had torn a big piece out of the map, a piece I needed. I could see where I was and where I wanted to end up, but everything in between was gone.

But I practically had the map memorized from studying it so much. I knew two important things. I now stood at the north end of a very long, narrow lake, or two lakes really, connected by a narrow passage of water, like a short river. From all my reading I knew that there would be rapids in the narrow part. Without that portion of the map, I didn't know any details. A portage trail skirted the rapids, but I couldn't remember on which side or how far from the rapids it began. After the rapids, at the end of the lake, I'd find that last tough portage to the ranger's lake. I was getting

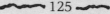

close, maybe two days to go.

And I knew that a long paddle lay ahead of me. At least it was a straight shot, as I remembered, nothing tricky about it except the rapids.

Rain fell lightly, steadily, and the breeze blew in the direction I had to go. That was one good thing—the breeze was behind me again. I wrapped the wrecked pack around my gear, trying to keep at least the sleeping bag dry. The trip before me now promised to be colder and wetter than anything I'd experienced so far. And what would I do for food?

I hunted up some more rocks for weight and pushed into the lake. I thought the breeze would be stronger in the middle, where it had a clear shot over the water, so I set a course there. The lake was narrow and straight, like a knife blade. Even in the murky weather I could see both shores easily.

SilverWolf moved smoothly, lightly, the water rippling musically against her bow. She felt almost like a part of my body, doing

what I willed her to do, like a hand or foot. I thought again that all would have been lost if I hadn't found her. There would have been two empty desks when school started. And I thought that if I made it out, I would keep her forever, that when I was an old man I would still have her. In the past few days, she and I'd shared a lifetime's worth of adventures—and they weren't over yet.

We passed through a cluster of islands in the steady rain. We were making good time, but there was still so far to go. I watched the gray mist drift through gray-green treetops. My pants were so wet they stuck to my skin. Knowing that I had no food made me feel hungrier than I was—I wondered if I'd be able to forget this hunger, or just get used to it. The breeze grew stronger and helped us. It was just about perfect. Time slipped away and disappeared behind us like the drops that fell from the paddle blade and vanished into the lake.

Gradually I became aware of a noise, a dull, steady noise like a train in the distance.

Soon I saw that the lake shores tapered in, making the lake narrower. SilverWolf and I, and everything in and on that lake, were moving toward the neck of a funnel. Our good pace had not been caused only by a breeze. Even though it looked still, the water was moving, carrying us. The whole lake flowed into the funnel. Figuring the rapids would be in this narrow part, I angled toward the left shore and kept SilverWolf close to it just in case I wanted to land in a hurry.

I watched the shore beside me and the lake ahead until the water moved fast enough and the rapids roared loud enough that I thought I should scout on foot before going farther with SilverWolf. As I landed her, I realized how fast the water was moving.

This shore was not great for walking. Steep and rocky and thick with brush, it made me follow a zigzag path, now up in the brush, now down on the rocks, wherever the going was easiest. And in doing this, by blind luck I came to the portage.

But I really wasn't that lucky. The trail twisted and climbed up the steep ground away from the rapids and went on and on, a killer of a portage. When the trail finally leveled, it looked like half the forest lay across it. The trees on this hilltop high above the rapids had blown down in the storm. Their needles were still green. Clods of soil still clung to their upturned roots. There was no portaging through this and no easy way around it.

So, now what? I was so discouraged I wanted to cry. So close to help, but everything was against me. I hiked back to the lake. I had to find another way. I climbed along the edge of the rapids. It began with a long stretch of fast, smooth water that picked up speed as the channel narrowed. Then it went over a little waterfall maybe seventy-five yards wide, but only about a foot high. Below the falls the channel was narrower and scattered with huge rocks. In places, the water boiled and churned against the rocks in a white froth. In other places, it ran fast,

but fairly smooth. A giant tangle of driftwood, whole trees and pieces of trees with
sharp, ragged branches jutting out like
spears, lay stacked along the right shore.

I turned back toward SilverWolf, not knowing what to do. Had I come this far and suffered this much only to meet a dead end?
With only part of a map, could I find another
route to the ranger's cabin?

Along the falls I had to pick my way
from rock to rock along the rapids' edge.
Sometimes I nearly crawled, holding on to
whatever I could. If I slipped into the fast
water, I'd get a rough ride into the rocks.
Imagining being swept into the water, I
thought I could probably survive the falls,
and if I could manage to get into the
smoother water on the other side, I might
possibly make it through.

This gave me a scary idea. I turned around
again and looked downstream. I could see
through the spray to the end of the rapids.
Beyond the rocks and driftwood the channel
widened and the water slowed into the still

lake. Could I get SilverWolf through it?

The portage was impossible. Finding a different route would take forever. If I could shoot the rapids, I'd be through in less than two minutes. In canoe class they told us that Rule #1 of wilderness canoeing is not to try fast water. If you smash your canoe and get hurt, you're stuck in the middle of nowhere with no help—like Alex. I was worried about two things. The first was getting over the waterfall. The second was staying clear of the rocks beyond it.

I felt nervous and excited at the same time. If I wiped out, Alex and I both might die. If I tried a different route with no map, we both might die. I probably wouldn't try the rapids if it was just for me, but for Alex, time was running out. I had no choice. I had to shoot the rapids. For a second, anger at Alex raged through me again. I had to risk this because of his screwup. But the risk was mine to take—and I wanted to take it.

The really bad water lay to the left side of the channel below the falls. If I hit the falls

at the right spot, about two-thirds of the way across, SilverWolf would drop into the easier water. She'd handle the falls okay if she hit it straight on. That was the key. We had to go over the falls at the right spot and then let the swift, smoother current carry us past the wild water, boulders, and driftwood. I chose the spot.

Heading back to SilverWolf, I felt like I was in the middle of a nightmare. Surely I'd wake up before going over the falls. This is not something you do in real life. But since Alex fell, I'd learned that some scary things happen in real life. You either deal with them or crack up. I'd done a lot already, more than I ever thought I could. *I might be able to do this too*, I thought. *I have to try.*

I took SilverWolf's bow rope and tied it tightly around the torn pack and then tied the pack to a seat so it would stay in the canoe if we spilled. I tucked the map inside my shirt and checked my pockets for my compass, knife, and waterproof container of matches. I carefully pushed off into the

water at an angle slightly against the current. In paddling against it, I felt its real
strength. I got lined up with my spot far
enough away from the waterfall so that I had
time to set a course and steer for it before
going over.

I took two wide sweeping strokes and let
the bow swing around toward the falls. The
current hit like a tractor. It pulled SilverWolf
with a force that wouldn't quit.

Sweat stood on my face in the cool, rainy
air. My hands gripped the paddle like they
wanted to crush it. If there ever was a time
I'd needed my life jacket, this was it! We
went faster now, as if SilverWolf were trying
to catch up with the speed of the water, not
easy-fast, but heavy-fast like a truck out of
control rolling downhill. Faster and faster
the water pulled until everything was just a
blur and a roar.

And now the current pushed SilverWolf
across the channel, away from my spot. I
couldn't do a thing about it. The water had
control. I fought with every ounce of muscle

to keep her straight over the waterfall. I saw the rocks beyond. At the last minute, I pulled the paddle out of the water and held my breath.

She went over like a torpedo, with just a good thump when she came down, perfectly straight. Whew! Just like I wanted! But the rougher water punched and kicked at her and swept her right at the mountain of driftwood. I dug hard at the water. Nothing. The paddle felt like a toothpick. I paddled as deep and wide and fast as I could, like a machine on high speed. SilverWolf edged slightly away from the jam. But a rock as big as a car jutted out from the water. I couldn't miss the wood and the rock, too. Too fast. No time. *Craa-Boom!* The bow hit the rock.

It threw me off my seat. SilverWolf rolled hard. Cold, churning water rushed into her, filling her nearly half full. Then the current pushed her sideways toward the giant snarl of heaped and jutting wood. I lunged out with the paddle to push her clear, and the force broke the blade off the shaft. SilverWolf

crashed broadside into the blunt end of a log with a groaning, smashing sound. I saw the center brace bend like a wire. Then she rolled backward against the current and dumped me into the sweeping water.

I tried to hold on, but I was underwater with SilverWolf on top of me. I had to let go. The current sucked me into and under the driftwood. I bounced, spun, and tumbled against the logs and tangled branches underwater for what seemed like minutes. Hard, sharp things raked against me. Then suddenly, I slammed into something and stopped dead. I couldn't move. Tons and tons of rushing water pressed me against it, trying to crush me.

My lungs burned, ached. *Drowning*, I thought, *I'm drowning*. I got one foot against something solid, then got the other foot on it, too, and shoved with all the strength I had left. I broke free. The current swept me into something else and pinned me again. *I'm dead*, I thought. Then I was moving again. I was about to black out. My lungs seemed to

be exploding inside me and just as I gasped, not caring if I breathed in air or water, I broke through the surface and sucked in air.

I wasn't completely conscious. Somehow I floated into the calmer part of the current, and when it had slowed down enough, I crawled out on the shore. I didn't cry, didn't even moan. I just lay there, gasping, shivering, thinking how close I'd come to drowning.

I felt beat up. My clothes were torn and I was bleeding from scrapes and gouges. My whole body was sore.

When I finally got up, I saw that SilverWolf was caught on some rocks in shallow water nearby. It surprised me. I don't know how she got out of the jumbled driftwood. My pack was still tied to her now-bent seat. She teetered on the rocks and with a shove from me she rolled and spilled most of the water that was in her. She was wrecked, bent-in like a huge weight had come down on her side. Maybe she could be repaired but not by me and not here. I wondered if there was

any way I could still use her, but then realized that I had no paddle. Mine was broken. Alex's floated somewhere on the lake. I looked for it across the water. Hopeless.

There was only one thing left to do now, and that was hike out. I knew that the rapids were more than halfway to the portage that would take me to the ranger's lake. I would have to hike this lakeshore to the portage, cross the portage, and hike the lakeshore to the ranger's cabin. It would take a long time, but maybe I could do it.

I pulled SilverWolf onto the shore, turned her upside down, and tied her to a tree. It choked me up. I felt like I was burying my last friend—and that I'd been the one who steered her into disaster. First Alex, now SilverWolf. I was completely alone.

The only things in the bear-chewed pack that I thought would do me any good were the flashlight and the light nylon rain cover for the tent, which I could use as a blanket.

The sleeping bag and real tent were too wet and heavy to carry.

Walking this shore in my wet clothes reminded me of looking for SilverWolf on the big lake, only now I felt so beat up and sore that I hobbled and dragged myself along. I walked the rest of the day. The rain stopped. The sky cleared. The sun helped warm and dry me a little. As evening fell and the long forest shadows reached across the water, I could see the end of the lake.

I stopped to rest, and looked at the map in a cove behind a good-sized island. I was back on the map now. The bear left me the part I needed to get from here to the ranger's cabin. I would have to hike around the end of the lake to reach the portage.

But looking at the map, I saw another possibility. Between this lake and the cabin it showed only forest, no lakes to cross or go around. I could hike cross-country straight to the cabin from where I was. I could skip hiking all the way around to the portage. Without a canoe there was no reason to follow a water route. Hiking the deep, pathless

woods probably wouldn't be much harder than following the shore. It was a lot shorter. It would have to be faster. I still had my compass. That was all I'd really need.

Then I had second thoughts. *What could happen in the woods with no trail to follow? What might be waiting for me?* I already knew it would be tough going, very tough, but it might save time, maybe a whole day. That could mean a lot for Alex, if he was still alive.

In the fading light, I set the compass on top of the map so that the compass needle and little arrow on the map both pointed north. Then a straight line from the island beside me to the cabin lined up with the southeast mark on the compass. In the woods I could use the southeast mark to point me in the right direction as long as I kept the needle pointing north. I figured I couldn't miss finding the ranger's lake. I'd have to come to its shore somewhere. The trick would be knowing which direction to go from there to find the cabin. I decided that any time I had to skirt around some-

thing in the woods, I would go to the right. That way the cabin should be to my left when I reached the lake.

I'd start first thing in the morning. Now I had to get some sleep. I drank some water and then found a level, mossy spot in the woods near the lake. I spread the rain cover out, lay down on part of it, and pulled the rest of it over me. It was just thin nylon. I was cold in my still-damp clothes and I was painfully hungry, but I fell asleep.

I awoke in the dark. What woke me? Was something there? I switched on the flashlight. Nothing. I tried to wrap more of the cover around me, but I couldn't stop shivering. I wondered if Alex was cold. I pictured him lying on the rock with his pain pills gone and his water running out. Counting the day he fell, he'd been there for four days.

I was wide awake. I don't know how long I slept, maybe two or three hours, but I knew I couldn't fall asleep again. I decided to start for the ranger's lake in the dark. I had to do something to get warm. I might as well start walking. The sooner I got there,

the sooner I'd get help.

I felt even more sore and stiff after resting than I had before. I went to the lake, knelt, and drank. I had no way to carry water. Then I turned back into the dark woods. It was just me and the flashlight and the compass now.

I tried to walk with the rain cover wrapped around me for warmth. It didn't work. I fell twice in the first twenty minutes. I hurt so much anyway that it didn't seem to matter. Darkness filled the woods so thickly that it was like something you could not only see but feel. Twisted, haunted shapes surrounded me. Trees reached out with long, spindly arms and spidery fingers. Big rocks and low bushes crouched as if beasts ready to attack. Everything looked strange, like I'd been dropped on an unexplored planet. The ground beneath my feet was just a dark mass. I couldn't see its details. And I couldn't use the flashlight too much. I needed to save it for the many times I would have to read the compass.

The forest itself prevented me from keeping a straight course. I had to go around the

fallen trees and huge boulders. But I needed to go straight southeast. I used the shapes themselves as a way to do it. I would stop and use the flashlight to read the compass. With the needle pointing at north, I looked into the darkness to the southeast and picked out a shape that lined up with it. Then I walked to that shape, whatever it was. If I had to zigzag to get to it, and usually I did, it was okay because as long as I ended up at it, I knew I was straight southeast of where I'd started. It was slow, but it kept me pretty much on course.

I tripped often enough to think that things were grabbing at my feet. If the ground was wet, I found out not by seeing mud or water but by hearing the splash of my steps and feeling cold trickles seep into my boots. I came to places too steep and rough to climb, thickets too thick to go through, and worst of all, huge heaps of deadfall trees. Trees of all sizes lay across each other in barriers as big as soccer fields, like some giant had stomped them down. All I could do was go around them.

At times I thought I must be stepping where no one had ever stepped before. I wondered what wild eyes might be watching me in the deep dark. If they were there, all they did was watch. Nothing moved. Nothing stirred. A silence as deep and heavy as the darkness lay across the night. Only my steps and stumbles, my breathing and talking to myself, broke it.

Every few minutes I switched on the flashlight to check the compass. Sometimes I shined it around me—sections of tree trunks, branches, chunks of mossy logs stood out weirdly in its narrow beam. I thought about food, all kinds of food, all the time while I walked. I kept imagining I had something to eat, like a candy bar, in my pocket. Over and over I reached for it. My stomach felt like it had caved in on itself.

Sometimes I pictured SilverWolf lying bashed at the end of the rapids. I felt guilty and sad, like I'd double-crossed a friend. I'd smashed her up and then abandoned her after she'd done all I'd asked. If it wasn't for her, neither Alex nor I would have had the

chance to see another birthday. I knew she could be repaired. If I could save Alex, I could save her. "I'll come back," I said to her through the darkness. "I promise."

After I'd walked a long time, I noticed something strange happening in the forest in front of me. At first I thought I imagined it— maybe I was too tired and hungry—but as I walked up a long hill I became sure of it. The sky was changing. The treetops started to glow with silvery-yellow light. I stopped. I wondered if I was about to have a close encounter with a UFO.

As I neared the top of the hill, I saw that the whole sky beyond it was glowing silvery-purple. I listened hard. Silence. I picked my way from tree to tree as if to sneak up on it, and when I got to the top I saw it.

It was the moon, bigger and brighter than any UFO, rising above the forest. It was so bright it hurt my eyes and, in its light, the forest's weird shapes turned into things I could see, things I knew. I could even see the needles on the pine tree beside me. I never paid much attention to the moon at home. I

didn't know how awesome it could be in a place with no light.

It changed everything. It didn't smooth the problems out of the forest, but it let me see them before I walked into them. And it let me see a way around them.

Southeast. Southeast. Southeast. Hungry, thirsty, tired, bruised, aching, I followed the compass for a long time. I thought about pizza and my mom's great dinners. I fought off the urge to lie down in the soft moss and rest by thinking of Alex and how close I was to getting help. "Keep going, keep going," I whispered to myself again and again.

Late in the night I climbed over damp, mossy rocks to get to the top of another long hill and started down the other side. Suddenly *two* moons were shining at me. One hung above the treetops and another shone through the trees in ripples of light from the bottom of the hill. It was a reflection from the ranger's lake!

First I drank. Then I followed the curving shore to the left as I'd planned. I crossed a point of land that stuck into the lake,

and from the other side I could see the ranger's cabin and dock standing dark across a silvery bay. My plan worked. I'd hit it almost dead on.

The first plane came in the morning, dropping out of the clear sky about an hour after sunrise. The ranger radioed for it during the night after hearing my story. It carried a woman and two men. They came into the cabin. The woman was a doctor. One of the men was the pilot and the other was a rescue guy.

The doctor asked what had happened and how long ago. She asked if what Alex said after the fall made sense, if his eyes looked like they could focus, if any broken bones poked out through his skin, and if he had enough water and food. She said I looked like I needed a doctor myself. She felt my arms, legs, and back, and gave me some salve for my cuts and scrapes.

A big map of the whole area hung on the

147

cabin wall. The pilot asked me to point out exactly where Alex was. The map was so much bigger than mine that it took me a minute to find the spot. The pilot said, "You understand how important this is. Are you sure?"

"Yes." I nodded. "I'm positive." And I really was.

They didn't waste any time. As soon as they had my answers, they left. I wanted to go with them, but I couldn't. The plane was too small. The pilot shook my hand, saying, "You've done enough for your friend. We'll take care of the rest."

I watched them take off to the west and turn to the north. I wondered how many minutes it would take them to cover the distance that had taken me four days. I tried to imagine how Alex would feel when he heard the plane taxi to the shore just below him. He *would* hear it, I told myself. But I couldn't shut out the idea that he might not be alive.

The ranger fixed pancakes and Canadian bacon and I was so hungry I ate, even though I felt really nervous about Alex. Dead

or alive? I'd know very soon now. I ate a lot. It was like having real food for the first time in weeks or like tasting something you love, like pizza, for the first time ever. During the night, after sending the radio message, the ranger had given me cold cereal with powdered milk. I was so hungry that even that tasted good.

The ranger's headquarters radioed to check on the rescue and say that reporters wanted to interview the boy who'd tried to save his friend. The headquarters guy said something about "waiting for the outcome . . ." and that worried me. After that the ranger tuned his radio to the channel the plane used and we listened. For a while we heard only scratchy static, but then the pilot's voice broke through. First he said some code words followed by "We've got him." I couldn't understand the other radio voice at all, but then the pilot's voice said "bad shape, but alive." My eyes went blurry with tears, and I turned away so the ranger wouldn't see.

Then the doctor's voice came on with some medical stuff. I think she was telling

the hospital what to have ready. All I could get out of it was that it sounded like Alex would live. A great comforting sense of happiness flowed through me. I asked the ranger where they were taking him. "Thunder Bay," he said.

The second plane came in the afternoon. It carried only its pilot and one passenger— my dad. I had mixed-up feelings about seeing him. I felt excited and embarrassed and worried that I might bawl like a little kid who's been lost at the mall. As the plane taxied to the dock, I remembered when I lost SilverWolf and thought I might never see my family again. But I also wondered how much trouble I was in.

I forced myself not to cry when my dad hugged me. Then he took a long look at me and asked about my scraped-up face and torn clothes.

We stayed only long enough for Dad to thank the ranger. Then it was on to the plane to fly to Thunder Bay. "Alex's parents are already there," Dad explained. "There's nothing we can do to help, but I'm sure you want

to see him." When I walked toward the plane carrying only the rain cover, he asked, "Where's all your stuff?"

"This is it," I said. He looked at me with a look that was both puzzled and proud.

During the flight I told him the whole story as the blue and green world of lakes and forest passed beneath us. Two or three times I started to choke up and I knew that he knew. He didn't say much. I could tell he was caught between being really mad at me for taking off with Alex, and being proud of me for doing so much on my own. Mostly I could tell that he was as glad to see me as I was to see him.

When we walked into Alex's room at the hospital in Thunder Bay, Alex looked at me, smiled faintly, and gave me the thumbs-up sign. He looked awful, really sick. His face was all bandages and scabs and his skin was a yellowish-gray. "You made it," he said weakly. He turned away and I knew it was his turn to fight back tears. I couldn't be mad at him anymore.

"You made it too," I said.

He nodded. "It got real hard when the pills were gone."

"Did you have enough water?" I asked.

"Yeah."

"What about that storm?"

"Oh, man . . ." he said.

"I saw a bear," I said. "It got my pack."

His eyes widened.

"So how long do you have to stay here?" I asked.

"Don't know," he said. He paused to rest, then asked, "Are you going home today?"

"Don't know," I said. "I had to leave SilverWolf in the woods. I was hoping maybe I could fly back up there first and get her." I glanced toward my dad. He looked at me for what seemed a long time, then nodded and smiled.